LITTLE WIFE LIES

KATHERINE COBB

BANDITO PUBLISHING

For anyone who has ever been
cheated on, lied to, and not loved the
way you wholly deserve…I hope you are
living your best life full of abundance,
joy, love, and anything else that
fills your soul.

P.S.
They say Karma never
forgets an address.

"WE CAN BE REDEEMED

ONLY TO THE EXTENT TO WHICH

WE SEE OURSELVES."

—MARTIN BUBER

PROLOGUE

HANK

SEPTEMBER 2008

I LUNGE AT ADRIENNE, slam her against the wall and pin her there. Her eyes bulge, wide with shock. I clench my hand around her delicate, pale throat and squeeze. A gurgle spurts from her mouth, the very mouth I'd eagerly kissed just a few weeks ago. Her hands claw at my chest in vain, not gaining any purchase. Through the sharp tunnel of my fury, a sense of calm emerges.

Snapshots of our life together parade across my thoughts. The memories I'd walled off in my brain buzz like static on the radio. They come in short, disconnected snippets. And then the night we met replays, and it's crystal fucking clear.

CHAPTER 1
HANK

A RUCKUS on the dance floor jolts me out of my trance, and I zero in on the couple arguing. A sexy brunette wriggles her wrist out of a man's grasp. He towers over her, eyes ablaze and spittle flying, but the band muffles his shouts. The pair's unfolding drama interrupts the nearest dancers, in full swing as The Hicks from the Sticks finishes up its second set on a rowdy Thursday night.

I clock the telltale signs as I near: this dude is about to blow. The female stands her ground, impressive despite her short stature. My lip curls into a one-sided smile and adrenaline rockets through me, my muscles expanding from the flood of oxygen.

The guy raises his hand, and I bridge the gap in six strides, inserting myself between the pair and forcing his wrist to his side.

"I suggest you scurry along, fella," I say, keeping a firm grip.

He glowers. "This isn't your business, and you better let go of my arm before my fist connects with your face."

Music to my ears. *Make your move, you redneck asshole.*

He bumps my chest with his own and endeavors to strike me with his untethered hand. I duck the punch and ram my fist into his gut on my way to standing.

While he's doubled over, I lean near his ear. "Hitting a woman is everyone's business, douchebag."

The man rights himself, bitterness flaring in his eyes. He points his finger at the gal. "That bitch is banging my best friend. She deserves whatever she gets." He turns away, then hauls off and takes another swing at me with his meat hook. I dodge it, the blow glancing off my shoulder. Like I didn't see *that* coming.

Time to get serious.

I slam the heel of my palm into his nose and a satisfying crunch resounds as I follow through. I fucking love that sound. He moans, and his hands fly to his face, attempting to stem the bleeding. *Good luck with that.*

I grab the scruff of his neck, herd him across the club's floor to the exit and push him out the door. He trips over his feet, landing face first in a puddle leftover from the afternoon thunderstorm. *Bonus.* "Consider yourself unwelcome at this establishment going forward. Enjoy the rest of your night, bud."

Scum like Mr. Nosebleed makes me dig my job as a bouncer at The Crazy Horse.

I inspect my bloody hand as I reenter the club and head for the restroom. Better not be one speck on my Tony Lamas. They're my favorite: expensive, square-toed, and made from caiman belly. I pass the door for Fillies and push open the one labeled Stallions. My heart rate slows as I wash up and steal a glance at my reflection. I'm no worse for wear—still the ugly mug I've always been—but I can't say the same for my chambray shirt. Dabbing at the red dots sprayed across one sleeve is a lost cause. I tuck my shirttail into my jeans and walk back to the floor to finish my shift.

Scanning the bar, I spot her easily enough. As I approach, she drains the last half of what appears to be a Tequila Sunrise.

"You all right, ma'am?"

Her head swivels, a perplexed expression on her lovely face. "Ma'am? Do I look like your grandmother?"

In that Daisy Duke outfit? Hell, no. "Not in the slightest. And ma'am is not a derogatory term, despite the offense y'all take to it. It's called manners."

"Is opening a can of whup-ass on strangers called manners too?" After a beat, she smiles, but I'm already grinning.

"Only the douchebags who rough up women."

"Do you work here, or are you some random guy who likes to hit people?"

"Both." I cock my head and rest one boot on the foot railing. "You didn't answer my question. You good?"

She motions to Noreen for another drink and glances my way again, giving me the slightest of nods. She seems more vulnerable than the feisty gal prepared to take it on the chin moments ago. Her eyes shine with unshed tears, their color and depth reminding me of the canyons back home. In stark contrast with her milky skin, they're mesmerizing.

"Thanks for stepping in before. Darren was drunk and out of line."

"My pleasure." *Really.* "You should let me escort you out when you're ready to split. That joker might still be lurking around, although I doubt it after the shape he's in."

She nods. "He okay?"

"Physically, he'll live." Why the fuck does she care after the way he treated her? And crap…why do I care what she cares? That's my cue to skedaddle. "Catch you later, *ma'am*." I turn to leave, but she grabs my hand. Static electricity sparks between us and we both flinch.

She rubs her finger. "Can I buy you a drink? If that's cool while you're on the job? It's the least I can do."

I scan the club for any sign of trouble and come up empty. My gaze falls on her expectant face, and I lob her a lazy grin. "I wouldn't say no to a beer." Nothing better than a cold brew after a fight and it should ease the sting radiating from my hand.

I nod at Noreen, who's probably eavesdropping anyway. She reprimands the pimply kid bussing glasses behind the bar—she can be a real hard-ass—and places a Shiner Bock on a coaster before me. "Thanks, Noreen, and thank you…?"

"Adrienne," she says, lifting her glass to mine.

Lovely name. "Hank McCallister, named after my mother." I drain half the bottle, and it hits the spot.

"Hold the phone. Your mom is named Hank?"

"Henrietta. Technically, I'm Henry, but that's not a handle I cotton to much. Been Hank since my rugrat years."

"Are you, like, a legit cowboy or something?"

She gazes at me from under a cascade of wavy brunette hair. I'm starting to enjoy looking into those eyes. Big and brown with lashes for days. My eyes drop lower to a full mouth begging to be kissed. Jesus, pull it together. She's got a boyfriend—even if the guy is a tool. And this gal is *way* out of my league. I can't imagine a hottie like her going out with a mutt like me. I can almost hear my mother whispering it in my ear.

"Hank?"

I snap out of my trance. "Not exactly. But I'm a born and bred Texas boy who grew up ranching."

She smiles like she's remembering an inside joke. "No kidding. Where in Texas?"

"Little town called Sweetwater."

"Priceless."

I cock my head, unsure what she implies. "What about you?"

"Nothing exotic. Virginia native…who's never left." She sucks the remnants of her drink through her straw then lifts the glass to her lips, the ice falling against her mouth. *Lucky ice.*

"You're out of state right now, darlin'—smack dab in our nation's capital, which, come to think of it, is not a state at all." I wink.

"Cute."

"I have my moments." The band's last set starts, and I place my empty beer on the bar. "Gotta make the rounds. Don't forget to find me, so I can walk you out." I need to slip away from this gal. Her spunk and fragility are a potent combination, especially with that body and gorgeous face.

She tips a pretend hat. "You got it, cowboy."

The rest of my shift remains uneventful, even though watching Adrienne gyrate on the dance floor in booty shorts is anything but. Hard as I try to ignore her and stay focused on my tasks, she has my head turned as if I'm under some witchy woman spell. I can't begin to figure her out. Who was the chump she came with? Did she cheat on him with his best friend? Is she still here drinking it up because of angst, or doesn't she care if her life is in shambles? I smell trouble—but the daggone scent lures me in anyway. And I need that kind of trouble like I need another ten-gallon hat.

An hour before closing, Adrienne prances over and tugs on my hand. "Dance with me!"

I shake her off. "No can do. I'm on the clock."

"Clock schmock." She giggles and trips.

I catch her before she lands on her ass. "Another time, darlin'."

"Say that again...I love how you talk."

"Maybe it's time for you to scamper." This gal passed way-over-the-limit drunk an hour ago. More than a few guys are looking at her like easy prey. I've seen it thousands of times and know how this story ends.

She pouts.

I also know just what to do with those lips.

She wavers, and I steady her again. "How are you getting home? Did you drive?"

"Nope. Came with Darren. But he's..." Adrienne giggles again. "Indisposed!"

More like disposed of, like trash. "I'll call you a cab."

She grabs me around the waist and gazes up at me. She's at least a foot shorter. "Why don't you take me to your place for the night?"

Tempting. And surprising. Then again, she's drunk off her ass. "It's not my style to take advantage of incapacitated women." I steer her over to a chair. "Wait here, darlin'. I'll be back to fetch you in two shakes."

When the taxi arrives, I help her into it, unable to avoid a close encounter with her voluptuous tits, straining against her red and white striped halter-top. My lower half responds instinctively, and I grimace at the discomfort.

She gasps, grabbing my arm. "Hold on!" She rifles through her purse, pouts, and stares at me wide-eyed. "I don't have any more money."

"I've got it." Handing the driver enough to pay her fare, I project my most menacing glare, so he understands I expect no funny business.

Adrienne clutches my face with both hands and presses her lips to my cheek. "Bye, cowboy!" She throws back her head and laughs, the sound echoing into the night. I rub my jaw, watching till she turns the corner, a tad remorseful I let this mystifying gal slip away.

———

Fazli Bukhari, Yellow Cab Co: One minute the lady was laughing and the next, crying. This is why sad people shouldn't drink. Alcohol is a depressant, and it's only a matter of cocktails until you drown in your own tears. What could I do? She only muttered incoherent sentences, something about her sister, I think. I'm one man trying to make a living. This is my second job. I can't solve the world's problems.

CHAPTER 2

ADRIENNE

MY CLOCK RADIO BLEATS, and I pounce to silence the contraption. Flopping back against the pillows, my heart thumps erratically from the rude awakening. I realize I slept in my clothes, and my now-wedged shorts are pinching my inner thighs. I yank them off and massage the ridges indenting my skin. My head pounds and my mouth's as dry as sidewalk chalk, further reminders of my drunken debauchery.

Remnants from the previous night flicker through my mind like snapshots in one of those old viewfinder toys. Darren coming home from work in a bad mood and starting in on a twelve-pack. *Click.* Darren pawing at me, irritated when I rebuffed his advances. *Click.* Darren driving us to The Crazy Horse in his rusted-up Ford because I thought a night out would be fun. *Click.* Darren making a fool of himself on the dance floor. *Click.* Sharlene telling Darren I screwed his best bud (skank totally wants Nate to herself). *Click.* Darren losing it, screaming in my face and grabbing my wrist—hard. *Click.* Then...cowboy Hank.

My headache eases at the thought of him. Tall, brawny, aggressive. Confident yet polite. An expansive, manly mustache. And a deep, panty-dropping voice. Not much of a looker, though, with a misshapen nose and an untamed unibrow. His eyes were a vivid cobalt but protruded from his face like a lizard's. Still, what he lacked in the eye-candy department, he sure made up for in charm. Plus, he met the requirements of Rule #1: Date a man uglier than yourself. The handsome, cocksure kind always break your heart. A man who worships your beauty will fall on his sword for you—and hadn't Hank already done something like that last night?

Yo, Adrienne! Concentrate on the here and now. What to do about the current boyfriend? He won't magically disappear—they never do. I need an exit strategy pronto. Darren is MIA, but with a broken nose and an even greater hit to his pride, it's only a matter of time before he shows up to settle the score. Plus, this apartment is ours...or technically his, if you want to quibble about the fine print.

Forcing myself upright, I bolt into the shower, unable to bask in its sobering warmth. I hasten to pull it together, then call the salon and leave a message I'll be late. Tess will be pissed, but someone else will have to accommodate Mrs. Tuttle's dye job this morning.

Grabbing the box of trash bags from under the sink, I shove the contents of my three dresser drawers into a couple. I cram my toiletries into a plastic laundry crate. Flinging open the closet doors, I hug the hanging items and deposit them over Darren's ratty recliner. My shoes and boots get tossed in another bag before I take a lap around the apartment for anything that's mine. It doesn't amount to much: some DVDs, a throw knitted by my Grandma Betty, my comforter and pillows. And I'm taking these goddamn fake flowers I bought to cheer up this dump.

It takes four trips, but I squish it all into my weather-beaten Honda Civic parked out front. My possessions are few, and only one matters: my sister's locket. I open the glove compartment and experience the same paralyzing relief I always do when it's still there. Lifting the lid on the small silver box, my breath hitches as my finger strokes the locket, patina discoloring the surface. Satisfied, I snap it shut and tuck it back where it lives.

Jogging up the stairs a final time, I take one last look around the place I've called home for the past seven months and mutter "good fucking riddance" as I close the door.

Craning my neck to ensure the coast is clear, I scramble to my Honda and get gone. Now to plot my next move.

———

Tess: I am so over Adrienne calling in late for work. I've put up with her irresponsible behavior because she's talented and clients love her. But more, something stinks—and it's not hair chemicals. I wouldn't be surprised if she forged her cosmetology license.

CHAPTER 3
HANK

TWENTY-FOUR HOURS LATER, Adrienne has fully hijacked my headspace. Those captivating brown eyes. Full lips. A tight body with all the right curves. And that beguiling combination of badass and damsel in distress. I wish I'd snagged her digits. Huffing out a mouthful of air, I wonder who I'm kidding. A babe of her stature can have any guy she wants...she sure as shit wouldn't choose me. I shake my head, hoping thoughts of her will fling out.

Wagner's classic "Ride of the Valkyries" thunders from the TV, jerking me back into my favorite scene in *Apocalypse Now*. My dog, Diesel, pads across the living room, tufts of his black and tan coat floating to the floor.

"What's happening, buddy?" I rub his head and the base of his long pointy ears, and his eyes close, tongue lolling out of his mouth.

"If only my life was as easy as yours. All you do is eat, sleep, and hump." I chuckle. "Heck, maybe we're more alike than I thought."

I click off the tube, my joints popping and cracking as I stand

and stretch. I'm still sore from last night. Glancing around the gloomy apartment, I note it could do with a woman's touch. Hell, so could I.

I wolf down a sandwich, grab my keys and split. My Dodge Cummings pickup fires right up, and Johnny Cash fills the cab. I pluck my grip strengthener off the seat and methodically squeeze it with my free hand in preparation for a Friday night at The Crazy Horse. I anticipate a drunk, rowdy, and stupid TGIF crowd venting pent-up steam from another workweek. If I'm lucky, I'll get to throw some punches.

An hour into my shift, fingers pinch my ass, and I whirl around loaded for bear.

Adrienne holds her hands up as if under arrest. "Whoa, cowboy!"

Customarily, such a flagrant impropriety would irritate me, but seeing this hottie again only makes my heart lurch and my mouth open into a wide grin. "You always greet people like that?"

"Only the ones I like." She flashes a dazzling smile and bats her eyelashes with exaggerated intent.

I forget my name, zip code and about everything else, but that dopey grin stays plastered on my face.

"I'm meeting my girlfriend at the bar. Catch you later, Texas."

"Sure thing," I mumble. "Stay out of hot water...Virginia."

"No need when you've got my back." She struts off, her full head of hair swinging like brushes in a car wash.

I enjoy her exit and her sass. *Double trouble.*

I track her whereabouts most of the night, drawn to her like a fruit fly to a ripe peach. One minute, she's laughing with her friend, throwing back shots, and another, she's moving her hips on the dance floor—and once, boot-scootin' with some idiot. When she catches me staring, she responds with pointed, flirty stares, reeling me in like a freshwater trout. And the wild way my heart flaps, I'm hooked.

While I still have the opportunity, I seek out Jimmy, my best bud and coworker. "I'm taking a short break. Cover me?"

He nods. "The girl?"

A smirk is my only answer.

I sidle up alongside Adrienne, sitting at the bar with her friend. "Dance with me, darlin'?"

"Thought you'd never ask, cowboy."

I take her hand and lead her to the floor, preparing to show her a proper Texas Two-Step and hoping I don't trip over my own feet from staring at her—she's so beautiful, it's like looking straight into the sun. My right arm slides around her back while my left hand holds hers at arm's length and muscle memory takes over. I guide her effortlessly to the music with two long steps followed by a shuffle. I'll throw in a twirl now and again if I think she can manage it.

"Figures the cowboy has moves," she mutters, a small smile edging her lips.

"This rodeo's just getting started." I gaze down at her and whip her into a spin.

She whoops, exhilaration lighting up her face. I could spend a lifetime watching that.

After a few more rounds, Adrienne is all smiles. She does not disappoint as a dance partner.

"Tell me about yourself, Hank. What do you like?"

"Besides luring pretty girls onto the dance floor?" I wink. "Fishing, trucks and my dog, not necessarily in that order."

"Your life seriously sounds like a country song."

"And that's a bad thing?" I twirl her again before she can answer.

"What kind of dog have you got?"

"A Northern Inuit. He looks like a ferocious wolf, but he's a total sweetheart. Your turn now, darlin'."

"I enjoy long walks on the beach, curling up with a steamy book in front of a fire and skinny-dipping on hot nights."

My eyes bulge, and I stutter a step.

"I'm kidding, cowboy. Didn't you ever read those old centerfold bits?"

I shake my head, laughing. "You're a little vixen, aren't you?"

I twirl her into a double spin right before the song ends, then pull her in close as a slow number begins. She doesn't protest. Our height proportions are awkward, but I soon forget with her face resting on my chest, brunette locks cascading around her. As I bring my head near hers, I detect the faint aroma of vanilla. My arms draw her in a mite closer, and she responds in kind. I let myself believe I have a chance with this gal—if I'm reading the signs correctly—and banish the Negative Nelly attempting to squawk.

The rest of my night features a parade of inebriated idiots. I break up three fights, toss an asshole slipping a roofie into a woman's drink (complete with a special beating I reserve for those types of dicks) and listen to one gal's elaborate sob story about her evil boyfriend that sounds like bullshit. Sometimes chicks say anything under the misguided belief I'll act, but seeing is believing, and my BS detector works fine.

I barely glimpse Adrienne after our slow dance, and as the club closes, I realize she never said goodbye.

I wash up, don my caramel-hued Resistol and join the staff at the bar. I guzzle the cold beer comped by management and try not to feel glum. Maybe I misread the situation. She probably went home with one of many guys fawning over her. Why that upsets me so much, I can't fathom. I hardly know her. But damn if she hasn't gotten right under my skin in an all-fire hurry. I catch the reflection in the mirrored backsplash and am reminded why she might prance off with someone else. She's *incredible*. And then there's me. I've got assets, but handsome ain't one of them.

Not in the mood to hang around, I bid my coworkers farewell and saunter out.

When I find Adrienne leaning against the façade, my heart splutters, mouth stretching into a shit-eating grin. Even despite the cigarette dangling from her fingers, which she quickly drops and stubs out with her toe. My eyes narrow in annoyance as I scan the area. This is a rowdy club, a Friday night, and come closing time, this is a prime way station for men hoping to get laid by girls too drunk to be choosy or protect themselves.

She presses off the wall and tugs on my brim. "You really are a cowboy. I'm digging the hat."

"What are you doing?" Her proximity is intoxicating, and my irritation takes a back seat.

"Waiting for you. I thought you'd be happy to see me."

More than you know. "I am darlin', but you shouldn't be out here. It's not safe." My eyes rescan the perimeter and return to rest on her.

She rolls her eyes. "I'm fine. Not to mention, all you burly bouncers are right inside." She inches closer and trails her fingers down my chest. "But I like your overprotectiveness. It's sexy."

My pulse beats double-time. Damn, this girl's a knockout. "I'm your man."

She tilts her head back, meets my gaze and flashes me a heart-stopping smile. "Wonderful, because I want to spend more time with you."

My dick twitches in anticipation, nature's warning sign I will soon be incapable of logical thought. I flash her an expansive grin. "Your place or mine?"

"Yours."

———

Jimmy: Hank's screwed. His chick radar is about 50-50. With a looker like Adrienne, I guarantee he's falling all over himself with gratitude, and that's bullshit. He's one of the good guys. Sometimes a little intense and cocky, but also a

VERIFIABLE FUCKING SWEETHEART. WHICH MAKES HIM A TARGET WITH GULLIBLE WRITTEN ALL OVER IT. I'D BET MY LEFT NUT HE'S GOT TUNNEL VISION, AND THE LIGHT AT THE END OF THIS ONE IS A TRAIN —THE KIND THAT RUNS YOUR ASS OVER AND SMILES WHILE SHE'S DOING IT.

CHAPTER 4
ADRIENNE

HANK STEERS me to an enormous black truck with one of those lift kits jacking it up even higher. I'm wondering how I'll climb into the monstrosity when he offers me a hand and helps slide me onto the leather seat. The immaculate interior combined with the shiny, pristine exterior is light years from my eyesore of a beater.

Hank appraises me from the driver's side. "I could get used to this. You look amazing in The Boss."

"You named your truck?"

"Doesn't everybody?" He arches that unibrow and flashes another giant grin.

I shake my head as he starts the engine and country music blares. He turns it down and we trade small talk as he heads to Arlington. We pass the high rises downtown and wind into the suburbs. My curiosity piques the longer he drives, especially when we enter a ritzy neighborhood. I hide my surprise when he pulls up to a gated estate surrounded by a formidable stone wall.

Jackpot.

He opens his window, punches a number into the keypad and the entry swings open.

"You're rich?" Please be true.

He chuckles. "Nah, I live in the carriage house. Hope you're not disappointed."

"As long as you can support me in the lifestyle to which I've become accustomed, we're golden," I quip before my memory reminds me that, as of eighteen hours ago, I'm living out of my car.

"You got it, princess." He steers his truck down the drive and parks next to a substantial cottage. Shrouded in darkness, I can only make out part of the main house perched on the hill. I reach for the door handle, but Hank orders me to stay put.

"I open doors for women. Manners, remember?"

A smile plays at my lips. "I could get used to this," I say, stealing his earlier sentiment and garnering another shit-eating grin under his sizable mustache. He's so dang nice and *almost* cute.

He lifts me out of the truck like I'm weightless. Taking my hand, which engulfs mine, he leads me to the door. He reminds me about his dog, not that he needs to. The canine bays from inside.

I hide my wariness as Hank and his fur buddy perform a greeting ritual before he introduces us. Dogs don't always like me or vice versa, and Diesel's wolf-like features freak me out. Tentatively, I offer my hand for him to sniff, hoping he doesn't bite it off. He takes a whiff and sits back, cocking his head to one side.

"Good boy," Hank says. "Now bed!"

"Are you ordering him or me?" I joke as the dog obeys.

Hank turns to me, zeroing in on my lips with a heated gaze. Wordlessly, he pins me against the nearest wall and kisses me hard. My body goes limp, sagging toward him. His strong arms hold me steady as his mouth sears his brand onto me, claiming me in a way I don't expect. Our mouths collide frantically, his hands roving over my backside as mine weave into his hair and across his broad shoulders. His dense muscle meets my soft curves as we escalate into a frenzy of gropes and caresses and tastes. The only sounds are our accelerated breaths, heady moans and the occasional *whoosh* of a garment coming off. When he tugs me flush to his torso, the preview of a promising erection presses against me and we both groan, grinding into each other.

Naked and breathless, we stare at each other with mutual lust. Hank picks me up effortlessly and I wrap myself around him. Kissing the entire way, he marches us into the bedroom and deposits me on his bed. His burning stare turns me into a puddle. Which almost never happens.

"You are fucking gorgeous," he says, kneeling before me, and I melt even more.

His mouth travels unhurriedly from my ankles upward, taking his time to lick and suck all the right places. I writhe with every flick of his tongue, every fluttery kiss. He tortures me slowly and deliberately, staving off my intermittent pleas. I forget everything. My pain. My hardship. My current situation. This is all there is.

His warm breath blankets my just-sucked breast, making it pucker further and ache for more. Raking my fingernails across his back, I plead in between broken breaths.

Hank's head lifts, a half-smile twitching on his lips.

"I need you inside of me," I whisper.

A full grin stretches his mega mustache wide. "Soon. But ladies first. Manners…"

I groan.

Hank licks my center and fixates his tongue on mission control. A finger slides into my gushing insides, then two, and I clutch at the sheets until I gain purchase. He has fingers in proportion to his ginormous size and oh em geeeeee. I widen my legs further, welcoming the relentless rapture this cowboy is dishing up. It doesn't take long before he cracks me open with his dual wizardry. I cry out as I quake with orgasmic fallout, undulating through me like the tail end of a roller coaster.

Panting as my body twitches through a decadent climax, Hank rises, hovering over me with reverence.

I reward him with a genuine smile. "Now?"

"It'll be my pleasure, ma'am."

I smirk at that stupid word. He fishes around for a condom, but I shake my head. "I'm covered and all that. You?"

He nods. "You sure?"

"One hundred percent. I want to *feel* you."

His stare burns into mine, and I don't have to ask twice. Hank plunges into me, and I gasp like a drowning victim. He drives into me again and again and again, waves of carnal bliss coursing through me with each thrust. Screwing after an orgasm is like having your favorite ice cream for dinner and a frosted triple decker cake for dessert.

Our groans punctuate every stroke as our bodies join, and I match him thrust for thrust. Lifting my head, I find one of his nipples and circle it with my tongue. It hardens instantly, and he curses under his breath. I smile against his chest then suck his other nipple into my warm mouth, which proves to be his undoing. Hank explodes, letting loose with a primal cry.

After we disconnect, we flop back on the mattress, our breathing ragged as we exalt in a new coupling devoid of first-sex awkwardness. That's one for the win column.

Two more delicious rounds and a shower later, the cowboy comes back to bed with a half-gallon of rocky road ice cream, and we spoon it right out of the carton into our mouths. I fall asleep in his arms as dawn breaks.

A noise coaxes me from my slumber. The dog. Hank rises, shushing Diesel as he slides on last night's jeans. The door clicks gently closed, and I tumble back into a dream.

Something new attempts to drag me from sleep. Fingers. On my skin. Lighting a fire. I snap alert. Hank's lips pepper my neck with kisses, followed by my chest and abdomen, then travel south.

Oh. My. Sweet. God. His mouth is back in all the right places.

This may be heaven. The cowboy's moves are smooth and don't require direction. His tongue flicks and sucks and licks until I'm floating, spinning, leaping, as every cell in my body awakens and screams with ecstasy. I explode as if shot into space and it's several minutes before I return.

Hank props himself up on one elbow, grinning at me with that walrus mustache, which is slightly dewy at the moment. "What's cookin', good lookin'?"

A smile creeps across my lips. His voice might be the death of me. So deep and masculine. And his accent, drawing out vowels and full of darlin's and good lookin's. Who can resist this shit?

His fingers reach over and stroke my hair. "Sleep well?"

I glance at him sideways. "What little there was of it, yes."

"What are you talking about? Half the day's gone."

"Not when you crash at dawn." I groan, cataloging his first obvious flaw: he's a morning person.

"How about some breakfast?"

"Didn't you just have that?" Closing my eyes, I shudder through another stretch.

"It *was* delicious but merely an appetizer. I make a mean ham and eggs..."

"Coffee?" Every ounce of my being yearns for it.

"Coming right up." He leaps up and disappears.

A glance around the bedroom in daylight reveals a tidy and organized space devoid of clutter. A king-sized bed, two end tables, a massive dresser and a bookshelf, all a deep shade of burnt umber. Everything is extra-large—like Hank.

Although I've never cared much for reading, finding it tedious, I crane my neck to view the titles on the shelf. War stories, mechanic's manuals, some biographies, and a Bible. He better not turn out to be one of those holy rollers or I'm out.

I drag myself upright and to the bathroom to inspect the damage. Bloodshot eyes, tangled hair, smudged makeup. I wash my face, smear toothpaste on my teeth using a finger, and borrow his comb.

Spotting one of Hank's button-downs on a nearby chair, I pull it on, the size dwarfing me. I scoop my hair from under the shirt and let it fall. As I roll up the cuffs, I summon my game face. Party time is over, a sobering reminder it's time to face reality. Again. I hope I haven't misread the cowboy.

"Mmm," Hank hums as I enter the kitchen, grabbing me by the waist and bringing me in close with his free hand. "That shirt looks a far sight better on you than me." He kisses me and gestures to a chair at the dining table, where a generous amount of food and a steaming cup of coffee awaits.

"Smells awesome." I'd be hungry if not for the churning in my gut, dreading what's on the horizon.

He scoops scrambled eggs onto our plates and sets the frypan back on the stove. "Dig in, darlin'," he urges, taking the seat across from mine. I swear, he's almost a caricature with his accent.

"Hank. I don't want you to think I'm...what I mean is, going home with you...without knowing you? It's not my norm. I'm not, as the saying goes, that kind of girl." The words flow with sincerity, even though I'm full of shit. It's more I wish I weren't that kind of girl.

"I sure as hell am glad you were last night!" He chuckles.

"I'm being serious." Although I'm not on the witness stand swearing on The Good Book either.

"I'm sorry. Listen, you've been crashing my headspace since I met you two nights ago. The one-nighter ain't my typical gig, but I like you, and I think you like me, so what do you say we just see where this thing goes?"

I nod, anticipating the rest might change his mind when it comes to light.

"What are your plans today?" He's so damn cheerful, smiling at me as he shoves a wad of ham into his mouth.

Here we go. "Finding a place to live."

Blue eyes pin me to the spot. "What?"

I take a deep breath and release it slowly. "The guy you put a hurting on the night we met? We lived together. Darren is an abusive douchebag, and I was ready to move on, but that night clinched it. I'm sure I can stay with a friend until I figure things out. I haven't had time to make any arrangements because I packed my bags yesterday, went to work, got caught up with you at The Crazy Horse and, well…here we are."

Hank slams his hand on the table, and I jump, my heart thudding in my chest. His face reddens, the vein in his jawbone pulsating like a strobe light. "Did that dickwad hurt you?"

I still my center, set down my fork and meet his gaze. "He laid his hands on me a few times. He'd say he was sorry, go back to the Mr. Nice Guy routine, and then do it again." He wasn't the first and probably won't be the last. "I'm not one of those pathetic females who sticks around believing bullshit lies—I planned on leaving him. I was still sorting it out."

Hank's expression grows steely as he stares at me a beat. "*Did you sleep with his best bud?*"

He remembers. I force myself to keep eye contact and my cool. "Of course not. Darren is a jealous bastard and says whatever he needs to justify his fucked-up behavior."

His broad shoulders visibly relax. "I know the type well, and I'm always happy to give those guys a taste of their own shit. What are your options? For the living situation?"

I exhale the breath I was holding. "I have friends at the salon who might let me crash with them until I can find a place." *Fat fucking chance.*

"What about family? I thought you were from Virginia."

I stare into my coffee. "The only relative I have left is my Grandma Betty, and she lives in Pamplin, a town in the middle of bum-fuck-nowhere a few hours from here. I sure as hell don't want to stay there."

"Jesus." Hank shakes his head and wipes his mouth with a napkin, dislodging the egg stuck in his mustache. "What about your parents?"

My armpits are so damp, a sticky seal has formed in the creases. I close my eyes, muster some mojo and open them again. "My family died in a fire when I was eleven. My mama, daddy and baby sister." My eyes flick to his face and his expression triggers a sadness I rarely allow myself to experience.

"Adrienne…that's horrific. How did it happen?"

I pinch my hand hard under the table to keep my emotions in check. Sadness is for weaklings. "My parents were drunks. One of them passed out with a burning cigarette, and we lived in a Cracker Jack shack, so it went up in flames fast."

"Jesus." Hank scrubs his jaw, disbelief etched on his face. "Did you escape? Or were you not there?"

"I was there," I whisper. "Playing in the woods. Far enough away that I didn't know what was happening…until it was too late." My face falls into my hands as I try to force back the emotions.

Hank holds out his arms. "Come here, darlin'."

I scoot out of my chair and into his lap. He envelops me in his embrace, murmuring condolences and kissing my forehead as it rests on his chest. A few tears escape.

I'm so fucking tired. And I don't miss my asshole parents, but the loss of my sister is like a sinkhole that can never be filled. It steadily consumes refrigerators and delivery trucks and double-wides…and yet it's never enough, never stops, never abates.

The longer he holds me, the more I dissolve. Before I can shove it back into the murky bowels of my existence, the dam breaks and I'm sobbing. Fuck all.

Hank continues holding me, rocking me, cocooning me in his protective orbit.

Too many minutes tick by, and I fight to pull myself together. "It was my fault," I choke out, the sound muffled by his shirt.

"What? How could it be?"

"Annabelle was my responsibility. I should have been looking out for her."

"Adrienne." Hank's fingers rub my back and trail up my hair, pulling it away from my face and laying it over one shoulder. "You were a kid. You may have been her older sister, but you can't blame yourself. You were not responsible for her...your parents were."

My parents don't deserve the title. My mother buried us in insults and servitude, and my father's crimes were a violation of the worst kind, compounded by my mother turning a blind eye. I was all Annabelle had.

His embrace tightens, and I feel safe in his arms, which is crazy since we're damn near strangers.

"It's not your fault," he whispers. "Life dealt you a bad hand. Not many people would make it through unscathed."

I'm not unscathed. But I'm still standing.

"Where did you go...after it happened?" he murmurs.

"My Grandma Betty's. She was a blessing, and a far better parent than either of my own."

Hank rubs my back as I melt into him. "An angel of mercy."

"Yes," I whisper.

His arms are so sure around mine, so comforting. Something about it, about him, fills me with the slightest ray of hope. Maybe Hank is the one to finally make me all right, make me whole again.

"Stay with me," he says.

I jolt upright and swipe my wet cheeks. "It's too soon. I don't want to take advan—"

He lifts my chin and stares into my eyes. "Stay," he repeats.

———

GIRL AT THE BAR: IT FIGURES HE WENT HOME WITH THAT CHICK. I WAS WAITING OUTSIDE TOO, READY TO MAKE A MOVE. HANK'S SWEET. WE'VE TALKED A FEW TIMES, AND I THOUGHT WE HAD A CONNECTION. BUT OF COURSE, HE CHOSE HER. SHE'S GOT THE BODY, THE FACE, THE WHOLE PRETTY, SUPERFICIAL PACKAGE. WHEN SHE

FLASHED HER TITS AND TOUCHED HIS CHEST, I DIDN'T STAND A CHANCE. BUT SOMETHING TELLS ME HE DOESN'T EITHER. WHY DO GUYS ALWAYS FALL FOR THOSE KINDS OF GIRLS? I DIDN'T PEG HANK FOR THE SHALLOW TYPE, BUT I GUESS HE THINKS WITH HIS DICK LIKE EVERY OTHER MAN.

FLASHED HER TITS AND TOUCHED HIS CHEST, I DIDN'T STAND A CHANCE. BUT SOMETHING TELLS ME HE DOESN'T EITHER. WHY DO GUYS ALWAYS FALL FOR THOSE KINDS OF GIRLS? I DIDN'T PEG HANK FOR THE SHALLOW TYPE, BUT I GUESS HE THINKS WITH HIS DICK LIKE EVERY OTHER MAN.

CHAPTER 5
HANK

IN THE PRIVACY of my shower, I'm kicking myself. My offer was impulsive, reckless and downright stupid considering I've only known the woman two days—*known* being rather a misnomer. But dang if she hasn't already hooked, lined and sinkered this fish. I shake my head and rub a squirt of shampoo onto my melon. It's not like I asked her to marry me. This is a temporary arrangement, a way to help her out of a jam. I can always kick her out if things veer south, but a part of me hopes it never comes to that.

There's something about her…she's rocking my world. And I'm not talking about my dick, although she is the sexiest damn woman I've had the privilege of sharing a bed with, and I'm mesmerized. Her vulnerability just now? Mind-blowing. I want to wrap my arms around her like a shield and protect her from any further atrocities. As I scrub my body with soap, I admit I've never wanted to love a woman so much in my life.

I need to get a grip.

Once I'm dressed, Adrienne and I unload her car. We move her non-essential items into the garage, and I make room in closets and the bathroom for the rest. She's jittery while unpacking and concerned about respecting my space. Maybe she's reeling over the bomb she dropped. It's a lot to process.

I find her fretting in the bedroom.

Wrapping my arms around her, I whisper, "Relax." I sweep her tumbling mane off one shoulder and press my lips into the curve of her neck, breathing in her heady scent. "I can ease those nerves for you. Just call me Dr. McCallister."

Her breath catches. "Can you fix what ails me?"

"I'm fixin' to. No time like the present."

I flip her so our bodies face each other and kiss her inviting mouth. Our tongues dance, mine probing and greedy, and heat scorches through me in seconds, like a simmering pot fixin' to boil. I back her onto the bed and strip off my shirt, boots and jeans. She scrambles out of her clothes, and we merge in fervor.

She rolls me over and climbs on top, stroking my chest. She kisses her way down my throat to my nipples, stopping to suck and bite both. They respond like soldiers, immediately at attention, igniting every erotic nerve ending and reminding me of our first bang. My eyes shut, giving in to her swirling tongue and soft lips as they travel south to the magic kingdom.

Holy fuck. *This girl.* Her warm mouth. Her deep throat. Her silky hands. Watching her unravels me. I groan when I teeter too close, and she smiles knowingly. Shifting, she straddles my midsection and inches me deep inside her. The expression of rapture on her face etches into my brain. She begins a slow grinding and rocking atop me, and I forget my own name. Groaning, I grasp her hips and begin to thrust from below, near-wrecked at the sight of her head reared back with pleasure. I'm not going to last; this girl reduces me to rubble. I explode like a grenade and twitch as the shrapnel settles. Adrienne flops across me, our chests heaving as we regain our breath.

"Dayummm," I mutter.

"Dayummm indeed," she agrees.

She dismounts, sliding her head into the crook of my shoulder. I tug her in closer.

Her fingers trace imaginary lines along my torso and it's almost better than my orgasm. Almost. I am two seconds from falling asleep.

"I hardly know anything about you," she says.

My brain jolts from post-sex narcosis, but my eyes remain closed, still lulled by her touch. "Ask away," I mumble.

"What's Texas like? What are your passions? What do you want to be when you grow up?"

"Is that all?" I chuckle, opening one eye. "I love Sweetwater—"

"I can't believe that's a real place. It sounds like Disneyland or something."

"It's as genuine as it gets in the good old US of A. My folks live on the outskirts, not in town, because they own a sizable cattle ranch. I have four brothers, and two of them help run it."

Adrienne repositions herself, swatting hair off her face. "Wow, that's a lot of testosterone. Where are you in the lineup?"

I take her hand and coax her into caressing me again. "Smack dab in the middle. Shelton and Samuel are ahead of me, and Wyatt and Eli are the youngest." My mother loves to remind me I have *middle child syndrome*. But there's a reason it exists—we're the forgotten kids, wedged between automatic favorites on both ends.

"Weren't you pressured to join the family business?" Her fingers travel toward my navel, and I stifle the urge to flinch.

"Sure was, but I became a diesel mechanic instead. I've always enjoyed solving mechanical riddles, so I learned the trade and vamoosed."

Adrienne folds her arms across my chest and rests her chin on top, peering up at me. "Why Virginia, and weren't your parents upset when you left?"

I reach around and stroke her back, loving its silkiness under my hand. "My mother wasn't happy about my decision—she expected me to help run the ranch. But Texans are tough as leather, so she hid her tears if she shed any. My father believes every man needs to make his own way, and he supported me one hundred percent. I think he took a similar road in his younger years. As for how I got here, after growing up in a smaller town, I wanted to experience the city while having some countryside nearby. The nation's capital seemed like the right fit. I live and work in the metro area but can still go fishing someplace off the beaten path in an hour or less." Sizing Adrienne up, I wonder if she can bait a hook.

"Do you like it here...or wish you were back in Texas?"

"I've never been sorry I left, not that I'm saying I'll never go back. Texas is in my bones and heart. It's a part of me and I miss her all the time, but I've enjoyed the heck out of exploring this area of the country and examining you city folk. Y'all are peculiar."

Adrienne hits me playfully on the shoulder. "Whatever, hick."

I respond by flipping her onto her back and tickling her until she begs for mercy.

We laze on the couch watching TV, the remnants of a large pizza growing cold on the coffee table. Diesel sits erect and barks four times, focused on our new roommate.

"Your dog doesn't like me," she says.

I wave my hand. "He doesn't know you yet. He'll be eating biscuits out of your hand in no time."

She raises an eyebrow and rearranges herself so she's laying with her head in my lap. "I wish you didn't have to work tonight."

"Me too, now that you're hanging around. You're not gonna rob me blind, are you?" I smile down at her.

"And ruin a perfectly good meal ticket? I doubt it."

"There's that sass I like."

"Hey, do you mind if I smoke in here?"

I wince. "About that..."

Her face scrunches. "Why do I feel a lecture coming on?"

"It's a nasty habit that *kills* people. I kinda like you. I'd rather you stick around," I say, chucking her under the chin. "So, no, you can't smoke in here. And if I'm being honest, smoking is a deal-breaker if we're going to be together."

"Whoa…that's a bit ultimatum-y for a first date."

"Just telling it like it is, darlin'. I lost my grandfather to lung cancer, and I fucking hate the taste of cigarettes in that beautiful, amazing mouth of yours." My fingers shift the hair off her forehead, travel down her cheek and lightly outline her lips.

Her mouth opens, and she sucks on my finger. I groan, my dick springing to half-mast.

My finger slides out of her mouth, and she licks those enticing lips. "I'll quit."

"Really?"

She nods her head, smiling slyly when she realizes the effect she's having on me and Hank Jr. "It's not a big deal. I'm not addicted to them or anything."

"I think I'm already addicted to you, gorgeous. And I'd like nothing better than to feed my habit," I say, thrusting my hard-on her direction, "but I've gotta ramble."

She pretends to pout.

I pull on my boots, stand and stretch. "Do me a favor and let Diesel outside for a spell."

"He won't run away, will he?"

"Nah." I bend down to meet her face. "And don't you run away, neither." I kiss her hard, reminding her of what I have to offer, or perhaps convincing myself she isn't a mirage. I rub Diesel's ears, tell him to be nice to the little lady, and head to work.

When I enter The Crazy Horse, it's vibrating with Saturday night energy. Musicians perform a final soundcheck, bartenders restock the booze and condiment caddies, and cocktail waitresses wipe down tables. I walk to the back and place a few items inside my locker while trading barbs with Jimmy and Finn. I'm glad these guys are working tonight; I trust them to have my six.

Within an hour, hundreds have packed the joint. The Should've Stayed Single band turns out to be a crowd-pleaser with its peppy, original bluegrass tunes. My toes are tapping as I scan the club.

To my right, an inebriated customer weaves into another guy and drinks crash to the floor. Yelling and shoving ensue as I hotfoot it to the scene. When punches are thrown, I step in and tell them to break it up or leave. The sober one argues while the drunk's wild expression telegraphs more to come, and seconds later, he takes another crack at him. I intervene, hitting him in the jaw and then the gut, manipulate him into a full nelson and usher him to the exit. Jimmy arrives in time to hold off the other guy, making it clear we'll toss him next if he keeps mouthing off.

On my way back inside, I witness a man give a woman an unwelcome pinch on her ass. I grab his junk hard, remind him how gentlemen behave and tell him where to find the door if he tries it again. Ever.

Blame the full moon, the whiskey or the energetic band, but it seems on this fine evening women came looking for love and men came looking for a fight. In the end, nobody wins, and the police haul off more than a few, including me.

Noreen: There's only one word to describe the club tonight: mayhem. It wouldn't surprise me if dead bodies were unearthed in the men's room. Even so, Briggs was torqued about having to bail out Hank again. Said he was ready to fire him for being such a loose cannon.

CHAPTER 6
ADRIENNE

HANK LEAVES, and I'm restless, flicking through endless channels broadcasting nothing interesting. When Diesel stares at me and bays, I slide open the door and he scurries out.

Now that I'm up, may as well check out my new digs more thoroughly. I'm like an alien in a strange land. In the kitchen, I explore drawers and cabinets, wondering if they contain only essentials or fancy gadgets. The fridge holds typical bachelor fare: beer and OJ, smoked ham, Chinese takeout leftovers, a couple of decaying apples and half a bottle of barbecue sauce. Hank's decidedly not gourmet.

I wander back into the living area and start reading the DVD titles on the built-in shelves, but they're action and western flicks. Hard pass. More books. Yawn. A vast collection of albums and cassette tapes but no CDs. Spotting ancient hi-fi stereo components, I sense my new roommate doesn't care much about emerging technology.

I want one of those "smart" cell phones advertised but can't afford the gadget or associated service plans. My landlines, when I have one, are usually disconnected, but it's not my fault the phone company overcharges for its stupid long-distance calls, making their stupid, overpriced bills impossible to manage. I've learned the best way to handle it is to skip out and move somewhere else. A change of address solves a whole host of financial problems. If you ask me, the system is broken and the American Way unfair to most Americans. If someone must pay, it sure as hell isn't going to be me.

I experience only a twinge of guilt before entering the bedroom, where I yearn to snoop most. Bedrooms are where secrets are kept and I'm dying to know Hank's. The sheets and comforter lay twisted and unkempt, signs from our earlier romp, and the musky aroma of sex lingers.

I start with his closet—the picture of organization with button-down shirts, hanging belts, and a floor rack housing cowboy boots and shoes. Rows of hat boxes line the top shelf. Pulling one down, I discover a fancy, jet-black Stetson. I try it on for size and check myself out in the mirror. The hat's humongous on me but I rock the hell out of it. The others hold more cowboy hats in different shades and styles, all similar.

The massive dresser is ornate with carved details on each of its vertical corners. Undergarments fill the top drawer but no baggy boxers in sight, thank God. The second bulges with tee shirts folded precisely in thirds, followed by another containing stacked shorts. Hank is neater than a chick. Which makes one of us, as cleaning is not my strong suit. The next compartment screeches open, housing plain work jeans and some fancier pairs with designer stitching. At least my cowboy has some style. The bottom drawer holds promise—revealing letters and documents, photo albums, coins and a pocket watch.

I pull out an album and flip through it. Family photos—mostly old. No mistaking five brothers with a through line of similarity, including that prominent, unsightly unibrow. My fingers itch for a pair of tweezers. It's easy to pick out Hank; he's the mutt of the litter. His parents appear stoic, although his mother sports Texas big hair. Will we ever meet? Will they welcome me? Accept me? The McCallisters strike me as a close-knit bunch. Undoubtedly not keen on girls like me, not that I care.

The shrill ring of the phone makes me jump, and I drop the stack of paper in my grasp. Hurrying toward the nightstand, I pause. Should I answer? It's not my house, but it might be Hank. I debate for three seconds then grab it.

"Hello?"

"This is Henrietta McCallister. Is my son available?"

"Oh, hi. Hank's at work."

"And to whom am I speaking?"

"Adrienne...Adrienne Barlow." I spout my last name because she did and that irritates me. "I'm Hank's..." Hmm...I'm not sure what I am. Yet.

"I know who you are," Mrs. McCallister says in a clipped tone. "My son tells me you've run into trouble, so you're staying with him for a few days?"

"He's been quite generous." I grit my teeth. Don't let this shrew hijack your happy place.

"That's my boy. We raised him right. Were you, Adrienne?"

This woman has balls, but if she takes this bull by the horns, she might wind up impaled. "With all due respect, Mrs. McCallister, I don't see how that's any of your business. I do wonder why you're interrogating me though, especially while Hank isn't here. Did you think I'd go to pieces?"

"Evidently not, dear, but I guessed as much." She chuckles so quietly I almost miss it. "Now tell the truth and shame the devil, do you have designs on my son?"

I laugh, some of my hostility escaping. "Not at present, but things are moving fast. You never know when I might wind up your daughter-in-law."

She snorts. "You got some snap in your garters, I'll give you that. And please don't take this call the wrong way. I merely wanted to ascertain whether you intend to do my boy harm. I'm protective of my brood. I'm sure you can understand, or will one day, if you have children of your own."

I roll my eyes. "Certainly. We all want to protect our own interests."

"Best of luck with your troubles. Then again, you present like a gal who can take care of herself."

In spades, bitch.

"Please give Hank my love."

"It'll be my pleasure." I hang up, tapping the receiver a few times with my index finger. Trampling that woman's confidence and becoming a thorn in her paw are reasons enough to marry Hank. Do I have *designs* on her son...did she forget to leave the 1940s?

Diesel's barks intensify, and I hasten to the front door. Wolf-dog eyes me warily but steps over the threshold and glides into the bathroom, where I overhear him slurp water out of the toilet. *I'll win this battle too, buddy.*

I return to the bedroom and resume investigating my new bunkmate.

When I finish with the memorabilia, I yank the drawer out to put it all away and a black case pokes from underneath an army blanket. I flip open the catch, revealing at least a dozen pocketknives ranging in size. Why does Hank have so many? I noticed he wears one clipped to his jeans pocket. I close the case and slide it back into place, and another knife clatters against the wooden surface. This one gives me pause. Weighty and measuring about a foot, I unsnap it from its leather sheath and find a menacing, serrated blade that reminds me of something Rambo would carry.

Repositioning everything back where it belongs, I stand up and stare at his dresser. My gut tells me there's more. I reopen the sock drawer and rifle around. When my hand grazes metal, a chill crawls up my spine. Hidden underneath the undershirts is a gleaming silver pistol.

———

Shelton McCallister: When he called about some chick moving in, I thought our mom would blow a gasket. Only Hank can rile the matriarch from fifteen hundred miles away. And you're goddamn right it bugs me. I'll never understand why she gives a crap who he's hitching his wagon to… it's not like the kid stayed, which shows how little he cares about what he left behind. And once again, big brother is stuck dealing with the fallout.

CHAPTER 7
HANK

I'M TIRED, sore and smelly. Spending a night in a holding cell with a bunch of baboons reeked, literally and figuratively. Getting chewed out by Briggs after he showed up and convinced the police to release me into his custody only added to the fun. Briggs lectured me all the way back to The Crazy Horse, saying he'd fire me the next time I hit someone without it being self-defense. Any dickhead can press charges if lines are crossed, but most guys provoke the situation and are too plastered to remember the details.

Here's the thing sticking in my craw: I don't go off half-cocked on dudes that don't deserve it. The boss questioning my integrity roasts my nuts. I've got more honor and principle than everyone working at the club combined. But what-the-fuck-ever.

As soon as I'm in my truck, I open the windows, clearing out the stench. I pull into the nearest drive-thru and order breakfast chow and an extra-large Coke, which I chug, attempting to obliterate the stale tang in my mouth.

I'm still peeved. A night in the slammer. A boss who blames me for doing my job. And likely a pissed-off girl to face once I make it home.

No one understands how much I thrive on serving justice or how well a beat-down delivers the message. It's a release, akin to why the earth muffins probably dig yoga or that aromatherapy bullshit. I'm glad people aren't privy to what's in my head. My detailed fantasies of doling out the proper payback to these idiots would completely freak out the layperson.

I love my Crazy Horse gig. I don't need the dough, but I appreciate the physical outlet it provides. Now my gainful employment hinges on one more mishap. Not an if, but a when, unless Briggs gets his head out of his ass.

I open the gate and pull up the drive, bracing myself for the wrath of Adrienne. Our history may be brief, but something tells me I'm tangling with a tiger.

She lets loose the second I enter.

"Where the fuck have you been? And don't lie to me—you worried me sick!" Adrienne shrieks.

From my side, Diesel barks at her three times, his own display of outrage.

She glares at him, then me. I quiet my dog and approach my new roommate, gorgeous even while raving.

"Good morning to you, too," I say, falling back on the couch.

"Asshole."

I squint at her. "That's not the worst thing someone has called me in the past twenty-four hours."

She scrutinizes me in silence. "I'd think you were out boning some other chick except you look like crap. What's going on and why the hell didn't you call?"

"I spent the night in jail, charged with assault and battery after breaking up a fight where I threw a couple of punches." I close my eyes and rub my temples.

"Isn't that your job?"

"Ideally, violence is a last resort, used in self-defense only. Sometimes the line is...blurry." I lurch forward and tug off my boots and socks, appreciating the immediate relief.

"That's ridiculous." Her voice softens, and she scoots closer to me on the sofa. "Are you hurt?"

Not any more than usual. "Nah, just bushed." I take her hand. "Listen, my boss got me out about an hour ago, and I came straight home after I got my truck. I couldn't call you from lockup, and I thought you might still be asleep this morning, so I didn't try once I got released."

She nods. "Let's not make this a habit."

"Dang. I love going to jail." I give her a half-smile, cradle her head and bring her toward me, kissing her softly. "Forgive me?"

She pulls away, wrinkling her nose. "Maybe after a shower."

I chuckle and drag myself upright, feed Diesel his kibble and head into the bathroom. In less than thirty minutes, I'm sprawled on the bed, too tired to even get it on.

I wake to a beeping smoke alarm, burnt odor and yapping dog. I fly out of the rack and find Adrienne frantically fanning the screaming device with a dishtowel while gray plumes pour from the oven.

"Sorry! I was trying to make you a decent meal."

After a quick assessment, I turn off the broiler and ask her to get the front door. Fetching some mitts, I open the oven, stepping to the side as acrid smoke fills the kitchen. I grasp the pan, which holds a charred, indiscernible blob, march it outside and set it on the stone walkway.

"I figured a Texas cowboy might fancy a steak," says Adrienne, chagrined.

I glance back at the blob. "There are only two proper ways to treat a steak, darlin'. One is on the grill, and the other is in a cast-iron skillet. But I appreciate the effort." I pull her into my arms and rapidly become aware I can satisfy my hunger with only one thing. "Let's put supper on the back burner. I fancy something else at the moment."

I scoop her up and carry her to my bed for an hour of lovemaking.

Afterward, both of us reluctant to leave our little oasis, we order Chinese takeout.

"Glad that's settled," I say, leaning back against the pillows as my stomach rumbles loud enough for her to hear.

"Sorry, again, about the whole dinner mess." Adrienne reconfigures herself to sit cross-legged facing me, tucking the sheets around her lower half.

"Don't give it another thought. And I hope this doesn't offend you, but can't you cook?"

She shrugs. "Not much. Grandma Betty showed me a few things, but she mostly made stuff from boxes."

I fight back a grimace. I'd been raised on damn fine food growing up on the ranch. Fresh eggs, beef and pork, vegetables from the garden, my mama's homemade bread and pies, and milk and butter from the dairy down the road. I feel sorry for anyone reared differently, and a tad disappointed. I like a woman who knows her way around the kitchen.

I chuck her under the chin. "Ain't no slack in my rope—I know a thing or two."

"Which means what exactly?"

"I can cook."

She props her hands behind her and leans back, giving me a hell of a view. "I've got other talents."

"Ain't that the truth." I leer, and she swats me. "Aside from putting every woman this side of the Mississippi to shame, what, pray tell, are these 'other' talents?"

"I can cut hair. And trim that mustache threatening to take over your face."

I stroke my stache. "Excellent. Are you my personal stylist now?"

She shrugs. "If you want me to be."

Damn, her tits are distracting, nipples puckered and poking straight at me. "Will you do it topless?"

"It'll cost you extra, cowboy."

I grin. "I'll pay. Where do you work?"

"Tess's Tresses. And not only is Tess a royal bitch, but she also can't style her own hair. I'm amazed anyone books her." Adrienne's fingers comb through her own long locks.

"Is that your dream...the hairstylist thing, or owning your own place?"

She shrugs. "Maybe. What about you?"

"My job or my dream job?"

"Both."

"I manage a shop servicing heavy commercial vehicles. I'm responsible for the workflow, but I still get my hands dirty. I can repair tractor-trailers plus power farm equipment. Not sure it's my ultimate gig, but it suits me for now."

"Does that mean you can fix my car?"

"Child's play," I say.

"Will you do it naked?"

Pouncing on top of her, I kiss her smart, sexy mouth.

Adrienne pushes against my chest. "I almost forgot. Your mother called."

Oh, shit. I sit up, still straddling her legs. "You spoke with Hank Sr.?"

"Didn't I."

I wince. "Uh-oh. How'd that go?"

Adrienne closes her eyes and grimaces. "She thinks I have *designs* on you."

I laugh. "What?"

"I take it she's worried I'm suckering you into a relationship or something. She came across a tad…overprotective."

Perceptive. "Ma can she-bear it up."

She gives me the side-eye. "That's putting it mildly."

"Don't let her scare you off." I lean down and kiss her with more tenderness this time.

"I can handle your mother, who by the way, sends her love."

A knock at the door interrupts us, and we scramble to our

feet, throwing on the clothes we'd shed an hour earlier. I pay the delivery kid and leave the door open to encourage the persistent bitter odor to dissipate.

I unpack the brown bag containing our feast while Adrienne fetches plates, napkins, utensils and two cold beers. We dig in. As I inhale my chow and gaze at the fetching gal across from me, the most vivid of statements crowds out all the others in my head: *she's the one.*

———

Mrs. Hawker: As an attorney, I've got a bead on people. And not that it's any of my business as Hank is my tenant, but when I saw the woman he brought home, the flags were all red. It's easy to understand why any man would be drawn to her because of her exterior assets, but she reminded me of the orchid mantis. Are you familiar with those? Beautiful and flower-like in appearance, it lures the typical pollinators like bees and butterflies. Once they flit too close, the cunning mantis snatches its prey out of the air and eats them for breakfast.

CHAPTER 8
ADRIENNE

HALFWAY TO WORK, I curse after glancing at the gas gauge. I'm cruising on fumes, already behind, and the last thing I need is another one of Tess's stony-faced lectures. I pull into the nearest station and mutter a litany of profanities as the slowest pump in the world drips five bucks worth of fuel into my tank.

I skulk through the back door seventeen minutes late.

"Nice of you to join us," my boss says. Tess has dyed her hair an ugly shade of orangey-red, and I try not to stare at the debacle.

"Traffic sucked. Couldn't help it."

"Your tardiness is one hundred percent your responsibility. Leave earlier. Plan for delays. You don't see the other stylists habitually delinquent. I won't tolerate this, Adrienne—don't let it happen again."

Bitch! I bite my tongue and mumble a platitude as Tess strides from the back room. I stow my purse, pour a cup of coffee and take a few deep breaths to shake off my resentment. I prep my station, crank up my curling irons and greet my first appointment, patiently sitting in the reception area.

The morning flies by. At twelve-thirty, I duck out to grab a quick bite and find Nate leaning casually against the wall, waiting for me.

My insides seize as I glance furtively around. "What are you doing here?"

He flashes a lazy, sexy grin and opens his arms wide as if I'll run into his embrace. "Aren't you happy to see me? I've missed you like crazy."

I stop him with my hand. "Not here."

He shrugs. "How about my ride? It's parked up the street."

Your fuckmobile? Nope. "Fine. But only for a minute."

Hurt flares in his eyes as he cocks his head.

Nate's faded blue van can only be called an eyesore. Rusted, dented and sporting a cracked windshield, it's a miracle it runs. After he climbs into the driver's seat and leans over to unlock my door, I scurry in.

"What gives, baby?"

"I'm not your baby, Nate. We screwed a few times, that's all. And if you recall, we did it covertly since you're Darren's best friend."

He chuckles. "I remember all right. He's still plenty pissed off about it, and you splitting."

"Whatever. He's the one who fucked up."

"I thought if Darren was out of the picture, you and I—"

"You thought wrong. And I'm not trying to be a bitch. You're a decent guy, Nate, but I've moved on." I inspect my fingernails, which need trimming and shaping.

"What do you mean?"

I stare at him straight on, not an easy task with his blinding hotness. "I've got a new fella."

His jaw clenches. "Don't you get around."

"I do what's necessary."

"Why not me, Adrienne?" His voice wavers.

I pause. "Truth? You have nothing to offer—and Darren will always be in our rearview mirror. That's no life."

"Because I'm not rich and I'm out of work? That's temporary.

I think I love you. If I'm not mistaken, you have feelings for me, too."

Not feelings, just attraction. Vast difference. His gorgeous face competes with his chiseled hardbody. Best not stare at the muscles popping out of his clinging shirt much longer or I'll be a goner. "Nope, I don't."

His eyes narrow. Before I can say a word, Nate presses his mouth to mine and holds my head firmly in his grip. I fight him initially, but then my double-crossing lips give way to his. I moan as his tongue works its magic and my insides turn molten. My fingers weave into his wavy chestnut hair and one of his hands travels south, under my sundress. I gasp and he pounces. In no time, he's got me pressed against him on his bed in the back, thrusting into me with a vengeance I neither stop nor want to try.

————

NATE: ADRIENNE CAN SAY WHATEVER SHE WANTS, BUT SHE DOESN'T FOOL ME—SHE'S AS INTO ME AS I AM HER. I'M NOT GOING TO SIT BACK AND WATCH HER SAUNTER OFF WITH ANOTHER SWINGING DICK. I'LL SHOW HER I'M ENOUGH. AND I WASN'T BULLSHITTING WHEN I SAID I LOVED HER. THAT'S A WOMAN YOU CAN'T JUST TASTE ONCE AND WALK AWAY. SHE'S GOT ASS, SASS AND CLASS.

CHAPTER 9
HANK

I WHISTLE a tune as I clock out for the day. I'm in a stellar mood. Playing house with Adrienne suits me fine. Besides the extraordinary sex and how easy she is on the eyes, I enjoy her candor, sense of humor and the way she dishes it back when I tease her. She already showed me her vulnerable side, sharing about her past. And she quit smoking, which means everything... because it means she wants us to work. Bottom line: she's the full package.

Nothing can bring me down today, including wading through the always craptastic commuter congestion. I crank up Deana Carter and tap to the beat on my steering wheel, a stupid grin on my face.

Diesel greets me at the door when I arrive home. I give him a quick rub and let him out. Adrienne raises a limp arm in greeting from the couch, huddled under a blanket.

I kneel by the sofa and move a length of her hair blocking those beautiful eyes. "What's wrong, darlin'?"

"Terrible headache."

I lean over and kiss her forehead. "Poor thing. Did you take ibuprofen?"

She nods. "And a hot shower. It helped."

"Know what else can make you forget about the pain?"

She smiles wanly. "That's not happening tonight, cowboy. Not with this throbbing in my temples."

"Just trying to make you smile," I say. "Can I get you anything…water? Tea?" She declines so I fetch a beer from the fridge. "How was work?"

"Uneventful, aside from this headache smacking me down. It's probably from those damn hair chemicals—or my micromanaging battle-ax boss." She winces and rubs her forehead.

"Why don't you find another job?" I sink into the leather recliner and tilt it back. I love this damn chair, most comfortable contraption I've ever owned.

"I should. How was your day?"

"My co-workers commented on my improved disposition."

"And to what do you attribute this new mood?" she asks with a raised eyebrow.

I place a palm on my chest. "A sexy siren who's stolen my heart."

Adrienne's face brightens. "You've run off with mine too, cowboy."

My turn to grin like an idiot. I relax while I finish my beer, then pamper my sick gal the rest of the night, including suffering through one of her favorite chick flicks.

We crawl into bed early. Her smooth, naked body ignites my fire as I pull her against me, spoon-style. "Sure you're not up for the royal treatment?" I whisper, Hank Jr. raring to go.

"Sorry, baby, not tonight. I'll make it up to you tomorrow."

I content myself with her womanly scent, her silky skin.

"What are you thinking about?" she asks in the dark.

"You."

Adrienne places her hand in the one I have wrapped around her waist. "Don't think I'm crazy, but do you think we might be soulmates?"

"Mmm hmm." So much it spooks me. But I still can't shake

the feeling our time is limited, that I'm a distraction for her. I'm trying my damnedest not to get my hopes up.

"Ever think about the future? Like, do you want to settle down, marry, have kids?" She shifts, her satiny skin stroking mine.

"I think about it sometimes. When the time is right, I want those things," I say.

"Have you ever been in love?"

"Once. And I've also dated knowing it wouldn't amount to much. How about you?"

"Same."

Dang, she feels sublime. The perfect pea to my pod. "Do you want all that stuff…marriage, babies, grandkids?"

She jerks her head in my direction. "Whoa! Marriage and a couple of kids, yes. I can't think about grandchildren yet. I'm only twenty-two!"

"You're darn near over the hill." At twenty-four, I can't believe *I'm* thinking so long-term about Adrienne.

She thrusts her hips backward in protest.

"Watch the family jewels, darlin'." I ignore the discomfort and rearrange my package.

She giggles.

I kiss her goodnight and listen to her breathing turn steady as she falls asleep in my arms. I stay awake another hour, envisioning what a life together might look like. I hope it includes at least two nitnoys running underfoot. Not that I'm ready, know this girl from Adam, or believe she'll stick around.

SHARLENE: I WENT OVER TO NATE'S—LOOKING HOT, I MIGHT ADD. I BROUGHT HIM A SIX-PACK, FLIRTED MY ASS OFF AND PRETENDED TO HANG ON HIS EVERY WORD, YOU KNOW? WHAT DO YOU THINK THAT GOT ME? JACK SHIT, THAT'S WHAT. I MAY AS WELL HAVE BEEN INVISI-

BLE. ALL HE WANTED TO TALK ABOUT WAS ADRIENNE, AS IF I COULD GIVE A CARE. I'M EMBARRASSED TO ADMIT THIS, BUT I GOT DESPERATE, YOU KNOW? THE ONLY WAY TO PROVE MY WORTH OVER HO HIGHNESS WAS TO CRAWL ON MY KNEES AND OFFER HIM THE BEST BLOWJOB HE'D EVER RECEIVED. LET'S JUST SAY HE DIDN'T DISAGREE.

CHAPTER 10
ADRIENNE

I MAKE it to work on time after forcing myself out of bed without snoozing the alarm once. My nagging bitch-boss doesn't acknowledge me or my punctuality.

My first appointment is a wash and set for Mrs. Haniford, an obese woman who calls me sweetie and dispenses unwanted advice each month. I tolerate her.

My second booking is the perky Shay, a young newlywed who wants chunky highlights and regales me with the dramas dominating her life. I pretend to care.

Don arrives next. I trim him up every four weeks like clock-work. He's quiet, polite, an above-average tipper. Somewhere in his mid-thirties, I suspect he might bat for the other team.

My last appointment before lunch is Mrs. Fite, a woman on her fourth husband who can't resist telling me each speck of juicy gossip she's accumulated. I adore her. She quickly picks up on my terrific mood and bombards me with questions, prying out of me most of the story about Darren, Nate and cowboy Hank. Good thing she's in for a permanent wave or time would have run out to discuss it all.

I place cotton around the perimeter of her hairline to protect her skin and apply the perm solution, squirting it on the neat rows of rolled hair. The door pings with a new arrival, which I ignore, focused on my task. If I miss one strand, it won't curl.

Mrs. Fite purrs. "Who is *that* hunk of man?"

I glance up and lock eyes with Nate. Damn him for showing up here *again*, and for my heart lurching in my chest as he flashes his pearly whites. He is not the one, girlfriend!

"That's Nate," I whisper in Mrs. Fite's ear.

"Yummy," she hums. "No wonder you're in a lather."

I finish with the solution and cover her hair with a plastic cap.

"Go on with yourself, honey. Find out what he wants...but don't forget about me processing over here."

I set the timer for twenty minutes. "Be back in a jiff."

Peeling off my gloves, I throw them in the nearest trashcan and address Nate at the counter. "How can I help you?" I say sweetly—and loudly—before murmuring under my breath, "And what the fuck are you doing here?"

"I'm interested in booking a service," he answers with a sly smile. If I wasn't so annoyed, I'd be enchanted.

I close my eyes and summon strength. Refocusing on him, I give him the death stare. "You can't keep showing up like this, Nate. It's not cool, and I'm with a client."

"It's almost lunchtime. Meet me outside when you're finished, and we'll talk."

"Talk? That's what you said yesterday."

His lip twitches on one side. He stares at me hard, unleashing the full power of his sea-green eyes, dark hair and...that mouth.

I swallow. "Fine...when I'm done with this customer. Until then, please leave." I make a production out of handing him a salon brochure listing our services.

I smile as I pass Mrs. Fite, who raises her eyebrows and likely salivates to hear the details. I lock myself in the bathroom. *Fuck!* Why does Nate have to complicate my life? And why does the gravitational pull have to be so strong toward him? He is nothing but a pretty face with no assets, no future. Not to mention his friendship with Darren. He equals a dead end—unlike Hank—and I need to handle this once and for all.

I finish Mrs. Fite's perm. When I confess I'm ending it with him, she clucks about how I should ride that stallion one last time, making me laugh.

Forty minutes later, I walk outside and find Nate kicking a rock against his shoe like a Hacky Sack. He glances up and the pebble falls to the sidewalk and bounces off the curb.

"Hi, gorgeous. Thanks for meeting me."

"Like I had a choice." I canvas the street like an escaped convict.

He chuckles. "Back to the van? It's right around the corner."

This garners him the side-eye. "Someplace out in the open is fine."

"You want to do it in public, huh? I like your style."

I roll my eyes and gesture to a nearby bench. "Let's sit here." I swiftly reconsider when I realize someone might see us. Call me paranoid. "Wait, the van works, but we're *only talking*, got it?"

"Roger that, Batman."

Dork.

"You look beautiful today."

"Don't, Nate."

"Don't compliment you? Why not?"

"Just...don't."

We walk in silence the rest of the way.

Once inside the vehicle, Nate taps a fresh pack of Marlboro's against his palm, unwraps the cellophane and lights one up.

"Can I bum one of those?"

He flips the pack toward me, a few cigarettes sticking out of the opening. I snag one, put it to my lips and he lights it. I inhale deep into my lungs, and it's fucking bliss.

Taking a few puffs, I steel myself. "I can't see you anymore."

He opens his arms and grins. "I'm right here, baby. Look all you want."

I stare out the front windshield at the everyday bustle of people probably living normal lives. "I'm serious. I can't date you, have sex with you, any of it."

"Why not? I like you. You like me. Nothing else matters." He reaches for my hand, and I shake it off.

"You're wrong. I need more. I want a relationship with someone stable, ambitious and committed."

"And in exchange, you're willing to give up hot sex?"

I glare at him.

He holds up his hands in surrender. "Sorry. And baby, it may not look like it, but I can be that guy. I don't have it all figured out right now, but I will." He clasps my hand and this time, I let him. "I want more with you, too."

My heart melts a fraction. If only I believed it could work.

"Can't we simply be with each other and give it some time?"

"I told you, I'm with someone else."

He strokes my cheek. "Does he know how to push all your beautiful buttons like I do?"

I can't answer or argue. He has the unfair advantage of the full package, sans brains. And he understands exactly how to use his assets. My mind blanks—I can't even remember what I like about Hank.

"Don't decide today," he whispers in my ear, making my insides twinge. "You can call it quits later, but give this a chance, or a moment, this fucking day, if that's all it winds up being." He kisses my forehead, cheek, neck.

"Nate..." My resolve is slipping, my breath catching and stuttering. I can't think straight.

"Please, baby," he murmurs. "Let me worship at the altar of Adrienne and treat you like the goddess you are. I will burst if I can't have you right now." His lips crash down on mine, and I respond, knowing I will indulge him one last time. And possibly more.

. . .

I return to work, exalted (he had indeed worshipped at the altar of moi) and disappointed (where is my resolve?). My skin tingles from Nate's touch and my wet panties are a tangible reminder of a tryst I'd intended—and failed—to avoid. Is it wrong to want *both* of them? I haven't pledged exclusivity, and together, they make the ideal man. Hank would never go for the idea, but Nate would absolutely accept sloppy seconds. It wouldn't be the first time in my life I'd walked that tightrope. I cringe, remembering I'd promised the cowboy sex tonight after feigning a headache the night before.

The door chimes and a courier delivers a dozen long-stemmed red roses. For me. From Hank. Like a karmic warning. My throat constricts as I read the card: THINKING OF YOU AND HOW PERFECT YOU ARE. YOURS, COWBOY HANK. I clutch the vase and carry the flowers back to my station, avoiding eye contact with the other stylists.

I limp through my remaining appointments, pasting on a false smile and pretending to care while listening to my clients' endless confessions and trivial blather.

At closing, Tess announces the health department is inspecting the salon at the end of the week. This means verifying our cosmetology licenses are up to date. As she outlines her expectations for staff in preparation of the visit, I tune out. This chick will be long gone.

TRISH: I WAS EATING LUNCH AT FRANK & STEIN'S WHEN ADRIENNE HOPPED IN A VAN WITH MISTER FINE-ASS WHITE BOY. YOU REMEMBER THE SAYING, *IF THIS VAN IS ROCKIN', DON'T BOTHER KNOCKIN'?* COULDN'T HAVE BEEN TEN MINUTES LATER, THAT EYESORE ON WHEELS WAS GYRATING LIKE A CHRISTMAS TREE NEEDLE-SHAKING MACHINE.

Then the tramp comes back to work and the other idiot she's seeing sends her roses—the expensive kind. I can't imagine what those guys see in her unless she's one hell of a lay. Or as Santa says: Ho! Ho! Ho!

CHAPTER 11
HANK

I PULL in next to Adrienne's car and another goofy grin spreads across my face. I've got a pep in my step and only one thing on my mind. Diesel tackles me, and I give him the bare minimum greeting. No offense to my best friend, but Adrienne takes center stage right now. Al Green croons "Let's Stay Together" throughout the cottage, and the roses I sent stand elegantly arranged in a vase on the dining table. My lovely roommate is nowhere in sight, but then I spy small pieces of paper. Upon closer examination, they trail down the hall leading to our bedroom.

"Hot damn," I murmur. My pulse races as I pick up the first one.

HURRY, it reads.

I scoop up the next. LOVER.

I move faster now, stumbling over my feet as I race to read them all.

IT'S... NOT... POLITE... TO... KEEP... A... LADY... WAITING... AND... I'VE... BEEN... WAITING... A... LIFETIME... FOR... YOU.

The notes end at the bedroom, where I eagerly push open the

door. Adrienne is sprawled on my California King clad in a lacy black getup, staring at me hungrily.

"Hi, cowboy. Wanna go for a ride?"

My cock strains against my jeans as I whip off my shirt and boots and extricate myself from the rest.

She crawls on all fours across the bed and inhales my throbbing dick between her plump lips. Ready to explode, I force my thoughts to something bland, so I last longer than a pussified two minutes. *Carburetors. Guitars. WWII.* Her mouth is warm and slick as she works her magic tongue up and down my shaft with perfection. One hand lightly strokes my balls as she sucks me deeper and deeper, so far I bottom out in her throat. *Little League. Dogs. Fishing.* I'm going to detonate any second, and nothing would make me happier...except I desperately want to bury myself in her sweet center. She goes downstairs, gently sucking my cashews—the whole shebang getting the royal treatment. Holy mother of fuck, this is next level. No chick has ever done this. I'm gonna lose it. *National Geographic. Rattlesnakes. Go Cowboys.*

Adrienne releases me but before she can ramp back up, I push her back on the bed and sink into her. "Sweet Jesus," I breathe.

She's so wet and velvety inside, it's like fucking ice cream. Wrapping her legs around me, she moans with each thrust. *Cheetos. Star Wars. Rodeos.* I'm hanging by a thread, but I can't stop pounding into her, she's driving me so crazy. Her creamy depths, her vexing eyes, her sexy black lingerie, that moaning mouth. I plunge into her with a force and velocity I can't control, all of her taking all of me. *Foghorn Leghorn. Socket wrench. Duck hunt—*

I unhinge, my pelvis grinding into hers on autopilot as the universe explodes and I am lost in her once again.

"Goddamn," I murmur, unable to move.

Her legs release me, and I lift my head to see Adrienne's lips curve into a smile. I roll off her and onto my back, and she shifts to rest her head on my chest. I stroke her hair, contentment permeating me from head to toe. "So much for ladies first. You sidetracked me with your wily woman ways."

She smiles against my skin. "I'm perfect, cowboy. I don't need a thing."

"We'll see about that. And I'm starving, but I ain't leaving this bed with you in it."

"I'm perfectly happy right here myself." Her breath tickles my torso, and I quiver.

She sits up, straddling me. "You're ticklish?"

"No," I lie.

"Then you won't mind if I do this…" She traces nondescript patterns with her fingers down my skin.

I fight it for as long as possible before my body jerks and twitches, and I succumb to unmanly snickers. Turning the tables, I flip her underneath me and dole out my own tickle spree until she begs for a truce. Staring down at her radiant face, flushed and lighthearted, I know I've scored the woman of the century. My mouth seeks hers, the contours of our lips sealing against each other.

––––––

The non-driving maggots in the DC Metro Area are asshats, and I'm way over their infinite road transgressions. I jerk my truck into the left lane to maneuver around a jackwagon who appears to be grooming himself. *Douchetard.* I tap my steering wheel as vehicles inch forward. These idiots block intersections after the lights turn red, cut people off and extend no courtesy. Unlike them, I possess manners. Sometimes I wonder if those only exist in Texas. Thank God I'm an excellent driver; it helps me anticipate their bassackwards ways. The only thing keeping me sane is doling out my brand of justice to these unsuspecting fuckwidgets in my personal fantasies.

As I crawl through rush-hour traffic, I am once again stymied by how many morons have personalized tags, one of the stupidest ideas known to man. Try escaping from the law or an agitated driver when your tag is memorable. It's not as if cars or even trucks are discernible from one another nowadays—everything looks pathetically the same. But slap on RAD GRL or N2 DISCO and you might as well be a fucking lighthouse.

The pace finally picks up, and the impatient ass with the gelled hair in a gray Lexus cuts me off for the second time after weaving through traffic, attempting to move ahead. I lay on the horn, and he flips *me* off. Classic.

Dragging him out of his car, I replace him in the driver's seat and grip him by the collar with my left hand. Holding his face against the pavement, I press the gas and take him for a ride.

I'm stopped at a red light and witness three shitballs blocking the intersection. When it turns green, we sit as immobile as the Grand Tetons instead of moving along seamlessly. If their brains were leather, they couldn't saddle a flea.

I ram through their blockade, their demolished vehicles flying out of my way like pins in a bowling alley.

The poor sucker in the Jeep (SOCR DAD) chalks up multiple offenses. Not only does he appear lost, drifting in and out of other lanes, but he can't maintain the speed limit for longer than two seconds and no self-respecting Jeep owner would profess to be a *soccer dad*. He should just put LOSER on his plate, turn in his man card and buy a fucking minivan.

Strapping him against a chain link fence, I pelt baseballs at him as he flinches and ducks.

If only my imagination became reality.

My thoughts drift to Adrienne all morning, making it challenging to focus on paperwork, jobs and parts orders. The sexy number she wore, her tantalizing pose on the bed, those saucy little notes leading me to the bedroom, and most of all, that she wanted to please me…it makes my stomach somersault revisiting it. Talk about winning the lottery. If it lasts. *Let it last.* Those inner voices are getting louder. I need a top-notch fantasy beat-down for them.

I call Adrienne at work during lunch as an excuse to hear her voice. "What's cookin', good lookin'?"

"I think I'm coming down with something."

"It's probably a Hankover. Get it? Hank plus hangover…I've plumb done you in."

She manages a weak laugh. "I feel rotten. Feverish, chills, the works."

"Why don't you go home, sweetheart? Dr. McCallister will fix you right up."

"I'm trying to make it through the day, but I'll take the doctor up on his proposal later."

"It'll be my pleasure. Take it easy, and I'll see you back at the ranch."

"Thanks, cowboy."

I stop by the store after work and stock up on groceries and over-the-counter medicines. When I arrive home, Adrienne's on the couch cocooned in a blanket, staring at the television. I ditch the bags and sit on the edge of the sofa.

"You all right, darlin'?"

She shakes her head. "Miserable."

I lean down and touch the tip of my tongue to her forehead.

She flinches. "What are you doing?"

"Best way to check for a fever. You're cool as a cucumber."

She shivers. "I've got the chills and my stomach hurts."

"I bought some stuff that might help. You relax." I caress her cheek. "Where's Diesel?"

"Outside. He wouldn't stop barking, so I let him out a while ago."

I'm surprised he didn't come running when I pulled up. Must be off the grid. I stash my purchases, tidy up and put fresh sheets on the bed. My dog reappears, and I give him a pig's ear to gnaw on after he eats his kibble. I whip up a quick dinner—hot dogs for me, soup for her—and we dine in front of the TV.

After I finish, I stretch my legs on the hassock and cross my feet.

"You working tonight?" she asks.

"Unfortunately. I'd rather stay here with you. Not to mention, I'm beat."

I close my eyes and force myself to catnap for twenty minutes, which gives me the boost of energy I need. I drag on my boots and kneel by Adrienne.

"You gonna be okay?"

"I'll be fine. Just don't be flirting with all the single ladies." She smiles wryly.

I chuck her gently under the chin. "I've only got eyes for one single lady. Or are you no longer available, perchance?"

"I believe I'm taken." She coughs. "What say you, cowboy?"

My heart leaps. If I had a tail, it'd be wagging like a mofo. She wants to be exclusive. With *me.* "That dills my pickle, darlin'!" The grin on my face is so immense, it might break it.

"I swear, the way you talk."

I wink, dipping to kiss her forehead. "You've made me one happy man tonight. I don't deserve you."

She flashes me a look I can't discern, almost like sadness.

———

Mrs. Hawker: I was out walking the property when someone shouted. I hurried toward the carriage house, where Hank's lady friend was yelling at poor Diesel. To his credit, he

STOOD HIS GROUND, HOWLING AT HER. THEY SAY DOGS HAVE A SIXTH SENSE ABOUT PEOPLE AND CAN RECOGNIZE BAD EGGS. WHEN SHE REALIZED I WAS THERE, SHE HID HER CIGARETTE, PLASTERED ON A SMILE AND WAVED, AS FRIENDLY AND WHOLESOME AS DORIS DAY. LET'S JUST SAY I'M WITH THE DOG ON THIS ONE.

CHAPTER 12
ADRIENNE

MY FAKE ILLNESS lasts two weeks, with a short-lived revival sandwiched in between. I deliver a flawless performance, not overdoing it while throwing Hank a bone in the sex department on days I'm "well" enough, keeping him happy and engaged. Using a little feminine persuasion, I charm an urgent care doctor into prescribing an antibiotic during week two of my "flu." The cowboy is no dummy, and the meds provide veracity to my scheme.

When rare smidgeons of guilt arise, I shove them down. A girl's gotta do what a girl's gotta do—and my little white lies don't hurt my new beau one iota.

Hank wonders how I can miss so much work. While I offer up reassurances Tess wouldn't have given me in a million years, I can't continue working at the salon with the inspector situation. It's too risky with my bogus license. Plus, I hate my fucking boss and I'm sure she hates me, even more so after ghosting her. I hated ditching my clients, but self-preservation reigns.

With my health back to "normal," it's time for Act II. As I prepare for the fake return to Tess's Tresses, I cycle through my morning routine relaxed and unhurried.

I drive near the salon and dither around for a half-hour, enjoying a syrupy mocha latte while people watching. Has Nate returned in search of me? My nether regions twinge as I relive our last van hookup. I allow this little indulgence, knowing I've slammed that door shut.

Enough. It's time.

It takes a few minutes, but I conjure up some tears, dry them and repeat. Bonus points for smeary mascara. With a final FU, I flip off Tess and her salon and drive to Hank's workplace.

He spots me before I enter the building, his expression transforming from joy to worry. "What's wrong? What happened?"

I sniffle. "Tess fired me."

"For missing work? I thought she approved it."

"She lied."

Hank places his hands on my shoulders. "That's illegal. We can fight this."

I lean into his chest. "I don't want to. She's a bitch, and I hated working for her."

His arms draw me in, holding me tightly. "For crying in the drink, Adrienne," he says, bending his head against mine, his breath warm. "She can't terminate you without just cause."

I disengage and rummage in my purse for a tissue. "She said I'm unreliable. And she's the boss, two-faced skank."

His hands clench at his sides. "What are you going to do?"

I shrug and blot my eyes. "I can do cuts on the down-low until I find another salon, or waitress for a while."

The muscle in Hank's jaw flexes as he rakes a hand through his thick locks. "Jesus! I've half a mind to drive over there and tell her a thi—"

"No! Don't," I say. "It's not worth it and may make things worse if I need a reference." As if. I've got a better chance of winning an all-expenses-paid trip to Bermuda for two.

"You sure? It's against my nature to let people get away with unethical bullshit." He crosses his arms, his lips pressed into a thin line.

Nodding, I wipe my remaining tears.

"I'm sorry, sweetheart, but I need to get back to work. There's a mountain of problems to solve—it's a real shitshow today."

"I shouldn't have come. I'm upset, and you always make everything...brighter." I do my best to look helpless.

"I'm glad you did." Hank pulls me in for another embrace and kisses me on the forehead. "You all right to drive?"

I nod again.

He walks me to the car and opens my door.

Hesitating, I turn and caress his cheek. "I know it's probably too soon to say this, but I love you."

A smile stretches his mustache across his face, and he picks me up, bringing me up to his height. "Damn if I don't love you right back." He sets me down and presses his lips urgently against mine, passion and emotion swirling into one.

Relief hits as I steer the car home. My plan worked. I'd left a salon I hated. Not a soul, aside from my Grandma Betty, is aware I live at Hank's, eliminating any way for Nate or other hangers-on to find me and Armageddon everything. And when I told Hank I loved him, he responded the way I anticipated. It isn't a lie, per se—I *want* to love him, I truly do. The important thing is, I bought myself some time. I can breathe. The cowboy will let me stay at his place for as long as I need.

I wish life wasn't always a series of tightrope walks. For once, just once, I'd like smooth sailing. Isn't it my turn for easy street? I deserve it, don't I?

Maybe not. Maybe this shit is my lifelong penance for my sister.

For the next couple of weeks, I provide hairstyling services for friends and longtime clientele at their homes. When I impress Hank after cutting his hair and trimming his mustache (not topless, although I let him cop a feel), he sends me half a dozen new customers, too. All the while, I search for jobs, finding salon positions and plenty of waitress gigs at restaurants and night-clubs. The cowboy voices his displeasure at the idea of a cocktail server, but it's easy money, coincides with him working at The Crazy Horse, and this gal has no cash reserves. I'd be in deep kimchee without Hank paying for my room and board, and his ignorance is essential to keep me from falling off the high wire.

I'm hopeful, and grateful, to find myself on an upward trajectory. I sense I'm through the worst of things, climbing out of the pit always threatening to pull me back in, believing smooth sailing *is* on the horizon, in my grasp.

Then disaster happens.

———

DR. LANCASTER: I'VE BEEN UNABLE TO RID THAT YOUNG WOMAN FROM MY MIND, TRY AS I MAY. STRIKING, WITH A POUTING MOUTH FLANKED BY PLUMP LIPS. THE OPPOSITE OF MY WIFE, WHOM I LOVE, BUT WHO'S NEVER SATISFIED MY NEEDS IN THE BEDROOM. THE WOMAN WAS LIKELY A HYPOCHONDRIAC, AND ADAMANT ABOUT GETTING AN ANTIBIOTIC DESPITE MY FINDINGS TO THE CONTRARY. I BENT TO HER WILL, MESMERIZED BY THE EYEFUL SHE PROVIDED OF HER LARGE BOSOM AND HER INVITATION TO GROPE HER UNDER THE GUISE OF FINDING A LUMP. I WAS QUITE THOROUGH IN MY EXAM, ALLOWING ME TO REASSURE HER I FOUND NOTHING. EVER SINCE, I'VE BEEN UNABLE TO THINK OF LITTLE ELSE THAN PLACING MY MOUTH—AND MORE—ONTO THOSE TWO MAGNIFICENT ORBS.

CHAPTER 13
HANK

A DELICIOUS AROMA envelops me as I come through the door. I don't care how progressive, feminist or whatever the hell guys profess to be nowadays, there ain't a man alive who doesn't love their gal rustling up a meal.

I plant a kiss on her sweet lips. "Smells mighty fine in here!"

"I made a chicken casserole. Hope you like it." Adrienne wrings her hands together, like she's nervous about cooking for me, and damn if my heart doesn't stutter.

My stomach rumbles in response, like a bird dog on point. "I'm sure it's fantastic." I make quick work of washing up, while she carries a salad to the table, the bowl clattering on the surface when she drops it.

I open the fridge and snag a beer. "Want one?"

"Uh...no thanks. Although I could chug a twelve-pack right now," she mutters.

"Bad day?"

She shakes her head and busies herself with spooning a mound of casserole on my plate as I slide into my chair.

"You have no idea how much I appreciate coming home to this, darlin'."

She smiles weakly. "Dig in."

I attack my dinner, murmuring compliments between bites. When I come up for air, Adrienne has hardly touched her food. Maybe I should remember my manners and slow the hell down. I scrape another forkful in my mouth.

"Hank..."

I look up mid-swallow.

"I've got to tell you something."

My heart leaps in my chest. *Crap, she's leaving.* "Should I worry?"

She waits a beat, then drops a bomb. "I'm pregnant."

Pregnant? *Pregnant?* How is that possible? Okay, dumbass, you know how. But how did you let it happen? You never should have removed the goalie. You always practice the golden rule: sheath your steed. You got sucked in, lost your head. Yeah, both ways. Fucking moron. Jesus...I'm not ready for a kid. Later on— sure thing. But now? I'm only twenty-four! *I'm* still a kid. Will she consider an abortion? Am I a total asshole for asking? My mother is going to blow a fucking gasket...

Adrienne stares at me, waiting. I've got to say something, but this is one time I don't have a fucking clue. "Give me a minute. I'm trying to absorb this...news," I say.

She nods. "Tell me about it."

"What happened? I mean, you're on the Pill. I thought it was foolproof."

"Ditto, and it's never failed until now. It might have been the antibiotics. I found out some make birth control less effective, which would have been helpful knowledge ahead of time. *Thanks, doc.*" She rests her elbow on the table and leans her head into her upturned palm, closing her eyes and letting out a long breath.

"Have you thought about what you...want to do?"

Adrienne eyes flash open. "You mean keep it or not?"

I nod, unable to vocalize either.

"I'm not ready to be a mom, not by any stretch. It scares the hell out of me. But if you're asking about abortion, the answer is no fucking way."

Any coherent response leaves the building. I've lost the ability to formulate words.

"So, that's it, Hank? You've got nothing else to say?"

"I…" My brain freezes, going utterly blank.

"You're an asshole." Adrienne runs from the room and moments later, the bedroom door slams.

I stare at my plate of half-eaten food and push it away, my appetite vanished, along with my unfettered youth. Darkness fills the cottage, and Diesel treads over and lays his snout on my leg. Absently, I stroke his head. My mind is whirling like a dust devil as I try to process this monumental turn of events or even move from this spot.

––––––––

Janelle: It's not every day someone buys three pregnancy tests *and* a paternity test. I don't like to judge, but she also bought two packs of cigarettes, and she shouldn't be smoking if she's pregnant. You couldn't pay me for her troubles. Although having sex with more than one guy sounds like a problem of prosperity. Just sayin'.

CHAPTER 14
ADRIENNE

I'M HOLED up in the bathroom, sobbing. It's pathetic but the dam opened and now I'm trapped in the whitewater rushing through the abyss of the gorge known as fucking *feelings*.

It's a rare day I can't control the waterworks or the chasm of sadness I quell on autopilot. Stupid pregnancy hormones. All the crap from the past month. And now being in this ridiculous, avoidable predicament. My sister's face appears unbidden. The tears flow fresh as pain reaches into my chest and squeezes my heart. My parents materialize next…my father with his grabby hands and leering eyes…my worthless mother, hard lines denting her face, her steely gaze ignoring the conspicuous evidence for years. Parents of the fucking year.

And now I'm going to be one. *Fuck, fuck, FUCK!* How am I going to navigate a baby? And single motherhood? I can barely take care of myself. And Hank thinks abortion is the answer? Typical. Men are so self-serving—and predictable—when you give them the key to the crypt. They're more than happy to divest themselves of the burden and responsibility of birth control, but when things go south, they're the first to suggest killing off the nuisance of children. *Wouldn't want to trouble you,*

Hank. I made that choice once in my life and I'm not doing it again. Not that I'm one hundred percent sure Hank's the father. Because nothing I do is ever fucking uncomplicated. I hug my knees to my chest as waterfalls gush from my eyes and roll down my cheeks.

He knocks, and I snort in disgust. "Go away."

"Please open the door," he pleads.

Fuck him.

"Please," he repeats.

Fine. I crawl over and unlock the door. He can do the rest.

Hank eases through. Using a handful of wadded up tissues, I blow my nose, avoiding his gaze.

"Adrienne."

My eyes focus on a blemish in one of the tiles. "Although this wasn't planned, it's happening, with or without—"

"I'm not saying—"

My head swivels toward him. "That's right. You're not saying *anything!* You're being such a dick."

"Let me finish. I needed time to think. You rocked my world."

"And mine isn't?"

He sits on the floor next to me and takes my hand. "We're going to figure this out together."

"This isn't a crossword puzzle!"

"That didn't come out like I meant." He lets out a whoosh of air. "We've known each other all of five minutes, but I've got to believe this happened for a reason."

Did I hear him right? I glance up at his face.

"Everything in my life led me to this moment, here with you, with this tiny heartbeat of another human we made growing inside of you. Is it perfect? Nope. We didn't plan it, aren't ready for it and have only begun to enjoy ourselves. But none of that matters now. Our little boy or girl is coming into the world in less than nine months, and we can give our little person a good life."

My fragile heart lurches. More droplets trickle down my face, and he dries them with his free hand.

"You are so beautiful," he says softly. "And I'm not going anywhere."

Fresh tears spill as Hank pulls me into his arms and holds me while I weep. I'm sure he thinks I need soothing, but these teardrops are a combination of relief and awe. His sentiments humble me.

It doesn't change the enormity of the situation: I'm pregnant. The father is either Hank, or God help me, Nate. No matter the truth, I must guard this information with my life, and take it to the grave, much like the other weighty secret I carry like a sack of cement. But at least I won't have to go it alone, so long as the cowboy thinks the baby is his.

And maybe, probably, it is.

———

Henrietta McCallister: In this world you've got two kinds of people: the workers and the shirkers. I guarantee the harlot shacked up with my son is a shirker looking for her next meal ticket. She lost her pathetic excuse for a job. Wouldn't put it past her to get knocked up and sever my boy's future like a wolf's leg caught in a trap. Hank's too gullible. Always has been. Try as I might to toughen him up, he still needs to grow a pair and escape that floozy's hold before it maims him forever.

CHAPTER 15

HANK

"FOR HEAVEN'S SAKE, she swindled you!" My mother takes the news about as well as I predicted. Once again, I'm *a moron, a pushover, a patsy*.

"Ma, you haven't met her yet. Can you give her a chance, please?"

"You're thinking of marrying her now, am I right?" Her tone remains acidic.

"Of course. She's having our baby. You raised me to believe that's what any responsible man would do."

"I thought I raised you to be smart first. I don't understand how you let this happen."

Touché. "It was an accident."

"You *accidentally* had intercourse?"

I wince.

"Remember me telling you not to throw your life away for five minutes of pleasure?"

If my father only gives my mother a measly five minutes of sexual satisfaction, no wonder she's so irritable. Not like I want to picture *that*. "Ma, this one's a keeper."

"And you know this because of *all* the time you've spent

together? I had one short conversation with the gal, and I'll bet I understand her better than you do!"

Highly likely. Who can figure women? "It's important to me you like and accept her. And she is carrying your grandchild."

My mother sighs so loudly it's a phrase all its own. "Are you certain it's yours?"

I bristle. "It's mine."

"Do yourself a favor and take a paternity test."

"Drop it, Ma." God, this woman is impossible.

"Fine, I'll buck up. But mark my words, she's slicker than a boiled onion, so don't say I didn't warn you when this all blows apart."

"Thanks for your vote of confidence." As usual.

"I'm confident in *you*, son. And I love you more than a hog loves mud, but this is not what I wanted for you. Not at this stage of your life."

"Believe me, Ma, I understand. But the chips have fallen, so they're going to lay where they may."

"Apparently."

We pause. It's awkward.

My mother clears her throat. "When can we meet her?"

I hoped she'd ask, and I'm ready with an answer. "How about Thanksgiving? I'll take off work and we'll fly out."

"Fine."

"Great."

"We miss you." Her tone's lost the edge.

"I miss you, too." *Even though you're a hard-ass.* "And Ma? Thank you."

She pooh-poohs me, then fetches my father and brothers, so I can pass on my news. More gracious than my mother, they offer congratulations and lob me some good-natured ribbing.

With that over, I turn my attention to planning my proposal. It's not every day a man asks the love of his life for her hand in marriage.

———

Elias McCallister: Hank's a champ at taking the heat off, even from three states away. He always manages to find himself in a mess of trouble, especially with Ma. She's fired up, going on about oversexed boys without a God-given brain, what she's done to deserve this, and the embarrassment of one of her sons having a "dadgum shotgun wedding." I'm staying out of the line of fire, but I'll stick up for my brother after she simmers down. He's true blue and a gentleman. If he says this gal's worth it, then she is.

CHAPTER 16
ADRIENNE

I'M CLEARING the dinner dishes when Hank leans in for a goodbye kiss before his shift at The Crazy Horse. He's got a strange gleam in his eye.

"What?" I ask.

"I left you a note. Make sure you check it out." He winks and slips out the door.

I find it on the bed and sit on the mattress to read it: Surprise plans tomorrow! Dress comfortably and be prepared to walk.

My lips curve into a smile. What's my cowboy cooked up? Although my bun-in-the-oven announcement rocked our boat, Hank weathered it like a gentleman, and the last few days, even seems animated about the prospect. It makes me hopeful. I stand and rummage through my wardrobe, trying to figure out what to wear for this outing.

I happen across the brown bag hiding the paternity test. Holding it in my hand, I decide I don't want the truth. Right now, I have plausible deniability, plus Nate's a dead end and Hank's a willing and capable provider. He's the father, no matter what biological evidence exists to the contrary. I stick the accusatory box back in the sack and shove it to the bottom of the kitchen trash. I'll think no more about it.

The next morning, Hank catches me checking myself out in the bathroom mirror. The cool November air calls for jeans, which I've paired with a blazing red V-neck sweater and matching Chuck Taylor's since we plan to walk *somewhere*. Thigh-high boots are more my style, but practicality wins out.

"Is this outfit okay? You haven't told me enough! Where are we going? You realize that's a bona fide form of torture for a woman, right?"

He merely smiles, still not giving anything away. He's worn the same satisfied expression all morning. It's maddening, but I admit, fun.

Rubbing Diesel, he mumbles how he wishes we could take him today and promises to make it up to him. Try as I may, wolf-dog hasn't warmed to me, so I'm glad he isn't joining us.

Hank hoists me into the truck and closes the passenger door. When he hops in, his chipped-tooth grin is firmly in place.

"Ready?" He turns the key in the ignition.

"Cute," I mutter. I'm dying of anticipation—and the cowboy is milking it. "What's in the backpack?" A sizeable one sits between us.

"Uh uh uhhhh...none of your beeswax. And no peeking!" He clicks on the radio, immediately singing along to some country tune about a lucky man. Twangified yokel music isn't my thing, but I refrain from making a negative comment, refusing to dampen his mood.

Hank croons as he drives, shooting me teasing glances under the brim of his hat. After a short trip through Arlington streets, he speeds up as we merge onto the lush, tree-lined George Washington Memorial Parkway. Fifteen minutes later, he pulls into a parking lot adjacent to the Potomac River, grabs the backpack and helps me out of the truck. We walk across the pedestrian bridge to Theodore Roosevelt Island.

"I've never been here," I confess.

"It's one of the coolest spots in DC," Hank says. "Teddy is my favorite president, and this island is the ideal tribute to him. Now I get to share it with my best gal. That's called the trifecta of perfect."

His unbridled cheer forces a smile to my face. He takes my hand as we stroll up the hill to Memorial Plaza, which features an animated sculpture of Roosevelt with his arm extended in greeting, tailcoat flowing. Adjacent fountains bubble, and two bridges arch from the plaza to other parts of the island.

"Check these out," Hank says, positioning me in front of the first of four large columns etched with some of Roosevelt's most famous sentiments.

I skim the quotes about nature, manhood, youth and democracy as he eagerly awaits my response.

"He's amazing, right?"

I don't want to disappoint him but reading about history isn't my jam. "For sure."

"Every American should visit this place and read those words. We'd be a better nation for it." Spoken like a true patriot.

As we meander along the island's wooded trails, the Potomac flows around us, the sun filters through the plentiful trees and Hank elaborates on why he admires our former president. I can't remember one fact about him from my years of public schooling, including whatever graced the shoebox diorama I'd created about him in fifth grade. But the cowboy is a fountain of knowledge, reviewing Roosevelt's legacy, philosophies, desires and efforts. What little I'd learned about Hank jives so much with Teddy, it's no wonder he idolizes him.

We segue onto the Swamp Trail, which includes a suspended walkway to navigate the marshy areas. He points out the Kennedy Center and notorious Watergate Hotel through the trees. A fawn prances across the path and into the woods, and a hawk perches on a nearby tree branch.

We close the loop and wind up at the main plaza again, and

I'm wondering why he brought me here aside from sharing something he loves. Not exactly surprise worthy.

He steers me to a bench. "Eyes closed, darlin'." After indiscernible rustling noises, he says I can look.

I open my eyes, taking in the scene: a picnic of sliced salami, cheeses, olives and crackers, chocolate-covered strawberries and sparkling water in tiny bottles.

It's sweet, but…God, what's wrong with me? Why do I have such lofty expectations? Why am I such a bitch? Plastering a smile on my face, I lean over and kiss him. "This is lovely. Thank you."

"My pleasure. Dig in." He bends down to my stomach and adds, "You too, kid."

We eat the tasty tidbits in silence for a minute.

"This is the memorial I dig most, but what's yours?" he asks.

"Lincoln. I love how it butts up to the reflecting pool. It's so impressive with him sitting in that enormous chair, larger than life."

Hank whips out his pocketknife and slices salami with it.

"Why do you carry that thing wherever you go?"

He wipes the blade on his jeans and closes it with one hand. "Comes in handy. I don't go anywhere without it." He admires the knife. "This Kershaw's my favorite."

I take advantage of the opening. "You have more?"

"Sure. Including some handed down by my PapPap. They're a right of passage in the McCallister family. My father gave me my first when I was seven or eight." He caresses my belly, a gleam in his eye. "Eventually, whoever's cooking in here will score one too."

I recoil. "They're too dangerous."

He shakes his head. "Nah. Pocketknives are tools. I use mine several times a day for all kinds of things. It's indispensable. And you can't beat it for protection that fits inside your pocket. It's a scary world full of bad people. As the Boy Scout motto says, 'Be prepared.'"

I roll my eyes.

He changes the topic before I can ask about the gun in his drawer. My nagging inner voice wants proof I haven't jumped in bed with a lunatic. When my brain stops processing where that may lead, Hank's in the middle of a dissertation about the Marine Corps War Memorial depicting the flag-raising at Iwo Jima, just up the road.

Despite living a mere Metro ride from Washington, DC for years, I'm embarrassed to admit how much I've missed. Hank is worldly. He reads books, gets carried away about presidents, sings the words to most country songs by heart, and exudes a true enthusiasm for knowledge. My biggest asset? I'm fantastic in the sack.

And I realize, with some appeasement, while I may not be as schooled as the cowboy, I have what he wants.

He feeds me a chocolate-covered strawberry and leans in for a kiss, licking the sweetness from my lips and groaning in pleasure. He pulls back, staring into my eyes. "I love you so goddamn much."

"I love you, too," I answer.

Nuzzling my neck, he groans again. "I need to quit, or I'll have my way with you right here on the island."

"You might get voted off."

"No worries. It's time for our next destination." Hank jumps to his feet and extends his hand.

I take it, and he hoists me to standing. "There's more?"

"One more stop." His shit-eating grin returns.

He drives us into DC, exits onto Constitution Avenue, and parks in a metered spot near the mall.

Holding hands, we stroll toward the Lincoln Memorial, pausing at the immense rectangular pool reflecting the day's stunning blue sky, billowy clouds and from straight ahead, the long, slender pillar of the Washington Monument. Hundreds populate the area, milling about the memorials and monuments. A couple kisses nearby, sharing a private moment, while a harried mother scolds one child in her large brood as they pass. At least three school trips are in progress, one group gathered around a park ranger speaking on the steps leading up to the memorial.

"You brought me here because it's my favorite?"

Hank cocks his head. "Of course."

How thoughtful. More, honestly. He's a good man, not a madman.

We enter the shrine made of glistening white marble. No matter how many times I visit, it takes my breath away. We view the precision-carved statue of Abraham Lincoln, read all the passages etched into the walls, mingle with other visitors, and emerge back onto the steps into the sunshine.

Halfway down the stairs, he pauses, catching my hand.

Before I can question why we're stopping, he bends down on one knee, reaches into his pocket and presents a blue velvet box.

Oh my god! Is he…?

Hank opens the case, and sunlight glints off an exquisite, marquise-cut diamond ring in a platinum setting.

Gawkers from the throngs at the memorial stop to stare. They blur as tears prick my eyes and dam-breaking emotion fills my center at what is unfolding in such a public, demonstrative way. My hand flies to my mouth and my heart flutters in my chest like a trapped bird.

Hank's face projects pure adoration. "Adrienne, I know things are happening faster than a prairie fire with a tail wind, but you're it for me. You're everything I could ever want or ask for in a woman. I love you and want to spend the rest of my days waking up next to you and only you. Will you marry me, darlin'?"

I don't stop two seconds to think about it. "Yes! *Yes!*"

The crowd erupts in applause. Hank bellows a "Yee-ha!," sweeping me into his arms and off my feet. We share a long, heartfelt kiss under the brim of his hat to more cheers, whistles and well wishes.

"You've made me the happiest man alive," he whispers in my ear.

———

GRANDMA BETTY: THE NEWS TICKLED THIS OLD GIRL PINK! AND ANYONE GETTIN' THEIR KNICKERS IN A TWIST OVER IT SHOULD SHUT THEIR PIEHOLES. CONSIDERING A BAMBINO'S ON THE WAY, HANK'S PROPOSAL WAS A STAND-UP MOVE. LET'S HOPE ADRI CAN MAKE THIS ONE STICK. AND FOR THE LOVE OF PETE, LET'S HOPE SHE DOESN'T BURN THE...OOPS, DARNED IF I DON'T SUFFER FROM DIARRHEA OF THE MOUTH SOMETIMES. SCRATCH THAT LAST BIT.

CHAPTER 17
HANK

ADRIENNE DOZES against my shoulder on our flight to Texas, and I'm engrossed in *Lone Survivor: The Eyewitness Account of Operation Redwing and the Lost Heroes of SEAL Team 10.* Except for the woefully inadequate legroom for a man my size, having my gal, a first-rate book and a beer all within a two-foot radius is my idea of nirvana.

Turbulence wakes sleeping beauty minutes before our descent.

When she realizes the time, she wigs. "Why didn't you wake me? I need to be presentable!"

I quirk an eyebrow. "You look gorgeous."

She shoots me an irritated glance, grabs her purse, shimmies across me into the aisle and hurries to the lavatory. Women can be so ridiculous.

The plane lands—Adrienne doesn't look any different to me—and I take her hand as we exit the Abilene Regional Airport. Seconds later, I spot my brother. He gets out of an idling black Dodge Durango with a huge smile, and we hug, slapping each other on the back.

"You're looking tip-top, kid," I say.

"And you're just as ugly as I remember," Wyatt answers with a grin.

I gesture to my gal. "Wyatt, meet Adrienne, who I admit is far prettier than me."

"You ain't kidding a bit." He shakes Adrienne's hand. "Welcome to the best state in the union."

Her eyes ping-pong between us. "The family resemblance is striking."

I slip my arm around Wyatt's shoulders. "We've heard that a time or two."

The McCallister boys split down the middle: Wyatt and I inherited our mother's flaxen hair and blue eyes, but he is shorter and leaner. My three other brothers are dark-haired and brown-eyed, like our father. I'm the mutt of the bunch, but probably the smartest. I can outbrain them all.

We load up the SUV with our bags and head to Sweetwater, chatting amiably the whole way. We pass wind turbines, livestock operations, the occasional armadillo (alive and dead), and dusty fields stretching to the horizon. It hits me how much I've missed home.

An hour later, Wyatt turns down the road leading to the ranch. My insides ease as the first fence post pops into view. I absorb the grassy pastures and scrubby post oaks peppering the landscape with their crooked trunks reaching for the sky. Three thousand acres of loamy soil stretches before me, with ponds and streams making me ache for the uncomplicated days of my youth. Not that I'm old, but...I'm getting married with a rugrat on the way.

Wyatt reaches over and slaps me in the chest. "Welcome home, brother."

He pulls through the arched wooden entrance signifying McCallister Cattle Company and down the sandy gravel road leading to the house.

"This is where you grew up?" Adrienne asks, awe in her tone.

It *is* awesome. "Ain't she a beaut?"

"It's huge. And sort of how I pictured it. Except, where are the cows?"

I turn toward her. "It's cattle, darlin'. Cows refer to females, and we've got cows, bulls and steers. They're around somewhere —the ranch is massive."

Wyatt parks on the circular drive in front of our parents' expansive log home. The door opens and my brothers descend before I can fetch Adrienne from the car. After more backslapping hugs, introductions and good-natured ribbing, we move inside.

I clasp Adrienne's hand, sensing her palpable nerves, and give it a reassuring squeeze. It isn't every day you meet your soon-to-be in-laws and get hitched—all in the span of seventy-two hours. Leave it to my mother to concoct that scheme. I'm grateful, and full of hope my mother embraces my gal once and for all.

My parents greet us in the great room. I've missed them more than I realized, and their warm embrace shows the feeling's mutual.

I present my fiancé.

"It's a pleasure," my father says, shaking her hand. "Welcome to Texas and our home."

"We meet at last," my mother adds. She's polite, but her tone's glacial. "How are you faring after the long flight?"

"Fine, thank you."

Ma glances at Adrienne's stomach. "And the baby?"

My gal pats her belly. "So far, so good."

Let's hope it's the same for my mother and bride-to-be.

My mother's arm encircles my waist. As I gaze down at her, I note a few grays peppering her scalp, blending in with the mass of golden strands she meticulously coifs every day. My family may be ranchers, which is gritty, dirty, hard work, but my mother always brings her A-game when it comes to personal grooming.

She squeezes me twice. "Why don't you settle in? Dinner's in about an hour."

"Whatever it is smells delicious, Ma."

"It's your favorite, you idiot," Shelton says. My oldest sibling rivals Wyatt for the biggest mouth. "The prodigal son returns, so he gets a standing rib roast."

"Hot damn! I guess you don't mind too much either, do you, Shel? Sounds like we all win."

He grins. "I'll ride your coattails for a day or two, young'un."

Our mother is quick to respond, wagging her finger at us. "Nobody is riding anything around here but horses. There are no favorites in this house."

My brothers and I guffaw in chorus, knowing full well Eli is the favorite. But as I'm getting special treatment, I lean over and kiss her on the cheek—a smart son knows where his bread is buttered.

My family gathers at the immense mahogany table in the dining room for dinner. It's enough to seat my parents, brothers, two sisters-in-law, two young nephews and the newest addition, a niece I hold in my arms for the first time. Her tiny fingers grab my thumb, and I'm awed, humbled one of these doofers is coming my way soon. I hand her back to mom as the massive spread materializes under the glow of the antler chandelier suspended above.

My mouth waters as I fill my plate with prime rib, smashed taters, okra, collards, corn pudding, and homemade rolls. My mother proves once again the way to a man's heart is through his stomach. And I'm damn happy to have a longneck Lone Star back in my hand to wash it all down.

We dig in, conversation taking a noticeable back seat.

"This is delicious, Mrs. McCallister," Adrienne says.

"Amazing, Ma," I add between bites. "You're a saint."

She rewards me with a small smile.

"It's too bad y'all couldn't come next weekend and hit a Mustangs game," Wyatt says.

"Friday night lights, baby!" Eli chants.

Eli played all four years on the high school varsity team, but every McCallister logged time on the gridiron. It's dang near a requirement in Texas.

"The Mustangs are the Sweetwater High team," I explain to my bride-to-be.

She nods. "Is football a big thing here?"

A few forks clatter as all eyes rest on my fiancé.

"It's a religion in these parts," my father answers. "And all across Texas."

I quit stuffing my face long enough to chime in. "Football and the Rattlesnake Roundup are the two biggest deals in our county."

Adrienne's head swivels. "What is *that*?"

My mother answers. "Every March, Nolan County holds what's now become the world's largest Rattlesnake Roundup. There's a parade and carnival, gun shows and contests. People go on guided hunts to find rattlers and bring them back to the event to sell or donate. Toward the end of the festival, awards are given for the longest snake and most pounds of snakes, et cetera."

My father snaps his fingers. "Don't forget about the Miss Snake Charmer Pageant."

"I'll bet Hank didn't tell you he dated Miss Snake Charmer 2002," Eli says.

Adrienne shoots me a look. "He hasn't mentioned it."

I shrug. "Ancient history."

"Was she...*charming*?" Her eyebrows rise with the last word.

"Not like you, darlin'." I lean over and peck her on the cheek.

Adrienne takes a sip of water, but I can sense her wheels churning. "What happens to all the snakes?"

"They're kept in the pit during the roundup, then later slaughtered," my mother says. "They milk the venom, then sell the meat and skins, so nothing is wasted."

My gal shudders next to me, and I place a steadying hand on her knee, realizing this fish is way out of her water. There are rattlers under every rock in Texas, but I keep that tidbit to myself.

Over dessert—three kinds of mother-lovin' pie—Ma outlines

the next few days. Thanksgiving festivities tomorrow, wedding preparation on Friday and the nuptials on Saturday. The following day, my new bride and I fly home.

Back in our room, Adrienne sits on the bed and sighs.

I take off my shirt and glance at her. "That wasn't so bad, right?"

Her lips curve into a smile. "I've never heard so many drawls and y'alls."

I chuckle. "We're just getting started."

"Your family is so...genuine, and fun, and seem to truly love one another."

I snort. "We might look sweeter than stolen honey now, but we shed plenty of blood in our younger years, believe me."

She toes off her shoes and rubs one of her feet. "Your mother hates me."

"Nah. Y'all just aren't acquainted yet. Be yourself, and you'll win her over in no time." *I hope.* My mother's not a warm woman, even to her five sons. And she's never made it easy on the women trying to date or marry us. She's judgmental, quick tempered, and a control freak. But she's my mother, and I love her, flaws and all.

She looks dubious. "Your father is sweet."

I murmur my agreement. "He's also fair and rational with a quiet strength I've always admired."

"You are too, Hank."

Her words bring a smile to my lips, but for better or worse, I've got a healthy dose of qualities from both.

Adrienne leans back on her elbows. "Do you think your parents are happy?"

I shrug. "Seems like it. Why?"

"Because we're doing the deed in two days, and I don't—"

"You getting wedding jitters?" I go to tackle her on the bed, but before I can, she bolts upright and sprints to the bathroom.

———

SHELTON: Adrienne's one horny-looking broad, the kind who gives a lap dance rather than the one you bring home to your mama. Bet she's a hellcat in the sack. Sure hope she doesn't have a cheatin' heart—and that my brother's thinking with the right head.

SHELTON: Adrienne's one horny-looking broad, the kind who gives a lap dance rather than the one you bring home to your mama. Bet she's a hellcat in the sack. Sure hope she doesn't have a cheatin' heart—and that my brother's thinking with the right head.

CHAPTER 18
ADRIENNE

I NIBBLE on bland crackers and sip ginger ale as I prepare to wed Hank. T-minus one hour until I'm Mrs. McCallister. I've erupted in bouts of morning sickness on and off since arriving—and not only mornings, as the moniker implies. It wrecked my Thanksgiving and threatens to make my wedding day memorable for all the wrong reasons.

I sit on a stool in front of the full-length mirror applying makeup. Staring into my own eyes, sadness engulfs me. Grandma Betty can't be with us today. She's my last surviving relative and significant in all ways—the only one who's ever genuinely cared about my welfare. But she's old, arthritic and probably has lung cancer the way she hacks every time we speak. A trip like this would only be a hardship and burden, and I'd never obligate her. My sister's face surfaces in my mind, and I gulp down the lump in my throat. Annabelle would have been my maid of honor…if still alive. I wonder what she'd look like all grown up.

I brush away the thoughts as I stroke rouge across my pallid cheeks. This is no time for grief. I am marrying a wonderful man, someone better than I deserve. Hank is kind, loving, genuine, and a gentleman. I believe in him, his goodness—and that it can rub off on me.

I have no one to walk me down the aisle, stand up for me or next to me, but I guess this wedding isn't exactly traditional. When the cowboy told me his mother's brainiac suggestion we marry this weekend, I balked, wondering why we couldn't quietly elope. But how could I obliterate his unbridled enthusiasm at the idea?

We agreed to keep it a small affair with the McCallister family, relatives and friends.

I didn't have the money for an elaborate gown, or even a plain one, but Hank's generosity allowed me to purchase a simple ivory dress, discounted at a bridal store and ready off the rack. Body hugging with a deep V-back and asymmetrical hem, it suits me.

I've just stepped into it when Henrietta knocks on the bedroom door, asking to come in. She's treated me cordially—but with that same chilly undercurrent—thus far. She wouldn't dare behave like a shrew an hour before I marry her son. Or would she?

She enters cradling a hatbox and sets it on the bed. In her elegant black gown and pearls, her coiffed blonde hair sprayed into paralysis, she plays the Texas matriarch part to a tee. The fine lines on her face, smoothed by foundation, only add to her beauty.

Her eyes appraise me top to bottom. "You look lovely. Need a hand with the zipper?"

"Please."

"I'm sorry you don't have any family here." Henrietta finishes and moves to face me. "With your blessing, I want to offer something old, something new, something borrowed, something blue. Call me a traditionalist."

This takes me off guard.

Reaching into the box, she retrieves a velvet case and flips open the lid, displaying an exquisite necklace with a large oval turquoise stone. "This will cover the borrowed and blue. May I?"

I nod and she clasps it around my neck. The weight of its presence is comforting. "It's beautiful. Thank you."

After a rustling, Henrietta shakes her head and holds out a transparent plastic package containing a black garter. "Hank wanted you to have this. That takes care of something new."

I roll my eyes and chuckle.

"And this will give you something old." Henrietta produces a vintage, white satin headpiece with a short veil. "I wore it at my wedding, and I hope it brings you both luck for a long and happy marriage."

Although I'm not the crying kind, pregnancy appears to override all normalcy and tears threaten. Again. I smother them, for the sake of my makeup—and my pride. Her thoughtfulness touches me, though an undercurrent of mutual mistrust stands unspoken between us. "Thank you, Mrs. McCallister. It means a lot."

She gently clasps my forearm. "I know we're all strangers. Even you and Hank are still relative strangers. But we're family now, and I only want the best for my kin. I am fiercely protective of my flock, but if we're on the same side, then we're on the same team."

I nod, acknowledging her veiled warning.

"Don't break his heart, sweetie, or I'm coming for you." She flashes her bleached teeth, reminding me of the Grinch's evil grin before he schemes to steal Christmas, and pats me on the arm again like we're mother and daughter.

She turns on her heel and makes a swift exit. I squeeze my eyes shut, almost unsure if all that just happened. Whether she comes bearing gifts or making threats, that woman is a two-sided, domineering bitch.

I shove those thoughts aside. It's showtime.

Clutching a tasteful bouquet disguises my shaky hands as I take measured steps toward Hank. My life flashes in snippets as I take each step: brushing my sister's golden curls, catching tadpoles in a mason jar, picking blackberries in my grandmother's backyard, my first kiss with Mickey Poplar in seventh grade behind the gym, getting drunk at keggers with my best friend Ashley, learning to texturize in beauty school before I dropped out, my first disastrous marriage, the cowboy arriving in my life like a knight in shining armor.

Hank, dressed in an elegant black suit and matching cowboy hat (I've never seen so many in one room), waits for me in front of the massive stone fireplace stretching floor to ceiling in the great room. Next to him stands his brother, Wyatt, and behind them, the pastor from the McCallister's church, who is presiding over our ceremony.

As I near, guests stand from the three-dozen chairs assembled for the occasion. I keep my eye on the prize and listen to the final words of the country song, "I need you," resonating in this grand space. Hank made an impassioned plea to play this instead of the traditional junk. Sung by Tim McGraw and his wife Faith Hill—some hick music power couple—it's sweet. Besides, the "Wedding March" can suck it.

My eyes meet Hank's, and I only find love and devotion shining back at me. I can love him, can't I? He's a decent, polite, strong man. He'll be a loving husband and father. He'll never hit me. He'll never cheat. He's not a deadbeat. This can work. *Please let this work.*

The ceremony passes in a blur. Quick, to the point, with all the usual promises and religious references. Hank lightens the mood when he tacks one of his quirky sayings onto his vows: "Long as I got a biscuit, you got half," garnering laughs from the audience. Two "I do's" and a ring exchange later, we kiss to applause, yee-haws, and rowdy whistles.

The reception includes a buffet of barbecued meats and sides, a gorgeous, tiered cake, plenty of alcoholic beverages, dancing and meeting more folks than I'll ever remember. My new husband remains attentive and by my side, whether swirling me around the makeshift dance floor, being a gentleman during the cake-cutting ritual or attending to my every need. I stave off baby nausea the entire affair.

Guests stay through early evening. I finally beg off, itching to be free of my dress and turn in, exhausted but happy, after all the festivities. Hank tucks me in but rejoins the party to visit longer with his family.

My lids close but my brain still races, churning through the day's activities: Henrietta's warning, marrying a man I scarcely know, and glad-handing with strangers, a fair number who probably think I've hoodwinked the cowboy. Maybe—hopefully—this will prove to be my ticket to happiness, a shot at redemption, the chance to do something right.

———

JAMES MCCALLISTER: IT'S A SPECIAL MOMENT IN A FATHER'S LIFE TO WITNESS HIS SON MARRY. ALTHOUGH WE RAISED HANK LIKE THE REST OF OUR BOYS, HIS HEART HAS ALWAYS SEEMED MORE VOLATILE THAN THE OTHERS', WHICH MEANS IT'S EASIER TO BREAK. I CAN'T PREDICT THE FUTURE, BUT I HOPE THIS SUDDEN UNION IS SOUND, AND MY BOY'S HEART IS SAFE AND SECURE. I WOULDN'T TRADE ONE DAY I'VE SHARED WITH MY SWEET BRIDE, NOT EVEN THE HARD ONES. THAT'S HOW MATRIMONY SHOULD BE.

GRAN MCCALLISTER: SHE WAS THE PRETTIEST LITTLE THING BUT THIN AS A FIDDLE STRING. MARRIAGE AND BABIES WILL FATTEN HER RIGHT UP. AND SHE WAS CLEARLY DAMAGED GOODS—YOU DON'T HAVE TO BE DR. PHIL TO SEE THAT.

CHAPTER 19
HANK

OUR FIRST ORDER of business upon returning to Virginia is finding a proper home for our budding family. Adrienne and I decide to rent a place in the suburbs until we can afford to buy. Finances are tight with me bringing in the lion's share of income, and the Washington Metro Area's inflated living costs only make it tougher.

Due diligence pays off, and we find a cozy three-bedroom rancher painted sky blue that will be all ours on January 1. The rooms are small but sliding glass doors in the dining room and master suite make them appear larger. The sizeable, fenced back-yard clinches the deal with its stone patio, lawn space and a huge oak tree we fall in love with. Our child will swing from it, climb it and sit in its shade while Diesel roams nearby.

I got choked up when I walked into the yard for the first time.

When Adrienne questioned me, I told her, "This is going to sound like some cheeseball sentiment, but this tree is a good omen. I feel it in my bones. This great oak is like us, a living beacon of strength and beauty—and darlin', you're the beauty in this equation. Now we're putting down roots, much like this tree."

In that moment, I'd never loved her more nor seen our future so clearly.

Adrienne's not showing yet as we prepare for the move. A planner by nature, I create a timetable and mental to-do list for a seamless and efficient process. I'm the kind of guy who works smarter, not harder.

I bring home empty cartons from the office, showing Adrienne how and where to label them and discussing proper packing techniques.

Every morning, I leave hopeful. But every evening, my wife hasn't touched a damn thing. Since she also doesn't make dinner, clean the house or work much, I wonder what the fuck she does all day.

Today is no different. She's sprawled on the sofa, watching a dumb show and popping pretzels into her mouth.

I glance at the unfilled boxes cluttering our living area. "You didn't pack anything?"

Adrienne rolls her eyes. "Nope."

My chest tightens, hands flinging into the air. "Why? We're moving in two weeks!"

"I'm nauseous and miserable. You try functioning when standing up makes you want to hurl."

"I've worked with fevers, broken bones, and bleeding wounds, so it sucks to be you, but shit has to get done and you're the one who's home all day." I don't buy a measly upset stomach is preventing her from goddamned life. Obviously, I don't have a clue what it's like to be pregnant but give me a fucking break and suck it up.

"You have no empathy."

Whatever that means. "It doesn't change anything. We're moving, and you need to help pack. Moaning about it only makes it worse," I snap.

Her lip curls. "You think you're so much better than everyone."

"That's horseshit. I just don't allow mamby pamby excuses to prevent me from taking care of business." The vein in my jaw pulses in time with the second hand on the clock.

"Fine," she says, making a show of dragging herself off the couch and grabbing a box. "I'll suffer. Let me pack up your shit, *take care of business*."

"Fantastic," I say with sarcasm. "And it's *our shit*, sweetheart."

Adrienne's burst of energy is short-lived and half-assed. Two nights later, I accept my lot and commence with packing up the joint myself. The whole thing blows beets, but I'm done arguing about it. I focus on the task, my resentment growing.

A week before the move, Adrienne shuffles into the kitchen. "You're gone all day, and when you come home, you pack until you go to sleep. *And* you work weekends! Can you take a damn break, please, so we can spend some time together?"

I stop rolling glasses in newspaper and glare at her. "Have you lost your ever-loving mind?"

She flinches at my volume. "Don't yell at me. That's uncalled for."

I funnel my frustration into my right foot and kick the tar out of an empty cardboard box. It flies past her into the other room, destroyed. "I'll tell you what's uncalled for: your lack of helping with *anything* around here! You're like a fake wife. You look like my wife, you sound like my wife, but you don't do fucking shit. You don't cook, you don't clean, you won't help pack. You scarcely take care of yourself!"

"Bastard! I'm carrying your child. It's not my fault I'm sick!"

I move inches from her face and speak through gritted teeth. "You're not sick. You're pregnant. Millions of women across the globe manage productive lives while expecting a baby. You're acting like a lame-ass! Pull it together and contribute something!"

She shrinks back. "You're exactly like the rest."

I glower at her, the adrenaline threatening to pop out of my veins. "What the fuck does that mean?"

"You're abusive!"

Bullshit, bullshit, bullshit! My jaw clenches and, like a chain reaction, my muscles tense from my neck down. "You're crazy. I haven't touched you, and I never will. I'm not like any of those jerks you've dated. I respect women. The irony here is, I'm not sure you respect yourself!" I spew, spittle flying from my mouth.

Adrienne picks up a glass and hurls it at my head. I duck, smirking at her.

"Asshole!" she screeches.

"Yeah, this is all *my* fault." Unbelievable. And so fucking typical.

"I'm leaving!" She flounces toward the door, and I resist the temptation to block her.

"That's rich."

"You're nothing but a bully and a tyrant!"

And you're a lazy, self-centered psycho. "Hey, Adrienne?"

She pauses, glancing back at me, hostility radiating from her face.

"Don't let the door hit your ass on your way out!"

She slams the door behind her, and I put my fist through the wall. *Perfect, something else to add to my fucking list.*

Everything inside me is wound tight. Punching through the drywall helps relieve the pressure. I'm fucking pissed Adrienne split like she did. And to accuse me of such crap...why do women always resort to pressing buttons instead of taking responsibility for their shit? My mother's voice worms its way in, dragging me back to my childhood. *You're a bully, Hank. You're out of control. You embarrass me.* I shove it back in the box deep within me, slam a beer and debate calling in sick to The Crazy Horse. I've already redlined, and it won't take much to blow the engine. But I don't shirk my responsibilities *like some people.* And I want to hit someone.

• • •

I pound another brew before my shift begins, then put my wife out of my head. It's surprisingly easy, although nagging anxiety never fully leaves, evidenced by the volume of visual laps I make scouting the entrance, hoping she stops by to make up.

Two hours in, the Friday night bozos give me what I need. I am a wrecking ball, obliterating one asshole after another for any infraction. These are the real scum—not me. How can Adrienne be so dense?

One jizz stain buys a woman a drink and won't leave her alone. I'm on it. Another peckerhead forces himself on a gal by the bathroom, kissing her while she claws at him to stop. *Let me help you with that chore, miss—it's my pleasure!* A couple of shit-faced morons start throwing fists after bumping into each other on the dance floor. Jimmy and I break it up, clocking both dudes and tossing them out on their asses. The final straw is when a dickless wonder gropes a woman at the bar. I witness the whole thing, arriving as she backhands his arm, and he leers at her. Not cool.

"This guy bugging you?" I ask her.

"Hold up. She's been flirting with me all night, coming on to *me*," the man interjects.

The woman balks. "He grabbed my breast! And he's lying—we met fifteen minutes ago." To the perp, she says, "You're dreaming if you think I want anything to do with you!"

"Twat! That's not what you said—"

I grip the back of his neck. "You're my problem now, dickwad."

"You and what army?"

I roll my eyes. They are all so disappointingly unoriginal.

He spins and breaks my grasp, leaving us facing each other. He attempts a strike and misses. I take a swing, and he dodges it. He kicks a roundhouse, but I thwart it, twisting his ankle until he falls on his ass.

"Had enough?" *Please say no.*

I let go and he rises, wavering unsteadily, then surprises me with a blow landing low in my torso. *That's it…pour gas on the fire.* I answer with a throat punch, rendering him speechless and gasping for air.

"Cat got your tongue?" I say.

He gags and doubles over. Then he lunges, a knife in his grasp. He jabs and I whack the hand holding the blade. It skids across the floor as my fist connects with his jaw. The crunch of bone as it gives provides instant, euphoric gratification. Another bag of garbage to throw in the can.

Briggs and Jimmy materialize. Briggs places a firm hand on my shoulder. "My office. Right now. Jim, deal with this."

What the hell?

I trail my boss to his office. When he shuts the door, I can tell he's steamed.

"You're done, McCallister. Fired. You overstep too often."

"Wait a goddamn minute. The guy pulled a knife on me!" I fling my hands into the air, floored.

Briggs makes eye contact. "That's a serious situation. But you throat-punched him and likely broke his jaw, son, and it's not the first bone you've broken belonging to a patron. We're trying to keep the peace here, not create mayhem. This isn't your personal fucking *Fight Club*."

"I'm doing my damn job." I fold my arms across my chest, squelching the temptation to hit my boss.

"You've been an asset…most of the time. But Hank, you've got some anger issues to resolve—and this isn't the place to do it." His stare is unflinching.

"So that's it? I'm gone, just like that?" I pantomime going up in smoke.

He shakes his head as if *he's* frustrated. "I warned you, more than once. Now it's time to part ways. Clean out your locker and exit the premises immediately. I'll mail your final check."

I rake my battered, swollen hand through my hair, and it hurts like hell. My mind boggles. I give Briggs one last scornful glare, turn on my heel and split, slamming the door behind me.

———

JIMMY: I love Hank like a brother, but I agree he can escalate the situation. I think he gets off on it in some weird way. But in his defense, most of the creeps we deal with deserve a smackdown with the stunts they pull. Does it mean he has 'anger issues'? Sounds like a load of psychobabble bullshit to me. People are quick to condemn violence, until they need someone like us to save their ass.

CHAPTER 20
ADRIENNE

SPEEDING THROUGH THE STREETS, details of the battle churn in my mind, Hank clearly in the wrong. At the sight of the first mini-mart, I buy a pack of smokes, an extra-large Snickers and a grape soda. I unwrap the cellophane from the cigarettes, rip open the foil and chain-smoke as I drive, slower now. I refuse to succumb to guilt—a little nicotine won't affect the baby, for chrissakes. And Hank can suck a bag of dicks.

My husband was way out of line tonight. Does he have any clue what it's like to be pregnant? Nope. Like every other asshole in the universe, he places the order then sits back and twiddles his thumbs until the main event. How dare he judge me in any way? Walk a couple of miles in my shoes, buddy. The constant need to pee, the dread of an impending hurl session, don't forget to give up the booze and cigarettes and, oh yeah, eat healthfully and responsibly…for two!

I unwrap the candy bar and inhale it while a few stupid tears escape down my cheeks. I chase it with the soda and burp. Gross —now I sound like the cowboy too.

My husband erupts in bodily noises often. Sneezes in earthquake proportions so deafening I jump. Nose honks that blare like an out-of-tune trumpet. Incessant belching. He always excuses himself—masked behind his gentlemanly premise—which does little to make up for my enduring it. Maybe it's hormones or pregnancy emotions, but I wonder if I can bear a lifetime of his disgusting habits.

He should be treating me with reverence for carrying his precious cargo, not screaming at me for failing to pack up a few stupid boxes.

I'm aware of the direction I'm heading, but don't acknowledge it. Once I arrive, I sit in my car, debating for the slightest of moments.

Fuck Hank.

Inside is a man who will treat me right—and that's what I need now...to feel loved and beautiful, like a queen.

I knock on the door.

Nate answers, a beer in one hand, a cavalcade of emotions crossing his face.

"Well, well, well...if it isn't Adrienne Barlow, Miss MIA."

I put one hand on my hip and cock my head. "Are you going to stand and stare, or can I come in?"

Holding the door, he steps back and gestures me in with a bow. "By all means."

I shouldn't have screwed Nate, but Hank pissed me off, and it's the easiest way to gain the upper hand I find so gratifyingly necessary. It was the teensiest bit slutty...and being a married woman brings an added moral violation, I suppose. But philosophically speaking, no one person owns another, wedding ring or not. We are free agents with free will. What matters is whether I can live with myself, and the answer is, was, and always will be a resounding yes.

———

NATE: ADRIENNE WAS ON FIRE, AND I'M TALKING FIVE-ALARM. MADE ME FORGET HOW MAD I AM AT HER. FACT IS, SHE CAN'T STAY AWAY FROM THE GREAT NATE. AND THAT TELLS ME I'M STILL A DOG IN THIS HUNT.

CHAPTER 21
HANK

MY JAW ACHES. I massage both sides, prying it apart. I scrub my bleary eyes next, a brief respite from glaring at the door the last six hours straight. The ache in my churning gut remains constant. *Merry Christmas Eve.*

The morning light filters through the blinds as tires crunch into the gravel driveway. I assume—hope—it's Adrienne. Willpower don't fail me now...because I am hankering to unleash a fresh verbal assault on her.

She enters, eyeing me warily.

I press my temples with one hand and squeeze. *Stay calm.* "Where have you been? I've been worried out of my fucking skull."

She shrugs. "Nowhere. I mostly drove around." She tosses her keys, and they clank against the tabletop.

Her indifference sends me sky high. "And you think that shit's okay, to just not come home? No call. No fuck-you-very-much?"

She places a hand on her hip and rolls her eyes. "You pissed me off, Hank."

I leap to my feet, heart racing like a tornado, spite lacing my words. "Right back atcha, sweetheart."

Adrienne takes a step back. "What's your *problem*?"

I close the gap and point my finger in her face. "My problem," I enunciate through a clenched jaw, "is my wife and unborn child were MIA. I thought you were dead. I called every hospital and law enforcement agency in the tri-state area."

She responds with the death stare. "Well, we're alive."

I inch closer and Adrienne shrinks toward the wall. "Where did you sleep?"

"In my car," she squeaks.

My chest tightens like a noose, shortening my breath. Touching my fingers to my head in utter frustration, I fling them away, leaning in further to close the gap. "Your idiocy boggles the mind. Can you possibly understand why that wasn't a good idea, a stone's throw to what—in the not-so-distant-past—was nick-named the Murder Capital of the country?"

"I guess."

I want to shake some sense into her. Some fucking emotion. Some goddamn responsibility. I loom in her face, my voice thun-dering. "And pregnant?"

She glares. "Stop being so melodramatic. I'm fine. The baby's fine."

I slam my hand hard against the wall and she flinches. "That's my baby in there, too. You don't get to put our child in harm's way. I won't tolerate it." I cross my arms in front of my chest, trying to keep my raging insides from exploding.

"You've got an anger problem, Hank," she says shakily, her eyes misting. "Some sort of violent streak. And I won't tolerate *that*."

I register this is the second time I've heard that in a matter of hours, which only torques me more. We face off in a staring contest, chests heaving, neither of us saying more. Time suspends.

Until my heart cracks from some invisible fissure...and damn if I don't squirt a few tears. I swallow hard to stem the tidal wave threatening to unleash. What the fuck?

Leaning back against the wall, I slide to the floor and drop my head into my hands. No chance forcing the shit down now—it tumbles forth in waves as my sobs ring out in the stillness of the cottage. I'm blowing this, scaring my wife, acting the opposite of everything I should be. "I'm so sorry," I choke out. "Please forgive me."

"Hank." Adrienne's tone softens as she drops beside me and wraps me in her arms. "I'm sorry, too. What I did was shitty. Super shitty. Of course, you were worried."

Emotions ricochet through me. She holds me as I struggle to regain my composure. "I shouldn't have yelled at you," I whisper. "I love you, baby...I love you so much. So much it hurts." And this fucking hurts. Like someone stabbed me with a KA-BAR blade right through the heart.

"I love you, too," she croons in my ear. She kisses my forehead, smooths my hair.

Our foreheads touch and I exhale, through the worst of it. Our lips lock, tasting of bittersweet pain.

"I hate fighting with you," I murmur. "Especially on Christmas Eve."

"Me too."

Shifting her brunette locks away from her face, I gaze into those gorgeous eyes. "Let's make love and crash."

She nods, her mouth finding mine again. "I need to shower first."

"I'll join you."

We shed our clothes and come together amidst the heat and steam raining on our skin, every moment as raw and scorching as the emotions coursing through us. As our bodies slide against each other and merge into one, the water washes away our trespasses.

We dry off and hit the rack. I'm dead asleep seconds after my arms wrap around her.

. . .

When I wake up, it's midafternoon. Adrienne faces me, gorgeous even as she sleeps. A gray sky mutes the light as a steady drizzle falls. Diesel's head bobs up once I move.

"Hey, boy," I whisper. He hasn't made a peep all day, poor dog. I creep from the bedroom, giving Diesel a pet and opening the door, which he scuttles through.

I pass the hole I punched in the wall and grimace. The old tapes kick in, reminding me I'm a loose cannon, and if I'm unable to control myself, I'll lose this woman. Hell, I don't know how I hoodwinked her into marrying me in the first place. Relief hits seeing Adrienne's keys and purse on the table and knowing she's home safe. I used to believe marriage provided security, but there are few sure things in life. My thoughts turned irrational last night. When she didn't return, I jumped to the worst-case scenario. This broad owns a part of my soul—something far greater than I can remember sharing with another human being prior to now. I don't want to lose it.

I gulp down a glass of water and saunter back to the bedroom. Adrienne opens her eyes.

"Hey, sleepyhead," I say.

She smiles. "Hey yourself. Been up long?"

"Nope. Bet I could sleep another five hours." I flop on the bed, emitting a weary groan. Reaching over, I trace light strokes from her forehead to her cheek. "But we can't lollygag around here forever. We have reservations at six. I'm taking your fine ass out to a fancy dinner."

She beams. "Ooh, nice."

"Anything for the woman I love, and I love you, Adrienne."

I kiss her tenderly then make love to her with every ounce of my being.

. . .

Christmas Day dawns cold and clear. Adrienne dang near glows, whether from the pregnancy or our spectacular make-up sex, I can't be sure. I give Diesel a massive rawhide bone to gnaw on in our absence. I hate leaving him behind, but we've got a long day ahead with the four-hour drive to visit Adrienne's grandmother.

As we hit south-central Virginia, it reminds me of Texas in its straight-up country appearance. Expansive fields, homesteads miles apart, the occasional highway taking you off the beaten path, and no towns in sight except for the sporadic gas station/store combos advertising everything from fried chicken and lottery tickets to butchered meat and fresh bait.

We arrive, and I pull up next to an aging farmhouse surrounded by towering pine trees. Mint paint peels from the exterior boards, and the porch has caved in on one side. A garden surrounds a stone walk leading to the house, but most of the plants are dormant for winter, the grass a wheat brown.

A fake wreath with candy cane ornaments hangs on the front door. Before we can knock, Grandma Betty opens it wide and greets us with a shout.

Her skin is milky, like Adrienne's, only wrinkled across every surface. Tight gray curls pepper her scalp, of which I have a birds-eye view; she's as short as her granddaughter.

"Look at you two! I'm so tickled y'all are here!" she says, her voice smoker rough. She grabs Adrienne and brings her in close for a hug then stands back to inspect her belly, not that there's anything to see yet. Turning her attention to me, she takes my free hand in hers and pats it a few times. "Hank, it's my good fortune to meet you."

"Pleasure's all mine, ma'am."

"Call me Grandma Betty, hon. We're family now." Her eyes sparkle as she gives me a thorough once over. "Aren't *you* a handsome devil?"

I lean in conspiratorially. "Maybe I picked the wrong gal."

Grandma Betty chortles. "Maybe you did. Better keep an eye

on this one, Adri, or your old gran here is going to take this cowboy for a ride."

My neck heats, and damn if I can't think of a smart retort to *that.*

Adrienne raises her eyes to the heavens. "I warned you she's a pistol."

Grandma Betty winks at me. "I think I may be too much woman for Hank. But he's a keeper, Adri."

"He's too charming for his own good, is what he is," my wife answers.

We trail after Grandma Betty, who hobbles as if every step requires effort. Inside it reeks of stale cigarette smoke and a cloying floral scent, like those air fresheners that make me gag. Depositing our packages with our coats, we follow her into the living room.

I understand Adrienne's ways better as I take in the mess. If my mother were here, she'd call it a "hoorah's nest." Piles of books, magazines, and papers take up space on most surfaces. Pillows and throws overrun the two couches and adjacent chairs. An eclectic assortment of decor crowds the room. Next to an aging television, a plastic Christmas tree blinks with multi-colored lights.

Adrienne sits by her grandmother on the sofa. I sink into a chair among the debris and try not to worry about what may live underneath. Three cats eye us from their various perches before the Calico behind the tree slinks off.

"It makes my heart burst to set eyes on you two *newlyweds*! I hated missing your nuptials. If it weren't for this damned arthritis, I would have showed up for the whole shebang. You know that, right, sugar?" She lights a cigarette and takes a deep drag.

Adrienne nods. "We understand."

Grandma Betty descends into a coughing fit, waving us off when we try to help. It's all I can do not to snatch the cancer stick in her hand and extinguish it. I'm damn thankful my wife quit this nasty habit.

Adrienne sprints to the kitchen and comes back with a tumbler of water, rubbing her grandmother's back before sitting down.

"Look what I brought," she says, rummaging through her purse and producing a handful of prints. "Pictures from the wedding."

Grandma Betty places a hand on her cheek. "Here come the waterworks." She dons the glasses hanging from a beaded chain around her neck and reviews each photo with careful consideration. The jet-black cat with the white paws gives me the stink-eye. I give it right back.

"Aren't you precious?" she whispers, clasping Adrienne's knee and dabbing at her eyes with a tissue she fishes out of her pocket. "Here I go, getting all spongy. Told you I would." She continues cycling through the photos, clucking and sighing. "How I hated missing this. Here I am, your only kin, and I missed your big day."

Adrienne holds her grandmother's hand. "Please don't be sad. We wish you'd shared the day with us too, but we're together now. I can't ask for a better Christmas gift."

"Me either, child. Now tell me everything. What's been happening? How's the baby?"

Grandma Betty prepares our holiday meal, refusing our help aside from allowing me to heft the spiral ham from the oven and carve slices onto a platter. When I catch sight of instant mashed potatoes and canned green beans, I stifle a frown. Bagged rolls and a salad mix with a pale tomato round out the dinner.

Raised to be gracious, I accept helpings of every item but don't have to fake enthusiasm for the meat and bread—or the pecan pie and cheesecake I pile on my dessert plate.

Grandma Betty is an adept conversationalist, regaling us with funny and intriguing stories throughout the meal. I enjoy learning more about young Adrienne, and her adoration for her granddaughter endears me. I won't be surprised if the woman hacks up a lung by the frequency of her fits, yet she seems undeterred in plowing through a pack of cigarettes.

Adrienne excuses herself for another trip to the bathroom, leaving us alone.

"I'm tickled you two stumbled across each other. My Adri needs someone like you in her life."

"It's a blessing for us both." I'm uncomfortably full but still scoop the last two bites of pie into my mouth.

Grandma Betty smooths the tablecloth with her hand, much the way I've seen my own grandmother do countless times. "That child's had it rough."

"You mean the fire? Losing her family?"

"That and a lot more. Her mother—my daughter—was hateful. I can't imagine why, truth be told. I raised Caroline to be a kind and decent woman, but I swear she was born with a chip on her shoulder. Even as a youngster, she picked on others and hollered all the time. I often wondered why she seemed so miserable. Whatcha got to be unhappy about before you're grown?"

I bob my head in agreement.

"She grew up cranky and unpleasant and later found a fella to marry. I didn't think much of him, but I hoped he'd make her happy, teach her about love. But nope. She bossed him around, made him think himself inferior. No wife should do that to her man. Or vice versa."

"I concur."

"I'm all for women's lib and whatnot. But Caroline was abusive, cruel and perpetually annoyed—for no reason. When she had the girls, I thought *now* she'll learn about love and being selfless. There's no greater devotion than a parent to a child, except perhaps to the man upstairs."

I smile, knowing how protective I am about our unborn baby.

"But that backfired. Much to my alarm, she went the opposite way, treating those two young'uns something terrible, making them believe they were never good enough. I sometimes wonder if she was jealous of them. Both those babies were so lovely." Her voice trembles. "Adrienne still is—just look at her. And Annabelle, well, she was such a light." Her eyes well, and she pauses.

A heaviness settles inside me. What I don't know about my wife is cavernous. She's gotten a raw deal, something no kid deserves. I nod, encouraging Grandma Betty to continue.

"Every day, Caroline yelled and cussed and fussed at them— and worked them to death in their free time. What five-year-olds need to scrub floors? They should be out chasing toads, getting dirty, having tea parties, twirling on tire swings! I did my best to drill some sense into her, but she'd snap at me to mind my business."

I look at the floor, my insides twisting, heart aching. "Your daughter sounds horrible, if you'll pardon my criticism. I had no idea."

"Adri doesn't like to talk about it, and can you blame her?"

She doesn't wait for me to answer.

Grandma Betty raps her hand against the table. "By the time she came to live with me, the damage was done. I tried so hard to reverse it, to help her understand she was perfect. But those were challenging years."

"I can imagine." Only I can't.

"I was heartbroken when Adri married Kyle. But I sort of understood it, after all she'd been thr—"

"Adrienne was married?" A needle being pulled across a record screeches in my head, and the seductive yank of adrenaline sparks in my belly.

"Oh, dear. I didn't realize..." She shakes her head.

"Please continue, Grandma Betty," I implore. *Please.*

"I reckon she ought to tell you the rest, hon. But I will say this: Kyle was her high school sweetheart. And although I pegged him for a son of a bitch, Adri thought the world revolved around him. I couldn't talk any sense into her. Figured it wouldn't last, and it didn't."

"What didn't last?" Adrienne asks, re-entering the kitchen.

"Your first marriage," I say, unable to keep the spite from my tone.

She stares at her grandmother, then me. "I leave for ten minutes, and this happens?"

Grandma Betty casts her eyes downward, repentant. I glare.

"Hank, that relationship meant nothing. It lasted all of a minute." She starts clearing the table.

"You should have mentioned it. Don't you think that's an important detail?" The anger careening through my body is trapped, like me. All I want to do is launch something across the kitchen and stalk out.

"No, I don't."

"You led me to believe you'd never been hitched."

"If I did, I'm sorry. I don't like thinking about it." She avoids my gaze and busies herself with rinsing dishes and stacking them in the dishwasher.

I clock her every movement. "If the tables were turned, wouldn't you want to know?"

She finally glances at me. "Fine. Got any skeletons rattling around in *your* closet?"

"No. I didn't want to marry anyone until I met you."

"Not even Miss Snake Charmer?" She smiles, trying to lighten the mood.

"Not even a little." Maybe a little.

Adrienne wipes her wet hands on a towel embroidered with a gingerbread man, walks over and kisses me tenderly. Part of me resists kissing her back. "Let's forget about it, okay, Hank? I love you, you love me, and we're married now. That's all that matters. The rest is ancient history."

I'm forced to smother my anger and dismay to allow the remainder of the visit to unfold peacefully...but I can't shake feeling duped. It lingers and simmers under the surface of my fake, plastered-on smile.

On the way home, my wife dozes to a backdrop of Christmas

tunes, but my thoughts are adrift with the news I'd learned from her grandmother. When her first marriage came to light, it was like careening on the downslope of a roller coaster. You can't jump off, can't steer—you can only hang on and go along for the ride. Was this what being married to Adrienne promised? I can't help but wonder what else might be around the corner, and how many more peaks and valleys I'll be forced to navigate before we reach the end. Pulsing through my veins is the one question I can't answer: what else has she lied about?

———

GRANDMA BETTY: THE PARALLEL OCCURS TO ME AFTER THEY LEAVE. I USED TO THINK MARRIAGE, AND LATER KIDS, WOULD CHANGE CAROLINE FOR THE BETTER. NOW I FIND MYSELF THINKING THE SAME ABOUT ADRI. I'M NO FORTUNE TELLER, SO IT MIGHT BE FAR-FETCHED. BUT PERHAPS THEY ARE THE VERY THINGS THAT WILL SAVE HER FROM HERSELF...IF IT'S NOT TOO LATE.

CHAPTER 22
ADRIENNE

HANK'S BOUNCER buddies help us move into our new house. After they unload the trucks, the guys put a hurting on a twelve-pack and a couple of pizzas. While they rehash favorite ass-kicking moments at The Crazy Horse, I survey the chaos, dreading putting everything away. Ten bucks says my anal-retentive husband has *a plan*. I groan inwardly. I hate moving, and I hate being pregnant. Pairing the two is a special subsection of hell.

I make my fortieth trip to the bathroom, staring at the hideous pink and black tile combo. Another residence in the life of Adrienne Barlow, er, McCallister. I pray this time won't end with me skipping out on an abusive asshole or outrunning the electric company over an unpaid bill.

I flush the toilet and glance at my reflection as soap washes the grime off my hands. I hope the cowboy and I make this crazy, shotgun marriage work, and that this house helps us plant those roots he talked about.

I collapse on the sofa next to Hank, and he reaches over and gives my thigh a squeeze.

"Have you given any more thought to Friday Night Fights?"

Jimmy asks, throwing two jabs in Hanks' direction.

My ears perk up. "What are you talking about?"

"Jimbo's been bugging me to do this for a while. Guys show up for organized bouts but it's all legit—in a ring with gloves and a referee, and prize money if you win."

"And this appeals to you?" It's beyond me.

His eyes gleam. "Heck yeah."

"Sounds dangerous. What if you got hurt?"

The men guffaw.

Hank shrugs. "I can't predict the outcome, but I can put a hurtin' on another guy. I'm not worried about me."

I roll my eyes.

"The next one's in two weeks," Jimmy says. "Think about it. You've got to be missing that loving feeling since Briggs bounced your ass."

"You're kicking at an open door, brother," Hank says.

"Unless you've turned into the giant pussy I always suspected you were," he adds.

Finn points to Jimmy then Hank. "Nail, meet head."

Hank motions to his package. "All y'all can suck my king-sized dick."

Men are so stupid, and this ranks at the top of the stupidometer. My husband acting like a cocky son of a bitch doesn't help. All I can picture is him in a hospital with brain damage.

After his friends leave, Hank ushers me outside. It's cold and I'm drained, but I follow. Standing in the frigid January temperatures for what appears no reason, I stare at him expectantly.

He swoops me up into his arms, and I squeal. "What are you *doing*?"

"Giving my bride a proper beginning." He carries me across the threshold, kicks the door closed and kisses me.

"You're a true romantic, cowboy."

He gingerly sets me down. "I have something else for you. For us. A housewarming gift."

"What is it...a new bed?" I smirk.

He chucks me under the chin. "Not a bad guess." He leaves me to wait on the sofa and darts off. He returns with two rectangular boxes the size of paperbacks and hands me one. We open them together, revealing identical Apple smart phones.

My first cell phone!

"I think these are important for us to have now," he says. "Not only because you're pregnant and in case of an emergency, but to give each of us peace of mind. I went nuts the night you didn't come home. I never want to feel separated from you again or worry if you're safe."

"Great idea. I'm so excited to have one of these!" I turn the phone over, inspecting it. The screen is covered with a graphic showing little icons for the apps.

"One more thing."

I tear my gaze away from the gadget, giving him my full attention.

"I've been mulling over what marriage means, what matters, what my parents figured out. I think it all comes down to commitment. To do whatever it takes to work things out when the going gets rough—and appreciating what we have the rest of the time."

My heart melts a little as he clasps my hands. "It's easy to bail when shit's going wrong. It's harder to stay and fight for what you believe in, or to give up something in the name of peace or compromise. But that's the stuff where real love endures. I want us to commit to that kind of love. We should never go to bed angry at each other or let bad feelings fester. I want us to be open and honest and pledge we'll always work it out, no matter what. You with me?"

I nod, tears pricking behind my eyes. This is the kind of man I need. A good man. Responsible. Respectful. Loving. "All I've ever wanted is to be in a mutual, loving relationship, and you've shown me what that can be."

We embrace, his devotion surging through me. Maybe Hank can give me what I need—and help me give it in return. Except...

I pull away. "Hank."

"Yeah, darlin'?"

"If you want honesty, I need to tell you something weighing on my mind since our last fight."

"Lay it on me."

"Your temper. It scares me, especially when you're physical. You punched a hole though the wall, and that's not rational." I wait, unable to gauge his reaction.

"It was extreme," he admits, "but anger is a normal emotion. I haven't a clue how to be angry any differently than I am. Do you?"

I pause, considering. Irritatingly, I'm forced to agree. "I guess not. But my anger doesn't involve violence."

"I'm not violent."

I'm dumbfounded, almost speechless as examples parade through my thoughts. "Hank. You beat the living crud out of my boyfriend the night we met. You've hurt countless others at the club. You want to hit people in a boxing ring."

"But I'd never hurt you." His eyes soften, pleading. "That's what I meant."

"Even so...I'd rest easier if you'd see someone about it."

Hank's eyes widen. "You mean like a headshrinker?"

"A psychologist." I give his forearm a gentle, reassuring squeeze. "Or find something else, like one of those anger management classes."

He strokes his mustache while he considers my words.

"Think about how much this benefits not just you and us, but our child," I argue.

He sighs. "If it's that important to you, I'll look into it." He meets my gaze. "But I'm not making any promises."

I fling my arms around him. "All I ask is that you try."

"If you stay here in my arms much longer, I'm going to have my way with you, Mrs. McCallister."

"The bed's not even made yet." I groan. "Ugh, guess we better get to it."

We heft our aching bodies and grind out the most essential tasks. Hank uses his pocketknife to slice through all the taped boxes we need to unpack. He tackles the kitchen and I pull the bedroom together, starting with the bed, upon which I will collapse ASAP.

As the top sheet flutters in descent, I time-travel back to my first marriage, which I assumed would be for eternity. I was so naive and unsure then, not understanding my place in the relationship or Kyle's expectations. Raised without any concrete examples, I floundered, swimming in the deep end of the pool before learning how to tread water. I know better now.

Kyle was a bad boy through and through, and attractive as hell. Long hair, tattoos, rode a Harley. He got me hooked on cigarettes and used to score us booze even though we were underage. We screwed like rabbits, drank too much, and worked low-paying jobs. We barely covered the rent on our dingy apartment or our basic needs. We were young and dumb enough to think love conquered all, but the fantasy soon shattered.

The short span we dated in high school, Kyle sometimes grabbed my arm too tight or pushed me into screwing or blowing him when I didn't want to, but nothing to cause me alarm.

Those indicators only got worse during the sixteen months we lived together after exchanging vows. He expected sex whenever he wanted—as if I owed it to him—and forced himself on me the few occasions when I brushed him off.

I recoil, remembering the sting of his palm against my cheek, how he shoved me into the wall then dragged me to the bedroom one night after getting drunk. He pushed me face down onto the bed and pinned me with one hand while he hiked up my dress, ripped off my underwear and raped me, demanding it was my duty.

Kyle suffered from a power trip and used force and violence to drive home he was the boss whenever the mood struck—worse if alcohol was in the mix. His blend of tender, loving husband juxtaposed with the crazed, pain-inflicting one confused me.

He was always remorseful after an episode, blaming the booze, but I saw a pattern emerging. Not long after, I hitched my horse to a new wagon and got the hell out of Dodge.

I can't fathom why Grandma Betty blabbed about it. She has a kind heart but a big mouth. Despite sticking her nose where it doesn't belong, I can't stay mad at her.

I finish making the bed, smoothing the duvet and fluffing the pillows. I shut the door on my past and take comfort in knowing Hank is not Kyle. He may be quick to display aggression, but he'll never hurt me.

The cowboy and I settle into a new rhythm, one that includes me doing my best to lend a helping hand. I attempt to straighten up and cook meals. I'm a far cry from Martha Stewart (and Hank's on-a-pedestal mother…how I'd love to push her off), but it's better than nothing. I've also started walking in the neighborhood at the suggestion of my obstetrician. This has resulted in meeting a bevy of nosy neighbors asking too-cheerful, probing questions, which I detest. When fatigue, boredom or laziness hits, I retreat to the sanctity of the couch and mindless television.

Hank accompanies me to my ten-week appointment. I'm due for an ultrasound to check on the baby's health, which means a photo op for Baby McCallister. I hope he agrees to let the doctor reveal the gender to us. My husband is a stickler for tradition but since he also likes his wife happy, that's the card I'll play. I'm bothered the nursery remains bare. Without knowing whether a boy or girl is on the way, I can't fully plan or execute the décor.

A nurse registers my weight, takes my vitals and leaves me to change into a floral cotton hospital gown.

Hank saunters over and trails his fingers across my skin through the opening in the front. "We could squeeze in a quickie…"

The chill forces my nipples into hardened peaks and my

breasts flare with tenderness. "Don't be absurd." I swat him away as Dr. Swann enters and I scramble to pull myself together.

She greets us in her professional yet friendly way and runs through her standard questions. I like her overall vibe and with each visit, my comfort level increases, at least about her delivering the kid. After asking me a series of questions, Dr. Swann helps position me for the ultrasound, reminding me of the process as she squeezes gel on my stomach, which is just beginning to bulge.

My eyes follow hers to the screen, waiting for images to materialize as she operates the wand in a circular motion and pauses, the machine making an alien *wow-wow-wow-wow-wow* staccato noise. A black splotch appears, followed by another.

"Would you look at that," the doctor muses. "And then there were two."

"What?" Hank and I say in unison.

"Mr. and Mrs. McCallister," she beams, "you're having twins."

That's impossible.

"That's incredible!" My husband laughs and squeezes my hand.

I try to regain my composure, but I'm sweating buckets, my brain frozen. "Are they the dark blobs on the screen?"

Dr. Swann points to each spot, indicating two babies.

Hank and I gape in awe.

"But...how?" I blurt. "It was one before."

"Twins typically show up after eight weeks, but often longer. I understand it must be a shock."

My husband chuckles. "That's an understatement."

Wrapping my head around this is like wading through peanut butter. "Are they going to be identical?"

"Too soon to tell. Once the sex of each fetus is discernible, we can usually answer that question. But you might have to wait until they're born to be certain."

"How long before you can cipher the gender?" Hank asks.

"Usually around eighteen to twenty-one weeks, sometimes sooner. Twins aren't always the same sex. And some same-sex siblings are fraternal versus identical." She pats my leg. "Get dressed, and we'll talk more."

We reconvene in her office, where Dr. Swann explains with twins in the picture, monitoring my prenatal care is more intensive. I'll return for ultrasounds once a month, focus on my nutrition, take my vitamins and need extra rest. She says I might be more tired or sick than with a single fetus. The babies have their own placentas, which is less complicated than if they shared one. We discuss risks, the likelihood of cesarean birth and how to prepare for not one, but two, children. She loads us up with pamphlets and resources, and we leave.

Although I've never been in combat, I'm certain this resembles shell-shock. Hank seems bizarrely chipper, taking the news in stride.

On the ride home, he exclaims, "I knew I was potent, but two babies with one shot? That's stud power!" He turns up the music and taps his fingers on the steering wheel, already trying to corrupt our kids—plural—with his hick tunes.

Meanwhile, I wonder why the universe constantly conspires against me.

———

MRS. KINCAID: I SPIED ON THEM THE WEEKEND THEY MOVED IN. THE HUSBAND HAS ONE OF THOSE GIANT MUSTACHES, THE KIND STRETCHING ACROSS HIS ENTIRE FACE LIKE A 70S PORN STAR.

MRS. BROWN: OH, GLADYS! WHAT WOULD YOU KNOW ABOUT PORN STARS? I LIKE THE MAN. HE'S FRIENDLY AND HAS ONE OF THOSE DRAWLY ACCENTS. HIS WIFE WAS A LITTLE CHILLY FOR MY TASTES, AS IF MY SIMPLE QUESTIONS IRRITATED HER. IT'S CALLED BEING *NEIGHBORLY*. SHE ACTED LIKE SHE'S BETTER THAN THE REST OF US, EVEN THOUGH SHE SMACKED OF TRAILER TRASH.

CHAPTER 23
HANK

I TURN off my alarm and hold Adrienne in my arms, my first thought about the two hearts beating inside her womb. *Twins.* Talk about going from zero to sixty. And I was petrified at the thought of raising one kid. The universe possesses a twisted sense of humor. Nothing to do but roll with it.

I love holding my wife. Everything about it—her waterfall of cascading hair, the faint perfume of vanilla, skin like satin and the healthy glow pregnancy brings to her face.

Our relationship has improved since our conversation. She's more attentive, putting in a concerted effort. The twofer announcement rocked her world, but she'll work through the surprise and fear and slay motherhood like a boss.

Adrienne's request weighs like an anvil on my mind. As an investment in our commitment and a show of good faith, I'm tackling it today and attempting to stay open-minded. But inside, I'm dragging my feet and screaming bullshit.

With reluctance, I disengage and hit the shower. As I soap up, it occurs we should live it up a little—go on dates, take a short trip, have some fun while we can still freewheel.

Adrienne stirs as I dress.

"I have an idea," I say.

She rubs her eyes and glances at me sideways. "More sleep?"

I sit on the bed next to her and stroke her cheek. "You snooze all you want, your highness. I'm thinking we need to kick up our heels before Frick and Frack arrive—"

"Frick and Frack?" She raises her eyebrows.

"Catchy, right?"

She laughs.

"Let's do something fun once a week, like dinner and a movie. I'll suffer through your dreadful chick flicks, and you can endure my action movies."

"Great idea." She beams. "I pick dancing."

"I'll Two-Step with you anytime, darlin'." I slide into my work boots and Adrienne gasps, a hand flying to her belly.

My stomach lurches. "What is it? You okay?"

"Hank!" She grabs my forearm. "The babies moved!"

For a second (and only one), I would give anything to be in her shoes. "What's it like?"

"An ocean current, kind of…it's hard to explain." Her eyes light up, wondrous. She inhales sharply. "There they go again."

"You're killing me, Mrs. McCallister."

She reaches over and places my hand on her belly.

I wait and wait…but get jack squat.

"It's subtle, like a hand drifting through water."

I love her expression at that moment. Her awe, beauty and glow make for a potent combination.

"I'm sorry you can't feel it," she says.

I flip my hand over and give hers a squeeze. "I did, through your eyes."

"Don't worry. These two monsters will undoubtedly start kicking me anytime—and *that* you'll be able to experience."

I kiss her goodbye. "Gotta shake, rattlesnake."

"See you later, alligator."

I do my goofy gator dance move and she laughs, loud and unrestrained. It's one of my favorite sounds.

. . .

During my lunch break, I lock my office door and force myself to investigate *anger management,* which smacks of a phrase coined by some cheesedick white-collar therapist.

The internet provides plenty of research avenues, and I plan to take the easiest, smoothest route once I've done due diligence.

I wade through psychologists in the region but can't fight the internal tantrum waging over the idea of someone trying to pry into my life, prodding me to relive my childhood or some such crap. *Next.*

I find classes. Control your anger before it controls you! A ten-part series taught on Saturdays for *only* $499. Three *months* of weekends held hostage? That I *pay* for? *Not a chance.*

A surprising number of book titles exist on this topic. *Huh.* This shit must really be a thing. Of course, Americans become more pussified by the second. We used to have thick skins. Now everyone gets offended every millisecond, thinks all kids should earn a trophy, and lacks personal responsibility. No wonder so many books exist on how to control anger. Where are the selections about how to not be a jerk or antagonize others? I make a mental note to stop by the bookstore and thumb through its selections.

Ah, here we go. A website with strategic approaches. I scan the introduction and subsequent list, agreeing with the first sentence: "Managing your anger doesn't mean you never get angry." *Bingo.* "It means you learn to recognize and express your anger in healthy, effective ways."

I read more mumbo-jumbo and "strategies" to "appropriately express" my "feelings." And there it is…the pitch for cognitive therapy, which requires a headshrinker. *Fuck that.*

I peruse the ten approaches.

1. Identify triggers. *Um, everyone and everything—the world overflows with idiots.*

2. Recognize warning signs. *Whenever someone does something stupid, like write a book about anger management.*
3. Step away. *It goes against the Hank Playbook, but I guess that's the point.*
4. Talk to a friend. *Negative, Ghost Rider, the pattern is full.*
5. Exercise. *Friday Night Fights, anyone?*
6. Manage your thoughts. *Hello, fantasies! According to this, I've been practicing anger management for years.*
7. Redirect your thoughts. *Like thinking about history or football when you're trying not to shoot your wad too fast? Got it.*
8. Relax. *Have more orgasms.*
9. Explore your feelings. *Hard no.*
10. Create a calm kit. Suggestions: scented hand lotion, a photo for meditation practice, a spiritual passage you can read. *Kill me now.*

I can work with some items on this list. Maybe. With a little creative license. Let's hope Adrienne buys it.

———

BENJAMIN: THE MASSIVE DUDE WITH THE HUGE MUSTACHE, THE ONE WHO LOOKED LIKE HE COULD KICK MY ASS WITHOUT MUCH EFFORT? YEAH, HE FREAKED ME OUT. WHEN HE ASKED WHERE TO FIND THE ANGER MANAGEMENT BOOKS, HE SCOWLED IN THIS WHOLE INTIMIDATING WAY. AND I GOT DISCOMBOBULATED, BECAUSE I'VE ONLY WORKED AT BOOKS-A-GO-GO FOR A COUPLE OF WEEKS AND WE HAVE, LIKE, TONS OF CATEGORIES AND A BEHEMOTH STORE. I COULDN'T HELP THINKING, *DUDE, YOUR FISTS ARE PROBABLY YOUR BEST TOOL.* BUT YOU KNOW, I KEPT MY MOUTH SHUT. THEY'RE ALL ABOUT CUSTOMER SERVICE HERE. DUDE WAS POLITE, THOUGH. JUST SORT OF A WALKING CONTRADICTION.

CHAPTER 24
ADRIENNE

HANK WOLFS DOWN HIS DINNER, imparting workday details between bites. "Wait until you hear this," he says, a dab of lasagna sticking in his mustache.

It's bound to be far more interesting than anything happening in my world.

"Guess who got busted banging Monica in the body shop?"

"Who?"

He stops shoveling food in his piehole, looking like a proud cat dragging home a dead mouse. "The boss."

"No!" I set my fork down. "I knew that girl was bad news, and your prick boss isn't any better, cheating on his wife with some tramp."

"What do you have against Monica?"

"Hank." She levels a stare at me. "She's got a thing for you. And she obviously possesses no qualms about screwing a married man." I'm one to talk.

"Nah. You're imagining things," he says, blowing me off. Men are clueless.

"Look out just the same. You might be next on your assistant's to-do list."

"I'm *happily* married. That shit won't fly with me."

It's the truth. We eat in silence for a minute before I say, "Brings new meaning to the term *body shop*, doesn't it?"

We snicker conspiratorially.

Hank gulps his beer and helps himself to another serving of lasagna. "I researched the anger thing today."

I'm shocked, in a good way. "Yeah?"

"There must be a lot of pissed off people in the world because I found a crap ton of information on the topic. And some of it smacked of horseshit." He pauses to inhale a couple more forkfuls while I swallow a snarky retort. "Some suggested strategies might improve my response when I'm ticked. Some I already practice."

"Such as?"

"Like relaxing. This guy knows how to kick back and decompress." He leans in. "And what's more calming than an orgasm? I'm willing to have a lot more sex in the name of anger management."

I shake my head and smirk. "What a hardship."

He nods, scraping the remains of his meal onto his fork.

"What else?"

"Learning your own warning signs, which sounded like a no-brainer. Another was walking away when the alarms sound, giving yourself a chance to regroup without taking it out on someone."

"You formulated a game plan yet?"

"Working on it, darlin'. There's one more strategy I'd like to give a go, but you've got to promise to hear me out."

"Uh oh. It must be bad if you're starting with that. What?"

"Exercise."

I eye him suspiciously. "I'm all for it. Why the big preface?"

"Not sure you'll be on board with the type I'm proposing. I want to try my hand at amateur boxing. I'm a decent fighter, and this is a legal avenue to have physical interaction without repercussions."

I vehemently shake my head. "No fucking way. You risk serious injury, Hank. That's a huge consequence."

"This outlet works for me, and I mean perfectly. It couldn't be more tailor-made, but I need your blessing. Please give this a chance."

I hate it.

Hank's eyes beseech me. "You were the one who asked me to work on this. Now that I present you with a solution, you're going to yank the rug out from under my feet?"

He's got me between a rock and a hard place. "Fine. Try it. But don't come crying to me if you get brain damage."

He raises an eyebrow. "More than I already do?" His grin stretches fully open, pulling his gargantuan mustache with it.

Exactly. "I'm not joking. The first sign of injury, and you're quitting."

"Yes, ma'am." Hank stands and flexes his biceps. "No need to worry, darlin'. Those other morons won't know what hit them."

Monica: What a day. I'm like one of those Hollywood actors busted for making a sex tape, only I'm not famous. Why did I let Peter talk me into screwing in the body shop? Because...I got carried away. The danger, the excitement, the taboo of it all. And since men are worse gossips than chicks, everyone's now privy to my sex life. I overheard snickers and mumblings all day. Hank didn't treat me any differently and was the only guy who asked about my well-being. He's a true gentleman as opposed to the other cretins who work here. I've always liked Hank. Maybe I should have slept with him.

CHAPTER 25

HANK

I CUT out of my job early to get primed and pumped for my first appearance at Friday Night Fights. Once home, I pack my new boxing trunks and shoes into a gym bag, then puke my guts out.

Adrienne mopes as we travel to the venue, but I can't expend any energy to deal with it. Pumping my grip strengthener to a backdrop of country music settles my nerves until we arrive, but ramps right back up once I steer The Boss into a parking space.

Adrenaline rushes through my veins, making me hyper aware of every sound and movement in my line of vision. It takes effort to slow my stride into the arena, so I don't leave my wife in the dust. Inside, Adrienne stakes out seats while I check in, fighting to restrain a maniacal grin and the intensity churning under my surface.

Officials weigh me, determine my class, and outfit me with proper gloves. They outline the rules and I sign a waiver assuming responsibility for any injuries or death. Until registration closes and my bracket's announced, I'm stuck sitting around, about as happy as a fly in a glue pot.

I find my wife at center stage a few rows back from the ring, which sits flush on the floor instead of on a raised platform like on televised fights but otherwise, it's legit. Jimmy and Finn soon join us, and we speculate about who showed up to throw down.

When they announce the brackets, I'm in the fifth bout against a guy ranked in the top ten of our class. I will rank after I fight, and if I win, advance to a second and final match.

The first three matches, I assess the skills of each boxer as a frenetic energy pulses through me like my own personal soundtrack. The contestants range in ability and dexterity, a mix of novice and more seasoned fighters. I assume Mr. Top Ten will throw down, and I'm itching to find out.

Before the fourth bout, I gather my gear and lock eyes with Adrienne. "Time to get scrappy."

Her expression remains cryptic. "Knock 'em dead or out or whatever."

Jimmy fist bumps me. "KO, brother."

Finn claps me on the shoulder. "Remember, I got green riding on you. But no pressure."

"Blow me." I say, heading for the locker room.

I ditch my street clothes and slide on my shorts, staying shirtless, per the rules. I tie my shoes and glance in the mirror. No question I'm a sizable dude, but the black trunks throw me, making me look like a pro with the thick white waistband and trim, the Everlast logo blasted larger than life. Despite my lacking fitness regimen, I look sturdy and strong.

Time to mentally prepare. I think of memorable scumbags I pounded at The Crazy Horse, the dickwads who cut me off in traffic who deserved their faces mashed into the ground, and people like Adrienne's mother, who had no business having children with the sick shit they did to their kids. I let my anger and disgust amp me up, fuel my need for physical release and stoke my true desire to deliver the corporal punishment fitting the crimes of these supreme assholes.

An official laces up my gloves. I smack them together, testing them out, as he reads me the rules. No hitting below the belt. No holding. No tripping, kicking, head-butting, wrestling, spitting or pushing. No funny stuff. He waxes on for five minutes until I'm nearly pawing the ground like a bull.

The announcer says my name, age and weight over the booming PA system, and I emerge from the locker room to the uproar of cheers and jeers. I blank it all out and zero in on the ring. It's a fucking rush. Tugging down the ropes, I step in. A light sheen coats my body, and I move side to side on my toes, my neck cracking as I flex and shrug my head and shoulders. The energy pinballs through me and I harness it, ready to brawl.

Let's go, motherfucker.

I don't acknowledge the other fighter as he enters the arena, focused on staying warm and loose. When my opponent steps into the ring, I scrutinize him. About my size, but shorter and stouter. Dark-skinned, with Garcia for a last name. My heart hammers in my chest. Nerves jangle as if exposed. Turbulent power streams from my pores. My inner chatter reminds me to keep my head in the game. *It doesn't matter who he is or what he looks like, you can take this motherfucker downtown. Do it —decisively.*

The referee calls us to meet in the middle and touch gloves. "Let's have a fair fight," he says before ordering us back to our corners.

An instant later, the bell dings to start round one.

Go time.

We do the bob-and-weave dance, assessing each other. Garcia throws the first punch, and I dodge it with ease. He fires off another; it glances off my shoulder.

C'mon, Garcia. That all you got?

He strikes low, and I reverse to avoid it. He lodges another swing and a miss. I haven't thrown a damn strike yet, letting him do the work, tire himself out, show his hand. He telegraphs most of his moves, and I'm a quick study.

The bell rings, ending the round.

I sit on the stool that appears, and my handler squirts a stream of water into my mouth, drapes a towel around my shoulders, and wipes the sweat from my eyes. No time for anything else in the sixty seconds allotted.

Round two.

I leap to standing and trot to meet Garcia in the middle. When he jabs, I swerve, but quickly plant my feet. Drawing strength up my legs, through my hips, and along my torso, I channel it into my gloved right hand, hitting that sucker in the chin with everything I've got.

Garcia goes down like a felled tree. He rolls to one side, attempting to rise, but never manages to do more than flop. The referee hunches over him, counting the seconds out loud. He reaches ten, and I pump my fist to the sky at my first amateur knockout.

The official grabs my arm, lifts it in the air and pronounces me the winner. I find my cheering section, where Jimmy and Finn are grinning wide, pointing their index fingers at me and shouting I'm the man. Adrienne stands, awe or shock in her expression. When our eyes meet, she beams a genuine smile.

I touch gloves with a groggy Garcia and scramble out of the ring, sweaty and breathless. My friends slap my back, gushing praise. My lips collide with Adrienne's, and she tells me I'm amazing.

Guzzling down water, I can't stop my body from moving as the next contests ensue. I recover as the excitement subsides, going from ninety miles per hour to idling about forty-five.

For my final fight, I have underdog status once again. This time I face Clanahan, another Scot like myself. Leaner in stature and covered in tats, he stands a few inches taller and has the brawn to back up his number one ranking.

We perform the dance as I gauge his abilities. Clanahan proves to be a smart, aggressive boxer. We exchange several blows in the first four rounds, but land few, more evenly matched. I respect his dexterity but remain steadfast in my purpose: shut this cocksucker down.

During the fifth and final round, my lack of cardiovascular fitness becomes glaringly apparent. I gasp for air, my breathing labored. My arms are leaden, legs throbbing as if in constant muscle spasm. I intensify my focus, knowing without it, I'll lose. Leveraging a gargantuan right to his gut, I follow it with a left hook to the jaw. Clanahan stumbles back against the ropes, and taking full advantage, I rain down more blows. Through the haze of fatigue, I find renewed motivation and launch an all-out offensive until the bell rings. Clanahan sways on his feet, grasping at the ropes for stability.

We retreat to our corners, where I all but collapse, while the judges score the fight. The handler wipes me down and gives me fresh water as I struggle to regain my bearings. One eye is swollen partway shut. Aches and pains scream from various body parts. My legs are like jelly. None of it matters.

The referee calls us both into the center of the ring. "By unanimous decision, the winner is Hank McCallister!" he announces, holding my arm up in victory.

My perpetual grin hurts my cheeks. I search out Adrienne in the crowd, and she blows me a kiss. Is she crying? Jimmy and Finn bow my direction, using worshipping hand gestures and yelling something unintelligible.

The rest is a blur. Strangers congratulate me, hand me their cards, ask if I want a trainer, a manager, a whatever. Crazy shit. I only want to rejoin my people and clean up. When I return my gloves, the organizers hand me my winnings: fifteen hundred in cash. That's even crazier. Getting paid to punch people. *Living large!*

When I make it back to our seats, the guys can't shut up about my performance or stop hooting it up. But Adrienne clings to me, and through the commotion, I sense the need to whisk her out of here.

Despite the damage to my left eye and utter exhaustion, I drive home, knowing my wife can't manage The Boss. She's only half as big as a minute.

I take her hand. "Tell me what's going through that beautiful head of yours, please."

"It was scary," she says.

"Worried I'd get creamed?" I squeeze my fingers around her palm. "Oh ye of little faith."

She stares out the passenger side window. "The first fight went so fast, and you knocked him out. But the second one...it went on forever. I hated watching you getting hit."

"But in the last round, I kicked ass."

"You did, but by then, you were hurt. Look at your eye...and you're not supposed to be a punching bag, Hank. You're acting like this is some casual, everyday event."

My battered face doesn't reflect my euphoria, which I'm tamping down for her benefit. "I can tell you're upset. And I took a few tough hits, no question. But damn it was a rush. I felt fucking invincible. I dragged ass somewhere in the third or fourth round and couldn't catch my breath. I'm out of shape, but I've got more mental strength in my pinky toe than most people do in their entire body. I can withstand pain, suffering, fatigue, lack of oxygen..." I stop to grin. "That's a huge advantage over the other pussies throwing down."

Adrienne remains despondent. "I hated the whole thing. I don't want you volunteering to get beat up."

"Sweetheart, I'm fine. And we're fifteen hundred dollars richer!"

She manages a weak smile.

I grip her hand again, trying to reassure her. I doubt I can make her understand fighting—and winning—is a high. Despite a few knocks, it was as satisfying as hitting my first out-of-the-park home run or besting my older brothers in roping after years of attempts. *I made those opponents my bitch.*

"You're not doing it again, are you?" she says.

"Fucking-A I am." I can't wait.

———

AIDAN CLANAHAN: I'M NOT STUPID ENOUGH TO THINK I HAVE EVERY FIGHT IN THE BAG, BUT I TOOK ONE LOOK AT THAT ROOKIE MCCALLISTER AND THOUGHT I'D WALK AWAY WITH THE W. I'VE FACED HIS KIND BEFORE...A COCKY BAR BRAWLER WITH NO FEAR. HE LACKED BOXING SKILLS AND WAS UNCONDITIONED. BUT THE ROOKIES ARE WILDCARDS. YOU DON'T KNOW WHAT THEY'RE FIGHTING FOR, AND IT GIVES THEM AN EDGE.

CHAPTER 26
ADRIENNE

HANK'S EYE turns a gruesome purplish green along with many spots on his torso and arms. He spends most of the weekend recuperating on the couch in front of the TV or fooling around in the bedroom—nothing stops my husband's sex drive. By the time Monday arrives, he's back to work, like everything's golden.

Watching him recover, I don't understand his attraction to the boxing gig, nor do I support it. Unfortunately, he's hell-bent, playing the "you wanted me to have an outlet for my anger" card to the hilt, so I shut my mouth. For now.

Mid-morning, I take a stroll through the neighborhood because it's supposedly healthy for me and the babies, not that I harbor any illusion it's going to help my shape. It seems like overnight, my belly size doubled. I feel swollen and fat. I'll probably rival the size of a hippopotamus before it's all said and done with two in there. I also don't relish these arctic temps, but at least it keeps the blue-haired busybodies inside.

I turn down a new block in our subdivision. So many houses look the same. It reminds me of *Edward Scissorhands* with its identical homes in pastel colors, where husbands mowed their yards in synchronicity, drove similar cars and waved goodbye to their homemaking wives as they headed to the office.

This trend to decimate a patch of perfect land, build rows of uninspired dwellings, replant trees and have the nerve to label the streets something natural like Elm, Arbor and Maple disgusts me. Yet here I am, residing in one. I shouldn't complain—I couldn't wait to ditch country life. And built in one of the older sections, our home is no McMansion. Although, damn it, it *is* pastel blue.

A navy minivan drives past and pulls into the driveway a few doors up. A woman with a chic bob a pretty shade of auburn exits the car as I walk by. I smile at her, thinking I'd never pull off that cut with my expansive mop.

"Hi!" she calls out. To my surprise, she approaches and holds out a gloved hand. "Tami with an i."

I clasp it. "Adrienne."

"Are you new around here?" Tami's hazel eyes might have been plain with any other hair color, but the red makes them pop. Next to her, I suddenly feel ordinary.

I nod. "We moved in earlier this month. We live over on Oak."

"You must be freezing. Why don't you come in for a cup of coffee?" Tami's entire demeanor conveys warmth.

I shock myself by agreeing, and she seems delighted.

Standing inside the foyer, we shrug off our coats. When she spies my small baby bulge, she blurts, "Are you pregnant, too? I'm sorry. I shouldn't be so presumptuous, should I? Sometimes I speak before thinking. You don't know me from Adam, either. For cripes sake, now I'm babbling!"

"It's fine," I reassure her. "I *am* expecting—*twins*. God help me." I pantomime the sign of the cross.

Tami grasps my arm. "Oh, my! That's…a handful. I'm three months along. You?"

"Same!"

"How fabulous we can commiserate! Is it fate the universe brought us together or what?"

Indeed. Something nice for a change. I could use a friend.

She leads me through the dining room, and I admire the contemporary black table, scooped white chairs and elegant chandelier. A chalk-colored sideboard sits underneath a bank of windows, reflecting light against the stylish gray walls.

The kitchen colors follow suit: grey cabinets, granite countertops, a creamy backsplash. For such boring shades, it's anything but. I lack interior decorating skills, so her talent impresses me. If this friendship works out, I'll tap her for help with our house.

Tami invites me to sit at the modern dinette while she busies herself with bringing coffee, creamer and sugar to the table.

I take a sip. It's high end, like this house. I want to bathe in it.

"Where did you move from?" she asks.

"Arlington. After getting married and knowing a baby was in the picture—two babies, I mean," I say, shaking my head, "we needed a bigger house, and we liked the neighborhood."

"This is a super area, and we have good schools. You'll love it." Tami sips from her mug and I glimpse her big-ass diamond ring. "So...twins! Wow. Are you completely freaking out?"

I put an imaginary gun to my temple. "I can't wrap my head around it. I've been trying to read up, attempting to prepare for the onslaught of double everything, but sometimes I zone out in front of the tube and deny it's happening."

"Honey, you better do all the chillaxing you can. You're about to go a million miles an hour."

My lips poof as I release an exaggerated sigh. "Is this your first?"

"Sure is. Rod and I hope to have a few. How about you guys?"

"Hank and I didn't exactly plan this, so we're rolling with it. But I think with twins, we might pump the brakes until we find out how things go."

"Good call. How long have you been married?"

"Since November." Bet she's silently doing the math. "How about you?"

"Rod and I wed about five years ago. We were high school

sweethearts." She stands and disappears around the corner, returning with a framed photo. "Try not to judge."

I peer at the image of their wedding day. Her hair, longer then, was teased and sprayed in place, what those of us in the industry refer to as *prom hair*. She had a gaudy white dress to go with it, probably in style at the time. Rod is striking, slick and dark, dapper in a classic tuxedo. "You make a handsome couple. And your cut is fabulous right now. I don't know if that's your natural color, but it's perfect for you."

Tami gives her head a swish and every strand falls back in line —bob perfection. "It's au naturel. Yours is divine. I'd kill for those waves."

I smile, not only at her compliment, but because I like her.

When she grips my arm again, I peg her for one of those touchy-feely people, but I don't mind. "Hey—why don't you and your husband come for dinner this weekend? We can hang out!"

"We'd love that."

"I'm tickled we met, Adrienne. I hope our men like one another because this just feels right, doesn't it?"

"It does. And if the guys don't become BFFs, who cares? We can still be friends."

We chat for a while and swap phone numbers before I leave. On the walk home, my spirits rise, hopeful about this budding friendship.

Hank drives us the few blocks to Tami and Rod's Saturday evening. Tami answers the door, ushering us in as her husband joins us in the foyer. We dispense with the introductions, and Hank hands Rod a six-pack of imported beer. The guys launch into a discussion about their favorite brews while us girls head into the kitchen. I groan at the divine aroma and my new friend beams.

She offers me water, the pregnant woman's drink of choice,

but dresses it up with fresh lemon. We settle into comfortable conversation as she finishes up elements of the meal.

Rod pokes his head in the room. "Honey, we're headed downstairs so you can have some girl time." He winks and disappears.

Tami rolls her eyes. "He's trying to sound magnanimous, but in truth, he's showing your husband the bar so they can consume booze and college football."

"At least they're predictable," I say.

"There is that. How are you?" She slices a baguette in half lengthwise and smears it with butter.

"Tired. Enormous. And wary—I'm not even halfway."

"Right? My legs swell daily, another joy of impregnation. But, ahem, you're *not* enormous." She sprinkles fresh garlic and parsley on the bread.

Dismissing the compliment, I caress the outside of my belly, which has become second nature. "I love it when they move, though. It's one of the coolest sensations, a reminder life is growing inside of me."

"I agree one hundred percent. That's been the best part...and the cravings. I've sent Rod out for some peculiar items." She laughs. "You having any?"

"Nothing major...except suddenly I hate beef. Weird, right? Just the sight of it makes me gag."

"I wish I hated ice cream and cheese puffs. I'm eating for, like, four," she says with an exaggerated grimace.

I help her bring dinner to the table, and she calls the men up from the dungeon to join us.

Hank kisses me on the cheek. "Miss me, gorgeous?" he asks as he pulls my chair out for me.

"Always," I say.

Tami snorts. "You can spot the newlyweds in this group."

Rod feigns offense and tries to recover. "Miss me, baby?"

She guffaws. "Every second of every day, stud."

We cycle through the usual get-acquainted topics: where

we're from, how we met, college attended, what we do for a living.

Rod is a CPA for what he calls a "Big Four" firm. Tami works in finance, but she's already quit her job in preparation of staying home with the baby. Hank talks about being raised on a cattle ranch and how he transitioned to a diesel mechanic and now manages the shop. Before I can reveal my profession, my husband brags about my hairstyling skills.

"Lord, and I showed you our wedding picture. My hair was hideous," Tami says, "and you never let on."

I flash her a sly smile. "Professional courtesy."

"Do you make house calls?" Rod asks, locking eyes with mine for a minute. "I'll give you a try."

Is he flirting? "Be happy to, if your wife approves." Emphasis on *wife*.

He chuckles. "She won't mind. She's always bugging me to trim it."

She agrees, giving me a reassuring glance. "You'd be a godsend."

Hank and I rehash our evening on the way home. He likes Tami but says the verdict's out on Rod. Calls him a "vain, white-collar pansy." My verdict is also out on him, but for reasons I keep to myself. The vibe I caught, one I'm well-versed in, has philanderer written all over it. Moreover, he is damn attractive, another one of my downfalls.

————

Rod: I can't fathom what she's doing with good ol' boy, Hank. Adrienne is a fine piece of ass, even pregnant. I would nail and bail on that any day of the week.

CHAPTER 27
HANK

I LEAVE work to meet my wife at Dr. Swann's office for the gender reveal—at least we hope. The doc made no promises. I chuckle remembering how Adrienne convinced me to overturn my old school values and agree to this. Pussy rules the roost again. Lest we mere mortals forget, women are *always* in charge.

I experience a pang of regret about not learning my children's sexes the old-fashioned way, but planning the nursery is driving her insane. It's a small concession, and *happy wife, happy life,* right?

I still can't believe I'll be a father in five months. Life sure has a way of showing you who's boss. I'd be lying if I said I don't care what we have. Fingers crossed for boys. One of a quintet of brothers, I have a handle on how to raise a boy. But a girl? A few bats of the lashes and I'm a goner.

Adrienne's on the exam table when I'm ushered in, and Dr. Swann's not far behind. The doc does the ultrasound routine, squirting gel onto my wife's belly and gliding the probe around. My heart rate ticks up a notch, and I hold my breath, the curiosity almost smothering. As the picture appears on screen, I lean closer, not that I can decipher a damn thing.

What previously looked like blobs now reminds me of the Rorschach test, with two near-mirror images: my babies. Little Frick and Frack.

"Well?" asks Adrienne. "I'm dying over here."

Dr. Swann clears her throat. "Just another minute."

We wait, the only sound coming from the machine, emitting its bizarre alien chant.

C'mon, Doc. What's the verdict?

The doctor turns and faces us for a moment, a small smile gracing her face. She points to the screen. "Twin one, on the left, is a male."

Yes! My fist pumps into the air.

Shifting her pointer finger, she says, "Twin two, on the right, is a female."

What? My mind blanks. My daughter's already messing with my head.

"Wow," Adrienne exclaims. "A boy and a girl."

"This means your twins are fraternal."

My brain is still buzzing. A girl...who will become a woman...who will become some guy's...

"So, they won't look alike?" Adrienne asks, snapping me back to the present.

"They may resemble one another, such as any other sibling. Fraternal twins are formed by your body releasing two eggs at the same time with each being fertilized by a different sperm," explains Dr. Swann.

I can't help gloating a little. I'm a potent motherfucker. My boys sired two of those suckers!

"Because of this, they only share about fifty percent of their chromosomes, like other siblings. Time will reveal what characteristics they split."

My wife's face lights up. "Cool. What do you think, honey?"

I'm a little disappointed...no, nervous...I didn't put a stem on that second apple. But I keep those thoughts to myself. Gazing down at my wife, my hand finds hers and squeezes. "It's amazing, darlin'. I couldn't be happier." I return my attention to the doctor. "Are they healthy? Can you tell us more about what we're seeing on screen?"

She nods. "They appear in good physical condition. At this point, they are approximately a half-foot in length and weigh about five ounces. Their facial features are now in position and will continue to become more refined. They can detect light and some sounds."

"Whoa! If we talk to them or play them a song, they'll hear it?" I say.

"It's possible, and certainly can't hurt."

"Unless my husband pollutes them with his country music." Adrienne smiles, and I flick her playfully on the arm.

Dr. Swann points to a circular area on Frack. "This is your daughter's heart."

We soak that in. And I thought my mind was already blown.

"You should also begin to sense fetal movement now, if you haven't al—"

"I have!" My bride beams.

I shake my head and shrug. "I've gotten diddly squat."

"The babies will become more active now, and when they start kicking and jabbing, you'll be able to feel plenty, Mr. McCallister," the doctor says before directing us back to the monitor. "This membrane separates the twins, so each of them can move in utero. As they wiggle, these shift with them. Right now, their arms and legs are developing and becoming more proportional."

Adrienne shifts on the clinical table. "I don't understand how they're both going to fit in there. Aren't they in danger of banging heads or something?"

"As we discussed, there are concerns but you're more at risk as the mother, predominantly for high blood pressure and gestational diabetes. Taking care of yourself is paramount. We'll carefully monitor the fetuses, but you might be surprised how resilient they are, even when space becomes cramped as childbirth approaches," she says. "So far, you have a healthy baby boy and girl, and your vital signs are exemplary for this stage of your pregnancy."

I stroke Adrienne's hair and she smiles up at me. I'm suddenly stupidly confident we can handle anything—even a chick.

Adrienne is downright animated as she gets dressed. "Now we can finish the nursery. And pick names!"

"How about a neutral paint color, like blue? No McCallister is growing up in a pink bedroom."

"How about the walls in blue with clouds on the ceiling?"

"Sounds artsy." Something I'm not.

"I can do it. I found a technique online."

I glance at her. "You're up to it? In your condition?"

She swats my arm. "You don't seem concerned when we're screwing on the kitchen counter."

I tip my hat. "Guilty as charged." I check out her beautiful breasts before she covers them with her blouse.

"I might stencil the walls, too." Adrienne's stare turns unfocused, as if she's daydreaming.

"I reckon we better hammer out names. Let's each compile a list and powwow in a week."

She agrees, reaching down to slip on her shoes. "I hope we're on the same page."

"We'll work it out. We've got millions to choose from," I say with reassurance.

———

I'm exhausted after days of trying to name Frick and Frack, examining every option like a scientist with a rare cell mutation, burdened by the awareness we only have one shot to nail this.

I nix the idea of naming them after my folks, Henrietta and James, or anyone else in my family tree. I favor strong names, and prefer those with a southern or southwest flair, but haven't yet begun to whittle down some concrete options. I despise the trendy (Jayden, Ryan, Tyler, Makayla, Chloe, Brianna), overused (William, David, John, Sue, Lisa, Laura) or those without a nick-naming option (Evan, Grace). Girls create additional hurdles. If a name conjures any connection to a gal I've known or dated or remember as sleazy, I eliminate it. It's also a hard no on any sexpot hooker names such as Misty, Candy or Raquel.

But Rapunzel works. It suits me fine to lock up my daughter in a tall-ass tower until she's thirty *and* give her a buzz cut, just in case.

I pull into work and shut off the machine churning this shit around in my head. Between a packed schedule, employees out sick and backordered parts, I need to stay focused and juggle the firebombs.

Monica fetches me lunch and makes me take time to eat it. Punctual, efficient and first-rate at her administrative assistant duties, I'd be sunk without her.

"Thanks, Mon. Appreciate you," I say, taking a bite of my sub.

Leaving her perch on the chair across from me in my office, she steals one of my chips. "Someone's got to take care of you."

I attempt a smile with a mouth full of roast beef.

"How *are* you doing? You seem distracted."

I slug down some soda. "I'm one wheel down and the axle is dragging," I joke. "Lots going on here and, hello…expecting twins."

"I can imagine. Or rather, I can't. Adrienne must be getting huge."

"Her belly's expanding, all right. Between you, me and the fencepost, it freaks me out what's happening inside the whole womb room. It's natural and all, but you've got to admit, freaky."

Monica laughs and absconds with another chip. "Nature knows what it's doing, Hank. Been at it for centuries now. But I might be able to help with workplace stress."

In seconds, she's moved behind me and begins massaging my shoulders. Holy what-the-fuck.

"Hey!" My jerk reaction to shrug her off stalls; it feels too dang awesome. Instead, my body sags, eyes fluttering closed.

"Want me to stop?" she murmurs after a few minutes.

"Nope…as long as this is on the up-and-up." Adrienne probably wouldn't like it, but damn, I never get this treatment at home.

"If that's how you want it."

My eyes fly open, and I lurch forward.

"What?" she says.

"I don't want to mislead you. I'm a happily married man, and I'd never cheat on my wife."

"Of course. That's one of the reasons I like you—your integrity. And relax. I'm only fooling around!" Monica holds up her hands in surrender.

"Oh, right. I'm…" The moment turns awkward, and she bows out. As I finish my lunch, I dissect the situation. Monica's pretty, but our relationship is strictly business. I don't recall her being anything but friendly. I think. But she did bang the boss. Perhaps I'm reading too much into it. *Shit.*

I call my wife. "Yo, Adrienne!" I say in my best Stallone imitation.

"I'll take Rocky over Rambo any day. How's it going, cowboy?" Diesel barks incessantly in the background.

"Busy and plenty of fires. I'll be working overtime."

"That sucks." Diesel's woofing continues.

"What's with the dog?"

"Same ol', same ol'. He hates me and yaps all the fucking time."

"He doesn't hate you. He's used to being a one-man dog. I'll bet he comes around when the kids are born." I'd never admit it, but it cracks me up how displeased he sounds. It means he's true blue to me.

"I hope so. They say possessive dogs can bite babies."

I snort. "Stay off the internet, honey. Diesel wouldn't hurt a flea. Well, maybe a flea. You know what I mean."

"To what do I owe the pleasure of this phone call?"

"Just checking on my best gal." Who happens to be my wife...and assuager of guilt this second. "Better swish, jellyfish."

"Ciao, ciao, brown cow."

Despite the late hour, I still find myself in murder-inducing traffic on my way home. Not even George Strait, the King of Country, can fix this. I need a few stiff bourbons and beer backs to unwind from this hellish day. I visualize sitting on my leather recliner as Adrienne presents me with a hot delicious meal, eases my aches with her magic fingers, and, for the grand finale, tosses me a sexy smile before giving me one of her magic blowjobs.

Diesel meets me at my truck. "Hey, buddy. Roaming the neighborhood?" I rub his head and we venture inside, where it appears a tornado struck sometime after I left this morning. A large rectangular box sits on the floor, packaging materials and scraps littering the living area. I move into the kitchen where dishes fill the sink, and a burnt odor assaults my nostrils. Debris is stacked precariously on the dining table. The entire place is a sty.

My jaw muscle twitches. After the day I've navigated, I want to come home to a clean, orderly, welcoming haven—a respite from the rest of the world. Not this bullshit.

Then I see Adrienne's purse toppled on the floor. And plain as fucking day is an opened pack of cigarettes spilling out of it. She's smoking. And pregnant.

My fists clench, and the sparked fuse ignites.

Adrienne emerges from the hall, all smiles and sporting a blue smudge on her cheek. With a brush in her hand and clothes spattered with paint, she announces, "I got started on the nursery!"

Like Mount Kilauea, I erupt.

———

Your Home Center employee: We see a lot of do-it-your-selfers in our store, especially in the paint center. It's obvious when they're inexperienced. Everyone thinks they're a painter, and I don't try and dissuade them. We're supposed to encourage the DIYer, help them think they can. But this woman was clueless. She had no idea what supplies were needed, what a primer coat was, how to go about the process. I suggested she watch some how-to videos on YouTube, but I'll bet you a thousand bucks she went right home and started painting.

CHAPTER 28
ADRIENNE

HANK'S FACE contorts and turns three shades of red, like the coils on a stovetop escalating from cold to hot. My head screams *danger* but dismay roots me to the floor. My elation over the nursery project dissipates in an instant.

Hank's words come through gritted teeth. "You're fucking smoking?"

My mind races, eyes flitting around the room scanning for my purse. How does he know? *Shit!*

He reaches down and plucks the damning evidence from the floor, wiggling the pack in the air. "Answer me."

Crap. "I…well…just one, I swear!"

He peers into the pack, moving closer. "Looks like a lot more than one, just like your little lies." He shakes his head and crushes the cigarettes with his hand. "The lying is bad enough but you're fucking pregnant! You're hurting our unborn babies!"

He opens his mouth to say more, but only stares at me like he doesn't understand what he sees. It's terrifying.

"I'll stop."

"Goddamn right you'll stop. How are you so selfish, so

uncaring to those tiny, innocent, not-even-formed children inside of you?"

A few cigarettes aren't going to hurt anyone. Mothers smoked for years before the surgeon general got involved, and their kids turned out fine. My defenses are kicking in, but I keep my mouth shut. There's no answer that will satisfy him. I stare at him, bereft of what to do or say.

"And you painted the fucking nursery?"

I shrug. "Most of it. I wanted…to help," I explain. "You're so busy with work and it seemed like something I could manage." What the hell is his problem now?

"Something you could fuck up, you mean. Please don't tell me I married a Harry Homeowner who thinks they can slap paint on a wall then stand back and admire their subpar, lame-ass effort! Jesus fucking Chr—"

"It looks great, asshole! Go see for yourself." I cross my arms in battle mode.

He laughs, a mirthless, hollow sound. "Spoken like a real *pro*, he says, adding air quotes. "I guaran-fucking-tee you did a lousy job. The bigger issue is you did it without consulting me, and that's bullshit!" He punctuates the last word with a pointed finger a foot from my face and I flinch.

My turn to speak through clenched teeth now. "We already covered this. Blue, we decided! So, I bought blue. Just. Like. We. Discussed. Your boxers are in a twist because you missed out on picking the shade? Grow a pair and quit the patronizing caveman shit!"

Hank inches closer. "I am not the problem here, Adrienne," he says, his tone low and controlled. "You went full speed ahead with something we barely discussed, and I'll bet you never considered I might have more experience and a process to complete this. Did that occur to your pea brain? I doubt it, because you don't think about anyone but your—"

"What crap! I did this to surprise you, to pitch in since you're working all the time and—"

"Tell yourself what you want, sweetheart, but you were doing whatever the fuck you wanted. Just like the smoking. And just like," Hank surveys our surroundings and flings an arm toward the mess, "this goddamned house. It's a train wreck. What the hell happened in here, and why do I have to come home to this shit?"

My heart thumps in spastic intervals, sporadic breaths straining my voice. "Asshole! I bought some things for *our* babies! I got cribs and—"

"Un-fucking-believable! You are...I've got no words." Hank's hands fly to his head and when he removes them, his eyes bulge with such a blazing intensity, I wonder if they'll pop out of their sockets. "I'm the other parent here. Don't do another goddamned thing regarding their room or our kids without consulting me. Got it?"

"Motherfucker!" I scream. I lunge at him, beating him with my fists with every ounce of fight in my body.

He grabs my wrists with ease and bends them back toward me, forcing me to crumple to the floor. He grips them tightly, speaking to me with quiet menace. "Don't ever attack me again. I may be angry, but I am still being civil."

He releases me, and I sink to the carpet and rub my forearms. All the anxiety and emotions release, flooding my existence and taking me down with it. I burst into tears and Hank stalks off. He mutters something unintelligible from the hallway and storms out moments later, slamming the door with thundering hostility. I rush to the window in time to witness his truck flying out of the driveway, tires squealing halfway down the street.

———

Jimmy: When Hank called wanting to tie one on so late on a weeknight, I wanted to pass. Then I figured, how many nights like this do we have left now that he's saddled with the ol'

BALL AND CHAIN? PLUS, IT WAS OBVIOUS SOMETHING WAS UP. HE DIDN'T ELABORATE, AND I DIDN'T PRESS. THAT'S THE BEST PART ABOUT BEING A GUY—YOU CAN GET SHITFACED WITH YOUR BUDS AND NOT HAVE TO TALK ABOUT YOUR *FEELINGS* LIKE THE BROADS ALWAYS WANT TO DO.

BALL AND CHAIN? PLUS, IT WAS OBVIOUS SOMETHING WAS UP. HE DIDN'T ELABORATE, AND I DIDN'T PRESS. THAT'S THE BEST PART ABOUT BEING A GUY—YOU CAN GET SHITFACED WITH YOUR BUDS AND NOT HAVE TO TALK ABOUT YOUR *FEELINGS* LIKE THE BROADS ALWAYS WANT TO DO.

CHAPTER 29
HANK

I POUND the drinks over several rounds of pool against Jimmy at Get a Cue. I let my mind go blank except for the game. Chalk the stick, plan my shot, talk smack, take another slug, drag my feet, irritate my buddy and sink it—or more accurately, miss. This strategy keeps my angry, frustrated and homicidal thoughts at bay. I can't leave things hanging forever, but I'm not remotely ready to patch that shit up.

I stagger out of the bar at one in the morning. Too drunk to drive, I sit in the cab of my truck, careful not to insert my keys into the ignition. Checking my phone, I stare in dismay at twenty-two text messages from Adrienne and more lighting up my voicemail. *Fantastic.*

Through bleary eyes, I start reading. Typical female bullshit: vitriol, defensiveness, blame. Women can be such fucking psychos. The last one is the least hateful:

Where are you?

I don't bother with the voicemails, sure they're full of more screeching. After a few tries, I punch in a response:

Be home in the morning. I'm fine.

These damn phones are for munchkins, not big-fingered men. Or drunk ones.

Setting my alarm, I anticipate tomorrow is gonna hurt. Shortly after I kick off my boots and get horizontal, I pass out.

Scorching sunlight beams into the cab. I lurch upright, squinting, grimacing and off balance from my spinning head. I grab my phone. "Fuck!" I overslept and now it's almost nine o'clock. The dregs of last night's rocket fuel coats my tongue. Nasty. I call work and direct Monica to handle certain necessities until I arrive. I crank up The Boss and head home, stopping at the nearest gas station to buy an extra-large caffeinated soda to inhale on the way. It helps with the mouth fuzz but not the throbbing head.

I pull in the driveway. All quiet...on the outside. We all know the real *Jerry Springer Show* shit happens away from the public eye. With a heaviness, I exit my sanctuary and stumble into the house.

My mind blows with what greets me. Adrienne cleaned—the place damn near sparkles and a fresh lemon scent fills the air. No clutter. No dirty dishes. No boxes.

Why am I such an asshole?

"Adrienne?" Not finding her in the front, I walk down the hall, intentionally bypassing the nursery, lest I call forth the clusterfuck that got this ball rolling. I find her in the bedroom, sitting on the bed. She doesn't glance up when I enter.

"Hey."

No response.

"I'm sorry. I acted like a ginormous ass." *Except about the smoking.*

Still nothing.

"I'm falling on my sword here. Want to throw a guy a bone?"

She turns. "Okay."

"Okay?" I sink next to her. "Listen, this isn't an excuse, but yesterday sucked. Coming home, the whole situation was the nut strap that made this bull buck. It wasn't your fault." I put my arm around her.

She sniffles and glances at me. "You mean you're not mad?"

I take a moment. *Choose your words wisely, Hank ol' boy.* "I'm upset about the smoking. You hid it from me, and you're not only endangering yourself, but our babies, so that's non-negotiable...agreed?"

She nods.

"Sometime soon, I want to talk more about it, but not now. Regarding the nursery, I'm not mad, but I'm also not happy with how you went about it. I should have communicated better about my plans and expectations. Maybe you don't understand my process, but I spent considerable time thinking this through. I don't do anything willy nilly; I always have a plan, and I do shit right. If you understood my upbringing...suffice it to say I'm highly capable. Maybe guilty of perfectionism."

"I didn't know."

"How could you? I didn't communicate, and that's on me." I fall into those brown pools staring back at me. "I hate losing my temper with you."

"That makes two of us." She gazes toward the wall.

I put my fingers on her chin and gently coax her to look at me. "All I can say is I'll continue to try and do better. In exchange, I'd appreciate it if you would not go off half-cocked in these kinds of matters—and trust me to handle the work."

She nods. "I'm sorry."

My mouth finds hers and we kiss tenderly, lessening the ache in my gut.

Our mouths part and Adrienne draws back. "Where were you last night? You worried me."

"You mean, sometime after all the hateful texting?"

Her pretty lips curl into a guilty smile.

"I got drunk with Jimmy and passed out in my truck. I know it's not cool." Hoping I've served enough penance, I shrug and paste a pleading, puppy-dog-eye expression on my face. "Forgive me?"

"You expect me to buy that story?"

Does she think I stepped out on her? "It's the truth. I've ooooonly got eyes forrrrrrr youuuuuuuu…" I croon, badly.

She shakes her head.

Pushing her flat against the mattress, I press my lips to hers again, my insides flooding with relief.

She wraps her arms around my neck and pulls me closer, allowing our mouths to dispel the hurt. Soon our bodies move in a familiar concert, and the flame ignites.

She pushes her hand against my chest. My dick throbs in protest of the interruption. "Aren't you going to work?"

"I'm already late. Another hour won't matter."

She scooches the covers back and hikes up her nightgown, exposing her beautiful, ballooning belly. Overcome with how much I love this woman, I bask in her glory for a moment.

Hovering over her, I slide my index finger inside her slick center, groaning at how wet she is for me. Licking her salty essence, I duck down to pleasure her with my mouth. I make lazy circles with my tongue and suck on her bundle of nerves while my fingers keep up a slow and steady pace in what I've dubbed her tunnel of love. God, she's delicious. Perfect. A feast in all ways.

Her hips become frantic, nearing release, and my mouth rides her like a bucking bronc. Her legs stiffen and she screams, an orgasm rocketing through her as contractions clench around my digits.

I crawl up her body and ease my throbbing cock inside her. Our lovemaking is unhurried and sublime as we gaze into each other's eyes. We move in concert, natural and unscripted. Adrienne's supple hands and legs clutch my back as I go deeper, claiming all of her.

Our moans fill the room, and our breathing grows ragged as I head toward the finish line. When the pleasure is almost too much to bear, she squeezes her eyes shut. Mine stay focused on her rapturous face, and it sends me over the edge, helplessly under her spell.

The weekend arrives and I repaint the nursery, correcting the disaster my wife began. I'll be damned if she doesn't nail the ceiling—a smattering of puffy clouds floating against a blue sky. I assemble and install two identical cribs. We shop together for a rocking chair designed for nursing twins and score a changing table. We wait on making other major purchases, knowing family members will send gifts. We are way ahead of this deadline—even if Frick and Frack arrive prematurely, which we pray won't happen.

We invite Rod and Tami for dinner, and they ooh and aah over the nursery. Tami and Adrienne begin an animated conversation about baby prep, which drives us men to the living room to drink beer.

"What's this?" Rod asks, pointing to a medal.

I wave my hand as if it's no big deal. I'm nothing yet. "I won a couple of matches."

"You box?" He looks impressed.

"At an amateur level. Ever hear of Friday Night Fights?"

"Sounds familiar."

"Guys sign up, meaning regular schmoes like us. You're assigned to a weight class, so it's not like you against Goliath. You throw down in a ring with a ref and find out how you measure up."

"Ballsy." He fingers the medal, as if contemplating whether he'd do it. "And you weren't worried about getting your ass kicked?"

"Nah." Probably should have been, but I'm too cocky, stupid or both.

"You do this a lot, man?"

"Only once so far. My next bouts are coming up soon. Not sure how long I'll keep at it, but it's been a blast. Ever been in a fight?" My assessment of Rod: a vain pussy. He's got a pretty boy face, gelled hair and for God's sake, he's wearing skinny jeans. Ma would say he thinks the sun comes up just to hear him crow.

He shakes his head no. "Never had to, but I would."

Sure, buddy. And I'm Cinderella. "Give this Friday Night Fights thing a go—if you think it's your bailiwick." I can't help the smirk.

He laughs and swigs his beer, changing the subject. "You and Adrienne doing all right?"

I glare. What kind of fucking question is that?

"I know it's none of my business, but she called the other night, upset. Talked to Tam for an hour. Something about you two fighting."

Does this idiot not understand The Man Code? I dial up a penetrating stare. "We're good."

"Cool, man. Didn't mean to pry. You seem like a nice couple. Just looking out." Rod breaks eye contact and stares at the bookshelf.

Looking out for who? This tool is already on my watch list, but now he's earned his nickname: NimRod.

Our wives rejoin us, dispelling the awkward silence. The rest of the night goes pleasantly enough, but my weird vibe about the dude never dissipates. It may be my active imagination, but I swear his eyes linger on my wife. *That's why there's a watch list, buddy.*

———

Tami: I'm so happy I met Adrienne. She's sweet, genuine and pregnant, giving us plenty to commiserate about. I like her husband too. He strikes me as a man's man: pragmatic, polite, the right amount of rough around the edges. Rod thinks

Hank's a redneck and can't understand why Adrienne hooked up with him. Granted, Hank's not pretty like Rod, but what does that have to do with the kind of person you are? My husband can be so shallow and elitist. And if I'm being honest, a bit of a wimp. I think Hank intimidates him, which he'd never admit.

CHAPTER 30

ADRIENNE

I PULL on Hank's two front belt loops and gaze up at him with my best forlorn face. "Take me dancing tonight, pleeeeeeeeeease. I'm desperate for fun before I can no longer walk."

His lip twitches underneath that walrus mustache, and he leans over and kisses me. "I'm happy to swing you around, darlin', but only if we're Two-Stepping—not any other nonsense."

I envision my cowboy trying to dance to pop or R&B and stifle a laugh. "As long as I'm dancing, I don't care. Crazy Horse?"

Hank makes a squeamish face.

"Forget Briggs. You'll get to see your buddies."

He's silent and I wait, showcasing my best pout.

"All right. Let's do it. You changing?" He turns to his closet and fishes out one of his many hat boxes.

I sigh. "If I can fit into anything decent. I'm a fat cow." My figure, formerly my greatest asset, now disgusts me.

His eyes find mine. "You're pregnant, sweetheart, not fat. And you're gorgeous."

I stifle an eye roll. My husband regularly says my pregnant

bod turns him on. Lies! As if anyone could find this deformed mess sexy. I open my closet and sift through my outfit options. One flowy dress might work and would be cute paired with the mocha and turquoise cowboy boots Hank got me for Christmas.

We look like a bona fide country couple when we leave the house, and I love my husband in his black Stetson. He's almost handsome.

It's been months since we stepped into The Crazy Horse. The gang's all working—Jimmy, Finn, Noreen—and they give us a warm greeting. I'm dying for a Screwdriver but have a better chance of becoming a brain surgeon with eagle-eye daddy scrutinizing my every move. Once we hit the dance floor, I forget all about it and the twins somersaulting in my belly. I come alive as Hanks steers me around in his deft grasp. There's no shortage of grins from either of us as we whirl, twirl and Two-Step in each other's arms.

Breathless, I request to sit a few out, and Hank finds us a table. He heads to the bar to snag a beer for himself and ice water for me. Sitting, a haze settles over me, my head spinning uncomfortably. I duck between my legs, trying to stop the dizziness. I'm too fucking hot. Grabbing the small plastic food menu, I fan myself, but it's not enough in this steamy, suffocating club. I search for my husband in vain. Lurching to my feet, I scurry to the exit, desperate for fresh air.

Once outside, I lean against the façade and inhale deep breaths. Closing my eyes, I'm cooled when a faint breeze rustles through my hair and skitters across my damp skin. Heaven.

"Looky what we have here. If it isn't miss runaway."

My eyes shoot open at the voice. *Darren.* Warning bells clang in my head.

"Cat got your tongue, bitch?"

"What do you want?" I retort, faking more spunk than I have.

"What I've got coming to me." Darren steps on the cigarette he's flicked to the ground, grinding out the embers.

"I owe you nothing, you piece of shit." I push off the wall, still wrapped in a dizzy haze. Fear slithers up my spine, penetrating my muddy thoughts.

He holds his hands up like a question, steadily approaching. "Is that any way to greet an old lover? Seems to me you're all about spreading the love…and your legs. You fucked me, my best buddy, and I hear moved on to someone new. Sounds like the exact definition of whore."

"Don't come any closer. You're never touching me again, asshole." My eyes flick toward the entrance, imploring Hank to materialize.

"I beg to differ," he says, lunging at me in one movement and grabbing my hair so hard it's a miracle it doesn't rip off my scalp. I shriek into the night, my arms clawing at him as I lose my balance and tumble to the ground.

Darren drags me across the sidewalk, a firm grip on my long tendrils, barely struggling against my kicking legs. Wide-eyed, my heart thudding wildly in my chest, my throat strains with each scream. Why does no one hear me?

Dear God. Why is this happening? And what the fuck is wrong with Darren? Please don't let me die, or my babies…

In full panic mode, I flail again until my hands gain purchase. I dig my nails into his flesh with all the fight left in me. He cusses, pauses, and smashes a fist into my jaw. Through the stars speckling my vision, my husband emerges from the bar, and I cry out.

Hank is upon us in seconds, pausing only to scoop up the lid of a nearby industrial trashcan at the curb. Wielding it like an armored dark knight, he attacks. Blood spurts from Darren's head on impact, and I'm released from his death grip. I scramble away on my hands and knees, turning in time to catch Hank smashing the metal lid into Darren's opposite temple.

My ex falls to the ground and Hank swiftly straddles his torso, pinning him to the sidewalk and wailing on his head with blow after merciless blow.

I'm glued to the scene with a combination of alarm and awe.

My husband spews a litany of insults, punctuated by heavy grunts as he unleashes his furious wrath.

Darren's head is a pulpy, bloody mess. I'm not sorry. But…

"Hank," I croak, my throat tight as shivers course through my body.

Silence.

"We need to go."

He turns, eyes ablaze, as if remembering I'm there. "Are you all right?" he asks hoarsely.

I nod, my lips quivering as tears prick the back of my eyes. "We've got to go *now*."

He glances back at nearly unconscious Darren and forces himself to stand. He holds out a hand and helps me up, and I take in the blood splattered on his clothes, face and hands. I cannot read the turbulent expression on his face.

"We need to hurry," I say, as sirens whine in the distance. The street appears deserted, muted music wafting from the club, so maybe they're not coming for Hank, but what if they are? Although he's not at fault, I question if the police will view it that way. Not when Darren isn't moving.

Hank picks up the bloody lid in one hand, I collect his Stetson in mine, and we hightail it out of Georgetown in The Boss.

––––––––

JAMAL: YOU EVER SEE *THE GODFATHER*…THE SCENE WHERE SONNY GOES ALL MOTHERFUCKING CORLEONE ON THE DUDE WHO BEAT UP HIS SISTER…USING A TRASH CAN? THAT'S WHAT WENT DOWN RIGHT IN FRONT OF MY APARTMENT. ONLY INSTEAD OF MAFIA, HOMEBOY LOOKED LIKE HE WALKED STRAIGHT OUTTA *THE GOOD, THE BAD AND THE UGLY* OR SOMETHING. HE PUT A *HURTIN'* ON THAT CAT. BUT CHECK IT, THE DUDE HAD HIS WOMAN BY THE HAIR, DRAGGING HER DOWN THE STREET LIKE A FUCKING CAVEMAN. SO, COWBOY WAS JUSTIFIED IN ANYTHING GOING DOWN. HE WAS JUST TAKING CARE OF BIDNESS.

CHAPTER 31
HANK

AS I LOG miles between us and Georgetown, fury and guilt ping-pong through my veins. And I don't know what the fuck to do with these *feelings* aside from shoving them further into the bowels of the ship. The adrenaline exits slowly, numbness settling in, my back slumping against the seat like a sack of potatoes.

I don't have an ounce of remorse over what I did to that fuck-tard. He dragged my pregnant wife down the street by her hair, an image I'll never forget. What if I'd been too late? I almost was...when I returned to our table, I assumed Adrienne was in the ladies' room. As time ticked by, my intuition urged me to search for her, go outside. My whole body shudders, chill bumps rippling across my skin.

Adrienne breaks the silence. "Thank you," she whispers, reaching for my free hand.

Glancing at her...her face beginning to bruise, brunette waves a tangled mess, my nerve endings crackle with rage. "I'm sorry," I croak, my voice strained and hoarse.

"Hank, no. For what?"

I clear my throat. "If you could see what I see, you'd understand. I didn't protect you."

She shakes her head, as if dismayed. "You *saved* me."

I inhale deep breaths, trying to shut off the internal looping replay. "Why were you outside?"

"I couldn't breathe. All the dancing, I guess. When I became dizzy and faint, I tried to tell you, but you were on the other side of the club at the bar. I couldn't wait, so I walked out front to get fresh air and, well..."

Fighting back a grimace, I squeeze her hand. "Please don't ever leave again without me knowing. I got frantic when I couldn't find you. And when I did...what he was doing to you...I—"

"I know," she breathes, her voice catching.

"That was your ex, right? The guy from the night we met?"

She nods.

"Walk me through what happened."

Adrienne fills in the gaps, leaving me seething and simmering with bloodlust all over again. I do my best not to crush her hand, safeguarded in mine.

"Do you think you'll be in trouble?" she asks.

I scrub my jaw and shrug. "It's hard to say. But douchebag would have a hell of a time explaining himself. I guess it depends on what he tells the police and whether there are any witnesses."

She rubs her belly with her free hand. "I was so scared, Hank. So worried about our babies."

The churning in my gut intensifies. "Do you think they're all right? Should we go to the hospital to be sure?"

Adrienne shakes her head. "They're fine. I'm fine. Shaken up, but okay. My knight in shining armor...in a Stetson, saved us."

I squeeze her hand, grateful I found her in time, and the hammering in my heart turns to something sharp. My eyes prickle, and I swallow those unmanly, sissy tears. I force myself to shift away from morose thoughts and what if scenarios to how I kicked ass. "Sometimes my...skillset...serves justice." Except true justice would ensure that cowardly, pregnant-woman-beating shithead lands in jail—or six feet under. He'll get off scot-free unless we step forward, but it's too convoluted now.

She squeezes my hand in return and we ride the rest of the way home in silence.

———

OFFICER CIRILLO: THE VICTIM'S FACE WAS BEATEN TO A PULP. HE SAYS HE HAS NO IDEA WHO ATTACKED HIM OR WHY, AND OUR CANVAS YIELDED NO WITNESSES. IT APPEARED AN OBJECT WAS USED IN THE ASSAULT, BUT WE FOUND NO PHYSICAL EVIDENCE OF SAID OBJECT. WE'RE AT A DEAD END, BUT WE'LL KEEP DIGGING. BECAUSE THERE'S CLEARLY A STORY HERE…WE'RE JUST MISSING SOME OF THE CHAPTERS AND CHARACTERS.

CHAPTER 32
ADRIENNE

INSPECTING my belly in the full-length mirror, it now rivals the size of Santa's sack, and I still have sixty days to go. Deep red stretch marks mar the underside, another irreversible consequence of being knocked-up. I glower at my reflection, happy at least my face has returned to normal since the nightmare with Darren. An involuntary shudder weaves through me. On its heels, one of the babies throws a jab and I fold in half, eyes resting on my swollen legs and feet. Sucking air until I catch my breath, I fear we've created actual monsters by the frequency and velocity the dynamic duo kicks and punches. Straightening, I search for the antacids to calm my incinerating heartburn and pivot, because I need to pee. Again. *Kill me now.*

I finish dressing as Hank arrives home with his mother from the airport. Impeccable in slacks and a fitted top, every dyed hair in place, I try not to compare myself to her. It's not even apples to oranges. More like grapes to watermelons. It's also a mystery why she didn't wait to visit until after her grandchildren were born. Maybe she's here to prey on my vulnerabilities.

Henrietta treats us to an expensive dinner in Falls Church and catches us up on news from the ranch and gossip about friends and family. I struggle to keep up, clueless about most of the people she references. She speaks mostly to Hank but throws me a frigid smile on occasion. I'm too tired to care.

We drop her off at a nearby hotel—her choice but thank you, universe—and it doesn't come soon enough. I want to peel off my clothes, crawl into bed and sleep.

The following morning close to eleven, Tami calls in tears and begs me to come over. My husband understands, promising to smooth things over with his mother, not that she'll give two shits if I'm absent.

I speed to Tami's, thankful for an out with my monster-in-law. Cars clog up the street, so I park in her driveway.

She opens the door, all smiles.

Cocking my head, I level my gaze. "What gives?"

"I'll show you." She takes my hand and leads me to the living room.

"SURPRISE!" chants a chorus of voices.

I've been duped. Standing in stunned silence, my eyes scan the group. My heart lurches when I spot Grandma Betty. Next to her stands Hank's secretary, Monica, and Jill, the wife of one of his work friends. Henrietta is sandwiched between our nearest neighbors. Great...now I'm the heel. Jimmy and Finn's girlfriends round out the guests. My eyes well up again, knowing they've all shown up for me. Will a day ever go by again when I don't bawl over something?

I rush into my grandmother's arms and tears slide down my cheeks as we hug before I greet the others, expressing my utter shock and gratitude. Thankfully, I left the house in a dress with my hair and makeup done—all on account of my polished, stylish mother-in-law being in town.

Blue and pink balloons dot the ceiling, and more decorations fill the space. A small mountain of stacked gifts obscures a corner table with more on the floor.

Tami calls for everyone's attention, rubbing her own obvious baby bump under her chic maxi dress. "Thank you all for coming and helping us pull it off!" More claps and cheers erupt. "Please help yourself to refreshments before we play games, and then our guest of honor will open presents."

I groan. "Games?"

"Oh, yes," Tami says, laughing. "And our first one begins right now." She hands out pastel colored diaper pins. "Everyone must avoid saying 'baby' until we eat cake. If you catch someone uttering the B word, take their pin! The person with the most pins at the end wins a prize."

I affix mine, dreading whatever else my friend has in the queue, and busy myself with visiting. Tami admits colluding with my husband on the surprise, elated about pulling it off. I pretend to chide Grandma Betty and Henrietta for keeping secrets.

As the event unfolds, we're forced to play three guessing-type contests and a hilarious activity where ladies place a quarter between their knees and waddle to a jar to release it. It winds up being a surprising amount of fun and laughs.

Opening gifts, I become overwhelmed by the generosity. I'm given the Cadillac of dual strollers, two car seats, two bouncy chairs, and tons of adorable outfits, bedding, essentials and toys. The unbridled glee on these women's faces is priceless. The waterworks are in full force, as are the *oohs* and *aahs* from cuteness overload. The event ends with refreshments, including a celebratory cake frosted half blue, half pink.

Guests disperse about the time fatigue sets in. I hug Tami close, unable to aptly express my appreciation for her and my lovely shower.

Henrietta and Grandma Betty spend the remainder of the day at our place, and I'm relieved and irritated they find common ground. My mother-in-law shows me more graciousness than normal, making her motivations transparent. In this scenario, it's important she's perceived as magnanimous, generous, and welcoming. I wonder about the narrative she swallows to keep her shit smelling so fresh.

My grandmother stays overnight. As much as I yearn to visit

with her and confide about the *real* Mrs. McCallister, by the time my mother-in-law returns to her hotel, I'm so exhausted, I conk out right on the sofa.

We gather for breakfast on Sunday before Henrietta and Grandma Betty depart for their respective homes, and I never have Gran to myself. *Gypped again.* Prego life is an endless series of gyps.

———

Tami and I begin a five-week birthing class at the hospital. Our husbands beg off from attending, asking us to fill them in on their roles. Tami's annoyed with Rod over it, but I don't blame Hank one bit for opting out. My gal pal and I can be each other's partners when needed.

When Tami picks me up the first night, I can tell something's bugging her.

"What's going on?" I ask, struggling to fasten the seatbelt because...pregnant girl problems.

She pulls away from the curb, her lips pressed in a tight line. "It's Rod."

"Is this about him not coming to class?" *Let it go!*

"I'm still PO'd about him bailing on me, but he's incredibly unsupportive all the way around. And selfish, focused on himself, his needs. But the latest has to do with a text on his phone that sent me into another stratosphere."

"Uh oh. Details." I already need to pee and Tami hitting four consecutive manhole covers isn't helping matters.

"Some message to a colleague, but in a super flirty tone, totally inappropriate."

Scumbag. "What did he say when you busted him?"

"He blew it off, said they're friends and nothing more. Called it harmless banter and declared they all joke around like that at work. To top it off, he had the audacity to reprimand me for checking his texts!" Tami opens her mouth in theatrical dismay.

"How *did* you see it?"

"His phone lit up sitting on the kitchen counter. I looked, but only to gauge whether it warranted me tracking him down."

"Are you worried? You think he's lying?"

"Wouldn't be the first time."

"Well, shit. That sucks." Although unsurprising. I'd pegged Rod correctly from the start. "What are you going to do?"

"What can I do? We're about to have a baby together. I don't know if he's doing something behind my back. I've got nothing here, except my intuition coupled with knowing I'm at my least attractive. I'm a beached whale—with psycho, *Fatal Attraction*-y thoughts."

I nod in support. "Gotta love hormones." I reach across and touch Tami's forearm. "Maybe it's nothing. And if it helps, you're the prize in the Cracker Jack box—not Rod."

Her grimace disappears. "Damn straight I am."

"All ready to birth those babies?" Hank asks from the recliner when I return. Diesel sprawls near his feet, licking his paw. Other than a quick glance my direction, the dog ignores me. *The feeling is mutual, buddy.*

I bend down, hiss out a breath, and abort kissing my husband on the cheek. "Not quite. The instructor gave us an overview and covered the basics, including signs of labor since that's coming first."

"Hopefully not for another two months." He flashes an exaggerated chipped-tooth smile.

I fetch a glass of water from the kitchen. "I think you might be right about Rod."

"What's NimRod doing now?"

"Tami says he's flirting with a girl at work. She's worried it's more."

"I don't put anything past that dickless wonder."

I shrug it out of my thoughts. "Ready to go a few more rounds about the names? Otherwise, Frick and Frack might stick."

Hank groans, his face pained. "If we must. I might need another beer for this conversation."

I retrieve my list and hand him a Rolling Rock. "Suck it up, buttercup."

"Buttercup's out, even though I loved *The Princess Bride*."

"Let the aggravation begin." I sit on the sofa and kick off my shoes, the most marvelous sensation in the world these days. I scoot ungracefully against the armrest pillows and elevate my feet, my swollen legs resembling tree trunks. I luxuriate in the stillness before attempt number eighty-three, give or take, to identify our children. I muster my strength and launch my offensive.

Two tedious hours later, after my husband rejects names for every imaginable flaw or nitpicky reason (*Sadie sounds like a stripper, Levi is too popular, and aren't we over the name-your-kid-after-the-fifty-states fad?*), we agree on Tanner and Cassidy.

It's only taken four months.

"That wasn't so hard, was it?" he says.

I grab a sofa pillow and chuck it at him.

He laughs, lurching out of the recliner to kneel by my side. He leans over my belly and speaks. "Hey kids, hear the news? Mom and I have you covered. Y'all keep cooking until it's time to pop out." He inches up and kisses me. "Hank, Adrienne, Tanner and Cassidy—that's our family, pretty mama. Long live the McCallisters."

Smiling at his eternally sunny disposition, my hand strokes the taut skin protecting my babes. I hope birthing these suckers will be easier than naming them.

Hank leaves to walk the dog. I close my eyes and lean my head back, my thoughts returning to my conversation with Tami. Is Rod cheating on her? He seems every bit the type from the vibe I picked up. And he is undeniably sexy. From a physical standpoint, he runs circles around my husband. I can't help but wonder if Tami's not dynamic enough in the sack to hold him.

———

MONICA: I WENT TO THE BABY SHOWER AS A FAVOR TO HANK. I'D NEVER TELL HIM, BUT I DON'T LIKE HIS WIFE. IS THAT BECAUSE OF HER RIDICULOUSLY GORGEOUS FACE AND HAIR? HER PERFECTLY PROPORTIONED FIGURE—WHEN SHE'S NOT PREGNANT, THAT IS? OR BECAUSE I'M A LITTLE IN LOVE WITH HIM MYSELF? GUILTY AS CHARGED. IF THIS THING BLOWS UP, I HOPE I'M THE ONE TO PICK UP THE PIECES.

CHAPTER 33
HANK

TFIF—THANK fuck it's Friday. My third appearance in Friday Night Lights is in three hours, and I'm fired up and more than ready to hit someone. I crank up the tunes and tap my hands against the steering wheel as I fly home.

I'm sure George Swiger will be on the scene tonight, hounding me, expecting an answer about his proposed management contract. Signing one would bring more lucrative, strategic fights and bona fide training. Of course, he gets a cut of the winnings. I've staved him off to avoid going the rounds with my wife, who has turned into a crabby Abby.

Adrienne complains nonstop—about nothing and everything. Ain't no pleasing her, placating her, or reasoning with her. Then there's the volatile mood swings around sex where one minute she's insatiable, and the next, telling me to get the fuck away from her. And for the love of Pete, the woman has no tolerance for discomfort. When I told her to "Take some Triactin," she didn't get it. "Try acting," I explained. *That* didn't go over well.

I try to remember we were reared differently. I had solid guidance and structure by strict parents who taught me manners, skills, values and ethics. My wife mostly endured trauma and came out a survivor.

I accept more invites than ever for after-work stops at the bar, anything to delay going home to my irrational, beautiful tyrant. Her issues make *me* damn cranky, then we have two idiots going toe to toe. Plus, I'm restless. Part of me can't wait for Tanner and Cassidy to emerge. My heart soars thinking about it while my head brims with ideas about all we'll do together and what I can teach them. But I also experience a suffocating, inescapable sensation—the whisper of *your free days are numbered, buddy*. I'm about to be a father to twins and am still a kid myself.

As expected, Adrienne's demeanor is chilly, and she ignores me as I collect my boxing gear. Her vehemence against me fighting leads her to believe I'm irresponsible and selfish. How convenient to forget *she* requested solutions to my *anger issues*. And I don't dare bring *this* up—but weren't my fists downright handy the night her ex pulled his violent bullshit in the not-so distant past?

I'm trying, for chrissakes. She can't have it both ways.

I attempt a smooch, but she turns her head and my lips glance off her ear. "Don't be like that. I've gotta bail."

"Then go." Her head remains in its defiant position.

"You're being an asshole. But I love you anyway."

Cue crickets.

I move toward the door and ruffle Diesel's fur. "Love you too, buddy." I blow my bride a kiss she never catches, grab my bag and leave.

The high kicks in when I enter the arena, the momentum building as I register, weigh in and listen to the mandatory review. I pace and flex my hand grips waiting for the night's schedule. When they announce my first bout, it's against a new guy—like me, a few months ago.

Jimmy shows up with his girlfriend, Amanda, and we

analyze the first couple of fights. We fist-bump and I head to the locker room to prepare, checking my phone in hopes Adrienne texted me. She's still maintaining radio silence. I push thoughts of my irate wife out of my head; I need to focus. I don my boxing garb, psyching myself out for the impending battle, barely listening to the rules while a staff member laces up my gloves.

I enter the ring with one thought: *You're mine, motherfucker.*

I knock him out in two rounds.

Ten minutes later, George Swiger claps me on the back, firing off words at rapid speed. "Good fight, kid. Solid instincts. Your next one won't be a cakewalk. Jenkins is seasoned and he's got size. You watched him fight? Know what you're up against? Got a plan?" This man could talk the hide off a cow.

"Only to hit him as hard as I can, sir."

Swiger laughs. "This guy," he says to no one in particular, squeezing my shoulder a few times. "Do your thing. Don't think too much. Find me later, and let's talk turkey." He points at me as he walks away.

My wannabe manager shits me not. Jenkins is a giant. That's saying something, since most people think I'm one. This dude looks as menacing as Mean Joe Greene, and I understand how rivals felt lining up against him when he played for the Pittsburgh Steelers.

How Jenkins and I made it into the same weight class is puzzling, but the scales don't lie. His muscles bulge, shiny from sweat. I bet his body fat percentage is under ten. I don't want to think about mine—or how imbalanced we are. He glares at me, and I remind myself he's just another cheetoh-eating, butt-munching, jizz-breathed shit magnet.

Sizing him up, I only have one strategy: hit the fucker as hard as I can and dodge my ass off, so his shots don't land.

The bell rings for round one, and we do the boxing waltz: bob, weave, feint, eye contact. I elude a few of his punches. Sweat trickles into my ears. As I'm trying to figure out his rhythm and when to pounce, I spot his weakness, a split second when he's vulnerable.

I continue dodging and weaving but as the round nears its end, my opportunity arrives to take a shot. Every solid blow starts in the lower body, so I plant my feet and draw power up my legs and through my hips to release a monster motherfucking punch with my right. I hit the sucker square on his chin—a knockout strike if ever I've thrown one.

Jenkins merely grins, and in that moment when I realize he isn't going down, I stall like a bad motor. He answers with a left hook, connecting with my jaw.

Lights out.

Three days later, as I'm driving to work, my world comes zooming into focus as if night turned into day with the flip of a switch.

What the fuck? Where the hell am I? I can't remember getting in my truck or where I'm going. I crane my neck. This is some freaky deaky shit. What time is it? What day? I pull into a strip mall parking lot and haul my phone out of my pocket. The calendar reads Tuesday, May 20. What the actual fuck is happening? I've lost track of days. *Days.*

There are several missed calls and texts from Jimmy:

> Hey dipshit, how you doing?
>
> BRO! See a doc about your concussion?
>
> Don't be a little bitch.
>
> Call me, man. I'm getting worried.

The fight floods back. I got knocked out, and I mean, LIGHTS FUCKING OUT. By goddamned Hercules, the Incredible Hulk or some combination of the two. I hit that asshole as hard as humanly possible, and he smirked at me, like, *That all you got?*

How embarrassing. I got my ass handed to me on a plate. Not just a plate—fancy fucking china. But damn if I can remember one thing since Jenkins threw his last punch. What the hell have I been doing from Friday night to now? How am I functioning without any memory of it?

I call Jimmy.

"What the fuck? I've been trying to reach you all week, man!"

"Sorry, buddy. This is going to sound crazy, but I just sort of… came to." A couple starts bickering in a foreign language near the dry cleaners and I roll up my window.

"What do you mean, 'came to'?"

"I'm out here driving in my truck like all systems go, but it's the first time I'm aware of *anything* since getting clocked by Thunderfuck. I literally lost three days of my life." Noticing a fast-food cup in the console, I pick it up and ice rattles when I give it a shake. No idea where this came from, but after an initial swallow —of what turns out to be magnificent, throat-burning Coke—I inhale half of it. *Liquid gold.*

"No shit? Totally messed up, bro."

That's putting it mildly. "Can you tell me what happened? Start with the fight."

"Dude hammered you right before the end of round one. KO'd your ass. You were out a minute or so. The ref used the smelling salts to raise you from the dead. You wobbled but got to your feet after a couple more minutes. You were out of it for sure; got your bell rung like a total fucking Nancy."

"Very funny, asshole." I drain the soda.

"The med crew checked you out, gave you the concussion test. You didn't pass. You were supposed to go to the hospital. We offered to take you, but you brushed me off. Hold on a sec." Forklifts beep in the background while Jimmy speaks to a coworker about moving lumber. "I'm back. Listen, you seemed fine. You were talking, joking around. And aside from your face taking a beating—eh, come to think of it, not much different than normal —I thought you were okay. You really don't remember?"

"Nope. Just that last punch. It hurt. And I punched Jenkins as hard as I've ever hit anyone, and he didn't even fucking wobble."

He chuckles. "Yup. Dude was a tank. I think you should go to the hospital, man. That's some messed up shit."

"You might be right."

"You telling Adrienne?"

Ugh. I'd rather pull out my eyelashes one by one. "Yeah."

"Keep me posted. Don't leave me hanging again, dipshit."

If I'm still alive once Adrienne has her say. "All right, *mom*."

"In your wet dreams."

We hang up and I debate how to proceed. I *should* tell my wife but argue that collecting all the information first would be smarter, making me armed and ready for a conversation. With a lunatic, because she's going to be furious.

I reach Monica and tell her I'm dealing with a non-life-threatening medical emergency and make her promise to keep her yap shut, including to Adrienne if she calls. Then I haul ass to the nearest hospital.

I leave the ER with more clarity. I don't have a concussion, and the doctor attributes my three-day walking dead act to transient global amnesia, a rare condition of temporary memory loss caused by things such as head trauma, pain and physical exertion. I hit the trifecta. Doc anticipated I'd be fine and advised closely monitoring my situation for the next few days.

Not much scares me—but telling my wife about this does. With a twinge of regret, I'm certain my boxing career is over. With kids coming into the world, no fight is worth my life or my health. Not by a long shot.

I text Jimmy an update and take the rest of the day off. On the way home, I debate what to tell Adrienne. On one hand, she'll be furious about this development and the danger I've put myself in. On the other hand, she'll be mollified about my decision to quit. I'll avoid any business and be a hero if I omit the first part, but that would make me a liar and a chickenshit. I can't do it, appealing as it sounds. Lying isn't in my makeup. I'll face the music and survive.

Now for some real music. Turning on the radio, Trace Adkins, Blake Shelton and Sugarland escort me home.

Fifteen minutes later, I pull into our driveway, and startle at the black Lexus already taking up space. Worse, the owner has a stupid custom plate: CPA MAN. My mind whirls. A thousand bucks it's NimRod. But what the fuck is he doing at my house at noon on a Tuesday?

———

MRS. BROWN: IN MY DAY, IT WASN'T PROPER TO ENTERTAIN A MAN AT HOME WHILE YOUR HUSBAND WAS AWAY. A MAN WORTH HIS SALT WOULDN'T EVEN TRY, BUT IF A WOMAN ENGAGED, IT IMPLIED HANKY PANKY. NOWADAYS, EVERYONE BREAKS THE RULES—THERE'S NO DECORUM ANYMORE. AS FOR THE MCCALLISTER PLACE...CARS COME AND GO ALL DAY WHEN HANK IS AT WORK, LIKE A FAST-FOOD DRIVE-THRU. AND CPA MAN APPEARS TO BE A REGULAR CUSTOMER, IF YOU KNOW WHAT I MEAN.

CHAPTER 34
ADRIENNE

WHEN ROD CALLS mid-morning and begs for an emergency trim, I acquiesce. What else am I doing except staving off labor, peeing every half-hour and putting my feet up so they don't swell as big as most male egos? And staying home—because pregnancy has robbed me of yet another life skill. I can't drive. What was previously short girl problems is now short, *wide* girl problems, which means I can't even reach the stupid pedals or strap in the seatbelt.

I can still manage a goddamn haircut.

I've cut Rod's hair twice—with Tami's blessing. Both times, he sat in a chair in their kitchen, and the three of us joked while I'd snipped and shaved. They'd called me a lifesaver the first go-round, saying he hated the rigmarole of finding a decent stylist and booking appointments every six weeks, so I scored a new client.

But Rod and I have never been alone, except once, briefly, when he dropped off some magazines and cookies from Tami. If he gets out of line, I'll put him in his place.

He arrives at my door ten minutes later. "Thanks so much for doing this. You're a lifesaver." That word again. *I'm a hairdresser, not Jesus.*

"No sweat." I usher him into the kitchen, gesturing at the chair sitting in the middle of our fake stone linoleum floor and drape him with a black plastic cape. "A trim, right?"

He meets my eyes. "Perfect. You look terrific, by the way."

I raise my eyebrows. "You're kidding, right?"

"Serious as the IRS in an audit."

That must be CPA humor...or an attempt at it. I shake my head. I'm gargantuan, my breasts ache and I mourn the loss of my svelte figure. I step back and assess his hair, avoiding his gaze.

"I'm pretty easy on the eyes, huh?" he says, nodding his head and grinning.

I roll my eyes and spritz water on his hair, starting at the front and working my way around in a circle. "How's Tami?"

"Ready to be done with this pregnancy business, I'm sure much the same as you. I'm amazed at how you ladies do this whole thing." He twists, trying to talk to me.

I reposition his head facing forward. "Try not to move. And we just deal. It's not like we have a choice." Remembering Hank's stupid "Triactin" comment, I begrudgingly admit there's truth to it. It's just irritating coming from Mr. Perfect In All Things.

"Tami's tits are getting huge. That's been a sweet fringe benefit. But you don't need any help in that department."

I pause.

"Too crass?"

"Yup." *These scissors are sharp and might slip.*

"I apologize."

"It's cool. My tits *are* spectacular." I shouldn't but can't resist. I continue grasping and snipping strands, working on the sides first. His hair is easy to cut—thick, lush and devoid of cowlicks.

Rod laughs. "I love your sense of humor. You're such a sarcastic smartass."

"Now you're talking about my ass?" I joke.

"Careful or I'll think you're flirting with me. Might take you up on it."

No doubt in my mind. "In your dreams."

"Been there, done that. You were magnificent."

Part of me knows I should steer this ship in another direction, but I'm enjoying the attention. "You've dreamed about me?"

"Many times."

I move in front of him, working on the crown of his head. This affords him a beeline view of my breasts, of which he takes full advantage. "Hmm…I've never had one about you."

"Ouch."

I smirk. Tangle with a tiger, baby, and you might get eaten. Circling him, I double-check my work then hand him a mirror. "You're all set."

He reviews my work, murmuring praise. I start to retrieve the mirror, but he holds it firmly, forcing me to make eye contact. "Thank you."

His penetrating gaze sears right into me and lodges itself in my loins. I swallow hard, irritated he has that effect. Goddamn handsome men, specifically the bastards with the impossible brown eyes. They're my kryptonite.

"Sure," I mumble.

He smiles, a hint of mischief in his expression.

As I remove the drape, Hank barrels through the front door and into the kitchen, loaded for bear. Rod and I swivel, caught off guard.

"Hey buddy," Rod says, standing and offering his hand to my husband.

I hurry to Hank's side. "Hi, honey. This is a surprise."

He throws an arm over my shoulders and leans down, kissing me long and hard. Then he shakes Rod's hand, still guarded, addressing him with a curt, "Rod."

"Adrienne saved my ass this morning. Now I need to motor, or I'll be late for my next meeting." Rod pulls out his wallet and hands me thirty bucks. "Thanks again." Heading for the door, he adds, "Good seeing you both."

"Later," Hank says as Rod slithers away.

My husband cocks his head, his arm tugging me closer. "I didn't realize you were giving NimRod a haircut today."

"Me neither. He called first thing, desperate for a trim. What else am I doing except waiting for these troublemakers to arrive?" I say, swiping a hand across my abdomen.

"I didn't like finding his car in the driveway. It worried me...not knowing who was here or if you were in trouble."

"It's only Rod, cowboy. Nothing to get worked up about." Is that a reminder for him or me? I give Hank's torso a comforting squeeze.

"He's a cumwipe."

My husband and his creative vocabulary. "Why are you home so early? Everything okay?"

Hank peers at the floor, then back at me. "Let's sit down and I'll explain."

He walks me through the past few days. *Unbelievable.*

I'm shocked but stutter out, "But you've been...talking, walking, showering, sleeping, driving...all like normal. How can you not remember?"

"It's bizarre, I know, but I'm telling you the God's-honest truth. You didn't notice anything different?"

"You were tired, napping a lot. Not abnormal, *considering.*" I let out an exasperated sigh. "Do you realize what could have happened? What if our babies were in the truck?"

He nods, morose. "I'd never forgive myself."

"You're never fighting again. No argument. Promise me right now."

He takes my hand. "I promise, sweetheart."

We clutch each other, the enormity of the situation hitting us both. A small, worrying twinge of a thought materializes, whispering...what happens to my husband's simmering pot of anger, ready to boil over at the slightest provocation, if we remove yet another outlet for its steam to escape?

———

ROD: I'M IN. IT'S JUST A MATTER OF TIME. ONCE SHE'S THROUGH THIS BABY NONSENSE AND GETS HER SHAPE BACK, WE'LL BE DOING THE DEED. I HOPE HER TITS ARE STILL GARGANTUAN. THEY ARE UNBELIEVABLE RIGHT NOW. IF THEY'RE ANYWHERE AS SPECTACULAR AS THE PAIR IN MY DREAMS, I'LL BE GIVING HER A PEARL NECKLACE.

CHAPTER 35
HANK

DIESEL FLOPS at the foot of my favorite recliner. I down another beer and stare at the tube, where the Texas Rangers and Mariners square off in a battle of the pitchers. Televised baseball has become my weekly respite while Adrienne and Tami attend their child-birthing class.

It's unfathomable we still have five weeks to go. Adrienne's belly looks like it's about to burst…and sometimes I think we are too. No matter how much I pamper her, cater to her whims and try to show her understanding, she remains as testy as a bull with its balls tied.

Wifey returns and I greet her cheerfully—even though inside, I'm tiptoeing on shattered glass. "How was it, gorgeous?"

She wrinkles her nose. "Don't call me that. I'm the size of an elephant. Two maybe. Did I tell you the latest? I'm so huge, I can only stand in the shower one way. If I turn sideways, my stomach pokes out of the curtain. I am bigger than the tub! *The tub!*"

I choke back a sarcastic comment. "You're beautiful, and you're carrying our twins. What do you expect? They take up some room."

"They're violent little suckers and kicking like a soccer game is in progress." She rubs both sides of her midsection.

"Chin up. You're in the home stretch."

She tries easing onto the couch but plops down ungracefully instead, emitting a growl through gritted teeth.

"Can I fetch you anything?"

"How about a stiff drink?" She notes my pointed stare and adds, "*Kid-ding*," in a singsong voice. "They discussed delivery complications tonight. Scary stuff, considering we're already at risk."

The stakes are high, making it impossible not to worry, but my job is to keep my wife's mind right. "Dr. Swann is on top of it. She's been monitoring you and the twins every step of the way. I'm confident she can handle whatever happens. But I predict smooth sailing."

Maneuvering her legs onto the couch, she leans against a throw pillow. "The relaxation techniques are a complete joke. They think a little steady breathing is going to thwart the agony of squirting out not one but *two* babies?"

I nod in compliance, agreeing they must be crazy.

"Here's their other pro tip: *relax*." Adrienne laughs, a contemptuous sound. "As if I can simply *poof!*, chillax. Great fucking suggestion."

I'm out of my depth. My advice is to suck it up. I know from experience that's not what she wants to hear—let alone execute. "The mental game is your friend, and it's the only constant you can rely on. It's all about being prepared, getting out in front of it. By accepting the pain and discomfort ahead of time, you won't be surprised or taken off guard when it happens. You can kick it to the curb and say, 'That all you got?'" I feign a few punches and an exaggerated scowl.

She grimaces. "I'm working on it."

"You've got this. You're a badass broad. I still have a picture of you in my mind from the night we met at The Crazy Horse. There you were, standing tall even though you're about as big as the little end of nothing, ready to fight some jerk. No fear. All spunk. I said to myself, 'there's a gal who'd charge Hell with a bucket of ice water.'"

My memory flicks back to the same jerk dragging my wife down the sidewalk and darkness filters in. Adrienne and I don't talk about the incident—haven't since the week it happened—but I still think about it...and the what ifs. I'm damn relieved the police never came knocking.

Adrienne smiles, lighting up the room and dispelling the shadows. "I've been a wretched, horrible person, haven't I?"

"You've had your moments," I admit.

"I'm going to be a terrible mother, like mine was." She buries her face in her hands, her voluminous hair cascading along either side.

I push out of the recliner to comfort her, easing her hands away. "I'm betting you'll be great for the same reason. And we're in this thing together now. I'll straighten you out if you're heading the wrong way, and I expect you to return the favor."

"But I don't know anything about being a mom. What if I wasn't born with the right instincts? Or I repeat the mistakes my parents made?" Her eyes shimmer with the beginning of tears.

I take her hand. "You're going to be the best mother you can. You're already aware of what you want to avoid and how your folks screwed up, and that's half the battle. Trust me, you're going to knock it out of the park. And if not, then we screw up Frick and Frack, and they'll survive, just like we did."

She swats my chest.

"Either way, we can't back out of this deal. We're kind of in it for life now." I push all my love into my gaze, trying to absorb the anguish reflecting in her bottomless brown eyes.

Adrienne shrieks and grabs my arm.

My heart stutters. "What is it?"

She pants for several moments. "Babies," she breathes, before uttering another anguished cry.

"Are you in labor?" *It's too early.* My thoughts churn in a hundred different directions. "What's happening?"

"I...don't...pain. Hank! Help me," she says, her voice weak as she tightens her grip. A second later, she passes out.

I spring into action as a deafening noise roars through my head and every stress response invades my being. We live fifteen minutes from the hospital. I can drive her faster than an ambulance. I shove my feet into my boots, grab my keys and pull her into my arms, carrying her as if I have the strength of ten men. She moans. Thank God she's conscious.

Murmuring words of love and encouragement, I hurry to the truck, finagle it open and set her on the seat. I race into the driver's seat. Before I'm out of the driveway, Adrienne slumps against me, in and out of consciousness. Hauling ass to the hospital, I dare the police to stop me, begging for God's grace through foxhole prayers.

I pull up to the ER entrance behind an ambulance and bolt through the automatic glass doors yelling for help. I'd better not face any lip-chipping asshats putting me through the bullshit insurance paces or suggesting she isn't in fucking crisis.

A guy in scrubs runs with me back to the truck, and as I fill him in, he rapidly grasps the gravity of our situation. When we reach Adrienne, she's unconscious again.

In a flash, a team transfers her to a gurney and hustles her into a curtained ER space. I back up against the wall while the pros take her vitals, start an IV and begin tests. One asks me her obstetrician's name and orders another to call Dr. Swann.

"What's happening? Is it the babies?" I can't hide my panic—or impatience.

"We'll know more soon," says the pipsqueak who appears to be in charge. He looks eleven, except for his facial hair. I hate the noncommittal double talk by medical professionals. Just fucking give it to me straight.

I stare at my wife, in and out of consciousness, and feel utterly helpless.

Time passes in a blur, agonizingly slow or on fast-forward, as we vacillate between a flurry of activity and waiting for results. I struggle to remain calm, wanting to punch everyone and everything one minute, on the verge of tears another. It's the unknowing. And this fucking powerlessness. Are Frick and Frack in trouble? Is Adrienne going to die? Why isn't anyone filling me in?

Dr. Swann enters, all business, and I jump to attention.

"Mr. McCallister, your wife has a placental abruption. This is a serious complication but also somewhat common. We need to perform an emergency C-section."

My heart jackhammers in my chest. "I don't understand. What's wrong?"

"An abruption is when the placenta separates from the inner wall of the uterus. This can block the baby's supply of oxygen and cause heavy bleeding internally, which has already begun. Adrienne and one of the twins are endangered, which is why the operation is necessary now. Because of the time sensitivity involved, we must also administer general anesthesia."

The breath I'm holding onto like a life raft releases in one loud whoosh. "Are they going to make it?"

"If we do the cesarean now, we should be able to deliver the babies safely and stop the internal bleeding. Time is of the essence. Do I have your consent?"

"You have it. Can I be there—to hold her hand?"

"I'm sorry, Mr. McCallister, that's not possible under these circumstances. But I'll find you once we're finished. I know this is stressful, but she's in good hands." With a curt nod, she exits the room.

I kiss Adrienne and murmur how much I love her. The tornado of medical staff leaves, whisking my wife and unborn children into the unknown.

———

HARRISON: IF I HAD A NICKEL FOR EVERY WOMAN WHO THOUGHT SHE WAS IN LABOR, I'D BE A RICH MAN. ACTUALLY, IT PROBABLY STILL WOULDN'T COVER MY MED SCHOOL TAB. BUT THAT LADY TONIGHT WAS NOT ONLY IN BONA FIDE LABOR BUT TROUBLE. HER HUSBAND LOOKED LIKE HE WANTED TO KILL SOMEONE. FOR A MINUTE, I THOUGHT MAYBE ME. HE SEEMED FAMILIAR...I SWEAR I SAW HIM FIGHT ONCE AT ONE OF THOSE AMATEUR EVENTS.

JESSICA: WHAT A RUSH! I STARTED MY OBSTETRICS ROTATION TODAY AND HERE COMES A PLACENTAL ABRUPTION! HOW COOL IS THAT?

CHAPTER 36
ADRIENNE

THE SENSATIONS INTENSIFY. Abdominal pain seizes my center and holds me in a tight grip. I'm dragged into a black, soundless abyss then re-emerge, assaulted with contractions—frenzied waves of mounting torture ebbing and flowing in a psychotic dance.

Am I dying?

I overhear snippets of conversation as I wrestle to stay focused. "…abruption… emergency C-section… supply of oxygen… internal bleeding… endangered… consent."

Save my babies!

Lights whiz past, reminding me of a carnival ride. Half-masked faces peer into mine. Tubes and needles poke and prod. A machine beeps at a steady interval. High- and low-pitched voices come and go like startled crickets in a cornfield.

Please, save my babies.

Dr. Swann speaks, but I can't hold on to her words. I slip away…and back. Another swell of pain. Bright light. The pressure of a mask adhered over my nose and mouth. A plastic smell mixed with antiseptic. Hands on my belly. A deep voice asking me to count backwards from ten.

Concentrate. "Ten, nine, eight, sev—"

Finally, sweet nothing.

———

Dr. Swann: Sometimes the weight of your entire career comes down to seconds. To save or lose a life. Or in this case, three.

CHAPTER 37
HANK

I LEAP to my feet at the sight of Dr. Swann, her expression unreadable. I didn't expect to see her so soon. Is that a good or bad sign?

"Everything went well," she reassures me. "Both babies are safe and healthy. Once they were delivered, it allowed us to stop Adrienne's internal bleeding and ensure the abruption caused no additional complications. She's in recovery now and should wake up soon from the anesthesia."

I impulsively hug her, relief coursing through me, and fight the urge to unleash a reservoir of tears being held back by the dam. "Thank you, Dr. Swann. I can't express enough how much." *And thank you, God. I owe you.*

She pulls back, understanding in her eyes. "Adrienne is weak and needs to stay in the hospital to be monitored. She'll likely require a blood transfusion. The twins are underweight, which is to be expected considering their early arrival. We have them in the neonatal intensive care unit, keeping them warm and monitoring their breathing—"

"They can't breathe?" My heart sinks.

"There are signs of apnea, which is common in preemies, and

often resolves quickly. And since their tiny bodies are prone to losing heat quickly, they are both in incubators to keep them warm. This is all standard and precautionary. We're keeping a close eye on them and managing their care until they're strong enough on their own. Rest assured, you and your wife will both be active key participants to their care and medical team."

I take a fraction of solace in her words. "And you expect Adrienne to make a full recovery?"

"All signs point in a positive direction. She's been through a lot though, and now she's facing nursing on top of regaining her strength, but youth is on her side."

"How soon until I can see her?"

"Likely within the hour. Everyone comes out of anesthesia differently. In the meantime, ready to meet your son and daughter?" She smiles.

My heart swells then dips. I never expected to greet them for the first time without their mother—or with them under duress. I shake it off. Knowing all three McCallisters are alive fills me with gratitude. "Lead the way, doc. I've never been more ready."

Dr. Swann connects me with a nurse that gets me set-up for entering the NICU. I'm given a special ID, briefed on protocol and steered to the wash station to scrub down and apply a harsh antiseptic. My nerves jangle as I shift between anticipation and not knowing what to expect. We're totally off plan at this point.

I'm checked into the NICU and hit with a barrage of stimuli. The room is gigantic, with babies encased in see-through plastic incubators circling the nurse's station. The babies are so incredibly tiny with tubes, wires and apparatus strapped to their little bodies as machines monitor their vitals, help them breathe, God knows what. It's noisy from all the beeping and whirring. There's zero privacy, as parents and staff attend to these sons and daughters in peril in their first moments of life, bunched together like refugees trying to get from one place to another. And in a way, that's what we are.

I'm guided to Tanner and Cassidy, side by side in separate

incubators. The nurse explains what they're monitoring and why. My heart lurches in my chest and tears trickle down my face as I see my children for the first time. They are dinky small, their skin almost translucent. Despite the noise and tubes and cuffs connected to them, both sleep peacefully, sprawled on their backsides. Clad only in diapers, I rake my eyes over these perfect miniature humans, absorbing every detail.

You don't realize how profound life is until you're watching newborns take their first breaths. It's life altering in a forever kind of way. "Welcome to the world, my little loves," I whisper, the tears flowing freely now. "What a big day you've had, what champions you are."

I reach through the holes built into the incubator and lightly rub Tanner on his arm and leg. My hand dwarfs his tiny parts but touching him is wondrous. "Hey buddy, it's your dad," I say softly. "You keep fighting in there because your mom and I have big plans for you. You haven't even seen the world yet or thrown a baseball or heard George Straight or caught a cricket or gazed at the stars. So, you heal up." I inhale a deep breath, unable to stop cataloguing every inch of his skin and scrunched up face. "You're magnificent, kid…destined for greatness. I love you, son."

I wrench myself away and shift to Cassidy, sending all my love into her with my gentle touch. "Hey, sweetheart. You did great today and I know you're going to ace life, starting with this grand entrance you made. You sit tight and let your body get its bearings because as soon as you're ready, we're blowing this pop stand. We've got so much planned for you, and I can't wait to get started and watch your glorious life unfold…you're already a star. You make me so proud to be your dad. I love you, honey. Sleep tight and let your body get stronger."

I stare at them a while longer. They are the tiniest little beings I've ever laid eyes on, so fragile and breakable. I wish I could whip them into my arms, but I can't. Not yet. Tanner's only 3 lb. 9 oz. and Cassidy's 3 lb. 5 oz. so they have some growing to do. But they're stable, their color and vitals are good, and they're safe and under expert care until deemed they're not in danger. I've got no choice but to trust the doctors and have faith. Cassidy's miniature blood pressure cuff inflates, followed by Tanner's, and I marvel at the miracle of science I'm witnessing. *Please, God, just keep breathing life into them.*

"I'm going to see your mama now. She'll be here soon, and everything is going to be all right," I rasp, overcome once again.

Outside the NICU, bright lights glare, and I squint. The hospital is surreal enough, its own kind of war zone…but the NICU is like a bunker, and coming out feels like being hit with shrapnel.

A female nurse wearing brightly patterned scrubs guides me to a room. Ten minutes later, a stout male nurse wheels Adrienne in on a mobile bed. My heart strains from navigating the volatile emotions of the past seven hours. Our eyes lock. She's pale and wan, but still the most beautiful girl in the world.

Nurse Todd introduces himself, adjusts the hospital bed until my wife is upright and comfortable, then leaves us alone after making sure we've got all we need.

Leaning over, I kiss her forehead. "I love you so much. I'm so grateful…" My voice falters.

"I know, baby," she answers, her eyes dewy. "I love you, too. Did you see them?"

I nod. "They're perfect. So small. A little prince and princess." I stroke Adrienne's hair. "How are you, darlin'?"

"Worried. Weak. And thirsty." I snag the cup of water and hold it to her lips. She takes a long drink. "Tell me everything, Hank."

I recite every detail from the prognosis to how the twins looked to the protocol to how it was in the NICU. We marvel how they were born one minute apart.

A new nurse enters and takes Adrienne's vitals, followed by a lactation expert. The babies are receiving feedings while she recovers, but they urge her to pump milk and start breastfeeding as soon as the babies are cleared. These early days are critical for babies to learn to latch on and drink their mother's milk and we are all hopeful this happens quickly.

Adrienne's physical condition prevents her from traveling to the NICU. It crushes her and all I can do is kiss her forehead and clutch her hand until she falls asleep.

Although I'm exhausted, I rally to make the requisite calls. My mother offers to jump on a plane but agrees to hold off until everyone returns from the hospital. Grandma Betty responds similarly and is almost inconsolable. The news shocks Tami, who volunteers to care for Diesel and help in any way possible, knowing we're in a holding pattern for the unforeseeable future. I touch base with Jimmy, and then work, filling in essential folks. And then I crash.

Due to Adrienne's surgery, the doctor orders pain medication for the first couple of days. She receives a blood transfusion, and it makes a marked difference. Her color and appetite return and, with it, her energy and stamina. The day she's able to sit in a wheelchair, I take her to the NICU. Witnessing her reuniting with Tanner and Cassidy out of the womb is a moment for the memory books.

Our babies spend a total of four days in the NICU—coming through with flying colors. I brag they're from good stock, with tough Texas blood flowing through their veins. Dr. Swann tells us their potential complications were minimized by not arriving severely pre-term. We are nothing short of elated. Despite the stress, difficulties and all the moving parts, everyone progresses beautifully.

With the McCallisters finally all together in one room, the four of us form an unbreakable bond. I spend most of every day with my brood, leaving only to shower, sleep and pay attention to the dog.

The twins learn to breastfeed, become stronger and encounter no further problems. Meanwhile, Adrienne and I learn tricks and tips for handling our babies regarding feedings, naps and routines. We won't have the help of nurses and experts much longer.

Seven days later, I bring my family home.

My wife and I each carry a baby inside. Still conked out from the ride, we place them in their basinets. We watch, on alert, as a curious Diesel pokes his head over the side of Tanner's cradle, sniffing him from head to toe before following suit with Cassidy. I speak in low tones to the dog the entire time, ready to intervene, if need be. Seeming to understand these little beings are part of the pack, he adopts them without much ado. He even nudges his head under Adrienne's hand, soliciting a pet. Dogs have a sixth sense about humans. Whether he senses her lingering pain or smells her recovering wound, he understands she needs loving. We turn on the baby monitors and bring one with us to the living room.

"I'm happy to be home," Adrienne says from the same spot on the couch where she last went unconscious. "And to be able to sit somewhat normal again." She strokes her significantly smaller belly, wincing when her hand flutters over the tender incision.

"I'm ecstatic." I rest my hands against the top of the recliner. "What can I do for you? Are you comfortable? Do you want a drink? Something to eat? You might have five minutes to yourself —if you're lucky—so you might want to jump on this."

"Since vodka's still out, I'll have orange juice." She leans back into the sofa.

"Virgin Screwdriver coming right up."

I bring out two OJs and sit beside her. "Here's to you, Mrs. McCallister. Way to be a badass."

She clinks my glass with hers. "Maybe the hard part is behind us, cowboy. You think?"

"We'd need to spike these with something higher-octane to swallow that fantasy."

On cue, one baby wails, setting off the other. Our eyes meet, and we know it's only the beginning.

———

TAMI: NOW ROD *HAS* TO ACCOMPANY ME TO CHILDBIRTH CLASSES. NOT TO BE INSENSITIVE ABOUT ADRIENNE'S SITUATION…IT'S TERRIBLE WHAT HAPPENED TO HER, AND THANKFULLY, SHE AND THE BABIES ARE FINE, BUT IT ALWAYS IRKED ME HOW HE TRIED TO GET OUT OF HIS HUSBANDLY DUTY. IT'S IMPORTANT, AND I DON'T WANT TO BE DOING THIS ALONE. I NEED A PARTNER—AND I'M NOT TALKING ABOUT ONLY THE BIRTH HERE.

CHAPTER 38
ADRIENNE

MANAGING the twins is a juggling act, but a hell of a lot less glamorous than Cirque du Soleil. While one is up in the air, Hank or I deal with the other, until the first one falls back into the rotation. Feeding, sleeping, peeing, pooping, crying, repeat.

Grandma Betty arrives for a few days. She fusses and dotes over Cassidy and Tanner—and me—with her special knack for making everything better. We visit, she makes my favorite foods, and she assists with chores and entertaining the minis so I can nap, bless her heart.

The cowboy keeps saying we are "rode hard and put up wet." I'm not versed in ranch jargon, but it sure sounds like our life. I experience mind-numbing fatigue, sleep deprivation and the area around my incision hurts like hell. The weight gain sucks, and my nipples are sore. I'm like Humpty Dumpty before all the king's horses and all the king's men put him back together again. Will I ever go back to normal? I'm not complaining—much—trying to remember we all came out alive and unscathed. And Hank shows up daily as a husband and father, chipping in and attending to us all.

Grandma Betty leaves and Henrietta takes her place, slipping into the grandmother role with a deft hand. I stow my wariness in exchange for help. Hank returns to work the day after his mother arrives, reassured I rest in capable hands.

We know from our time in the hospital the importance of getting the twins on a schedule for feeding and sleeping. Without one, I will have a baby sucking on a breast, awake, crying or requiring attention every hour of the day. There will be no breaks in the action, a moment's peace or the possibility of my aching, chapped nipples recovering.

Sounds great in theory. In practice, much harder. With Henrietta's help and a few days of failure under my belt, we figure out how I can breastfeed the babies at the same time. Having an extra set of hands is invaluable, and the impossibility of going it alone looms.

The twins sleep better if we nestle them in one crib instead of separate basinets. Cassidy and Tanner look and reach for each other and want to be together. I'd heard about the twin bond but seeing is believing—and astounding.

Henrietta and I settle the kids down for a nap and quietly exit the nursery.

"It's a beautiful spring day. Want to sit outside?" she asks, poised, as always, in crisp navy slacks and an unstained blouse.

My bar for clothing is set rather low these days: sweatpants and tee shirts. "Sounds nice."

We retreat to the screened porch, shaded by the giant oak which made us fall in love with this house. I place the baby monitor on the table, double-check the volume, and collapse into one of the wicker chairs Hank scored through Craigslist. Henrietta places a tumbler of lemonade in front of me and I take a few gulps.

"You always look so pulled together," I say, forcing the envy from my voice. "I'm such a mess."

She tilts her head. "I'm sure I looked a sight after birthing each of my sons," she admits.

Doubtful. "What was it like? Carrying five boys?" I lean back, savoring whatever seconds of relaxation I'm afforded.

Henrietta gazes into the backyard, seeming to reflect. "The pregnancies were similar. Some gave me morning sickness, others didn't. Most of them were kickers, including Hank. Samuel was the quiet one, still is. They all made my legs swell, which strained my veins and left them visible. Hideous looking, to this day."

I can relate.

"Shelton, being my first, set the bar for the other four. He went full term and took fifteen hours before gracing us with his appearance. I was about out of my mind. But obviously, not enough to stop there."

She shakes her head, as if not believing it herself. "I waited a while to get pregnant again. Samuel is three years younger than Shelton, and by that time, I'd repressed the hard parts. Sam was so content in the womb. When his due date came around, he popped out just shy of four hours, duping me into thinking this could be easy."

I laugh. "Then came Hank, right?"

"Yes, siree. He came a year later and was—and still is—the largest of my sons. He was cantankerous the whole way through and came out brawling. You should have seen his tiny fists balled up and trying to hit something. His little face was red and pinched, wailing like we'd smacked him. I think he must have been angry about leaving such a warm, dark place and being forced to contend with this new world."

"Think he still is. How much did he weigh?

"Nine and a half pounds. I thought he'd break me." Henrietta smooths her slacks with one hand, brushing a piece of lint on the ground.

"Ouch. And yet, you got back on the horse again."

She raises her head to the heavens. "A year later came Wyatt, arriving a full month ahead of schedule. Where Hank wanted to wait until the last second, Wyatt favored a head start. But there were complications. The umbilical cord had wrapped around his neck, making him a breech birth. They nearly did a C-section but were able to give me an episiotomy and deliver him safely." Henrietta hugs her arms over her chest.

"Sounds scary."

"It was. We didn't plan to have another, but—"

"Eli was a surprise?"

"Yes and no. Suffice it to say, I made sure he would be the final McCallister in our brood. We almost didn't make it to the hospital on time. He arrived in less than an hour."

"Oh, shit!" My eyes widen and I shrug. "Apologies for the language."

She laughs. "Mine was a tad stronger at the time."

My mind boggles. "Raising five boys. I can't imagine it."

"This might sound strange, but it's not as hard as you think. The more kids you add into the mix, the easier it almost gets. They take care of one another and play together. They even help teach each other things. Some of them caught on to using the bathroom quicker because they wanted to be like their older brother."

"Bet they also fought."

"Something fierce," she admits. "But the advantages outweighed the obstacles."

One of the babies cries out, but it's short-lived. I hold my breath, listening for more. Crisis averted, we continue our conversation.

"Tell me about Hank—the younger version."

Henrietta's lips curve into a small smile before collapsing. "He is my sweetest boy in some ways. He cares, sometimes too much. I used to worry he was too breakable. Still do."

I startle. Hank is not breakable. He does the breaking.

"He's plenty rugged," she assures me, reading my expression. "He ranched right alongside his brothers and did a darn good job at it, too. And while he's still got his bull-in-the-china-shop moments, he's sensitive, enough that I mothered him with a heavy hand to toughen him up.

"Learning came easy to him. Didn't have to ride herd on him like some of the others. He did his schoolwork, was whip smart, earned As and Bs without much effort. Could have majored in something complicated like engineering or mathematics, if he'd had a mind to."

"I'll bet working on diesel trucks and those tractor-trailers must have been challenging to learn." This sounds defensive, but Henrietta needs to hear it.

"Sure," she says, blowing me off. "That's what I mean. He can do anything. He chose this for the time being."

"You don't think he'll stick with it?" I imagine she'd like nothing better than for him to return to Texas, and her ranch.

She remains noncommittal. "Who knows? With his intelligence, he can change his mind and pursue other opportunities. Someday, he might even want to ranch again."

There it is.

"Hank excelled at his responsibilities at the ranch. I remember him working his little rear-end off to learn roping. We had a dummy all the boys practiced on. They learned to rope from the ground first, then graduated to a horse. It's not easy, but he picked it up fast. Became adept at herding cattle. He wanted to ride bulls, but I vetoed that nonsense." She pauses to sip her drink.

"Thank you." I envision broken bones, backs, necks. Reminded of his three-day blackout amnesia—which Henrietta knows nothing about—my heart palpitates.

"Hank was always reckless and unafraid. Made him dangerous."

"Did he have a temper?" *Because at times, he's a madman.*

She nods. "He's hotheaded by nature. As I said, he entered the world that way. Some of my boys have it and others don't. We had to take Hank down a peg or two in his formative years, get him to redirect his energy. With him, I worried about his rage being coupled with such a tender heart. But I figured, perhaps the two offset each other. How's it been on your end?"

I pause, thinking about his polar attributes. "I've seen both his anger and generosity. It's safe to say I prefer door number two."

She exhales a sound somewhere between a chortle and a huff. "No one's perfect, Adrienne. Maybe you know that by now, and maybe you don't. I can tell you this: knowing who your man is— his assets and heart and shortcomings and warts—far outweighs gambling on a man you don't know. The grass-is-greener mentality? Ignorant. It ain't any greener, it's just a different variety, so you're trading one flaw for another. In my mind, it's better to stick with the flaws you know."

Can't argue with her logic, which irritates me.

She gives me a pointed stare. "Hank's anger may get the best of him sometimes, but he'll never lay a hand on you or let anyone do you wrong. He is your fiercest protector, which is the opposite of the same coin. I hope you count your lucky stars because you hooked a good one with my son."

Before I can retort, the monitor blares with the cry of one baby, followed by the other, ending our discussion.

While I appreciate Henrietta's help, I can't wait for her to get on a plane back to Texas. She's passive-aggressive—a formidable presence cloaked in false pleasantries. How very Texan. She clearly reveres her role as the McCallister matriarch, but in my house, the title belongs to me, or will, once I stop stumbling around.

When I complain to Hank later that evening, he tells me to grin and bear it, reminding me her days are numbered and to give thanks instead. Of course, he sides with her, which annoys me on top of everything else. The way they dote on each other should be heartwarming…but sickens me.

As I brush my teeth before bed, I worry—again—how I'll manage when she leaves. The thought of it exhausts me. And I would kill for a real drink and a cigarette, which I'm supposed to avoid while nursing.

I snort. Like that's going to happen.

———

Henrietta McCallister: I still have an awful gut feeling about her—and my gut's never wrong. Mark my words, there is more to Adrienne than meets the eye, and it's only a matter of time until her true colors show. The worst part is waiting for the other boot to drop.

CHAPTER 39
HANK

SIX WEEKS IN, Adrienne and I resemble zombies, except with less energy. Independence Day—her original due date—comes and goes, the ultimate irony. With Tanner and Cassidy living a constant loop of needs and demands, our freedom is long gone, somewhere in the rearview.

Oh, sleep. I remember you fondly. How I used to take you for granted.

I shouldn't gripe. My wife takes the brunt of this two-for-one deal, hauling herself out of bed every time their piercing wails drive us awake. But what these babies want, only she can provide, and it makes her crankier by the day. If I'd thought her unreasonable during the pregnancy, I need my head examined. Wifey is off the rails now.

She blames me for getting her pregnant, accuses me of abandoning ship and rants about doing the lion's share of parenting. I receive angry texts while at work—and earfuls once I arrive home, when she thrusts the twins on me and stalks off. She professes to need alone time, stating it's her *turn*, like I do nothing all day except twiddle my fucking thumbs. And forget housekeeping or cooking. Adrienne can't even manage a shower most days.

Despite it all, I never dread coming home. Tanner and Cassidy blow my mind on a regular basis. They start moving their heads on their own and turning toward my voice when I speak. I love watching them yawn, stretch, smile and gurgle. I marvel at their near weightlessness and never tire of studying their tiny, defined features, down to the creases in their knuckles. Bathing them is one of my favorite rituals. Afterward, I like to gather them up, inhale their sweet, clean scent and recline in the easy chair, where I sing to them or watch them discover their new world. They are precious, incomprehensible miracles, and I am their creator and protector.

Adrienne flops on the bed. "They're down."

I roll on my side and rub her arm. "How are you, darlin'?"

"I'm alive." She closes her eyes. "Maybe."

"You're doing an amazing job."

She scoffs.

I let it go. "Did you see Tami today?"

"I tried, but our visit didn't last long. The twins liked the stroller ride, but once we got inside the house, all hell broke loose after twenty minutes."

"How's the baby?"

"Precious, and huge, compared to ours at the same age." Her eyes open, finding mine. "It almost made me cry."

I stroke her hair. "You had a different experience, but you've all pulled through with flying colors."

She snorts. "Tami's labor and delivery was totally devoid of drama. No near dying for her. She conceded I won."

I let that go, too. "How did Cassidy and Tanner react to Lexi?"

"Interested. They stared and kind of pointed. It was adorable until the wailing began. Once our babies triggered her baby, it turned into a shitshow. I packed them up and got the hell out of there. Of course, they conked out after one minute in the stroller, content as Bob Ross painting happy little rainbows."

I chuckle and graze my hand along her torso. We've passed the magic number of weeks to resume sex. Adrienne appears healed, and I'm salivating with need.

"I've got a happy little rainbow for you." My hand trails to the sensitive spot between her legs.

She bats my hand away. "No, Hank. I'm not ready."

"The doctor said it was fine now."

"I don't care what she said. I'm telling you how I feel."

An irrational response bubbles in my gut at the rejection. I replay a Japanese warplane getting shot down by the Americans, complete with sound effects. *Dut dut dut dut dut dut!* "Why can't we try? How do you know until we do?"

"I know. Trust me."

"I have needs, and whether you know it or not, *you* do too. Don't freeze me out. Don't freeze *us* out."

She chokes out a laugh. "You're kidding, right? I can't even find time to shower, let alone sleep. I'm exhausted caring for these tiny humans. My life is all about them, so ask me how much of a shit I give about your dick. Go ahead. Ask."

My chest tightens, and a telltale throbbing begins in my jaw. I shoot up and swing my legs over the side of the bed. "This is bullshit." I glare at her. "You're tired. I'm tired. Guess what? We're going to be bushed for months, hell, *years*. Better get used to it. It's no reason to avoid sex. It's the fucking payout!"

"Keep your voice down," she hisses, "or you'll wake the twins."

"I won't go without sex."

"What the fuck does that mean?" she yell-whispers, her face a mask of hate.

"Give me a break. I'm not talking about cheating. I'm saying making love is important to our marriage. Intimacy is *our time—* alone time away from the grind going on every other hour."

"I won't be bullied into sex. I said I'm not ready. My body's not ready, my brain's not ready, so jack off if you need to get your jollies." She stands and stomps from the room. A minute later, the front door slams. Un-fucking-believable. Could I have picked a more selfish, frail person to marry than Adrienne? The girl has no stamina, no clue, no ability to buck up and do life on life's terms. I am not going to stand for a sexless marriage. Not acceptable.

As for now, she can hug a nut. I crank on the shower, allow the heated water to flood over me and let my right hand go to work. A few soapsuds and thoughts of the sassy broad I'd bantered with in the drive-thru yesterday are all I need.

———

AMBER: THE BEST PERK TO THIS STUPID JOB AT FRY GUYS IS THE MEN. SO MANY FLAVORS...GORGEOUS, CHARMING, RUGGED. THEY MAKE MY DAY AND BREAK UP THE MONOTONY. I FLIRT, AND THEY LAP IT UP. TAKE THE COWBOY WHO ROLLED THROUGH WITH HIS DRAWLY ACCENT AND SEXY HAT. HE WAS SO POLITE AND GENUINE—AND THAT DEEP VOICE...MMM! I HAVEN'T STOPPED THINKING ABOUT HIM AND THE DAMAGE WE COULD DO IN HIS MONSTER TRUCK.

CHAPTER 40
ADRIENNE

MY QUAKING hands struggle to grip the wheel as I reverse the minivan out of the driveway. Once clear, I punch the gas, tearing down the street. Outside our subdivision, I pull over long enough to get my cigarettes out of their hideaway in the glove compartment and puff one to the quick. I light another and drive into the night.

Hank can be such a selfish prick. He has needs! As if I give two shits about his *needs*. I am knee-deep in the mud bog of motherhood, unable to do anything but wade through its murky depths inch by tedious inch.

It hits me I haven't experienced a whisper of horniness since before my last trimester. Would I ever *want* to have sex again? Do I care? Now sleep...*that's* something to get excited about.

Colorful fast-food joints light up the strip. On impulse, I swing into Fry Guys and order a large fries and vanilla shake. Might as well live it up for a change, add a pound to the unsightly wad pooled at my center. An annoyingly cheerful young woman hands me my food. I suppress a laugh when I see her nametag, reminded of the arduous task of naming our children with my anal-retentive husband. Hank would have vetoed Amber, calling it a stripper name.

I pull into a spot and turn off the ignition, leaving the windows down to let the muggy air flow through. I inhale half of my fries before the urge to murder anyone recedes. The winning combo of salt and sugar might be responsible. I light another smoke and suck down more of the creamy shake. A car pulls in next to mine and I glance over. *Fuck.* Rod's here.

He flashes a devilish grin. "Come here often?"

I can't even fake a smile. "Actually, no. I needed to get out of the house."

"I feel you! Stress eating." He holds up his Fry Guys bag with a maniacal expression. "Mind if I join you?"

I shrug. "You might be taking your life in your hands. I'm a tad homicidal."

He slides into the passenger seat after I scoop up the wrappers and debris resting there. "Tell Uncle Rod all about it."

For some unknown reason, I do, word-vomiting all the frustrations of parenting twins, often by myself, as he wolfs down a Big Guy burger, onion rings and a fountain drink. He is supportive and attentive, commenting between bites. Mostly, he listens.

He wipes the grease off his face and fingers with a wad of napkins and shoves them into his bag. A loud belch follows, with the requisite apology. "I get where you're coming from, and you should cut yourself a break. I'm only dealing with one kid and I'm ready to run for the hills. You've got double trouble. You're a candidate for sainthood."

His praise flatters me, but more, it makes me feel seen, validated. "Thanks for saying that."

"It's the truth. And damn if you aren't fine as hell doing it. If I didn't know you, I'd never guess you were grappling with all of this. You look like Miss USA." His eyes crinkle at the edges, meeting my gaze straight on.

"Please. I'm a complete mess." The proof is in my pink shorts with a forgiving elastic band and a loose tee shirt with today's baby spittle on it.

"Don't," he says, placing his hand over mine. "Don't minimize what I said. You're the best looking broad I've ever seen."

My insides twinge. "Th...thanks." I shift away from his penetrating stare, and snake my hand from under his, fumbling for my cigarettes.

"Can I get one of those?"

"You smoke?"

"Sometimes," he admits. "I didn't realize you did."

"It's a secret."

"I won't tell if you won't." He winks.

I laugh, but the double meaning is clear.

Smoke wafts out of the car and into the stale night as we continue airing our frustrations. I relax, grateful for the release of pent-up emotions.

He pulls out his phone and checks the time, sighing. "I'd better get back."

I glance at his screen, shocked that two hours have lapsed. "Me, too."

"Listen, if you ever want to talk or meet here or whatever, text me, okay?"

"Thanks." I reach over and touch his arm, my hand grazing the hard muscle bulging from his snug shirt. "I mean it. I appreciate you listening to me."

He leans over and kisses my cheek. "Anytime."

I return to Hank snoring contentedly in our bed. Asshole. I turn out the lights, brush my teeth and slide under the covers. Rod instantly invades my headspace. He'd shown me a new side tonight—a caring, compassionate one. Instead of telling me to suck it up, he displayed real empathy. I know he wants to do me, but there is more to him than the shallow, horny husband of my friend. And he is a far sight better looking than the cowboy with his refined dark looks and gym body. My insides tingle again at being wanted. I reach down and touch myself precisely where I'd rebuffed Hank a couple of hours earlier. Maybe I'm ready after all.

———

Rod: I am close to bagging the elephant. I can feel it. Did you see *Wall Street*? Remember when Bud Fox finally snags Gordon Gekko? Best movie ever.

CHAPTER 41
HANK

DRIVING HOME FROM A GRUELING, extra-long workday, I crank the AC and tunes. Although I'm generally a half-glass-full kind of guy, I predict no dinner, crying kids and a surly wife—perfect after a tedious day.

I'm sick of walking this tense tightrope the past two weeks, but neither Adrienne nor I appear willing to budge off our mountains built of stubborn pride. We remain polite, distant and silently pissed off, going through the motions—and the all-encompassing role of parenting twin infants.

Whether in defiance or relief, I continue whacking off in the shower. I've never been itchier to hit someone and long for my days at The Crazy Horse, when ass kicking was part of my weekly regime. My kind of therapy, if I believed in such crap. Raking a hand through my hair and hitting a snarl, I cuss loudly, tension simmering like lava in a volcano.

It will be up to me to end this stalemate. As usual. Adrienne is short on accountability. Everything is always my fault, or rather, anyone's fault but hers. I try to keep in mind her parents screwed her over and never taught her proper values, let alone the selfless basics. But should that be an excuse to behave like a jerk your entire life? No matter what hand you're dealt, take responsibility for yourself.

Turning the volume up another notch, I drown out my thoughts.

As I pull into the driveway, I give myself a pep talk. *Be kind. Play with the kids and offer her a break, even though you're dead on your feet. Fucking deal until you can go to bed…where you won't be having any sex for the next foreseeable century. Shit. Don't go there.* I turn off the ignition and heave my weary body out of the truck.

A charred smell assaults my nostrils as I enter the house. The kids are both bawling. I greet a frantic Diesel, tripping over baby crap as I head for the shrieks. The kitchen and dining areas look like a hurricane has blown through. I find Adrienne and the babies in the nursery. Her face wears an unreadable expression, some combination of panic, anger and depression.

"Take Cassidy," she says, turning the hip on which our daughter perches.

"Hello, beautiful girl." I wiggle her into the air and her cries turn to smiles.

My wife sits in the rocker. Tanner's mouth seeks her breast until he latches on, sucking greedily at her milk.

Bringing my daughter back to earth, I tuck her into my arm. "That's better. Everyone's happy now."

"Not mommy," my wife singsongs.

I maneuver to kiss her on the cheek. "Hi darlin'. Have I told you I love you today?"

"That Texas charm and deep voice won't win you any points."

"Rough one?"

"Every day is rough."

Tanner gurgles contentedly, and I gaze longingly at her bulging tits. I'd sure like to get some of that action. "Wanna talk about it?"

"Why? It won't change anything," she utters, her contempt palpable.

If I can get her to hear me, I can help her. I'm good at problem solving. "Listen, we're still in the early stages here. The kids are going to start sleeping through the night soon and will be less dependent on you. We knew the beginning was going to be hard. That's why we talked about getting ready up here," I say, tapping my head. "It's a lot for anyone."

"No one could possibly have the mental stamina this requires. It's a minute-by-minute five-alarm fire." She adjusts herself, Tanner none the wiser.

"Fire's out right now," I say with a smile.

Adrienne's eyes fixate on the wall. "I've decided to stop nursing. It's too much."

Decided? "You sure? Dr. Swann said the longer you nurse, the better it is for them."

She levels her stare at me. "She said a minimum of six weeks is what the babies need, which I've done. This juggling act is impossible, and my breasts are chapped and sore every single day. It's time. They're happy with the supplemental bottles, and if I can do one thing to make my life easier, why wouldn't I?"

"Uh huh…I get it. If you think it's the right move." Cassidy grabs my mustache, and I make a funny face. She giggles again, one of the sweetest sounds on earth.

"I made some mac and cheese if you're hungry."

"It's not the burned smell, is it?"

Adrienne casts me a withering glare. "No. That's from a Jell-O debacle."

"How the heck did you burn Jell-O?"

If looks could kill, my wife would be an instant widow. "I scalded the pot. I couldn't deal with it along with everything else, so I left it. Let's switch."

We swap babies and as I burp Tanner, I ponder how lame it is to screw up a five-minute dish where the only cooking involved is boiling water and stirring. My mother would have a field day.

"Let's go on a trip to the kitchen," I say to my son, heading out to the hallway. "Would you like that?" He studies me intently then laughs when I gallop to the kitchen with Diesel hot on our heels.

Closer inspection of the "debacle" reveals a blackened pot and cherry gelatin granules strewn across the counter. Congealed neon-orange mac and cheese sits near the pile of dirty dishes near the sink, the floor needs scrubbing, and a trail of debris (toys, pacifiers, crumbs and unidentifiable bits) leads into the living room.

"Well, this is one hell of a mess, isn't it, baby boy?" He bounces in my arms. I carry him to the living room and place him on the sofa. He kicks his legs as if riding a bike, which cracks me up.

Adrienne deposits Cassidy next to me. "I'm grabbing a shower."

"Can you hold off until I eat? Kind of starving here."

She audibly sighs. "Lay them on the floor under the mobile, and you can have your precious dinner while they entertain themselves."

"I wouldn't call it precious."

"Fuck you, Hank. I'm doing the best I can. If it's not good enough for you, there's the door."

"You're unbelievable."

"And you're an asshole." She turns, walks toward the hall and swivels. "I'm showering. I'm sure you can figure out how to negotiate your two children and stuff your face. I do it every single day."

I turn to the babies, muttering in a cheery voice. "Mommy's grumpy today, isn't she? I hope she's treating you better than she is me. C'mon, let's see if you like this." I place them on the blanket underneath a fabric mobile with several hanging plastic shapes they can touch. They gurgle, and Cassidy kicks her legs in the air.

I make a couple of ham sandwiches, snag a bag of chips and a cold beer and settle on the couch in front of the TV. The twins seem satisfied, which is more than I can say for myself.

Thirty minutes later, Adrienne flounces into the room, showered and dressed. Is she wearing makeup? "I'm going for a drive."

"At this hour? What the hell?"

"I'm tired of being cooped up in this tiny house with these tiny humans. I need breathing room."

"So go out back. Relax in a chair. I'll take care of the kids."

"No. I want out of this house for a while." She glances at the kitchen and grimaces. "Please. I'm desperate."

"It sure would be nice if you wanted to spend some time with me."

"Jesus, Hank. It's not always about *you*."

"It's not even a little about me, and that's the problem. I feel like you've given up on us."

"Don't be so fucking melodramatic. I just want a minute to myself. Can't you understand? No, you can't, because you log zillions of minutes on your own. You aren't here in the trenches with babies relying on you every single second. I need a break from time to time."

"You're calling *me* melodramatic? This is called parenting, Adrienne. Life. So go…run away and ignore us, your family—the people who matter—while you take some *moments for yourself.*"

"Bastard. You think you know everything, but you don't." She grabs her keys and slams the door. Tanner and Cassidy start howling.

———

DON'T KNOW WHAT HIT THEM. THEN AGAIN, KIDS TODAY AREN'T RESILIENT. IN MY DAY, WE WERE EXPECTED TO GET MARRIED, SPIT OUT A PASSEL OF CHILDREN AND CATER TO OUR FAMILIES. I WAS PREGNANT AT TWENTY-ONE AND KNEW MY RESPONSIBILITIES, EVEN IF I DID WANT TO POISON MY HUSBAND'S DINNER EVERY NOW AND AGAIN.

CHAPTER 42
ADRIENNE

I SEND THE TEXT, light another cigarette and wait. I'm ninety-nine percent certain Rod will meet me. We've shared a couple of innocent texts since our chance meeting at Fry Guys. I complain. He cracks a joke. Instant mood lift. Between the strain of parenting, debilitating fatigue and Hank's holier-than-thou attitude, I need a laugh.

CPA MAN pulls up in his sleek black ride, his professionally bleached grin flashing from the dark interior. I dismiss the hovering twinge of guilt and smile in return.

Rod lowers his window. "Wassup? Trouble in paradise?"

"Yeah. I bailed before I lost my shit."

"Never fear, the doctor is here." He grins and raises his eyebrows in succession. "Want to go for a drive, or hang here and talk?"

"A drive. Can we take your car?"

In response, he grins and says, "Your chariot awaits." He hurries out and holds open the passenger door to his Lexus.

My ass sinks into the leather bucket seat, and I admire the lush interior, inhaling a strong masculine scent. Woodsy. Rod pushes the ignition, and the elaborate dash lights up. The motor purrs, so quiet I can't believe the vehicle is running. It's a far cry from my dorky minivan.

"Where to?" he says.

"Anywhere but here."

He maneuvers us out of the parking lot. "What happened?"

"My husband is a judgmental motherfucker." Just rehashing his bullshit speech gets my hackles up. "He thinks I should be better able to manage the twins, the household chores, make his fucking dinner every night—and for the grand finale, be up for hours of passionate sex."

"Sounds reasonable."

I whack his arm.

"Kidding! I'm on your side. The guy obviously hasn't got a clue what your daily life is about."

"Right? He has no empathy. Instead, he lectures me about mental preparedness. As if *that's* the answer to my problems."

"Pretty unhelpful."

"Believe me, no one wants to live a day of my life. It's hell on steroids."

Rod chuckles. "It's difficult now, but it'll get better. You've got to hang tough a while longer."

I tilt my head toward the sunroof, dragging out a long, exaggerated sigh as I glimpse the night sky. "I know, but I need someone to throw me a goddamn rope."

He steers into Tilden Park. "Want to stop here? It's quiet."

"Okay." The dimly lit parking area is vacant, except for us. He opens the windows, the muggy air assaulting us. Light glints off the pond, but the surrounding trees are shrouded in darkness.

"Where were we?" he says.

"Me drowning with no life preserver in sight. I don't mean to sound selfish and ungrateful. I love my kids, but—"

"Of course, you do." Rod touches my hand, and I don't pull away.

"It's all a bit much, and Hank's not helping enough. His expectations are ridiculous. And now he's mad because I split."

"That's BS. Take a stand, state your needs and take care of yourself."

"You're so understanding." I lean my head against the seat, facing him. "I appreciate it...and not being criticized."

"There's nothing you could do to change my opinion about you. You're honest, straightforward and drop-dead gorgeous. But I'm preaching to the choir, right?" He strokes his fingers along my hand, and desire flickers in my core.

"I don't know anything anymore."

"Hey," he says, making me meet his eyes. "I'm not just sucking up here. You're an incredible woman."

I manage a half-smile.

"Can I make a confession?"

I tilt my head in silent permission.

"I've thought of almost nothing except kissing you since the day we met."

I lick my lips and swallow, my throat suddenly parched. "I had a hunch."

"My inability to stop staring at your tits give me away?"

"Among other things."

"Something tells me you won't mind if I do this then..."

Before I can answer, Rod's hands twist in my hair, bringing me closer, and his mouth finds mine. Molten heat blazes like a wildfire to my groin, and I fully succumb to his forbidden kiss.

We part, gasping, and collide again. Moaning as we explore new territory, our tongues intertwine, probing, flicking and tasting. His kisses are aggressive and intense and my body responds with a yearning dormant for months.

His hand slides under my shirt, caressing and squeezing my breasts, and I pant like an overheated dog. He pushes my bra aside and I lift my top, exposing myself.

"Spectacular. These are better than anything I imagined," he mumbles, admiring me first before sucking my nipples. Milk drips out and he laps it up. "That's hot and fucking delicious... I'm going to come in my pants."

I push him back in his seat and my hand rubs his bulge. Ooh, a promising girth. He unzips and his impressive cock springs to attention. Overcome with hunger, I go to work with my mouth, licking his silky head thoroughly, then taking him deep down my throat.

"So fucking good, baby," he mutters, his hands fisting in my hair. He doesn't last long, jerking his hips against my face, the fullness of him nearly gagging me as his orgasmic grunts fill the air.

I swallow, sitting upright and swiping at the trickle of salty release escaping my lips. Sweat glistens on Rod's face as his breathing returns to normal and he croons praise for my blowjob skills.

Regaining his composure, he leans in for a kiss. Taking my chin in his hand, he says, "Take off your shorts. It's your turn."

I love a reciprocator. I wriggle them down my legs, toeing them to the floor.

He strokes the outside of my soaked bikini underwear and pushes my legs apart, his gaze reverent. "Mmm," he groans. "Sopping wet...for me. Just what I like."

Yanking the material aside, he uses his other hand to plunge a thick finger inside me. I gasp, the air leaving my lungs. Unsatisfied, he shoves my panties down to my ankles, and I spread myself wider, granting him full access. He works in another digit and then a third, while his thumb strokes command central. I'm so turned on I'm thrashing and straining against every thrust, humping his hand without shame.

Rod murmurs as his slick, beefy fingers assault me in the best way. "Good girl. Beautiful," he rasps. "Come for me, baby."

I climax with such force, my scream echoes throughout the parking lot. He milks it, making the reverberations last five minutes.

When I can move again, I pull myself back together. Rod licks my essence off his hand appreciatively.

"Well," he says.

"Well," I answer.

I reach for my cigarettes. He snags the pack and lifts two to his lips, lighting them and handing one back to me. It's almost more intimate than the sex we just shared. We puff in silence, reveling in the aftermath.

He flicks his butt out the window. "That was amazing."

"Truth."

"You are a work of art."

I shake my head.

"Please tell me we're doing this again."

"Definitely." Hopefully many agains. Why did Hank have to be so lacking?

"You okay?"

"More than. You?"

"Golden, baby."

———

Rod: You ever hear the joke about why accountants make good lovers? They're great with figures. Adrienne has what I like to call an FF—a fuckable figure. The chick is built like a 70s supermodel, only shorter. Curves for days and huge jugs. I had a feeling tonight was the night. We didn't even screw, and she blew my mind. Can't wait for round two, three, four and more. I'm riding this train to the last stop.

CHAPTER 43
HANK

ADRIENNE WALKS through the door and her mood is markedly improved. I guess she did need a break. Maybe I've been too hard on her. I'm still pissed but can admit when I'm wrong. Begrudgingly.

"Kids down?" she whispers.

I nod. "Can we talk?"

Wariness crosses her face. She sets her purse down and kicks off her flip-flops. Her phone chimes.

"Who's texting you at this time of night?"

"Don't know, don't care."

"Aren't you going to look? What if it's an emergency?"

That earns me an exasperated glare. "It's probably Tami. I called her."

I follow Adrienne to the bedroom. "Listen, I'm tired of fighting."

"So am I. But you are totally ticking me off," she says.

"Truce?"

"Okay, but please be less critical and more compassionate. I get defensive when you tell me I'm not *mentally strong enough*."

She shimmies out of her bra under her shirt, a practice I enjoy spectating from my front row seat.

I move my eyes north to meet hers. "I'll try. I understand the pressure is getting to you. If you need to blow out of here some nights and take a drive or go for a walk, I'll manage the kids so you can recharge."

Adrienne perks up. "Seriously? That would be…helpful."

"You deserve it, and you were right. When I go to work, I have a different day than you. It's still stressful, but not in the same way as juggling twin bambinos. I imagine I'd go nuts if I was here all day with those two handfuls by myself."

Her mood thaws. "Thanks, Hank. I mean it."

I open my arms and she walks into them. Holding her, I lean over and kiss the top of her head. "Sorry."

"Me, too."

I make a concerted effort to exhibit more patience and empathy, both of which are unnatural. The payoff? My wife softens toward me by week's end, and we stop bickering and sniping at each other. She hasn't given it up in the bedroom yet, but I'm crossing my fingers for tonight. It's not only Saturday, so she'll have my help, but it's also my twenty-fifth birthday. The only present I care about involves us naked for an uninterrupted hour. If Frick and Frack scream their heads off, it won't exactly cultivate the mood.

After making bacon and pancakes, Adrienne offers to straighten up the house, so I carry Tanner and Cassidy outside. It's already sweltering with the stifling humidity summer brings. I use the hose to fill the baby pool partway, slather their sensitive skin with sunscreen and let them loll in the cool water with their floaties on. They love it—gurgling and splashing spastically with their hands. I keep my eyes trained on them and snap some adorable pictures, which I text to my parents.

The twins go down for their naps without a fuss. Adrienne shuts the door to the nursery, and I grab her around the waist, pulling her backside close and enveloping her with my arms.

"Here's my birthday present right here," I whisper in her ear.

She turns her face to mine and our mouths unite. My senses fill with my gorgeous gal—her vanilla-scented hair, warm lips, silky smooth skin. My body comes alive, yearning hungrily for her as I press her against me.

I raise her off the ground, kiss her at my height and carry her into the bedroom. "This okay?" I murmur.

"Yes," she whispers in my ear.

Depositing her on the bed, I slide off her clothes, my eyes roaming over her absolute perfection, before shedding my own. My mouth and hands seek her buxom breasts, and my heart is in my throat with the love and lust surging through me. God, I've missed this. I kiss her hungrily, my tongue tangling with hers and fueling my rock-hard boner, which presses against her abdomen like it's pounding on the door. I want to take my time but my urge to merge is pressing. Understanding, she parts her legs wide, and I plunge into her, melding our bodies together.

"Holy fuck," I pant out, paralyzed by the sheer rightness of us and how fucking amazing she feels.

There's no place like home.

Moving as one, our connection intensifies, both of us gasping and stifling moans as we reach the crescendo. Like a teenager, I come way too fast, not in control of any damn thing after being denied my craving for her this long.

I slump over her until our ragged breaths slow. "I love you so much," I whisper. "You are all I ever want or need. You're perfect."

"You too," she murmurs. "Happy birthday, cowboy."

I love it when she calls me that, and my lips find hers again. I roll off her and flop on my back only to realize we're half-finished. "Shoot, where are my manners? You didn't—"

"Sure did. How'd you miss it?" Her hand finds mine and she interlaces our fingers.

"Yee-haw. Fortune cookies all around." I close my eyes, blanketed by bliss.

I wake with a start, buck naked on the bed, one of the twins wailing in the distance. I pull on my discarded clothes and track down Adrienne in the living room.

"Sorry if we woke you," she says, holding a disgruntled Tanner. Our daughter babbles to herself in a bouncy chair on the carpet.

"What's up?"

She shrugs. "Beats me. I've tried feeding, changing and carrying him. Nothing is working. Shhhh, it's okay, Tanner."

"Let me try, darlin'."

I clutch my son and take him for a walk outside, pointing out trees and flowers. Within minutes, he settles down, reduced to only a few sniffles.

Stroking his back, I murmur, "That's better, buddy."

He hiccups, followed by a sneeze, sending snot flying across my face and shirt.

"Excuse you!" I say, and he gurgles in response.

When we return, Adrienne orders me to vacate the premises for an hour and begs me to take the kids.

"But w—"

"No asking questions on your birthday, Mr. Quarter Century. Shoo!"

My heart swells. After such a rough time lately, it's good to have some love showered my way. What does my beautiful wife have up her sleeve?

She packs up the diaper bag and sends us on our way. Within ten minutes on the road, the twins are snoozing. My parents call, and I swerve into the Tilden Park visitor lot to talk. They wish me a happy birthday and we catch up as I idly watch families enjoying themselves at the park.

When Adrienne texts the all-clear, I hustle home. Cars line the street near our house, including a few I recognize, and I grin like an idiot. My wife is throwing me a party. As I approach the front door, it flies open, and I'm bombarded with a chorus of well wishes, whoops and whistles.

I set down our kids, hold my wife's face in my hands and kiss her with ardor. "You little sneak." Between the makeup and clothes, she looks smoking hot. Perhaps too sexy for this social gathering…I want all her hotness displayed for my eyes only.

She winks and shoots her gun-shaped hand at me. "Gotcha."

I make my way around the room to greet my guests: Jimmy and his girlfriend Cathy, Finn, Noreen, Monica and a few other coworkers, Tami and Rod plus their newborn baby Lexi, and some of the nearest neighbors including the Kincaids, Wilsons and Mrs. Brown.

A huge potluck spread covers the dining table along with a sheet cake spelling out *Happy 25th Cowboy!* A cooler of beer accompanies bottles of booze taking up real estate on the kitchen counter. Streamers and balloons round out the decorations, making for a festive environment. I'm floored Adrienne pulled this off, flooded with a mixture of love and relief that she's gone to the trouble. I hope this means we've gotten through our scary rough patch, and I can lay those festering worries to rest.

I spend the next few hours enjoying myself, talking with guests, stuffing my face and blowing out twenty-five candles on a chocolate cake. The conversation flows. I swap bro-hugs and chug beers with my buddies and entertain the ancient Mrs. Kincaid, who admits she loves my mustache, of all things. I've a notion she was quite a pistol in her younger years.

Lexi is a godsend; the twins gravitate to her and vice versa. Rod and Tami take turns with Adrienne keeping the babies happy. Rod's a little too chummy with my wife for my liking, although her choice of outfit tonight is hard to ignore. I'm reminded how much I dislike the dickless asshat, but Tami is a gem. She's the genuine article, and seriously deserves better than NimRod.

A few hours later, Tanner and Cassidy's inconsolable cries clear the party. They are overstimulated and it's way past their bedtime. Adrienne attends to their needs while I say goodbye to our departing guests. Timmy and Cathy are the last to leave, and we promise to reconnect soon.

Locking the door, I stumble to the nursery, wobbly from too many beers and shots. Slumping against the doorframe for added support, I watch my wife feed the babies, who chug contentedly on bottled formula.

"Best surprise ever, darlin'-sweetheart-honey-pie-love-of-my-life. I'm riding the ol' gravy train with biscuit wheels."

She shakes her head and chuckles. "What on earth are you talking about?"

"I'm a lucky man with the bestest wife in the whole wide world. Loved my party. Love you too." Damn, I'm drunk.

"Glad you enjoyed yourself." She smiles and my heart lurches. She is so darned pretty. And hot, hot, hot in that skimpy outfit.

"If you hurry, I'll show you a...a helluva time, Mrs. McCallister."

She arches her eyebrows.

I lose my balance and catch myself. "Whoops. I maybe...might...should just go nighty night."

"Good idea. I'm right behind you."

I stagger to the bedroom, sit on the edge of the bed and shuck off my boots, which takes concerted effort. I flop back, and that's the last thing I remember.

———

NOREEN: GOTTA HAND IT TO THE CHICK HANK MARRIED. SHE CONTACTED JIMMY AND TOLD HIM TO ROUND UP FRIENDS FROM THE club for this little soiree. I enjoyed the reunion. But did you see that hooker outfit? I'm all for, 'If you've got it, flaunt it,' but have some self-respect. A family party is not the place for a miniskirt and halter-top. I may be wrong but I give this marriage two years, tops.

CHAPTER 44
ADRIENNE

THE BABIES ZONK out before finishing their formula. Tanner's bottle rolls to the side after his eyes close. Cassidy's mouth goes slack around hers after gaping a few times like a fish, as she succumbs to sleep. Gingerly, I settle them in their shared crib and stealth out, shutting the door most of the way. A glance in the bedroom shows Hank's passed out, fully clothed, snoring like a sputtering engine.

My phone pings, and I rush to grab it from the dresser, lest it wake my husband. Improbable, but possible.

It's Rod, and my heart zings.

> Can you text?

> Sure can. Birthday boy's out cold.

> I miss you.

> Back atcha.

Weirdly, I do.

> It was all I could do not to smuggle you
> into the bathroom and fuck your
> brains out.

A familiar, delicious twinge echoes in my gut.

> Ooh…a romantic!

> Put me out of my misery…did you sleep
> with him for his bday?

> Why do you care, Mr. Married Man?

> I want you for myself. You're mine.

My lady parts respond like a bitch in heat.

> So yeah…but I suffered through it, doing a
> supreme acting job. How do guys not
> know when we fake it?

> I'd fucking know. And you'll never have to
> fake it with me, gorgeous. When can I
> see you?

Hank should be willing to do me a favor after all I've done for him this weekend.

> Monday night??? What's your plan?

> Fucking you into oblivion.

I chuckle.

> "Where? Time?"

> Days Inn off I-66? 8ish?

> Sure you want to spring for a room when
> we only have an hour?

Would you rather fuck in the car like teenagers?

Maybe…

God, you're hot. Now I'm as hard as my granite countertop. Which is giving me more ideas about what to do with that perfect pussy of yours.

Will it involve a spatula?

I predict many…utensils.

So…

Are you wet right now?

Sopping.

Can I pop over now for a quickie?

Too risky.

Pity. I'll have to Lone Ranger it.

Pronto, Tonto.

Sweet dreams, hotness.

You too…dream about my glorious tits.

You're fucking killing me!

:) TTFN.

Rod out.

Monday, the twins go to their scheduled check-up. I don't love their pediatrician, although he came highly recommended by Dr.

Swann. He's stoic and ancient—I'd guess his sixties—with ruddy pink skin highlighting oversized pores and a bad combover.

Dr. Greenbaum examines the babies and assures me they're progressing well. While they're behind schedule compared to other kids their age, they'll still hit the predicted milestones, just a little later than average. Every appointment verifying their normalcy fills me with relief.

I secure Tanner and Cassidy in the backseat and slide the door closed. I never thought I'd be happy to own a minivan, but Hank was right—it makes transporting the McCallister family easier. Turning on a Disney lullaby CD, I loosen the reins and let myself relax.

Parenting is like being on a train I can't climb off. Some areas show signs of improvement, knock on wood. The kids are finally on somewhat of a feeding and sleep schedule, only waking once during the night to eat again. They aren't overly fussy or inconsolable like some babies. They entertain each other, which takes a smidgeon of the pressure off. And nothing can be done about the juggling act—double everything requires more than two hands. But at least I don't completely suck at mothering. I'm doing it, hard or not.

It's blazing out, but I need a cigarette. I slide the window down and light up, the sultry breeze taking the chill off my air-conditioned skin. While I'm relieved Hank and I formed a workable truce, my frustration lingers. Like most fathers, he lives on Easy Street, waking up refreshed every morning, enjoying a leisurely shower, eating breakfast without a second thought and skipping off to work for eight to ten baby-free hours. And Prince Charming has the nerve to question why the house is a mess, his dinner isn't made, and I'm not prancing around in lingerie, eager to satisfy his sexual appetite? I'm ready to kill someone, namely him.

Glancing in the rearview mirror, I confirm the babies are asleep. I light another cigarette and turn down the volume to stop myself from flinging this sappy CD out the window.

I speculate whether this would all be worth it if Hank was more attractive, but he is indisputably homely. I'd hoped it wouldn't matter because of all his other attributes, but being around Rod, who is gorgeous and has other notable…assets, makes me question if I need more than the cowboy can provide.

Ironically, my boy toy is making life with my husband tolerable. He's giving me something to look forward to, something that's all mine, something away from the drudgery of my life. He wants nothing from me except simple, uncomplicated, mind-blowing sex.

Rod is the perfect lay. Handsome face. Touch of scoundrel. Another smooth talker with dark eyes and hair. Irresistible.

I clear out the stench of tobacco and pop in some gum, the whole "pretend I don't smoke" routine also wearing thin.

Glancing at the clock, the excitement mounts—seven more hours until Rod and I come together. *Literally.*

As predicted, Hank doesn't put up a fuss about me taking "a drive" after dinner—a perk from our cease-fire. I dismiss the speck of guilt creeping in and kiss him lovingly on the mouth, promising to return soon.

I race to the hotel, pop in a breath mint and start changing into the clothes I'd stashed earlier when my phone buzzes with a text from an impatient Rod.

You coming?

I sure hope to be!

Are you making a joke, or are you saying
you've run into a problem?

Be there in five…and I never joke about
orgasms.

I've got your Big O right here, baby.

Counting on it.

Room 114.

———

Days Inn clerk: I'm not supposed to assume anything about our guests, but the guy in Room 114? He's been a steady customer the past few years. Books a room but never stays over. Bet he's not using it to meditate, if you catch my drift. I hope he's not one of those dudes into the freak show fetish sex like the dude we found once. Dead as a mouse on the wrong end of a trap from erotic asphyxiation. I'm ninety-nine percent certain pretty boy is getting laid. Must be nice.

CHAPTER 45
HANK

I'M WATCHING *True Grit* again, probably my twelfth time. The Duke's the man. The banging on bells and buzzers shifts my gaze to Tanner encased in the canary yellow three-hundred-and-sixty-degree walker. I check on Cassidy, sprawled on an activity mat kicking a foot toward hanging plush toys. Adrienne carries a basket of clean laundry into the living room and places it on the floor between us. Her booty shorts and tight tee snag my full attention.

I pull her onto my lap and cop a feel. "You are one sexy mama."

She swats my hand. "Hank, knock it off! The kids…"

"What about them? They're too young to understand what they're looking at. We could do the nasty right here on the sofa and it wouldn't faze them a bit."

"You're sick." She scrambles off and kneels on the carpet.

"You look fantastic, darlin'…not just your body, but your whole vibe lately. I don't know what's changed but hats off to you." I grab some clothes to fold. I have serious laundry skills.

"My weight might be normal, but my figure? Not so much."

"You're crazy. And smokin' hot. I'd like to take you for a ride right now. In the other room, if it makes you more comfortable. What do you say? The kids are content."

"Not now, honey. I don't like leaving them while they're awake."

The answer, lately, is always no. No, no, no, no, no, not now, later, I'm tired, no, no, no, no, no. It's wearing thin—and worries me. I'm terrified of becoming one of those sex-less husbands rumored to happen when kids crash your marriage.

"I've been thinking," I say.

Adrienne pulls the cowboy-themed pajamas my parents sent out of the pile and glances at me, raising an eyebrow.

"Let's carve out time for ourselves. Like a regular date night, just you and me, doing something without the nitnoys underfoot."

"How do you propose that?" She keeps folding.

"We find some sitters. Ask Tami for her recommendations, and I'll check around at work."

"I don't know. How can we leave the kids with total strangers?"

I stifle my irritation. "I thought you'd be excited about this idea, jump at the chance to spend quality time together. Two or three nights a week, you split almost as soon as I'm home to," I air quote, "'restore your sanity.' This would give us time alone, away from the fracas."

Her eyes flash. "Those outings do help keep me sane!"

"Well, guess what? My sanity involves the two of us...unchaperoned." I wink to lighten the mood.

She huffs. "It's always about sex with you. Which isn't the most important thing on my radar right now, cowboy. Sorry."

She's not the least bit sorry. "This isn't just about sex, Adrienne. This is about a husband and wife sharing private time. We can't lose ourselves because kids entered the picture. Our relationship requires attention. But while we're on the topic, intimacy *is* important. It's part of our marriage and how we experience love, affection and togetherness. Frankly, I'm starving over here for any bones you throw my way, which are far and few between. It's like you don't care about me, or us, anymore."

She closes her eyes and sighs decibels above normal, as if speaking with me is a strain. When did my wife become such a bitch?

"Excuse me if attending to your needs is not my priority. *Frankly*," she says, throwing the word back in my face, "sex is like another chore on my to-do list."

Her words are a slap to my face.

The phone stuffed in her back pocket rings, and she stands to answer it. "Hi, Gran." Pause. "No, it's a fine time. How are you?" She walks away, leaving me in stunned silence.

I call my mother the next day during my lunch hour.

"Is it normal for a mother to balk at entrusting her kids with a sitter?" I ask.

"Some new mothers find the transition difficult. It also depends on the babysitter. It's harder to leave your babies with a stranger than, say, a family member."

"But people do it all the time." I tap a pencil against the phone.

"What's going on, son?"

"Adrienne and I haven't spent much time together, and almost zilch alone. Caring for the twins is stressful and obviously, won't let up anytime soon. I think it's important for us to plan some date nights." *Tap, tap, tap.*

"You're right. It is."

"She's fighting me on it." *Tap, tap, tap.*

"Chalk it up to new mother jitters. Try not to get frustrated."

"Too late." I hurl the pencil across the room, and it splinters in two.

"Why not arrange for a sitter and whisk her away as a surprise overnight somewhere? Once she experiences it for herself, she'll pester you for more."

I rub my jaw, considering. "Not a bad idea, Ma."

"Do I ever have any?"

I'm too irritated to joke. "I wager not."

"What about Grandma Betty? Perhaps she'd be willing to come up for the weekend? If you think she can handle the twins."

"Two for two, Ma. And if we don't travel too far away…" My mind wanders as I sift through the surrounding states, the groundwork already underway. "Gotta run. You're a genius."

I pull up a map on my computer and review what possibilities exist in our proximity, something far enough away to lose ourselves but near enough to rush home in an emergency. We could head to West Virginia for history, or city shenanigans in Baltimore, or hit Virginia's beaches for sand and sun. Boom— that's the one.

I decide on Colonial Beach, which has a boardwalk, sand, kayaking on the Potomac River, and a downtown trolley. As perfect as it gets. Taking this bitch by the horns, I eye my work calendar and pick a weekend. Now to make another call.

"Grandma Betty, it's Hank."

"How are you, hon? Everything all right?"

"Fine as frog's hair."

"How are Adrienne and the kids?"

The picturesque scene calls from my screen. I can't stop staring at the promise it holds. "Didn't you talk to her yesterday?"

"I don't believe so, unless my memory's worse than I thought. I have my moments though," she says with a chuckle. "What can I do you for?"

Weird. "I'm hoping to ask a favor."

"Happy to do anything for you, hon, if I can swing it. Are you ready to divorce my granddaughter and marry me instead?"

I laugh. I dig Betty's firecracker personality. "In another lifetime, Grandma Betty, you'd be the one. As for my favor, I want to take Adrienne away for an overnight, but we don't know any sitters yet and she's worried about leaving the twins with a stranger. She's fighting me on all of it, but I think it's important for us to get away and share some time alone together. Would you—"

"Yes."

"What?"

"You want me to babysit my great grands, right? It'd be a joy! I am a little out of practice, though."

I could kiss her. "You remember our friend, Tami, from the baby shower? I'm sure she'll be happy to help should you need her in person or by phone. Both Adrienne and I will have our mobiles glued to our sides. And we'll only be about two hours away, so in case of an emergency, we can hustle home."

"Sounds like you've thought of everything."

"I'm trying. I'm also keeping it a surprise."

"You worried about her frettin'?"

Smart lady. "Indeed."

Betty chuckles. "Your secret's safe with me, Hank. Though she might feel ambushed."

"I'll take the odds. Because I'm winning this round."

We finalize the details and I promise to be back in touch. I gobble down the rest of my turkey club sub, alternating bites with searching for a suitable hotel and making reservations. All that remains is asking Tami for backup and surprising Adrienne in a few weeks. Come hell or high water, I am taking my bride to Colonial Beach. My internal radar screams our marriage depends on it.

———

Grandma Betty: I wonder why Hank thought I spoke to Adri yesterday. I have my daft moments, but I hope I can still remember something that only happened a day ago! When you live alone, it's harder to determine if senility's setting in. Might have to pay Doc Bailey a visit.

CHAPTER 46
ADRIENNE

I PACK up the necessary heap of baby gear and load Tanner, then Cassidy, into the double stroller. I stretch the awning over their heads to protect them from the scorching mid-morning sun. We'll be dripping before I've wheeled them the few blocks to Tami's, but driving isn't worth the hassle. Or is it? Going anywhere with twins is a rigamarole, whether on foot or by car.

I should feel ashamed about my continued friendship with Tami considering I'm banging her husband, but I genuinely like her. She doesn't deserve Rod's cheating, but that's on him. It's obvious I'm not his first rodeo. And I don't love Rod; he's simply a...pleasurable diversion. A lust connection. Orgasms give me release from the never-ending days crammed with vapid, tedious tasks. But being desired by a handsome hardbody amps up the forbidden factor. His hands, lips and enormous dick intoxicate me. Just thinking about it makes my lady parts vibrate.

Wheeling the twins up Tami's driveway, I spot Rod's car parked in the garage. He's supposed to be at the office. I debate turning around but the decision is made for me when Tami opens the front door and greets me with a hug. Time to get our acting on.

"Look at these precious faces!" she coos, peering closer at my sleeping babies. "Come on in. It's hot as Hades."

"Hotter." She helps lift the stroller inside, and I push it through the entrance, welcoming the cold blast of air conditioning. Parking it near the living room, where Lexi snoozes in her bouncy chair, I tiptoe after her into the kitchen.

"Coffee?" she whispers.

"Wine?" I counter.

"Bottle…or mug?" She pours us each a cup and brings it to the table. "How are you?"

"Seeing double. You?"

She grabs my hand. "Exhausted. Hoping someday I will have a life again. And my freaking shape back."

Tami's baby weight lingers. And here I am in ass-hugging shorts and a camisole showing off my boobs. I'm grateful my body magically returned to fighting form thanks to nursing and less food. The mind-numbing grind took away my appetite. "You'll be back to yourself in no time." It doesn't mean her husband will fuck her, though. Not while I'm around. Maybe I'm doing her a favor.

"You're giving me hope. Criminy, look at you. If it's possible, you look even better now than before having twins. Bitch."

I laugh. "Is Rod home? No mistaking CPA MAN parked in the garage."

She smirks. "He took a half-day off work to go to the DMV and handle some other stuff. But don't worry—I told him to steer clear, so we'd have our girl time."

I bet he shows up any second, unable to stay away.

Tami sips her coffee. "What's new?"

I lean back in my chair. "Hank wants us to have date nights." I roll my eyes.

"You say that like it's a bad thing."

I shrug. "I'm not sure I'm ready to leave the twins in a stranger's hands, and we don't know any sitters. Can you recommend someone trustworthy?"

She jumps up and fetches a pen and scrap paper. "Of course! I've already used a couple." She starts transcribing names and numbers from her phone book and glances up. "Hank's right. You should carve out some time. You need a break from eating, sleeping and breathing parenting."

"I guess so, but he irritates me so much lately."

Tami raises her eyebrows. "Maybe you're blaming him for getting you pregnant?"

The corners of my mouth twitch. "And ruining my life."

"It won't always be this hard. You don't want to drive a wedge between you and your husband because of the kids. I've heard enough of those stories to know they don't end well."

Being alone with Hank on a date sounds wearisome. And a hell of a lot less exciting than covertly meeting a married man at a hotel or the bathroom stall in a bar—where Rod and I did it last.

"Howdy, neighbor," Rod says, gliding into the kitchen and pouring himself a coffee.

Right on cue. "Hello yourself. How've you been?"

"Never better." He grins, and my heart melts a little.

Tami finishes her list and hands it to me. "Honey, can you do me a favor before you go to work?"

"I can try."

"I'm out of diapers; I picked up the wrong size by mistake. Can you pop over to the grocery store and buy some?"

He shakes his head. "I'm waiting on an urgent fax. I could stop after work, or I'll stay with Lexi, and you can go now if you need them sooner."

"I can't abandon Adrienne. I'll deal with it later."

"Psh! Don't be ridiculous," I say. "I'm happy to hang out. Go now while you aren't lugging a baby along. It won't take long, and you and I can pick up right where we left off once you return."

Rod's eyes gleam with opportunity behind Tami's back.

She hesitates. "You don't mind?"

I flash her an *are-you-kidding?* stare, pull her to standing and give her a playful shove. "Go!"

Promising to hurry back, she leaves. Rod waits until the front door closes, then flies to my side and seals his lips against mine. My body arches toward his, the flame lit instantaneously.

"What you're wearing should be illegal," he breathes into my ear, followed by nibbles down my neck. He rips my flimsy shirt up and I moan when one hand firmly grasps my tit, and his mouth claims my nipple. His other hand gropes the sweet spot between my thighs. "I'm going to fuck you so hard."

"Here? Now?"

"Here and now," he says, undoing his belt.

A baby cries, the universe laughing at us.

Tanner's the culprit, and the other two wake up like falling Dominos, one after the other. Rod places Cassidy in the kid corral while I bounce Tanner. He picks up his daughter, whispers in her ear and sets her beside Cassidy. The two girls giggle and gurgle, staring at each other.

My son quiets and Rod stares at me, tapping his watch impatiently. "Put him in the damn corral and let's get down to business. We don't have much time."

I settle Tanner near the girls under a hanging mobile and slither away undetected.

Rod eyes me like he hasn't eaten in days and I'm a rare steak.

"Are you sure this is smart?"

"Mmm hmm." He yanks my shorts and underwear down to my ankles and bends me over the kitchen table. Seconds later, he fills my sopping pussy, our stifled pants mingling together.

He dominates me with delicious thrust after thrust, and I gasp, unable to fully breathe. What we're doing is freaking hot, naughty and stupidly risky. I reach down and rub myself, my furious circles and the pounding of Rod's magnificent cock yielding an intense, undulating climax, forcing me to grip the table's edge with my free hand as I smother a scream. He follows, grinding into me as he unloads with a low, guttural groan.

Baby wails emanate from the other room, but lover boy stays slumped over me as we catch our breath and recover from our unexpected, wicked tryst. When the cries escalate, I nudge Rod to move. I waddle to the counter, tear off a couple of paper towels and use them to sop up the mess before disposing of them in the kitchen garbage, shoving the evidence down deep.

I right my clothes. "Time to be a mom again."

"Mom I'd like to…"

"Been there, done that."

Rod sniffs and leers. "Smells like sex in here."

"Fix it! Before Tami comes home."

He salutes. "Yes, ma'am."

The cries intensify to screams and I race to the corral. Cassidy is rolling back and forth, shrieking. Lexi howls, blood trickling down her face. *Shit!* "Rod, come quick!" Sitting on the floor, I pull my daughter into my arms and pat her back. I reach over and place a soothing hand on Lexi's belly, murmuring calming words to both girls.

Rod emerges, assessing the situation.

"Lexi's bleeding. Grab something!" I order.

He bolts, returning with a wad of tissues in hand. Retrieving his daughter, he dabs at her wound, and she howls louder. "What the hell happened?"

"Not sure. How bad is it?"

"Looks like a few scratches. Was it Cassidy?"

"God, I hope not." I inspect her hand as she sobs into my shoulder. Her nails are long, sharp enough to do some damage. I should have cut them. Who can stay on top of this never-ending mountain of mommy duties?

Rod rocks Lexi and I murmur into Cassidy's ear. Both girls soon hush.

"I'm sorry if Cass did that," I say.

"Yeah, not cool."

"She's an infant, Rod. She's not responsible for her actions yet. She can't control what she does."

"Like mother, like daughter."

"Fuck you."

"Anytime, sweetheart."

"Sometimes you're a Class A dick."

He smirks. "You like my dick."

I roll my eyes.

Tami arrives home with the diapers and absorbs the scene. "Did something happen?"

Several somethings.

"Cassidy may have scratched Lexi," I say, shifting her into my other arm. "I'm not sure."

"Her cheek was bleeding, but I've cleaned her up and calmed her down," Rod adds. "She seems fine."

Taking Lexi from her husband, Tami examines her daughter's face. "You didn't see what happened either?"

"Nope. Adrienne and I were talking one minute and the next, the kids were crying. Listen, I've got to check the fax machine." Rod kisses his wife on the cheek and practically runs from the scene.

Tami rocks her daughter, the silence stretching between us.

"Glad you got the diapers," I say.

"Yeah. Speaking of which, it smells like she needs a change." She fetches the diapers and carries Lexi into another room.

I exhale. Mine surely did too, since waking from their naps. A good mother would have attended to this already, instead of screwing her best friend's husband in the kitchen.

TAMI: THE WHOLE THING TICKED ME OFF. HOW DID BOTH ROD AND ADRIENNE MISS SOMETHING SO HUGE? MY DAUGHTER IS BLEEDING OUT AND THEY'RE *TALKING*? ACT LIKE RESPONSIBLE PARENTS. AND MAYBE I'M BEING PISSY, BUT I DON'T NEED MY GAL PAL FLITTING AROUND MY SPOUSE IN A SKIMPY OUTFIT, EITHER—ESPECIALLY WHEN I STILL LOOK LIKE A WHALE.

CHAPTER 47
HANK

ADRIENNE SLEEPS SOUNDLY, curled on her side, facing me. I can just make out her graceful features in the glow of ambient light. A whisper of dread reverberates in my core...something isn't right between us.

It took convincing, but Adrienne agreed to sex once we settled down for the night. I went to satisfy her first, more than ready and willing to bring her to climax, but she shut it down. Who blows off an orgasm? She countered by saying she wanted me inside of her—and it worked, getting me amped up and aiming to please her at least this one way. And you don't have to ask me twice to merge our bodies, lips and minds.

I couldn't put my finger on it last night. But now I'm realizing she was present in body, but not spirit. She went through the motions but lacked...passion, as excited as a block of wood. An empty vessel.

I knew something was off but Jesus, it had been so long, I thought I'd burst at how achingly familiar and decadent it felt to be inside of her. Like coming home after a tour of duty. Damn if I can argue with the playback.

What the hell is going on with my wife?

I call Tami from work on Monday, and she answers on the third ring.

"It's Hank. Got a minute?"

"Sure. Everything okay?"

"You alone?" My foot taps a steady rhythm against the floor, and I press my hand into my leg to quiet it.

"Aside from Lexi, yup. What's up?"

"Have you noticed anything different about Adrienne lately? Do you think she's all right?"

"She's stressed and overwhelmed by the twins. We don't talk or visit as much, but she's tired and pedaling as fast as she can, I guess."

"Nothing else?"

"I don't know. You're with her more than I am. What's going on?"

"I feel like she's going through the motions. I don't know if I should be worried." I prop my elbow on the desk and sink my forehead into my hand.

"Give her some time to adjust, Hank. Two babies are a lot."

"Yeah. I'm impatient for us to return to normal."

Tami laughs. "I've got news for you—this may be your new normal."

I lean back in my chair. "Can I ask a favor?"

"I will not wash your truck."

That garners a half-smile. "Duly noted. Not where I was headed."

She chuckles. "Shoot."

"I'm taking Adrienne away for a surprise weekend and her grandmother has agreed to babysit the twins, but I'd appreciate it if she can count on you for backup."

"You bet. And Hank, that's a terrific idea. You're thinking like a husband. Want to give mine some pointers?"

Sorry, Tami, but there's no hope for that asshat. "Uh oh. Is Rod slacking on his husbandly duties?"

"He's not whisking me away on any getaways."

"Maybe this will inspire him. And thanks for your sitter recommendations. We'll be using some of those in the future."

"There you go again, making my man look like a heel."

Nope. He does it all by himself. "You should schedule a date night, darlin'."

"Don't go dripping your Texas-accented endearments on me, or I might have to tell Rod and Adrienne to hit the road."

I grin on my end. "Can I ask something else? It's kind of inappropriate." I can't believe I'm going there, or my comfort level with it.

"Now I'm intrigued."

"I'm wondering if you…" Damn. Spit it out, Hank.

"Spit it out, Hank."

I chuckle nervously. "Adrienne hasn't been into sex. I wondered if you, uh, had a similar disposition since having Lexi."

"I'm gung-ho now, but that's a recent development. My birth was different than Adrienne's, of course, so she may have experienced something else. Pardon my candor, but not everything returned to its proper place or shape. It didn't exactly put me in the mood for amour. What's weirder is, now that I'm ready, my husband doesn't seem interested, and that's like hell freezing over, you know?"

Do I ever. "Guess we're in this together."

"Hopefully not for long."

"Right. Thanks, Tami. Appreciate you talking with me."

"Back at ya. You feel better?"

"I do." If this is the post-delivery norm, I'll deal with riding it out. She's worth it.

"Me, too. Text me your trip details."

"Don't forget it's a surprise."

"Mum's the word."

I hang up, perked up over my situation. Perhaps I'm imagining things. I'll see how our mini-vacay plays out and reassess, if needed.

. . .

I leave work Friday with excited anticipation and a sliver of apprehension. I still expect Adrienne might fight me on the getaway, but we're going to the beach *alone*. I've executed my plan with precision, from our itinerary to the babysitting to what we'd do in case of an emergency. In short, I've left my bride no room to argue.

I greet an exuberant Diesel and smile at my wife, who cradles Cassidy in the crook of one arm on the sofa. Tanner jabbers in the portable swing. "Hi darlin'." I lean over, kiss her cheek, and smooth our daughter's hair.

"Hi yourself."

"The kids look content. Good day?"

She purses her lips and nods. "Actually, yes. In the crazy world of mothering twins, I'd rate it a seven out of ten."

"I'm about to kick it up to a fifteen." Here goes nothing.

"You won a million bucks?"

"Maybe lower your expectations a tad," I say, illustrating by inching my thumb and forefinger together. "I have a surprise for you. For us. And before you say anything or interrupt, let me finish. I've arranged a weekend getaway to Colonial Beach."

Adrienne's mouth drops. "But—"

I wag my finger. "Your grandmother is coming this evening to babysit—and is delighted to do so. She'll be here in an hour. Tami's on deck, ready to help at a moment's notice. You and I are leaving first thing in the morning. This gives you tonight to visit with Betty and review all the baby stuff. Then the two of us are off to have a romantic escape alone. No kids. No cooking. A full night's sleep. And we'll only be two hours away in case of an emergency. Now, what do you say?"

Her mouth opens and shuts. "I'm stunned."

"In a positive way?"

"I'm not sure. We've never left the babies before, and they're still so tiny…and vulnerable. While I love Grandma Betty, I'm not convinced she's up to the challenge. They're a lot of work, Hank. If *I* struggle, how's she going to manage?"

"Give your grandmother some credit. She doesn't have a foot in the grave yet. Frick and Frack will be fine. They're healthy and, thank God, not too fussy. They sleep on a schedule. Betty is more than capable of feeding them bottles and changing diapers, and Tami is our ace in the hole. But remember, I picked a place close enough to hustle home if it's necessary. We'll be two hoots and a holler away."

"But—"

"No. No buts, Adrienne. I won't take no for an answer." I kneel beside her, touching her hand and gazing into her eyes. "I need this. *We need this.* It's only a short break, some time alone to reconnect. I feel like I'm losing you."

She avoids eye contact. "You're not."

I gently coax her face back to mine. "I'm drowning over here. You're distant and inattentive."

Her expression sours.

"It's not an accusation. I understand the kids are all-consuming, but that's why I'm begging you for this time together. To talk, sleep, breathe, make love and have some *fun.*"

She pauses but my eyes implore her. "Okay, Hank. We'll go. But if I catch one whiff the twins are sick or in trouble, we're coming home."

"Of course!" I take one of her dainty hands in between mine, marveling at its softness against my callouses. "You're happy about this, aren't you?"

She nods. "It's thoughtful, which is one of things I've always liked about you."

I hold her face in my hands and kiss her. "Go pack!"

———

HUSBAND WAS MORE LIKE HIM. ROD IS OFTEN SELFISH, CONDE-SCENDING AND ANAL RETENTIVE TO A FAULT. HE'S IN THE DOGHOUSE AT THE MOMENT, SO HANK'S PRINCE CHARMING IN COMPARISON, BUT HE ACTS LIKE ONE TOO, WITH ALL HIS OBVIOUS CONSIDERATION AND LOVE. A PART OF ME—MAYBE IT'S ENVY TALKING—DOESN'T THINK ADRIENNE DESERVES IT.

CHAPTER 48
ADRIENNE

HANK IS irritated when we hit the road. Mr. Particular wanted to leave earlier, but I wasn't going anywhere until I fed the twins and made sure Grandma Betty was settled. I struggled to tear myself away when the time came, but I did it somehow…kissed their little heads and walked out the door. Hank said his good-byes, completely untraumatized. *Men.* Unemotional robots.

He started to give me the business about taking my coffee, bitching not to spill it in his precious, pristine truck, but I silenced him with a glare and reminded him I'd been up with the babies in the night, unlike another person, who slept like a baby. What an oxymoron.

Hank's hick tunes waft through the cab as I gaze out the window, trees and towns whizzing past as we drive south on the interstate. Bright sunlight radiates through the glass, and I reach into my purse for my shades. My phone chimes with a text message alert.

No surprise, it's from Rod.

> WTF? Tami just told me you and Hank are
> going away for the weekend?

I steal a glance at my husband and punch in a one-word answer.

Yup.

What about OUR plans?

Canceled, obvs.

"Who's that?" Hank asks.
"Tami, wishing us a wonderful time."
Ping.

You're not going sleep with him, are you?

Are you serious???? GTG.

Wait. I'm jealous. I have feelings for you.

Not now.

Bitch!

I don't respond, shutting off the ringer and tucking the phone back into my purse. I plan to bang the hell out of my husband now. Color me spiteful, but no one, especially a cheating douchebag like Rod, is going to call me a bitch and get away with it.

"I like Tami. She's a good egg, and I'm glad you're friends. I hope you thanked her again."

"Sure did."

My husband slams the brakes and lays on the horn when a Mustang with New Jersey plates cuts him off. He speeds up, getting inches from the car's bumper.

"Hank!"

His eyes blaze, focused on the offending car. "What?"

"You're too close. You're scaring me!"

"He's in the wrong and I'm a damn good driver, thank you very much."

I glower. "You're going to make our kids orphans if you don't back the fuck off."

"Fine," he mutters, gunning it into another lane. He forms his hand into a gun and fires it at the guy as we pass. "Go back to Joisey, Yankee scum!"

I roll my eyes beneath my sunglasses and stare out the window to avoid the overwhelming urge to jump out of the damn truck. How, in addition to two babies, have I gotten stuck with two infantile grown men?

Hank shakes me awake. "Hey, sleepyhead. Look."

Navy blue water stretches before us as we cruise down the boulevard. The backdrop of aqua sky and plumy clouds makes my breath catch. Maybe this trip wasn't such a bad idea after all. "Is that the Chesapeake Bay?"

"Potomac River, but it feeds into the bay. We're in the Northern Neck region. Gorgeous, isn't it?"

"Beautiful."

He turns left and we pass shops and restaurants, glimpses of deep blue appearing between the avenues. The area gives off a quaint, beachy vibe without the stifling crowds.

"What's our agenda? Can we go to the beach first?"

Steering into a parking lot, he winks. "That's why I told you to put on your suit. I thought we'd hang until we can check into our hotel."

"Sounds like heaven."

We gather our gear and cooler and haul it the short distance to what, Hank informs me, is the second-longest beachfront in Virginia. Despite the sweltering August humidity, I kick off my flip-flops and delight in the warmth of the beige sand pushing between my toes with each step. I can't recall the last time I've set foot on a beach.

We pick a spot, and my husband unfurls a blanket. The shoreline stretches for miles in both directions and the place is relatively uncrowded for summer. We spread out our towels, and I strip down to my bikini.

My horny cowboy whistles appreciatively. "You could get arrested for indecent exposure, darlin'."

"Complaining?"

"Not on your life. But prepare yourself—as soon as we're in our hotel room, I'm hitting that hard."

I laugh and lie on my towel, the sun blanketing me in its warmth. It's positively sublime.

He kisses my flat belly. "Tough to imagine Frick and Frack were nestled in there not so long ago."

"No one's called yet? I can't believe we're in the clear."

"Believe it, darlin'. And *enjoy it*."

"Think I will." Closing my eyes, I allow relaxation to envelop me. It's fucking glorious.

"I'm getting wet."

"Mmm hmm," I answer, already half-gone.

Memories surface of fishing and wading in the rivers of my childhood, my sister and I discovering tadpoles near the estuary, and later, fighting when we played Crazy 8's and I was sure she'd cheated. My throat constricts. I wish Annabelle was here with me now. She should be alive, finding love, having kids and being a silly aunt to my own. I push those thoughts away and force my mind to go blank. Basting in the sun, free from responsibility, sleep lures me out of consciousness.

Cool droplets splatter my skin, and I startle. "Hey!"

Hank stands over me, dripping wet, mustache stretched across his chipped-tooth smile. "Come in with me. The water's mighty refreshing."

I sit up, sticky from sweat, groggy from napping. "I'm hot."

"You can say that again."

I smirk, taking his outstretched hand. He hauls me to standing, scoops me up into his arms and heads for the water, threatening to throw me in.

"Don't you dare!" I shriek, wide awake now.

"You're kind of cute when you're scared."

"You should be the one who's afraid, dear husband. If you have any hope of getting laid, you'll put me down this instant."

That gives him pause. He stops at the river's edge and places me on my feet. "Spoil sport."

I reward him with a kiss. Venturing forward, I poke my right foot in. Cold but bearable. I reach back, holding out my hand. "Come in with me, cowboy?"

"Anything for you, darlin'."

Clasping hands, we wade in slowly until the water covers my chest. I shiver and Hank pulls my body to his. I wrap my legs around his waist, and we share a deep, lingering kiss, forging a different kind of warmth.

He walks further out, wearing me like a flotation device. The occasional wake laps against us as we admire the view. A heron sits majestically on a boulder jutting from the riverbank, unfazed by the cries of gulls flying overhead. The sun's rays warm my exposed skin, while my lower half remains bathed in the coolness of the river.

"Is this heaven?" I wonder aloud.

"Anywhere you are is my heaven."

Our eyes and lips meet again, the water swirling around our torsos. Traces of guilt and betrayal slither through me as I'm reminded what I love about Hank. His kindness. Generosity. Worship.

Thirty minutes later, we dry off and walk up to the shops to find lunch. Settling on a little joint selling pit beef sandwiches and fries, we carry our haul back to our spot on the beach and devour every morsel.

. . .

Our hotel overlooks a stunning view of the Potomac and Chesapeake Bay, not that I admire it long. My husband makes quick work of hustling me into the expansive bathroom, where we shower our sandy bodies. His lips and fingers bring me to orgasm before the water turns cold. Turning off the spray, he lifts me against the wall and plunges into me, leaving me dazed, breathless and wondering, again, why I behave so terribly.

We crawl into the king-sized bed under a comfortable white duvet. Hank holds me in his arms, professing his love in whispers until he falls silent, his body slackening. It's not long until I follow, lulled into decadent sleep.

We awaken to the sun low in the sky. We both reach for our phones, checking everything's fine on the home front. A message from Grandma Betty confirms all is well and to enjoy ourselves. A second one from Tami reassures us she's checked on the twins.

Noting several texts from Rod, I gather my toiletries, covertly slip my phone inside the bag, and head to the bathroom. I sift through his messages: in turns apologetic, pleading or angry. He'd given up after six hours, but I don't kid myself. He'll be back. The whole thing ticks me off. I need to keep my ringer on in case of an emergency, and he's going to get us busted if he can't control his emotions, texting me like a lunatic.

I tap out a quick message:

> You are going to blow everything. Quit
> texting! We're fine. Chill!

He responds immediately.

> I can't stand the thought of his hands…
> and more…on you.

> Stop thinking about it. Your hands…and
> more…will be on me soon enough.

> Sorry.

Accepted. GTG. I attach a kiss emoji.

Hurry home. I've got plans for you and
that sweet pussy.

You better.

I stow the phone, rinse out my mouth, run a brush through my hair and apply fresh makeup.

Hank and I stroll to a restaurant overlooking the water and enjoy a fancy dinner with wine. It's so easy to take something like an uninterrupted meal for granted.

As the moon rises in the sky, we wander out to the end of the weathered wooden pier. He stands behind me, arms wrapped loosely around my midsection as we gaze across the horizon. "Happy?" he whispers in my ear.

"To the point I almost feel guilty." I glance back at him with a smirk. "Almost."

"You deserve it, darlin'. You're relaxed for the first time in months."

"I don't think I've slept so much since before the twins were born. A nap is unheard of and indulgent. And the beach, this gorgeous place…it's nirvana."

"Agreed."

He kisses my neck and murmurs words of praise and love. A flicker of self-reproach returns, but I swat it away.

After watching the light float along the current for a while, Hanks asks, "Ready to go back, wife? I'm not done with you yet."

I nod. It isn't hard to throw the guy a bone. As he believes I deserve this little vacation, he deserves something for his efforts —and he makes it clear exactly what he wants.

I sleep like the dead, waking up disoriented and grumpy in the middle of one of Hank's earth-shaking sneeze-fests. The sunlight radiating through the window pierces my eyes. I groan and roll over.

Hank trumpets his nose and pounces on me with all fours. "Morning, Mrs. McCallister! I've been waiting for you to wake up."

His morning-person cheer borders on obnoxious. Reality shovels itself in my face, and I burrow deeper into my pillow.

"Come on, Adrienne! We've only got today left, time's a wastin', and I'm starving."

I open one eye.

"Thatta girl!" He flings back the comforter, exposing me.

"Hey!"

"Hmm, we could skip breakfast..."

The thought of sex revolts me. I curl my lip at my husband, drag myself to standing and stagger to the bathroom in a groggy stupor. I calculate all the shuteye I've gotten since leaving home —somewhere in the vicinity of fifteen hours. Maybe there is such a thing as too much sleep.

I pull it together and we find a tiny café nearby to eat. I swallow a cup of coffee STAT.

Hank raises his eyebrows, his expression full of mirth. "Are we still a crabby Abby?"

I shut my eyes. It's going to be a long day. Opening them, I respond with a withering stare.

"I'll take that as a yes."

Our meal comes, and my husband attacks his chow as if he's been stranded on an island the past month. He eats too fast, speaks with a stuffed mouth and dribbles syrup and other debris into his food-collecting mustache. I try to divert my attention from the free-for-all across the table and focus on my own plate.

While Hank chews, he waxes on about our upcoming agenda: check out, go kayaking, drive to George Washington's birthplace, eat a late lunch and head home. It sounds exhausting. I'd rather zone out on the beach.

We finish breakfast and my head finally clears after four cups of caffeine. Back at the hotel, I'm gathering our belongings when Hank tackles me on the bed, pinning me uncomfortably. His bug-eyes forecast every lewd intention.

"Quit it!"

He stays put, sucking on my neck. "Let's take advantage of one more opportunity."

I buck in futility, no match for his size. "Not now." Why can't he leave me alone?

"Why not?" He presses up on his arms, and I catch my breath. He stares pointedly at me.

"I'm sore," I lie, softening my tone.

"Oh, jeez. I'm sorry." He climbs off, grinning like his sexual prowess is a superpower. "Kind of."

I return to packing, wishing we were already home.

I try to shake my mood but can't. Cranky and lethargic wins. I'd pay cash mo-nay to regain the contentment I experienced the day before but can't seem to find my way back. The kayaking is okay, but my apathetic limbs can't keep up with Hank. The tedious walk around the George Washington Birthplace National Monument bores me to tears as my encyclopedic husband prattles on about facts I couldn't care less about. George's great-grandfather this and when George lived in the house that. Who fucking cares about this ancient history? My guy, that's who. I tell him I'm parking it on a bench and to fetch me when he's finished. He looks crestfallen, but once I insist, he leaves me be.

Checking my phone, I discover Rod sent me a dick pic, and a familiar ache reverberates in command central at the sight of its robust size. Despite the inelegance of the male penis, and how few women want to ogle one, I can't wait to wrap my mouth around his...and welcome the drilling he'll give me after.

I type back a one-word response:

Want.

Next, I call Grandma Betty, who sounds harried but assures

me she has the twins under control. Confirming we'll be home on time or earlier, I sense we're both relieved. I miss my babies, which fills me with relief. Maybe I *am* cut out for motherhood.

When Hank returns, I press him to take us back, suggesting we do a drive-thru for lunch to save time. Despite his obvious disappointment, he doesn't fight me. He misses the kids too.

As he drives, my husband alternates between chattering about past presidents and belting out whatever country tune brays from his stereo. I silently ponder an exit strategy. I thought I could do this, believed it was what I wanted or needed, and convinced myself Hank—or marriage—would fix all that ails.

But now I'm not sure. I don't think I can stand looking at his ugly mug much longer, let alone forever. Or endure his alternately cheerful or raging moods. Or screw him when my heart isn't in it. The kids pose a new dilemma, but people divorce all the time. How hard can it be?

———

Tami: Rod was freaking moody as hell this weekend. Sometimes I worry I've married a mental patient. On Saturday, he went from sullen and angry to ravenous lover in about three hours. I can't tell you how long it's been since we had sex like that—hot, carnal, like there's no tomorrow. I guess his mood swings aren't a terrible tradeoff.

CHAPTER 49
HANK

MONDAY MORNING COMES TOO SOON, but nothing can slow my roll. Adrienne and I genuinely reconnected during our time in Colonial Beach. Not only with amazing sex, but emotionally and maritally. We needed a boost in the love department, and the extra shuteye didn't hurt. We returned rested, relaxed and close again, like all is right in our little patch of earth.

I admit I missed our little doofers. Once we had Tanner and Cassidy back in our arms, emotion coursed through me, all sweetness and light. Grandma Betty looked relieved—bet she went home and crashed ten hours straight.

I pull into the parking lot at the shop. Time to get back to the grind—one part of reality I didn't miss. My phone buzzes with a text message from Adrienne, brightening my mood.

> How about skipping lunch and fucking me instead?

Hot damn! It pains me to turn her five-star offer down.

Wish I could, darlin', but I can't steal
away. Put me on tap for this evening, you
gorgeous smokeshow!

She doesn't respond right away, so I head out to the floor to manage the workload.

Back in my office an hour later, I check my phone, hoping for another sexy text. My wife's only response is a thumbs-up emoji. Blood rushes to my groin imagining what I'll do to her, and I push the imagery from my mind to coerce Hank, Jr. to stand down. I don't need to be walking around the shop with a stiffy.

It's clear within seconds of arriving home I have a milkshake's chance in hell of getting laid. Adrienne's slumped shoulders, lifeless eyes and monotone voice broadcast her glum disposition. I can't believe this is the vibrant woman of yesterday. She stands in the kitchen, Cassidy on her hip.

"Hey," I say, kissing her on the cheek first, followed by my daughter. "Re-entry that bad?"

She shrugs half-heartedly.

"Is it the kids?"

She stares at nothing, her expression blank.

"Adrienne?" She's practically comatose.

She flicks her eyes back to my face. "What?"

"You're scaring me a mite. What's going on?"

"I'm tired, I've got vomit on my shirt, and they've been a handful today." As if realizing Cassidy is still in her arms, she walks to the swing, secures her in the seat and gives her a push.

"I'll take over for a bit. Why don't you grab a shower and change your clothes?"

She shrugs and shuffles down the hall.

Sometimes my wife needs to get a grip. I rub Diesel's ears, back and hind quarters since he got cheated out of his normal greeting and fill his dog bowl. Getting down to floor level, I squeeze Tanner's miniature hand. "Hey, little buddy. How's my favorite wrangler?"

He giggles, his face lighting up. I pick him up and roll on my back. Lifting my son into the air, I bring his belly down to my mouth, giving him multiple raspberries as he squeals with delight.

The rhythmic tick of Cassidy's swing stops, and her tears begin to flow. I speak to her in low tones, give her a push and reset the timer, but her wails continue. As I'm about to collect her, she nods off. Luckily, she doesn't spark Tanner's crying mechanism. When one bawls, it usually triggers the other. I place him in the activity station with objects he can bang on and fetch a beer. I tip it back, allowing the foamy liquid to slide down my throat. A quick survey of the kitchen yields no evidence of dinner in progress. What I wouldn't give to be in Texas right now scarfing down a Triple Meat Whataburger with jalapenos.

The kids secure, I venture to our bedroom and find Adrienne perched on the edge of the bed, hair wet, face bent toward her phone, texting. She slips the device under her leg as I approach.

"I don't want to assume, but it looks like we're getting takeout tonight?"

"Jesus, Hank, cut me a break, will you?"

"I'm not giving you crap—I'm asking a question."

"Takeout would be great," she huffs.

"Fry Guys? Angelo's Pizza? Something else?"

She shrugs, noncommittal. I might as well be married to a zombie.

I turn to leave but stop. I can't squelch that persistent nagging voice. "Who are you texting?"

"Why? Don't trust me?" Her eyes flare. Maybe she's alive after all.

"I'm curious. You're on that contraption a lot." *You sure as hell don't text me much.*

"Whatever. It's Tami. Satisfied?"

Nope. I want to see for myself, but don't push. Instead, I give her a curt nod. "I'm going to pick up the food, unless you want to."

Adrienne stands. "I'll do it."

She starts to whisk past me, and I catch her wrist. "I don't know what's going on with you, but this Jekyll and Hyde routine is wearing thin. One minute you're hot, the next you're cold."

She wriggles out of my grasp, brown eyes blazing, but stays mute.

"I thought we made headway this weekend. Remember how wonderful it was? Then you sent me a sexy text this morning… and now you're the bitchy ice queen. What the hell gives?"

"You wouldn't understand."

"Try me."

She tilts her head straight toward the ceiling and lets out an exaggerated sigh. "Let me go. And stop making such a huge deal out of everything. I'm tired, irritable and fed-up."

"With what?" Mothering, for God's sake?

"With this *life.*" She leans into my face and screeches the last word.

My neck pulses. Adrenaline spreads like syrup…fast but smooth, until it fills every orifice. "What the fuck does that mean?" I growl.

"I knew you wouldn't understand!"

I smack my palm against the doorjamb, teetering at the edge of no return. "I can't decipher your goddamn hieroglyphics by myself now, can I?"

"Chillax, cowboy. Don't have a conniption."

I want to smash her insolent face with my fist. I won't, but it eases the burning ache—ever so slightly—to visualize it in my head. "Don't say trendy, meaningless bullshit to me. Are you saying you're unhappy in our marriage?"

She shrugs, and I come unglued.

———

Mrs. Brown: I spy trouble in paradise over at the McCallister's again. Hank sped out of there so fast he left skid marks.

CHAPTER 50
ADRIENNE

MY BODY QUAKES uncontrollably as I stand in the hallway next to the wreckage where Hank stuffed his fist through the wall. Aside from the gaping hole, bits of pale-yellow paint and chalky drywall pepper the floor. He stormed out and slammed the door moments earlier, and both babies are in hysterics.

Fucking bastard. Hank's temper is uncontrollable and dangerous. He's always in my business and I'm sick of it. I don't answer to him—or anyone. Why can't men get that through their thick, impenetrable skulls?

And this…this is unacceptable. His punch missed my face by inches, crunching through the wall to my left. It scares me more than I will ever give him the satisfaction of knowing. *Violent fucking maniac.*

That's it. That's my out.

Suddenly, it's all so clear.

I dry my tears and make bottles for the twins. Tanner and Cassidy quiet once in my arms. I position them on the sofa and feed them, their sucking noises the only sound aside from the ticking of the mantle clock and my rapid heartbeat. I glance around for the mutt, noticing his absence for the first time. Hank must have taken Diesel with him. Stupid dog. He's been nothing but a pain in the ass, too, like his owner.

Wiggling my phone out of my back pocket, I text Rod.

You busy?

I spy the three revolving dots and pace, antsy for his response.

Kind of. Were you hoping for another round with the RamRod? I thought our nooner would tide you over.

I roll my eyes.

Need to talk.

Sounds serious.

IT IS. When?

I can't wait to message Hank next. Asshole.

Tomorrow? Noon again?

Fine.

You upset?

"Affirmative, Captain Obvious," I mutter. I can't afford to be snippy. I need him. Before I can respond, he texts again.

Want me to try and sneak away?

Nope. GTG.

I'm not in the mood for small talk or sexual innuendos. With the twins content on the couch, I pour myself a generous shot of vodka, then rummage for my stashed cigarettes and slip into the backyard. Watching the kids through the sliding glass doors, I puff three in rapid succession, blowing the smoke out of my mouth with force. I kick the rocks sitting on the patio and they skitter against the wooden fence backing the property. I want to hit something, or rather, someone. *My husband.*

I guzzle my drink and pick up my phone. My fingers fly over the tiny keyboard as I give Hank a piece of my mind.

> Your behavior is 100% unacceptable and total bullshit. If you want to act like an intimidating and abusive dick, you can do it by yourself, away from your wife and kids. I won't tolerate this shit from you…or anyone. I suggest you crash somewhere else tonight because I don't want to see your face right now. In fact, not sure when I will, so fucking call before coming back…period.

It shocks me when Hank doesn't come home or bother answering my text. I expected him to grovel like the sucker he's proven himself to be. I hardly slept, despite the babies only waking me once, and I look like it with a pallid complexion with purple semicircles under my eyes. I run a brush through my hair and pull it up into a messy bun. Should I be worried by Hank's disappearing act? I loathe the unease of losing control.

A tapping on the sliding door makes me jump. I hustle to open it and find Rod, freshly shaved and dressed for work in a crisp suit. I fling my arms around him, burying my head in his chest and fighting back tears.

He holds me for a minute and steps back. "What's going on, Adrienne? You look like hell."

"Thanks, asshole."

He throws his hands in the air. "Don't shoot the messenger. I'm worried about you."

I nod toward the kitchen. "Coffee?"

"Sure. Twins asleep?"

"For now." I pour us each a cup, and we sit at the dining room table.

Rod waits expectantly.

I get my bearings. It's go time. "How do you feel about me?"

His brow knits.

"It's not a trick question."

"Sorry—you took me off guard. I think you're fantastic, and you're the sexiest damn broad I've ever known."

Inside, I glow, my lips arching into a small smile. "I find you amazingly sexy too. I dream about your cock, and I'm pretty sure that's never happened before."

He reaches over and takes my hand, giving it a squeeze. "We've got a good thing going here."

About that. I pause for a beat, tilting my head and pinning him with a gaze I know drives men wild. "How would you like to take it to the next level?"

He starts to leer, then looks confused. "Wait...what do you mean?"

"I *mean* that I divorce Hank and you leave Tami, and we go fuck our brains out at a home we create together."

Rod jerks his hand away, blanching. "What are you talking about?"

"Ditching my dickhead husband."

"Did something happen?"

A million somethings. "Yes, but it's been a long time coming. I jumped into our relationship too fast. It's not what I want. I want...you."

He flinches. "Adrienne, I care about you. A lot. I think about you all the time. Truthfully, I'm obsessed. But I haven't given one thought to leaving Tami. We have a baby. You and Hank have two. It's complicated."

I need to close this deal, and unless my hunch is wrong—and it seldom is—I can. "Do you love me, Rod?"

He gazes into his lap for a moment. When he looks up, he

stares me straight in the eyes. "I do. And I fucking hate the thought of that redneck's hands on you. Makes me crazy."

Clasping his hand in both of mine, I lean forward. "I love you too, and I want more. I know it's messy, but I've got to break free of Hank and protect my babies. He's not right in the head. And last night, he came close to hitting me. It's only a matter of time before he does."

Rod's eyes narrow. "The fucker. I'd like to tear him a new one."

That's more like it. "Promise me you'll think about it. You and me, truly together." Standing, I place his hand on my crotch and begin to gyrate slowly. Closing my eyes, I raise my shirt, exposing my braless tits. Wetness seeps through my yoga pants and his eyes bulge, along with his pecker.

He groans. "I so need to fuck you right now."

"Not here," I whisper. "In the back." I lead him to the bedroom, where he yanks down my leggings and plunges into me from behind, screwing me with a ferocious desperation. We become lost in the moment, savoring the primal and raw emotions surging through us.

Caught up in the passion of our forbidden tryst, knowing we are on the verge of more, fills me completely, obliterating my senses.

As Rod's pace quickens, his climax imminent, Hank bursts into the room.

———

GRANDMA BETTY: I HAD THE WEIRDEST EXPERIENCE JUST NOW. MY FRIEND, SHERRI LYN, WAS GIVING ME A READING. SHE FANCIES HERSELF A PSYCHIC, BUT BETWEEN YOU, ME AND THE FENCEPOST, I THINK THE EXTENT OF HER *GIFT* IS SHE TOOK SOME QUICKIE INTERNET CLASS. ANYHOO, SHE'S DECIPHERING MY TEA LEAVES WHEN, ALL OF A SUDDEN, SHE JERKS BACK LIKE SHE'S SEEN THE DEVIL HIMSELF! I WAS ABOUT TO ROLL MY EYES, BUT SOMETHING ABOUT HER EXPRESSION

STOPPED ME COLD. WHEN SHE SPIT OUT MY DAUGHTER WAS IN TROUBLE, I CHORTLED AND TOLD HER THAT'D BE A NEAT TRICK, SEEING HOW SHE'S DEAD AND ALL. REALIZING HER MISTAKE, SHE CORRECTED IT TO GRANDDAUGHTER. AS SOON AS SHERRI LYN HOTFOOTED IT OUT OF HERE, I CALLED ADRIENNE, BUT SHE DIDN'T ANSWER. I TRIED HANK NEXT, AND HE DIDN'T PICK UP EITHER. I'M TRYING NOT TO FRET. AFTER ALL, THE LAST TIME I LET SHERRY LYN READ, I FIGURED SHE WAS ABOUT AS WORTHLESS AS GUM ON A BOOT HEEL WHEN SHE CLAIMED A LOVER WAS HEADING MY WAY AND NOTHING HAPPENED.

CHAPTER 51
HANK

I CAN'T FATHOM the scene confronting me. My wife—*my wife* —is letting that douchebag screw her. Nim-fucking-Rod. Dickless wonder Rod. Pansy-ass Rod.

"What the fuck?" My voice thunders throughout the bedroom. In a heartbeat, I descend upon fuckhead and grab him around his neck, squeezing with all my might. He sputters and chokes, and I slam him against the wall. When his knees buckle, I seize his throat, my eyes boring into his. "You are fucking unbelievable, the lowest form of scum on earth."

Wide-eyed, his gaze flits about the room. I have Rod's skinny ass by the balls, almost literally. His slacks and boxers circle his ankles—he hasn't even taken his goddamn shoes off.

The twins erupt in cries, a sound that pierces my heart. I register they're in the nursery but right now, they can wait.

"Hank! Stop it!" Adrienne screams from the bed—*our bed*—as she tugs her clothes into place.

"Fuck you, Adrienne! Or hold up, I guess someone already did!" I glare at her in disgust.

I return my attention to dipshit, who gasps for air. With some measure of pleasure, I ram my knee into his exposed groin. Rod howls and crumples to the floor in an agony I find only vaguely satisfying.

Before I can inflict further damage, Adrienne jumps on my back. "You fucker! Don't hurt him!"

I spin, flinging her off with ease. She hits the carpet with a thud and rolls against the wall. She whimpers, but I can't muster any sympathy—every inch of this is her own pathetic fault. I loom over her. "How long? How long have you been fucking this worthless piece of shit?"

She glares at me, not feigning one iota of remorse. Her lips curve, forming an evil smile. "Months. And you were too stupid to figure it out."

Her words punch me in the gut, and I stare at her like she's a stranger. "I can't believe you're the mother of my children."

Rod groans and staggers to his feet, grasping his trousers, attempting to cover his shriveled dick. He glowers at me. Wait, is he trying to make a move? Behold, Homo sapien moronica.

I advance and his pants gravitate back toward the floor. "Please, asshole. Make my day—give me your best shot." How's that for encouraging and supportive?

"Rod, don't!" Adrienne warns.

Hostility emanates from the pantless wonder in waves. NimRod swings, but like the mighty Casey at bat, he comes up with a big miss as I dodge it with ease. What a lame-ass, just like I always thought. I doubt he's ever thrown a punch in his entire pussyfied life.

I clock him hard in the jaw with my right and follow it up with a low left hook to the liver. As he falls, my wife flies at me, pummeling me with her fists. They remind me of mosquitoes, a nuisance to flick away.

I grab her wrists mid-flail and bend them, forcing her to kneel. "I told you once before never to attack me. If you don't want to end up like your limp-dicked boyfriend here, I suggest you back the fuck off!"

"I'm calling the police! I can't believe you're battering your wife, you coward!"

What a joke. "Don't forget to tell them you were fucking the neighbor. And better call Tami while you're at it and break the good news to her, too."

Rod moans.

Adrienne stands, hands fisted at her sides, spewing venom from the same brown eyes that roped me into this mess in the first place. "I hate you! In fact, I've *never* loved you!"

I shake my head, unable to comprehend this version of my wife, a completely different one than twenty-four hours ago, and miles away from the girl at the beach.

She glances at dipshit, now a crumpled shell on the carpet, his pants still bunched around his ankles, and shakes her head. "You're a real cocksucker, Hank!"

"I only see one of those in this room. Unless Rod swings both ways."

Adrienne shoots eye daggers. "You're crazy. And violent. And dangerous!" she screams, octaves above the twins' cries and the crazed, incessant barks from Diesel. She darts to the dresser, throws open the top right drawer, and with a shaky hand, points my pistol at me.

"What the hell are you doing?" I say evenly, hiding how startled I am.

She shakes her head, hate spewing from her eyes. "We're through motherfucker! Get the fuck out."

I take one tentative step in her direction, hand outstretched. "Give me the gun."

"Adrienne…" Rod croaks.

Adrienne's head swivels toward limpdick and I lunge and grab my 1911. I don't keep it loaded, but I have clearly underestimated my wife in vast proportion. She may have found the ammo in the closet. Maybe she's ready to kill me and run off with dipshit. She slaps my head and pummels me with her tiny fists. I swiftly holster the pistol in the back of my jeans and pin her arms to her sides. It only escalates the fury she's directing my way. I shove her onto the bed to put space between us. She flips on all fours and scrambles for the phone, punching in 911.

Through the roaring in my head, I force myself to focus. I better bolt. Slamming the door to the bedroom and hearing my life shattering behind me, I hesitate only a second as I streak past the closed door to the room holding my crying babies and crazed dog before storming out of the house.

———

MRS. KINCAID: WHEN THE POLICE CAME, SIRENS BLARING, AND WHIPPED UP IN FRONT OF THE MCCALLISTER'S, I WONDERED WHAT IN THE SAM HILL WAS GOING ON. AT FIRST, I ASSUMED IT WAS A MEDICAL EMERGENCY. GOD FORBID, ONE OF THE TWINS. NOW THE RUMOR IS DOMESTIC VIOLENCE. I CAN'T IMAGINE HANK AS A WIFE BEATER. IT JUST GOES TO SHOW YOU NEVER CAN TELL ABOUT FOLKS.

CHAPTER 52
ADRIENNE

MY CHEST HEAVES WITH EXERTION, my heart rate like machine gun fire as I attempt to answer the dispatcher through labored breaths. The angry chorus from Tanner, Cassidy and Diesel echo throughout the house. Why are they asking me all these fucking questions instead of getting here? I can't think straight.

"Uh…a Dodge something or other. Black…and jacked-up," I say in response to what Hank drives.

Rod, still prone on the floor, struggles to pull on his clothes, further indignity to the events that have transpired. His normally prominent cock is flaccid and withered—not a pretty sight. Revulsion ripples down my spine, followed by guilt. I should be helping him.

The dispatcher asks if Hank is armed. "Yes! He has a gun! He threatened me with it."

The twins shriek in a new key, and I'm on my last nerve, tethered to this phone via its cord and dealing with nothing short of a nightmare. "Look, I need to take care of my babies. Can you please send help...*now*?"

The male dispatcher rattles off instructions and finally lets me hang up. I move to Rod's side. "Are you all right?"

He stares at me with a fathomless expression, discoloration materializing on his face from Hank's handiwork.

"Can I help you?"

"No," he says tersely. "Get your children."

Giving him a long, lingering stare, I hurry from the room. When I push open the nursery door, Diesel leaps out, almost knocking me over. "I'm here, I'm here. Everything is fine," I say to Tanner and Cassidy, even though it most certainly is not.

Tires screech in front of the house and I freeze. Is Hank back? I haven't locked the door yet, as instructed. The phone jangles. Howls erupt from the dog. A new flood of adrenaline pushes me into the kitchen as I snatch the telephone from its cradle. A female informs me the police have arrived. My nerves raw and exposed, I exhale in relief.

I hustle back to the nursery. Diesel practically mows me over as he runs out the door. Pain thuds in my back as I pluck the overwrought twins from their crib—all from my husband throwing me against the ground like a sack of garbage. Venom swirls through my thoughts as I rush to the front and finagle the door open, no small feat with the crying cargo fastened in my arms and a frantic dog at my feet. Two squad cars flash red and blue lights, one in the driveway and the other in the street. Our busybody neighbors must be getting the gossip fix of their lives.

The officers approach as I jostle the twins to calm their cries. I'm sure they need bottles and clean diapers, but I can't do anything but hold them.

"I'm Sergeant Trainor," the imposing male says, "and this is Officer Gant. We're responding to a call about a domestic dispute."

"Thank God you're here." I step back to allow them entry.

Officer Gant's height matches mine, but she carries more weight around the midsection, the constricting uniform and bulletproof vest only adding layers. Her flawless obsidian skin shines and her matching hair is pulled into a tight, no-nonsense bun at the base of her cap. Sergeant Trainor towers over us, and gray hairs fleck his mustache despite him not looking past fifty. It's impossible to ignore a pink, amoeba-shaped birthmark on his cheek.

They run through the same initial questions as dispatch. I repeat my name, confirm Hank is not on the premises and reiterate that he's armed. I throw in he also owns lots of knives. The babies' cries peter out, long enough for me to hear myself think.

"He brandished the weapon?" the sergeant asks.

"Yes! And then he took it with him!"

"Did he fire the gun?"

"No."

"Are you alone in the house, Mrs. McCallister?"

"Uh, no. A…friend, who my husband attacked, is here." Backlogged tears began to fall as the full weight of the past hour seeps in.

"Where, specifically?"

"In the back bedroom," I choke out.

"Is he armed?"

"What? Of course not. Hank assaulted *him*!" My arms ache from holding my two babies.

"Do either of you require medical assistance?"

Performing a quick mental assessment, I wonder how to work this to my advantage. "My back hurts. My husband threw me across the room. I'm not sure what else…in all the commotion, I haven't had time to think about myself. Rod's injuries are worse. Oh, God. He might need an ambulance." I grimace, rewinding the violence in my mind.

The sergeant cautiously proceeds to the bedroom. Officer Gant stays with me but shifts her position to the hallway, maintaining a line of sight to her partner.

"Can you give me a moment to feed and diaper my babies?"

She nods. "Any other children here?"

I shake my head. "Just the twins."

I change their soiled diapers on the carpeted floor and prop them on the couch. Officer Gant follows me into the kitchen while I prepare bottles of formula. Her apparent distrust irks me. I'm not the maniac here. She remarks how cute my babies are and marvels how difficult parenting two must be, so at least she's somewhat empathetic.

We return to the living room, and I feed Tanner and Cassidy. They drink with gusto, their loud sucking punctuating the silence. I place one hand on each of their legs to ground me. Officer Gant perches on a chair and resumes her questioning. Poised with a small spiral notepad, she asks me to explain what occurred.

"It all started yesterday, when Hank punched a hole in the hallway. We had a fight, and he didn't come home. I was scared, unsure what he planned to do when he returned. Rod stopped by to check on me and find out why I was upset."

"And who is Rod?"

"A neighbor. Our two families are friends, we spend time together."

The officer scribbles in her book.

"I didn't want to wake the babies," I continue, "so Rod and I were in the bedroom, talking quietly. I was honest with him about my husband being a raging lunatic. After Hank punched a hole in the wall—and I really think he meant to hit me, because he did it inches from my head—I started thinking about leaving him. We're in danger. He's unpredictable and violent, officer." I wipe my palms on my yoga pants.

"Then what happened?"

"Hank came home, found—"

"What time?"

I try and rewind. "Nine? When he found us in the bedroom, he jumped to conclusions and went ballistic."

"When you say, 'conclusions,' what do you mean?"

"He assumed something…but it doesn't matter. What matters is he began punching and kicking Rod, and when I tried to stop him, he threw me across the room. I landed hard and slammed into the wall. He kept going after Rod, hitting him several times. I attempted to stop him again, and he grabbed my hands, crushed them and forced me to the floor." I pantomime the action. "I don't remember all the details, but you see how short I am. Hank is much bigger and stronger than me. And Rod, by this time, was completely incapacitated. I got away long enough to call 911. That's when my husband left in an all-fire hurry."

"When did Mr. McCallister brandish the weapon?"

"Toward the end."

"Did he say anything? Threaten to kill you or the other party?"

"I can't remember, but a gun pointed at me feels pretty fucking threatening."

"Let's back up a moment. You stated you were physical with Mr. McCallister first, correct?"

Huh? "Well, um, I guess, but only in response to him beating up Rod. And like I said, I'm far smaller than Hank, so he easily thwarted my efforts."

"Have you had previous physical confrontations with your husband, Mrs. McCallister?"

"He's never physically abused me before today, but he's been violent *near* me, which is just as frightening. And I've lost count of the times he's been verbally abusive, it's so frequent."

"Are you in fear for your life, regarding Mr. McCallister?"

"Yes! And for my babies' lives, too. They shouldn't be subjected to his abuse."

Officer Gant asks for Hank's full name, date of birth and criminal history. She requests an insurance bill to determine his truck's VIN and tag number, but I have no clue where Hank stores such paperwork. He pays all the bills.

She moves onto other identifying attributes. "Can you describe what Mr. McCallister was wearing when he left?"

My head throbs with the effort. "Blue jeans and cowboy boots. He wears Tony Lamas, and he's ridiculous about polishing the leather, once a week without fail. I think he had on one of his Crazy Horse shirts. He used to work there as a bouncer. Oh my God...you should talk to his old boss. He fired Hank for excessive violence." Nice touch, Adrienne!

"Does your husband have any definable characteristics or markings, such as tattoos, rings, etc.?"

"He's got a walrus mustache, crooked nose and chipped tooth. No tats. He wears a solid gold wedding band. And it's a sure bet he's listening to hick country music, wherever the hell he is."

"Anything else you can think of?"

"He sneezes constantly. I've never met a person who—"

"Please focus on identifying attributes."

Her tone irritates me. "He has stickers on his truck's rear-view window. One says, 'Don't mess with Texas' and another is a Dodge thing...'If you can't Dodge it, Ram it' or something stupid like that. There's a couple of brand logos too, I think."

She brings out a camera and asks to inspect my wounds, but upon examination, reports nothing visible on my wrists or back.

Sergeant Trainor returns with Rod, lurching along at a gingerly pace. He instructs us to wait while he confers with Officer Gant. I smile with forced politeness. The pair recedes into the kitchen, staying within sight but preventing me from eavesdropping on their conversation.

Once the officers are out of earshot, I whisper, "Well? What happened? Did he question you?"

He shrugs his hands. "Of course."

"What did you say?" He better not have blown this—we didn't have time to sync our stories before the cops arrived.

"As little as possible."

"Did you tell him we'd been...?" I make a hole out of my left thumb and forefinger and stick my right index finger in and out of it a few times, the universal sign for screwing.

He nods. He fingers the outside of his bruised jaw, causing him to wince.

"Fuuuuuuuuuuuuuuuuck," I hiss. "Why did you do that?"

"Why the hell else would Hank have attacked me? It's the only plausible reason, Adrienne. Why…did you lie about it?" His eyes bug out.

"Yes," I hiss again. "I thought you were smart enough to do the same! You're usually an adept liar." My glare says it all. "I told her we were friends, and you were consoling me because Hank's a violent jerk."

"I can't believe what your asshole husband did to me, and I bet he's already called Tami." His eyes water. I think he's close to tears.

"Pull it together, Rod. We've got to deal with this situation here. I'm hoping to file for a restraining order, and you can press assault charges."

He stares at the ceiling. "I'm not sure what I'm doing."

Unbelievable! Perhaps Rod and his dick aren't man enough for my needs. Why can't I find the male version of myself, only devoted and faithful? A smidgeon of sympathy kicks in. He did just get his ass handed to him by cowboy Hank, and right on the verge of an orgasm.

I stand and touch his arm. "Oh, baby. We'll work this all out, I promise. I'm so sorry this happened. You're a good man."

"No," he blubbers, "I'm not."

The officers return. "It appears we have a discrepancy," the sergeant says, his expression stoic. "Both of you, please take a seat on the couch so we can run through the details again."

Christ almighty.

He asks Rod to provide his version of the story first. Inwardly, I seethe at his compliance. I'm no dummy—now I'm forced to come clean or trap myself in a lie. When it's my turn, I backpedal, admitting Rod's consoling had turned intimate, weaving a heartfelt victim narrative in the process. I admit I avoided telling the truth the first time, scared of coloring the true crime in question. The pair scratch on their little notepads the entire time.

"Mr. Mason, did you witness what transpired with regard to the gun?"

Rod pauses and stares down at his lap. "I'm not sure," he hedges.

Atta boy.

"Did you see Mr. McCallister with the weapon?"

"Yes. I believe he took it with him."

"But he didn't point the weapon at you?"

He gives his head a small shake. "No, officer. The details are… murky." He shrugs, his shoulders slumping lower than before. "I wasn't in the best shape."

That's because he kicked your ass six ways to Sunday.

Sergeant Trainor sheaths his pad. "Right now, based on the information you've provided, we have enough probable cause to obtain an assault warrant against Mr. McCallister as the primary physical aggressor." He directs his attention to me. "In light of your fear of Mr. McCallister returning and the situation with having two babies in the home, you can file for an Emergency Protective Order."

Relief floods my body. "What does that do?"

"An EPO provides immediate protection by preventing your husband from contacting you for seventy-two hours. This gives you time to petition the court for a Protective Order, should you want to pursue one. Also, we strongly counsel you to leave this location and stay in a place where you'll be safe, in the event Mr. McCallister returns and things escalate. Perhaps a relative?"

I nod. That seems smart.

"We're issuing a BOLO for Mr. McCallister's truck, based on the information you provided," the sergeant continues.

"What happens when you find him?"

"Assuming we do, if he's still in the area, he'll be arrested. Based on your statement, you've met the threshold for probable cause of misdemeanor assault. But we will continue to investigate this matter to corroborate our findings."

To what extent would they go and what would they uncover?

I shove those thoughts aside. My asshole husband is about to be slapped with a warrant. "So, wherever he is, you can locate him by his truck?"

"If he's still driving it. But as this is a misdemeanor charge, this will be a non-extradition warrant."

"Meaning?"

The sergeant adjusts his vest. "Unless he's in Virginia, we won't be able to act until he returns. If he's found in another state, they'll call it in, but we won't extradite him."

"But he could be on his way to Texas by now!" Or lurking, waiting to come back. That slither down my spine reappears as Hank's angry face looms in my mind.

"Rest assured, Mrs. McCallister, we will do everything in our power to find him. As for you, Mr. Mason, you have refused medical transport and attention, although we advise you seek it. It's up to you to file formal assault charges as the evidence against Mr. McCallister is circumstantial. It's your word against his, and he's not here to represent himself."

"But I saw the entire thing, and I told you what happened!" I gesture at Rod with my outstretched arm. "Look at him!"

"I understand, Mrs. McCallister, but based on the situation with you and Mr. Mason, you're not a reliable eyewitness. Mr. Mason must prove beyond a reasonable doubt his injuries were sustained by Mr. McCallister in a court of law."

"That's ridiculous." What a bunch of legal mumbo jumbo.

"You're going to press charges, right?" I say to Rod. "Hank should go to jail."

Rod ignores me and speaks to the officers. "I understand. Thank you."

"But I have a case?" If I've got to put my husband in the slammer by myself, so be it. Screw weak-ass Rod.

"You'll also have to prove your case in court."

What a load of crap.

Sergeant Trainor reiterates his report, my next steps and safety precautions to take, and encourages me to relocate to a safe place, other than Mr. Mason's. The officers leave, and I lean against the door with a heavy sigh. Rod stands, his swollen face broadcasting a mask of bleak sadness. We hug and he strokes my hair.

Kissing my cheek, he murmurs, "Call you later."

"Where are you going?"

"Home."

He exits, and the prison I've erected around myself engulfs me.

———

SERGEANT TRAINOR: IT'S CLEAR MRS. MCCALLISTER IS LYING. I'VE SEEN THIS SCENARIO THOUSANDS OF TIMES. MY HUNCH IS SHE'S BEEN BANGING THAT GUY FOR A WHILE, AND THEY GOT CAUGHT. THE NEIGHBORS CORROBORATED SEEING MASON'S VEHICLE IN THEIR DRIVEWAY ON NUMEROUS OCCASIONS. IF IT WERE ME, AND I'D WALKED IN ON SOME MAN GETTING IT ON WITH MY WIFE, I WOULD HAVE TUNED HIM UP TOO. THE NEIGHBORS ALSO DON'T THINK HIGHLY OF THE WIFE BUT FAVOR THE HUSBAND. SOMETHING DOESN'T ADD UP, BUT WITH SO MUCH HAPPENING BEHIND CLOSED DOORS, WE MAY NEVER FIND OUT THE TRUTH.

CHAPTER 53
HANK

I REEL at the avalanche consuming me in waves, but I push that shit aside because I need to get scarce, and fast. Since my two-timing, whore-bitch wife called the cops, I'm sure my truck has a bullseye on it. My best bet is to hightail it to West Virginia. No way the West-By-God boys number as high as these ticket-happy Virginia cats. From there, I can drive straight through to Kentucky and on to Sweetwater. It's the only plan I have.

Once I'm on I-66 west, I connect with Monica, explaining tersely I have a personal emergency and will need a few days or more off work to straighten it out. She presses for details, but I cut things short. I'm sure I sound like a dick, but it's the least of my worries. I dread my next call, but it's got to be done.

Tami answers, buoyant and convivial as always. "To what do I owe this unexpected pleasure?"

Shit. "Tami, I…" How to even say this?

"Oh no, I can hear it in your voice. What's wrong?"

"I'm…fuck."

"Are the twins okay? Adrienne?"

Rip off the fucking bandage and just say it. "I'm so sorry to have to tell you this, especially over the goddamn phone, but Rod and Adrienne are having an affair." It takes all my restraint not to say *fucking each other*. Affair sounds way too clean.

"What?"

I hear the disbelief, and the full weight of shattering her world sits on my shoulders. "It's true. I wish it weren't, but—"

"How do you know?"

I clear my throat, willing my own emotions to take a back seat. "I walked in on them going at it." Remembering makes me want to punch a hole in my dash.

She cries out, a sharp, quick exhalation of pain.

"There's more."

Her breath comes in gasps, and I give her time. "What do you mean? What happened?"

"I went fucking apeshit. And I…well, Rod's in bad shape."

"How bad?" she whispers.

"Not sure. He might be on his way to the hospital." My knuckles, raw from the encounter, hang on the steering wheel. Not that I wouldn't do it all over again to the motherfucker.

She sobs, and I feel like the biggest shit-heel in the world. Except I shouldn't. Only two fuckheads are to blame for this disaster.

"I'm sorry, Tami. You don't deserve this."

"You don't either, Hank," she chokes out, followed by more muffled sobs.

She's breaking down and I'm clueless about what to do, so I hold tight.

"Where are you?" she finally asks.

"On the road. Adrienne called the police, so I'm sure I'm a wanted man." I'm grateful the day stretches ahead, as plenty of black pickups should be on the highway helping me blend in. I need to put hundreds of miles between me and The Commonwealth—and pronto. Passing a billboard with the state slogan *Virginia is for lovers*, I wince as if kidney punched.

"But they're the ones at fault!"

"Goddamn right. But the assault and battery are on me."

"I'm...speechless." She sniffles. "Did you...did you suspect this at all?"

"Not in the slightest. And I must be a total moron because she said some horrible stuff." I'm not sure how much to divulge—and only to spare her, not the other two shitheads.

"Like what?"

Deep breath. "Apparently, they've been at it for months. Told me I was too stupid to figure it out."

An injured cry leaves Tami's lips.

"Damn it! I'm making everything worse. I'm sorry."

"I had a bad feeling...recently," she admits. "Something happened here, and it didn't make sense. I was so angry with them both—"

"What do you mean?" Fresh adrenaline surges through my blood.

"Adrienne was here. Back when she was asking about babysitters, remember?"

"Yup."

"Rod was home, and I went to store to buy formula, no... diapers, because we were out. My husband couldn't go...some work thing, and I didn't want to leave Adrienne, but she urged me to go. Christ, now I know why," she says, her tone bitter. "I was gone no more than forty-five minutes and when I returned, Lexi was bleeding on her face. And neither Rod nor your wife had any idea how it happened. I had to ask myself how they could miss it if they were watching the kids. Right?"

I state the obvious. "They weren't watching the kids."

"It never set well with me. And I hate to say it but," she sniffles, "my husband is prone to being on the shallow side."

I huff out some air. "They're both lying, cheating assholes."

"Jesus, Hank...what are we going to do?"

"I don't know. I need to think. But listen, you call me anytime, day or night, okay?"

"'Kay. You, too." Tami says, despondent. "Thank you...for telling me."

"I'm so damn sorry."

"Me, too. And Hank?"

"Yeah?"

"Be safe."

I mumble a goodbye and drop the phone, unable to contain the careful control I've held over my fury another second. Like a blowout of crude oil, a geyser of pain and anger spews forth. I growl into the cab, a deafening sound, as my heart shatters into a million shards.

———

Mrs. Brown: I told the police officer I suspected hanky-panky between the wife and accountant. What with her running around half-naked and CPA MAN stopping in while Hank's at work...you don't need to be Matlock to figure that one out.

CHAPTER 54
ADRIENNE

OUTRAGE and frenetic energy fuel my every move as I spring into action. First, I call my grandmother and without going into detail, arrange for us to stay with her. Next I throw disorganized heaps of clothing into overnight bags and scurry about gathering other essentials, unsure how long we'll be in hiding from my maniacal, violent, soon-to-be ex-husband.

I impose upon the nosy Mrs. Kincaid to babysit for an hour or two. At first, I deflect her probing questions but, recognizing having her on my side is an asset, I exaggerate the assault to the hilt. Holding her rapt attention is child's play. Of course, I omit the part about screwing Rod, maintaining our friendship is platonic with a capital P. As I convey my urgency to file an Emergency Protective Order, her hand flies to her mouth, properly aghast.

At the police station, I swear out the EPO in front of the magistrate. I've even convinced myself of the story now in my head. The words Emergency Protective Order jump from the page. Oh, the power of holding this piece of paper in my hand! I snap a photo of it with my phone and place the document in my purse for safekeeping.

How is Rod faring? Does Tami know yet? Right...as if Hank wouldn't call her. He probably couldn't wait to tell her. How long before the ugly texts and calls come my way? Whatever. Rod's lack of resolve concerns me more. My plan involves us forging a life together, and it's no longer clear if he shares the same vision. I flash on the pitiful image of him crumpled on the floor and his reluctance to file assault charges. He's lost my respect in the past four hours, but not enough to bail.

After entering our neighborhood, I do several drive-bys until I'm certain Hank's not lurking. He's no dummy, but neither am I, and I can't afford to underestimate him.

With my heart flip-flopping like a gymnast, I run inside, grab our bags and cram everything in the car. Once I retrieve the twins, I latch them in their baby carriers. That leaves one other passenger: Diesel. His incessant barks stop when he spies the leash and allows me to clip it to his collar. Stupid dog. *I've got special plans for you, mutt.* I herd him to the back of the minivan, and he leaps into the remaining space in the cargo area.

In line at the drive-thru, I text dear hubby a copy of the EPO with one word:

Asshole.

Large coffee in hand, I head toward Pamplin, the godforsaken town I inevitably find myself running to whenever the shit hits the fan.

The twins suck on pacifiers as cloying Disney tunes lull them asleep in short order. No surprise after the trauma they've endured. I turn off the noise and chain-smoke, reliving the ordeal. Hank is an ogre. *Sayonara, fuckface!* Focusing on the future, I realize the stakes are high: me, the kids, our whole way of life. Divorce, attorneys and court dates loom. I will make my husband pay dearly, the sonofabitch. I hope I won't do it alone, but that requires Rod to find his balls and leave Tami.

Three hours later, we arrive in Dillwyn, another podunk town in the middle of nowhere—which describes most of south-central Virginia. Time to do something long overdue. I peel off US Route 15 and take a few turns down a winding side road. When I'm far enough off the main drag with no houses in sight—just tall oaks flanking both sides of the street—I pull over on the dirt shoulder and shift the car into park, leaving the engine running.

I walk to the rear of the vehicle and release the back hatch. Diesel springs out, panting and eyeing me in his irritating way, as if thinking, *why do I have to tolerate you?* I remove his leash and collar and toss them back in the van.

"Have a nice life, buddy—and good fucking riddance," I singsong. This stupid dog has caused me nothing but grief from day one. Gleefully, I turn on my heel and climb back into the driver's seat.

Diesel cocks his head, runs to my window and barks. I gun it, kicking up a dust cloud and hauling ass until he's no longer visible in my rearview.

ROD: TAMI'S TORTURED, ANGRY, BEWILDERED FACE IS AN IMAGE I'LL NEVER UN-SEE. I'M THE REASON FOR THAT FACE, AND SHE DOESN'T DESERVE ANY OF THIS. I LOVE MY WIFE, BUT I'VE NEVER BEEN FAITHFUL TO HER, EVEN BEFORE WE MARRIED. IT'S NOT HER. SHE'S AMAZING, BEAUTIFUL, SMART. I JUST GET...BORED. AND SO MANY LUSCIOUS, HOT, WILLING WOMEN ARE EAGER TO JUMP IN THE SACK. I CAN'T RESIST. BUT I'VE NEVER THOUGHT, NOT ONCE, ABOUT LEAVING TAMI.

CHAPTER 55
HANK

THE TEXT ARRIVES minutes after I cross into Kentucky. Fucking whoredog. She screws NimRod in our bed and then has the nerve to file an Emergency Protective Order on my ass? I only touched her in response to her attacking me. How am I the bad guy in all of this? The vein in my neck throbs as murderous thoughts bubble like molten lava, erupting and spewing forth. The minuscule amount of calm I'd achieved since fleeing Virginia evaporates.

With all confidence, I assume the police are searching for me. Did they issue an all-points bulletin? Am I now a person of fucking interest? If I'm arrested before making it to Texas, I'm screwed, more so with my pistol in tow. I can only imagine what BS she told the cops about that. And it's not loaded, but I'm still shocked Adrienne drew the sucker out and pointed it at me. Would she have *actually* pulled the trigger? Does she wish I were dead? I smack my hand against the steering wheel hard. Glancing at my watch, I should hit Sweetwater in seventeen hours. I pray —again—the law and I don't intersect.

The regrets sting deep. I can't think about Cassidy and Tanner without wanting to puke, so I convince myself they're safe with their lying cunt of a mother. Diesel's another story. Not only does he belong by my side…but *how* could I leave him in the hands of that hateful bitch?

Everything happened so fast. I panicked. Now my family is in the care of a woman I can't profess to know or trust.

I gotta call my folks but cringe, already hearing my mother's acrimony. Then again, once that she-bear is set in motion, watch out. There ain't no better person to have on your side than Henrietta McCallister.

I make the call.

My parents respond with shock, indignation, remorse and worry—about me, the kids, the future. They bombard me with questions, for which I have few answers. We end with my mother raring to contact the family attorney and my father making me promise to stay safe, avoid speeding and hasten my ass to Texas.

I continue my route southwest on I-40, fueled by resentment, Red Bulls and the occasional fast-food meal, which I can't keep down, so I quit trying. Small towns and iconic cities pass as I drift through Kentucky, Tennessee and Arkansas, watching day turn to night turn to day again. I'm fried, but afraid to stop and sleep.

Bleary eyed, I cross the state line into Texas. I've never been so happy to see Texarkana in my life. I'm still six hours from the ranch but reinvigorated by the end coming into sight. I've got to get my moving target of a truck off the highway ASAP, and I damn sure need more coffee.

I roll down the window to let the warm air blow me awake. Even at pitch-black-three-in-the-morning, I sense the soothing landscape of my native state. Maybe that's why my guard slips. Thoughts and images swarm likes bees from an upset hive, jumbling together the best and worst of times with Adrienne. I'd mostly drowned them out, but too tired to fight, the memories descend, stinging me mercilessly until I howl into the night like an injured animal.

———

Henrietta McCallister: I knew this day would come. And I will string that lying, cheating hussy up by her twat hairs and make her pay.

CHAPTER 56
ADRIENNE

SAFELY ENSCONCED at Grandma Betty's, we settle in the kitchen with steaming cups of coffee. The twins play on a nearby activity blanket, content and sucking on their pacifiers.

She pats my hand across the dinette. "Sweetie, what happened?"

"The short answer is Hank went bananas." I close my eyes for a moment and shake my head. "Rod and I were talking this morning…at the house. Hank wasn't there. In fact, he never came home the night before." God, was it only last night?

"Why not?"

"We had a fight, a bad one. But he's never stayed away like that, and it worried the heck out of me, even though I was still plenty mad."

"Why was Rod at your house?"

I sip my coffee and wave my hand. "We're neighbors. I was upset, and he stopped to check on me."

The quirks her head. "How odd. You're better friends with his wife, aren't you?"

My grandmother is so old-fashioned. "We're all friends. I'm

sure Tami was home with the baby, so Rod checked in on his way to work. It's no biggie."

"Hmm," Grandma Betty says, looking unconvinced. "Then Hank returned?"

I nod.

"What happened?"

"Hank started yelling and beating Rod."

"For just talking to you?"

I resent her judgy implications. "He's a jealous jerk."

"Can't blame him for being suspicious. It's not proper for a man to come calling without his wife present."

I tap my foot against the linoleum floor and fight back a comment. "Hank jumped to conclusions, like he always does. He didn't ask one question. He went straight to assaulting Rod."

"Oh, dear."

"I tried to stop my husband and you can imagine how well that worked."

Grandma Betty gasps. "He's twice your size! What did you do?"

"I leaped on his back, and he threw me off." I wrap myself in my arms.

Another gasp. I have her sympathy now.

"It hurt so much when I smashed into the wall. But I got back up and hit him with my fists. None of it mattered. He dispensed with me like a rag doll." I turn on the waterworks, letting some tears flow.

My grandmother blanches, pushing a box of tissues toward me. I take one and dab at my eyes.

"How's the neighbor fella?"

"Bad." I wince at the memory and wonder if Rod went to the hospital. "I should check on him."

"How did it end?"

"As soon as I called the cops, Hank fled, knowing he'd be arrested, the coward."

Her hands fly to her cheeks. "This is all so terrible. What did the police say?"

"They're filing a report. And they've got law enforcement across the country searching for Hank's truck right now. I hope they arrest his ass."

Grandma Betty makes another anguished sound as her tears flow. Now she's reaching for the tissues. "Oh, sugar."

My eyes bulge. "You're not feeling sorry for him, are you?"

She shrugs ever so slightly. "I'm heartbroken for both of you. What a mess."

"I filed an Emergency Protective Order so he can't contact me or the babies for seventy-two hours. But the police thought I should stay away from the house for at least as long."

"Are you worried Hank will try and hurt you?"

"Of course. He's a violent maniac!"

She sobs, blotting tears with a tissue, and says, "Does this mean you kids are getting a divorce?"

I set my cup down so hard it clatters. "Have you heard a word I've said?"

"It's just...you two were so great together. Hank loves you. I thought you loved him."

My mouth gapes. I try to speak but no words present themselves. I'm so irritated with my grandmother, I want to bite her head off. "We did love each other, but I won't tolerate violence, for me or the twins. Been there, done that, remember?"

"But the babies..."

"They're better off without a father like him. Jesus, Gran, you're kind of blowing my mind. Whose side are you on?"

She wipes her face again and honks into a tissue. "I'm always in your corner, honey. But these situations aren't necessarily black and white. You've got two tiny young'uns and no job. How will you manage?"

"Pshh. Hank will pay through the nose for our pain and suffering. I'll make sure of it."

—

GRANDMA BETTY: IT'S NOT A QUESTION OF WHETHER I BELIEVE HER. OH, HORSEFEATHERS! THAT'S PRECISELY THE PROBLEM. THERE'S ALWAYS MORE TO THE STORY WITH ADRI, AND SHE'S A SKILLED STORYTELLER—STEERING IT IN HER FAVOR. I'M NOT CONDONING VIOLENCE OF ANY KIND, BUT WITHOUT KNOWING WHAT OCCURRED, I CAN'T BURN HANK AT THE STAKE QUITE YET.

CHAPTER 57
HANK

MY EYES OPEN AND, for a disorienting second, my mind is blank. Then the wall of pain body slams me. I squint at the clock but have no idea if it's night or day. I barely remember arriving at the ranch or staggering off to bed. I heave myself up and pull aside the curtain. Evening but not twilight, the light casts a dull glow across the landscape. A bundle of neatly stacked clothes sits on the chair in the corner. My mother's doing, I'm sure.

Under a hot blast of water, I rinse off the last thirty-six hours, the ache in my heart spreading to every inch of my skin. I stand motionless, one hand propped against the shower tiles as my head hangs, stunned at the sudden twist my life has taken. I swallow hard to dislodge the tightness in my chest but can't stave off the grief threatening to devour me whole. Sliding to the floor, the pelting stream commingles with the flood of my tears, swirling together down the drain.

"Hank?" My father says through the bathroom door.

I can't stop sobbing, let alone answer.

"Son, you all right?"

I try to speak but only manage a muffled wail.

My father flings open the door. The water flow ceases, and a thick towel is placed around me as I struggle to gain control. I blubber and gasp, unable to breathe.

My father's reassuring hands press onto my shoulders. "I'm here, son. I'm here."

I sob harder.

The minutes tick by.

I take a few deep breaths, stemming the tide, and wipe my face, regaining my composure.

"Up you go." My father offers a hand, and I clasp it. Despite outweighing him, my dad is still as strong as ever. He pulls me to standing and shepherds me into the bedroom.

I wrap the towel around my midsection and sit on the bed. "Thanks, Pop."

He joins me, his hand finding a spot on my back. "I understand this is tough, son, but we're here to help you through this."

I nod a fraction of an inch.

"Let's get a meal in you. Pull yourself together and come eat supper."

I can't imagine eating anything or keeping it down, but I'll try. "Anyone here?" I'm not ready to face my siblings or their pity.

"Only Wyatt. We asked everyone to give you some room, but you know your brother. A bulldozer couldn't drag him away. He's worried about you."

I glance at my father, blowing out an audible breath. "Thanks."

He stands and kisses the top of my head, something he hasn't done since middle school, and quietly exits. More tears trickle down my cheeks and I blot them with my towel. I find my old sweatpants and a shirt in the clothes stack and don them, their scent reminding me I'm home.

Wyatt avoids his usual wisecracks and draws me in for a crushing embrace. My mother seizes the moment to hug me again as she eyes me with concern.

We convene at the kitchen table, my father making conversation about ranch business while my mother fills our plates. My family can't avoid staring, despite their valiant efforts. I'm sure questions gnaw at them, but I don't have much in the way of answers nor am I ready to speak. I push more food around my plate than I eat.

My mother sets down her utensils and our eyes meet. "Jack Dutton is coming tomorrow. He should be able to guide us with some legal advice."

Us? I grasp my parents are only trying to support me, but I'm in this shitstorm alone. "Thanks for setting it up."

"Do you want to talk about anything now?" my mother prods.

I shake my head. "Not yet."

She doesn't press, and for once, realizes the wisdom of such a choice.

After dinner, Wyatt and I watch *The Searchers*, an old favorite starring John Wayne, and start in on the bourbon. Halfway through the movie, I yuke up my supper and keep right on drinking. I only seek oblivion, and my old pal, Jim Beam, doesn't let me down.

Jack Dutton arrives on time, sporting a mess of new wrinkles and gray hair since the last time I saw him. A rotund man, his waistline is so large he resembles a ripe lemon. He's been our family's attorney from as far back as I can remember, every bit as much friend as counselor over the years. We shake hands and share a backslapping hug before filtering into the dining room. A crumb cake sits at one end with dishes, utensils and napkins—standard Texan hospitality.

Pleasantries aside, it's business time.

"Folks, if you could afford us a little privacy, I'm going to talk to Hank about his current troubles," Mr. Dutton says.

My mother bristles but acquiesces. My father pats my shoulder and follows her out. Mr. Dutton and I sink into opposite chairs.

He asks me to slice him a hunk of cake while he fishes around his briefcase, producing a leather-encased notepad and pen.

"I understand you might need counsel. As I'm familiar with Texas law, I can give you my general opinion, but Virginia laws may be different and likely will be."

"Yes, sir. Thank you."

"Why don't you tell me, to the best of your recollection, what transpired. Be as specific as you can." He inhales a whopping forkful of cake.

I struggle through the retelling, and reliving, of arguably my worst day ever—from the most excruciating part of finding Rod balls-deep in my wife to hightailing it to Texas after Adrienne called the heat. I manage to avoid the waterworks, although they hover, as a headache the size of Dallas presses into my skull.

"Your spouse texted you a copy of the order?"

"Yes, sir." I pull it up on my phone and hand it to him, tamping down my impatience as he reads.

"These family protective orders…they didn't have them when I started practicing law and I haven't seen many of them myself. And this, mind you, is an Emergency Protective Order, which indicates you must steer clear of contacting your wife and children for seventy-two hours from the time it was ordered. This gives her time to file for a Protective Order to be issued for a much broader timeframe if it's found justifiable."

"I don't want that to happen. What about my rights?"

"It depends. If there's a warrant out for your arrest, which I'd say is likely, you're going to have to turn yourself in and plead your case. You'll want to hire a reputable attorney to orchestrate your surrender. I've already investigated this in Virginia, and they arraign people right at the jail before a magistrate. Secure an attorney and bondsman, and you'll be able to focus on resolving this amicably. The firearms issue is sticky. If your wife contends you brandished your pistol or tried to fire it, you could be in a world of trouble, including this kicking up to a federal offense. Where's the gun in question?"

"Here, sir." Like the rest of my arsenal of shotguns and rifles. "In the safe. My 1911 was the only firearm I took to Virginia. It's an heirloom, my grandfather's from the war. I took it for protection only, and never had a cause to use it."

He nods.

"Keep it locked up and away from your person. Do you understand, son?"

"Yes, sir." Not a problem.

"As for the additional protective order, it's best if you're in court when it gets decided, showing you're a caring, decent man. If you're absent, a judge might err on the side of conservatism and award it to her. My recommendation? Be a man, get your tail back to Virginia and handle this."

"Yes, sir." I rub my eyes, the steady throb in my temples worsening.

"Let's talk a little more about what happened. You say your first physical contact with her was when she jumped on your back? And later, she hit you with her fists?"

"That's correct."

Mr. Dutton nods up and down like a bobblehead. "You might be able to charge her with assault, although, based on your testimony, you would be seen as the primary aggressor. Of course, there are extenuating circumstances most would discern. But these are details to pursue with your lawyer."

Talk about turning the tables. I'm somewhat mollified because it's a hell of a lot more accurate. "Yes, sir."

"Concerning the other fellow…are his injuries bad enough for him to press charges?"

I lean my head back, remembering, and snap it forward. "I reckon. The dude's such a pus…pansy, he might cry to the cops. Then again, he's proud, so it could go either way."

"He'll still have to prove the assault was by your hand."

"Won't Adrienne corroborate his statement?"

Mr. Dutton helps himself to another hunk of cake. "In this case, because of the extenuating circumstances, I'm not sure her remarks will be considered, based on the bias. It's your word against his."

Picturing Rod lying on the floor with his pants around his ankles gives me a surge of pleasure. Doubly so if he can't press charges. Scum-sucking douchebag.

Mr. Dutton presses escaped crumbs onto his index finger and swipes them into his mouth. "This may be hard to answer, Hank, but what do you anticipate will happen between you and your spouse from this point?"

I exhale hard, the air ruffling my mustache whiskers. This is the million-dollar question. "I'm not sure."

"Is it your assumption she might want to reconcile or is she gunning for a divorce?"

"She said we were through." Saying the words out loud stabs my heart in fifty places. "But Adrienne can be hotheaded and say things she doesn't mean."

He smiles in a knowing way. "Are you interested in staying married?"

I probably shouldn't be but tell this contraption beating in my chest. "I love her, even though right now I could kill her."

"Let's keep that phraseology to ourselves," Mr. Dutton says.

"I would never harm her. That's not who I am," I clarify. "Did I kick the snot out of Rod? Yes, but I would never hurt my wife or kids." My heart shears in half at the thought of Tanner and Cassidy.

"I believe you, Hank. Now this is simply an observation, mind you, but y'all met and got married in a real hurry, with babies on the way. Here you are, not yet a year into it, and you find her sleeping with the neighbor. Is it possible she's not the gal you think she is?"

"With all due respect, Mr. Dutton, I know my own wife. I'm not saying she doesn't have faults, but up to now, despite some major curveballs, we've been happy." Or have we?

He nods knowingly, and I fight back annoyance.

He's never met her before, so his assumptions come from his

ass. Now I'm questioning who she is. What if she isn't the Adrienne she purports to be? What if everything between us is bullshit lies?

"My point is, if this union is broken, it's smart to have your eyes wide open. You may decide splitting up is a better option for you."

"Yes, sir." I say this to be polite, but a part of me wants to wring his neck.

"To summarize, hire a credible Virginia lawyer in your own county. This person can find out what charges have been pressed against you, arrange for your surrender and represent you to ensure your rights are served properly. Stay away from any firearms, and let's not do anything else stupid, shall we?"

"I understand."

Once Mr. Dutton pulls his belongings together, we stand, and I pump his hand. "Thank you, Mr. Dutton. I appreciate the counsel."

"All the best to you, son."

My parents usher him to the door and return eager for a recap. It's time to ante up, so I do. Partway through, my mother stands and crosses her arms with a smoldering stare.

"What?" I ask.

"I'm so angry, I could kill her with my bare hands."

"Ma, stop. This ain't your fight."

"To hell it isn't. And you can't possibly want to work things out with your sorry excuse for a wife," she spits, her disgust as transparent as the nearby windowpane.

My shoulders slump.

"Hank, you must prepare for the worst. The woman is capable of any—"

"Enough, Ma. I haven't even talked to her yet, for chrissakes. A lot of shit has gone down, and I can't think straight. I love you, but back off and give me a little room, okay?"

She nods tersely and stalks off. I sigh.

My father squeezes my arm. "Be kind to her and yourself. We're all mighty upset."

I drag myself upstairs and flop on my bed. My head throbs and my mother, on the heels of Mr. Dutton, has kickstarted my anger meter. She knows exactly how to push the buttons she'd installed at birth. Dragging my ass to the bathroom, I swallow a handful of over-the-counter painkillers, strip to my skivvies and collapse back on the mattress. Closing my eyes, my thoughts swim with visions of the first night I met Adrienne. Fatigue overtakes me and I crash into the welcome blackout of sleep.

My phone vibrates on the nightstand, startling me awake. Through bleary eyes, I register Tami's calling.

"Did I wake you?"

I roll on my side. "Mmm hmm."

"I'm sorry. Want to talk later?"

"Now's fine." Swiping away crusty sleep granules, I blink to clear my vision. "How are you?"

"I've been better." Her voice wavers.

"Did you speak to…" I can't bring myself to say the fucktard's name.

"Rod?" She laughs, a mirthless sound. "He showed up shortly after you called."

"What happened?" I bolt upright, the first inklings of adrenaline spiking.

"I said a few choice words and told him to get the hell out."

She has more balls than I'd given her credit for. "Good for you, Tami."

"I also asked him why. It's baffling. I thought we loved each other."

"What did fu…he say?"

She scoffs. "He hasn't a clue what makes him do it. But claims he loves me and can't live without me. Like I would believe anything his lying ass would say!"

"What utter bullshit—If he doesn't know, who the fuck does? Be a grown fucking man."

"Exactly. Have you talked to Adrienne?"

"Not yet. She took out an Emergency Protective Order. Not supposed to contact her for seventy-two hours, legally."

Tami whistles. "She's a real piece of work. You okay?"

"Nope. You?"

"I'm devastated. Propelled by anger, mostly, but also sorrow. My daughter keeps me going. For her sake, I'm coping."

Angst torpedoes my chest again, thinking about the twins. I need to hold them in my arms. I need my dog by my side. And God help me, I still need Adrienne. Only all is lost…and partially my fault. The tsunami knocks against my skull. I'm holding it back with every shred of control I can muster. "Tami, I've gotta go," I choke out.

"Shoot…I upset you. I'm sorry, Hank. This is so freaking awful."

"We're both hurting and finding our way through it." I pause and force the tidal wave back. "Don't apologize. And stay in touch. I mean it."

"Thank you…and the same for you, 'kay? And be strong, Hank."

"You too."

The flood comes as my heart twists into knots. Fear engulfs me, filling my mind with worst-case scenarios. *Never seeing my babies again. My wife running off with NimRod and living happily ever after. My kids calling him Dad. Jail time. Love lost. A broken life.*

Fifteen minutes later, I splash water on my face and shove it all down. Fuck it. I'm talking to Adrienne. It violates her stupid piece of paper, but I don't give a shit. I'm sick of the unknown.

Goosebumps pepper my arms as I clasp the phone with a clammy hand. *One ring. Two.* My heart pounds with such ferocity it might flop out of my chest. *Three.*

"What do you want?" she says. No hello. No how are you?

"Nice greeting."

"What do you expect…you go ballistic and think everything is peachy keen normal? Not to mention, you're in violation of the protective order."

Still holding a hard line. "Give me a break. You know that's BS."

"The police don't think so."

A rush of energy surges through me. I need to keep my cool. Slumping toward the wall, I press my back straight against it. "Don't you see your part in this?"

She snorts.

So predictable, and a dead end. My head falls into my free hand. "How are the babies?"

"Fine." Every clipped response is laced with malice.

"Where are you?"

"None of your business."

Way to kick a man already down. "It's none of my business where my kids are? You're wrong about that."

"Where are *you*?" Smug bitch.

"Why…so you can turn me into the police?" My head thunks against the wall and I stare at the ceiling.

"They'll find you. The minute you step foot back into Virginia, you'll be arrested."

"How can you be so heartless and cruel?"

"You made it easy by acting like a homicidal asshole."

Leaping to my feet, I pace, keeping my voice level and calm. "You realize I've never harmed you, and never would, right?" She guffaws but I continue. "Or the kids. You can't be surprised I gave Rod a tune-up considering he was on the fucking down-stroke with my own wife."

"You did hurt me. You threw me across the goddamned room and forced me to the floor by almost breaking my fingers. Don't change the story to suit yourself or justify your warped actions."

Pot, meet kettle. I take a moment and gather my thoughts. "I'm sorry. But you jumped on me…*you* attacked *me*. I did the best I could without harming you. You think it was enjoyable?"

"It doesn't matter now, because that's the last time you'll lay hands on me."

"Meaning?" My heart is in my throat.

"We're done. I want a divorce."

I sag to the ground. "Adrienne…don't say that. I understand you're upset, but whatever problems we're having, we can work them out. We took an oath, and I'm prepared to honor those vows. We've got two tiny babies who need us." I wasn't sure myself until I said the words aloud, but of course that's the right thing, not only for Tanner and Cassidy, but for us.

"We're D-O-N-E done. I want no part of you and your violent craziness. Plus, you're a criminal—and a fugitive of justice. You're not the kind of man who is cut out to be a husband and father. I'm divorcing you and will go to any lengths to prevent you from having a relationship with these innocent babies."

Her words sledgehammer against my heart, obliterating whatever tenuous tape held it together. "No!" I croak.

"Goodbye, Hank. See you in court."

The phone goes quiet, and I stare at the blank screen as if it were an alien life form. It slips from my fingers as I roll into a ball on the floor and keen, a guttural sound so deep from within, I don't recognize it as myself.

Time slows, blurred pictures from my memory flashing by as I drown in my own misery. I press a fist to my lips to stifle the thundering howls trying to escape. My heart—my life—is busted beyond repair. I failed. I didn't protect and serve those closest to me. I didn't do my job as husband and father. I'm worthless. Defective. Unredeemable.

An unbearable, relentless agony stretches on the horizon. My torment scorches like Armageddon—and it *is* the end of the world as I know it.

It's too much.

I want the ache pummeling my heart to stop.

The agony to quiet.

A cease fire called.

I grope along the dresser for my Kershaw, my hand closing over its compact casing. It's been my trusty companion these last five years, my favorite pocketknife of all time, really. I flick open the blade with ease, having broken it in from near daily use. I stare at it fondly through watery eyes.

With my left hand, I finger the area of my chest poised over my hemorrhaging heart, and I plunge the knife in.

———

JACK DUTTON: I'VE BEEN AN ATTORNEY FOR FORTY-SEVEN YEARS AND HAVE SEEN A THING OR TWO IN MY TIME. I CAN ALMOST PREDICT HOW THINGS WILL GO FOR MOST FOLKS. IT'S SIMPLE HUMAN NATURE. IF I HAD TO GUESS, I'D SAY HANK'S WIFE TRAPPED HIM IN A MARRIAGE AND LIKELY DOESN'T HAVE A FAITHFUL BONE IN HER BODY. I HOPE TO GOD HE GETS A DECENT LAWYER AND EXTRICATES HIMSELF FROM THIS MESS, BUT IT'S ALSO HUMAN NATURE TO VENTURE INTO THE SPIDER'S WEB WITHOUT REALIZING YOU CAN'T ESCAPE.

CHAPTER 58
ADRIENNE

AS I PULL into our driveway, I'm hit by dual sensations. A part of me dreads the visual reminder of all hell breaking loose, but relief is palpably present. This is my home, and we belong here. I'm not concerned about Hank. He didn't cop to being in Texas, but where else would he hole up? Especially since the police haven't caught him yet.

Staring at our modest rancher painted sky blue with its trimmed shrubs and flowering plants—similar in size and upkeep to others on our street—one would never guess the secrets it keeps.

Mrs. Brown appears as I heft Cassidy's carrier out of the minivan.

"Everything all right, dear?" she says.

Busybody. I note her freakishly ink-black dye job, which does not make her look younger. *Time is marching on, sweetie.* I smile with false cheer. "Dandy. How about you?" I pick up Tanner, hoping she gets the message I'm not up for idle chitchat.

"We've been worried about you since the police were here, investigating things. You're not hurt, are you?"

"We're all fine, thank you. Now, if you'll excuse me, I need to move the babies inside."

"Of course. But Hank…what of him?"

I shouldn't take the bait, but why not give her something to talk about? "He can rot in hell for all I care."

Mrs. Brown gasps, and I whip around and stride to the front door.

I settle the twins in their playpen, turn on the TV for them and begin cleaning up the debris. I start with the easy stuff: washing dishes piled in the sink, trashing moldy food in the fridge, tidying up the baby paraphernalia covering the living room floor, replacing crib sheets, and disposing of days-old, rank diapers from the nursery.

Not able to put it off, I venture into the bedroom, instantly transported to the violent events of a few nights ago. Forcing it out of my thoughts, I get to work.

As I vacuum up shattered glass, my irritation with Rod and his mealy-mouthed ways grows. I'm good enough to screw, but not shack up with? We'll see about that. Picturing him moaning on the carpet with his shriveled dick doesn't make me empathize one bit. In fact, the opposite.

On my way to start laundry, I spy the dog bowls. I pitch them in the large bin outside along with Diesel's bed, toys and food and drag it to the curb for pick-up the following morning. I'm so happy to be rid of the stupid mutt. Man's best friend, my ass. I can only imagine Hank's expression when he learns of his dog's fate, not that it covers the retribution my violent husband deserves.

After pouring a glass of rosé, I sink into the sofa, placing my bare feet on the coffee table. I light a cigarette, free at last to smoke in my own home. The babies don't appear to mind, enraptured by the cartoons on screen.

Pulling my phone out of my back pocket, I check my messages.

Speak of the devil, Rod has finally checked in.

You okay?

Except for you.

We need to talk. Can you come by?

Instead of texting back, he calls. "Hey. Got your text." He sounds morose.

"Are you coming?"

"I'm at work. Is now good?"

"I guess. How are you?" I take a long drag and exhale, watching the smoke unfurl well above my babies' heads. It probably won't reach their little lungs.

"I've been better."

"How are your…injuries?" *Not to mention your pride.* I take a swallow of the pink wine, the fruity flavor snaking a cool trail down my throat.

"Healing."

"Did you press charges?" I'm poised like a tight spring anticipating his answer.

Rod coughs. "I decided against it."

I fucking knew it! I lurch to attention and violently stub out my cigarette. "Why would you let him get away with that?" I snap, my volume climbing. The twins turn toward me with disconcerted expressions.

"I don't want any more trouble, Adrienne."

"It helps my case if you level similar charges." *Man up!*

"What case?"

Is he daft? "I have an Emergency Protective Order, remember? I'm filing for longer-term legal protection and a divorce. It should be easy considering his violent offenses. Largely what he did to you, but also the gun bit."

Rod breathes, the sound amplified through the phone.

I wait. One Mississippi. Two Mississippi. Three Mississippi. He stays mute. "Well? You going to say something?"

"Calm down. I'm gathering my thoughts."

I can outlast you any day, asshole. Except I'm impatient as hell and now, add irritated. Four Mississippi. Five.

"Here's the thing, Adrienne. This has caused major anguish for my wife, and frankly, for me. I don't want further involvement in anything bringing more hostility from Hank or causing problems for my family."

I stand, my free hand balling into a fist. "You're a real piece of work, Rod. Are you deluded enough to believe you have a shot at keeping your family together?"

"I'm planning to try. And if it doesn't happen, I'm still not putting myself in a position to deal with your psycho husband."

I pace to avoid punching my own hand through the wall. "So just like that, you're willing to end everything between us?"

"I care for you. More, even. But—"

"Right!" I stomp to the bedroom.

"I do. But this…whatever we had, despite how great it was… has run its course. It's over."

"What crap! A few days ago, we were talking about our future, remember?"

"A lot's changed since then."

"How effortlessly you discard me. What do you think I am, some guilty pleasure like a triple cheeseburger you can throw in the trash, you fucking scumbag? Guess I was just another fuck to you, huh?" I punch the pillow on Hank's side of the bed.

"No," he says, just above a whisper. "I have real feelings for you. This is hard for me, too, but I think it's for the best."

"Bullshit. This is all about one thing: you're afraid of my husband." I chortle, glancing skyward. "All along, from the moment he met you, Hank said you were a giant pussy. He nailed that."

Rod sighs. "Let's not do this."

"Do what? Call a spade a spade? Oh wait, I think I need a bigger shovel for this shit."

"Take care, Adrienne. I mean it."

"Fuck you!" I scream so loud my throat hurts.

The line goes dead. He hung up. "Prick!" I hurl the phone into the pillows as the twins start to cry.

"Shut up!" I shriek, stalking back into the living room where my children wail louder, their faces scrunched up in agony "Shut up! Shut up! Shut up!" I shove pacifiers in their open mouths, but they refuse to latch on. They continue screaming, a sound crumbling my last shred of sanity.

And I snap.

———

MRS. KINCAID: I HEARD SHE HIRED ONE OF THOSE CONTRACT KILLERS TO RUB HIM OUT. AND WE HAVEN'T SEEN HIM SINCE, HAVE WE?

MRS. BROWN: OH, GLADYS, YOU'VE BEEN WATCHING TOO MUCH *CSI*. I'M SURE HANK IS LYING LOW AND LETTING THINGS COOL DOWN. MRS. MCCALLISTER LOOKS UNDISTURBED, SASHAYING AROUND IN THOSE TAWDRY OUTFITS OF HERS AS IF LIFE IS A BOX OF CHOCOLATES, AS A CERTAIN FORREST GUMP IS KNOWN TO SAY.

CHAPTER 59
HANK

I CAN'T BREATHE, and a fire burns in my chest. Why can't I breathe? Why can't I move? Holy shit-fuck. I'm horizontal, back to the floor, and something is terribly wrong. Am I dying? Without moving my head, I stare down my torso. The handle of my Kershaw stands rigid, the blade lodged deep into my chest. Fuck. Inching my hand toward it requires every ounce of my concentration. Sweat covers my skin like a soggy blanket. The edges of my vision darken. I'm gonna pass out. I pause, laboring for air, then resume, each microscopic advance bringing torment. Then my hand touches something sticky and wet. Blood. I need to call for help, but I can't fucking breathe. Or move. The blackness returns and swallows me whole.

"Oh, my heavens! Jim! Come quick! Oh, no. Please, God, no. Oh, Hank. What have you done, my sweet boy?" My mother drops to the floor beside me. "Jim!" she screams, her voice shrill. Her cold hand clasps mine, and she recites the Lord's Prayer between sobs.

. . .

Pressure grips my right biceps, and my eyes fly open. An EMT finishes taking my blood pressure and rattles off information to his partner.

"His eyes are open. Is he going to be all right?" My mother's tone is frantic. I imagine how horrific this must look.

"Let the professionals do their work," my father says, his voice strained.

"Hey, buddy. I'm Enrico and this is my partner, Wendy." A man with a brown complexion and matching warm eyes leans into view. His partner isn't in my line of sight. "Can you tell me your name?"

"Hank," I squeak, surprised I can speak.

Somewhere near, my mother gasps. "Thank the Lord."

"You've got quite the stab wound here, Hank. Can you tell me what happened?"

"I can't breathe. Something's…wrong."

"He can't breathe, Jim! So help me God…" My mother's weeping returns. "I can't stand here idly doing nothing."

The EMTs begin taping my chest. "I understand, Hank. We're working to stabilize you and control the bleeding so we can move you into the ambulance. Did you do this to yourself?"

Tears leak out of my eyes, and I wince from the instant pressure in my chest. As everything comes flooding back, the wall of pain smothers me.

"It's okay, Hank. Are you on medication?"

"No," I whisper, on the verge of passing out again.

They transfer me to the stretcher, and the metallic odor of blood makes me woozy. I think I'm gonna hurl.

We're moving fast, sirens blaring. Whatever I'm lying on is as stiff as wood. We hit a bump and shock waves reverberate throughout my body. I moan, the equivalent to getting punched in the chest. I want to claw myself upright but am powerless. Who is driving this crazy train? A certified motherfucking maniac like the drivers in Northern Virginia.

Enrico leans over and meets my gaze. "Hey, buddy, we're on our way to Rolling Plains Memorial Hospital. You're doing great."

Great would not be my word choice.

"Want to help me out? I've got to ask you some questions. Are you depressed, Hank?" And a minute later, "What's a good-looking guy like you have to be down about?" He winks.

Everything. More tears escape the corners of my eyes.

"Do you have a history of mental illness?"

"No," I croak.

"Ever hurt anyone else? Assault? Murder?" He monitors my vitals while he waits for a response. "I've got to burp your wound again, Hank. Hang tight."

Burp doesn't sound desirable. I try bracing but the slightest attempt causes excruciating anguish.

Enrico compresses my chest and stars dance around me, shooting every direction. "You're a tank, brother, Hank the tank."

He doesn't ask any other questions or impart any other details, like whether I'm dying. I guess that's not in the EMT customer service experience. I'm no idiot. If I can't suck air, I'm a dead man. We hit another string of bumps and as the scream leaves my lips, I slump back into the abyss.

I come to as I'm transferred to a different gurney. Enrico prattles a recap and medical jargon I don't comprehend to new faces in colored scrubs.

He leans over. "This is where I take off. Hang tough, brother."

A female introduces herself as Naomi and takes the helm. The gurney zips along, bright lights flickering overhead. Commotion abounds. I focus on counting, anything to distract me from the pain. One Mississippi, two Mississippi, three Mississippi, four…

Naomi pushes me into a room. The medical team descends,

checking my vitals, starting an IV and rattling off questions, the same Enrico sought answers to and more, and that I'm still not ready to answer. Could they focus on helping me breathe, for chrissakes?

The doctor orders tests: a CT scan of my thorax, abdomen and pelvis. Words like pneumothorax, intubation and OR float into my ears, but all I can hear is the deafening sound of my own suffocation. And the notion my babies will become fatherless, a thought worse than death. Enrico's comment rings back: *Hang tough, brother.*

They wheel me down the hall for the scan, which requires another excruciating transfer from my bed to the machine, shooting me up with something that makes me want to piss and zoofing me in and out of a contraption that looks right out of *Star Wars.* One Mississippi, two Mississippi, three Mississippi, four…

My parents are in my room when I return, and we listen to Dr. Lee explain how I have punctured my lung and require an immediate operation to remove the knife, salvage my lung and save my sorry ass.

"You're lucky you missed your heart," she says. "We probably wouldn't be having this conversation right now."

My mother sags against my father.

Lucky. And I have poor aim. "Am I going to be okay?" I whisper.

She doesn't answer. "Let's get you to the OR so we can fix you up."

"Doc?" I labor. "Can you tell them to save my knife? It's important to me."

She gives me a long, lingering stare. "If you promise not to stab yourself again."

"Deal."

My parents and I exchange I love you's. My mother kisses my

cheek, my father squeezes my hand. "We'll be here waiting for you."

I'm whisked away to the OR—and the unknown.

———

Wendy: Hank and I went to high school together. He dated a friend of mine, but I never understood the attraction. He was cocky and brash with a face only a mother could love while she was quiet and gorgeous—even won Miss Snake Charmer one year. Now Hank's brother, Wyatt? He's a tall drink of water. But Hank today...what a shocker. Never pegged him as the suicidal type. Made me sorry his life's taken a bad turn.

Terrance: It's more common than you might think to see a sharp force injury in the ER. People come through here stabbed with forks, screwdrivers, arrows, and all kinds of weird objects. This is the first pocketknife I've seen. Supposedly the guy did it himself, but self-stabbing is atypical for a suicide, probably because most people don't have the cojones for it.

CHAPTER 60
ADRIENNE

"THAT'S IT! I've had it!" I grab Tanner and march him to the nursery, leaving Cassidy to continue her own fit. As I shake Tanner's little body in concert with each emphasized, shrieked word, his eyes widen to saucers, and he gasps for breath through his tears. I drop him in the crib with such force, he bounces, then fetch his sister and chuck her alongside him.

"You can both come back out when you learn to be quiet!" I yell, flinging the door closed with a slam that shakes the walls and echoes down the hall.

They quit bawling twenty minutes later, a second before I strongly consider murder-suicide. It's all too fucking much. Screaming twins. A violent husband on the run. A lame-ass married boyfriend who won't level up. No friends—anymore. No family, aside from my grandmother. And no money saved. How is this my life?

I suck down another cigarette and glass of wine. I need to mastermind one hell of a plan. But tomorrow. I can't do one more hard fucking thing right now.

The television blares with the news New Orleans got nailed again by Mother Nature. Millions evacuate because of Hurricane

Gustav, and more than a million are without power. Now Hurricane Hanna is racing toward the U.S. Thank God we live inland, like sane people. I switch the channel, settling on *America's Got Talent*.

I chain-smoke through a sword-swallowing couple, savvy girl-child magician, and blue-haired octogenarian Salsa dancing with a lusty, twenty-something man. Now the house is too quiet, the only noise coming from this stupid box.

I creep to the nursery, weaving from the wine, and eke open the door. Cassidy sleeps, but Tanner's eyes fixate on me. My chest tightens. What the hell kind of mother am I? I pick up my son and rock him, humming a little song in his ear and whispering my apology. I change his soiled diaper, fix him a bottle and settle him in my arms to drink it. After burping him and placing him in the swing, I repeat the whole routine for my sleepy daughter.

As I hold her, I process my current reality.

I'm screwed.

Hank in jail is problematic. He can't provide behind bars, and I need alimony and child support. NimRod is clearly useless, so I'll have to cut my losses, although I might be able to milk him for dough with guilt. Until someone new presents himself, I'm forced to make my prevailing situation work to my advantage. Which means keeping my husband on the hook—while making him pay in every way possible.

———

TAMI: EVERYTHING IN ME WANTS TO PUNISH AND RESIST ROD, AND IT PROBABLY MAKES ME SOUND WEAK, BUT I STILL LOVE HIM. HE'S THE FATHER OF MY CHILD, LAVISHING ME WITH ATTENTION AND BEGGING FOR FORGIVENESS. AND THEN I IMAGINE HIS DICK INSIDE MY BEST FRIEND'S VAGINA...AND I WANT TO KILL THEM BOTH. SOMETIMES I FANTASIZE ABOUT SCREWING HANK. I BET HE'S A CONSIDERATE LOVER —WHO'D *NEVER* CHEAT ON HIS WIFE.

CHAPTER 61
HANK

A SYSTEMATIC, repetitive beeping wakes me. My eyes strain to open as my brain attempts to make sense of fragments, but it's like wading through a sea of marshmallow in a thick fog. Tubes are plugged into me, and a mask sits over my face. I can breathe!

My body is leaden and the pressure on my chest may as well be an anvil. I test moving my toes and fingers. They work, but anything more strenuous will break me. My mouth is dry, and a nasty film coats my tongue. With effort, I try shifting my head. Bad idea. It's eerily quiet aside from the machines.

The events flood back like a tidal wave: Adrienne. Rod. Cops. Driving to Texas. Tami. Sweetwater. My mother's face. My father's kindness. My heart, breaking like glass. My knife sinking in.

Christ, what was I thinking?

How much I love my wife, but she doesn't love me. Maybe never did. My throat tightens, my entire torso rebelling at that one infinitesimal action, and I wince. Note to self: keep emotions in check.

A smiling nurse wearing Super Mario scrubs appears. "You're awake."

I nod ever so slightly. Agonizing. "Water?" I croak.

She holds a cup and places the straw on my lips. "Small sips," she instructs. Her dirty blonde hair is pulled back in a ponytail. Wrinkles crease the corners of her eyes and mouth.

The cool liquid coats my tongue and travels down my throat. Heaven wrapped in searing discomfort. "Thanks."

"I'm Shawna, your critical care nurse. You're in the intensive care unit. How's your pain level on a scale of one to ten?"

Crushing. "Twelve."

"We've got you on morphine, and we'll continue monitoring you to keep your pain level moderate." Shawna's eyes convey warmth, but she's all business. She indicates a device near my hand. "You're on patient-controlled analgesia, which means you can push the button whenever your pain is too great, and it will administer medication through your IV. You'll hear a beep when you press it. However, only so much can be administered in a time period, which keeps you safe from overdose."

"If I press the button too soon, I'm SOL?" Every word is agonizing.

"Precisely."

Probably for the best. If it hurts like this with the morphine, I can't imagine where I'd be without it. "Can you tell me what's going on?"

She glimpses behind her. "Perfect timing. Dr. Lee will bring you up to speed."

"Hey, doc," I rasp.

"You're looking better." She glances down at my chart. Dr. Lee is a striking woman with subtle Asian features, her white coat overlapping dress slacks.

I grimace. "Depends on your perspective."

She meets my eyes, giving me a wry smile. "Your surgery went well. Your knife nicked your lung, which caused it to collapse."

No wonder I couldn't breathe.

"Fortunately, it missed your heart and the great vessels. We were able to repair the injury, but you'll be here until you're more stable. You're very lucky."

Perspective again. "Thanks for patching me up."

"You can expect to have some pain and discomfort for about a month, possibly longer. And you're going to have an interesting scar."

"How long will I be here?" Ow, ow, ow. Motherfucking *ow*.

"It depends. You should be out of the ICU in a couple of days and placed in another hospital room. But you'll undergo a psych consult. Are you suicidal, Hank?"

"No, ma'am. Never was."

She raises her eyebrows. "Why did you stab yourself?"

I pause a beat. Time to own it. "I thought if I cut my heart out, it would stop the pain."

She pauses and we share a lengthy, level stare. "It didn't occur to you it might cause your death?"

"I wasn't thinking straight." The tidal wave threatens. My chest tightens, and I fight for composure. A lone tear trickles down my cheek. "But I plan to stick around. Scout's honor. My kids need me." And I need them.

"Either way, you'll be talking to someone before you're cleared for release."

Great. Now a shrink is going to dig through my brain…like Adrienne wanted all along. "Did you save my knife?"

Dr. Lee smirks. "I did. But don't expect to get your hands on it while you're still a guest of RPMH."

My lids grow heavy as the doctor and nurse confer.

"You up for some company? I've got about eighty people in the waiting room who insist they're your family," Shawna says after another vitals check.

I muster a half-smile. "Yes, ma'am."

"I can only allow a few in here at a time. Parents first?"

"Affirmative, or your life might be in danger."

She shoots me a sideways glance as she adjusts my pillow. "You underestimate me, Hank—or any ICU nurse for that matter."

I chuckle, and pain ricochets through my chest. New note to self: no laughing.

Shawna ushers in my folks, who brighten despite the worry lines etched on their faces.

"You're going to be fine, Hank. The doctor said everything went well, better than expected," gushes my mother, taking my hand.

"Son," my father says, tenderness in his eyes. "How are you feeling?"

"Ready to rodeo," I joke.

Silent tears fall down my mother's normally stoic face. The sight slays me.

"I'm…I'm so sorry," I whisper.

My father places a hand on my thigh. "Hush now."

As if I could. "It was a dumbass thing to do."

My mom pats my hand.

"I wasn't thinking clearly."

"Are you now?" my father asks.

I nod. "I got my head right, boss," quoting a line from *Cool Hand Luke*, a McCallister family favorite. Goddamn it hurts to speak, smile…breathe.

My father gives me a wan smile, but his eyes are tired.

My mother squeezes my hand. "I'm grateful you're alive. That's what matters."

But I know full well that's not true. There's a mountain of shit to deal with. The tidal wave crests.

"We're here for you. Whatever you need," my father adds.

The heaviness returns, and I fight my lids closing.

"We'll leave you now to rest. When you're awake next, your brothers want their turn."

"Mmm hmm," I manage before sleep claims me again.

• • •

Three days after surgery, I'm moved from ICU and score my own room. That's the good news. The bad news: I'm in the psych unit because they think I'm a nutcase who tried to off myself. I've met with Dr. Nicholson once—more like a brief introduction—and dread whatever's coming. I don't need a stranger rummaging around my melon, nor believe it serves any purpose.

My family filters in and out, keeping me company, lifting my spirits, and turning my recovery into a rambunctious affair like only a rowdy pack of McCallisters can. Every brother and sister-in-law stops by. My parents remain the most attentive, and my mother seems reluctant to leave. I can tell she has a million questions she's fighting not to ask.

I hate the hospital. Nurses interrupt my sleep to poke, prod, and monitor me. Some are friendly, others surly. They're all bossy, forcing me out of bed to shuffle slow laps around the ward pushing my IV like a decrepit old man and suck on a spirometer (I call it a screwhanketer) to increase my breathing volume.

I'm back in the rack after a lap in the corridor, zoning out to a weekday game show.

Dr. Nicholson appears in his white coat, shutting the door behind him. He clasps a clipboard in one hand and stands at the foot of my bed. I hide my silent, full-body groan.

"How are you today, Hank?"

"Right as rain, doc. You?"

He gives me a disingenuous smile. "You like to joke around, don't you?"

He's already dissecting me. I start to shrug and am reminded that it's still a bad idea. "I like to keep the conversation light and upbeat."

"Let's talk more about what brought you here," he says, moving a chair adjacent to the bed and sliding into it.

I'd rather shake some Frank's Red Hot in my eyes, but the only way out of this is through. Getting my life back in order looms large. I have police to contend with, children to parent, a divorce to navigate and a gaping wound to heal in my chest, literally and figuratively. Nothing happens until I blow this hot dog stand.

"Fire away, doc."

"You stated you weren't suicidal and yet you stabbed yourself —through the chest cavity, near the heart—with a pocketknife. Can you elaborate?"

Hearing it out loud, I sound like a mental case. "It happened in a low moment after a hellacious twenty-four hours. It was stupid and impulsive, not premeditated."

He jots on his clipboard. "You weren't thinking, 'I'd like to end my life'?"

I shake my head. "I wanted to end the pain…in my heart. I thought if I could cut the damn thing out, it would stop hurting." What I like to call pragmatic. And why I'm in a psych unit.

"Have you ever attempted suicide?"

"Never."

More scribbling. "Contemplated it?"

"Never."

"Have you previously seen a mental health provider?"

"No, sir."

"Have you ever been prescribed medication for a mental disorder?"

"No, sir."

He moves the clipboard aside. "Are you currently a danger to yourself? Are you having any suicidal thoughts?"

I snort, sending another sobering ripple of torture through my torso. More like homicidal. "No, sir."

He jots a few notes and resumes his questions. "Let's circle back to the incident. What led up to the pain you were trying to stop?"

"I caught my wife cheating. Walked in on her. With a..." My body jolts into a full ten-hut. I lean my head back against the pillows, taking shallow breaths.

"Are you well enough to continue, Hank?"

I nod and push the tidal wave into the recesses.

Dr. Nicholson crosses his legs, his white coat falling open to reveal a polo-style shirt embroidered with a Longhorns logo. "Did you confront her, or the other party involved?"

Didn't I. Squeezing my eyes shut, I'm at a loss about what to do here. Tell the headshrinker the truth or tell him what I think he wants. I hate people in my business. Including this chucklehead, who doesn't know me and never will. "Yes," I say.

"What resulted?"

A shitshow. "An altercation. I became angry. My wife called the police and I left."

"Why did she call the police?"

Because she's a fucking two-faced whoredog. "Things got physical."

Furious scribbling. "Between you and your spouse?"

I shake my head. "Me and the guy banging her." I can't even think his name, or I'll lose it. "But she did attack me, and I defended myself."

"Is your wife abusive?"

What the hell kind of question is that? This is why I don't like shrinks. "Physically? Not usually. But obviously, she is not the woman I thought I married."

"How are you feeling about her now, or your situation?"

I vacillate between two emotions, like a coin flip. Heads: I hate the bitch. Tails: I can't live without her. "Confused. Hurt. Sometimes hopeful." The heart is a strange and powerful vessel.

"You have a lot to process, and it undoubtedly won't be easy. If you're released, is it your intention to cause harm to yourself or others?"

"No, sir." Then again, it's rarely *intentional.*

"That's enough for today, Hank," he says, rising. "We'll meet again soon."

"Can't wait, doc."

He gives me a curt nod and exits.

My eyelids droop as I lean against the pillows. The entire interaction sucked the life out of me, although not as egregious as anticipated. The million-dollar question is whether he'll sign off on my release—and when. The unknowns await, and the clock is ticking.

———

DR. NICHOLSON: HANK MCCALLISTER IS AN INTERESTING CASE. IN MY INITIAL OBSERVATION, HE PRESENTED AS CONFIDENT, POLITE AND STRAIGHTFORWARD, EXHIBITING MANY TYPICAL MALE CHARACTERISTICS. HIS RESPONSE REGARDING WALKING IN ON HIS WIFE WITH ANOTHER MAN AND THEN LATER, THE SELF-HARM HE INFLICTED, INDICATES A DISPROPORTIONATE LEVEL OF EMOTION. THIS LEADS ME TO BELIEVE HE MAY SUFFER FROM INTERMITTENT EXPLOSIVE DISORDER, WHICH IS CHARACTERIZED BY NON-PREMEDITATED VERBAL OUTBURSTS, ANGER OR VIOLENCE THAT IS OUT OF PROPORTION TO THE EVENT. USUALLY, THESE AGGRESSIVE ACTS ARE BRIEF AND MAY CAUSE A FLEETING SENSATION OF RELIEF, WHICH IS THEN OFTEN REPLACED WITH REMORSE. BASED ON MY CURSORY EVAL, I BELIEVED HIM WHEN HE SAID HE WAS NOT ATTEMPTING SUICIDE, AND IF HE IS A SUFFERER OF IED, IT WOULD PROVIDE FURTHER CORROBORATION AND EXPLAIN HIS RATHER UNUSUAL RESPONSE. MATTERS OF THE HEART CAN EASILY BRING ON SUCH A MENTAL DISORDER, ESPECIALLY IF IT'S GONE UNCHECKED, AS I SUSPECT HIS HAS. I SHOULD KNOW MORE AS I CONTINUE TO OBSERVE HIM AND CONCLUDE THE PSYCH EVALUATION.

CHAPTER 62
ADRIENNE

I PICK up my phone to text Hank. It's in my best interest to keep him off balance. I need him cooperative, not angry.

After a few minutes of debate, I decide to keep it simple.

> I'm sorry.

That should placate him.

I wait for the three revolving dots to appear but get bupkis. Guess he's *super* pissed off.

I try again.

> Can we talk?

> I'll be nice.

Silence. I purse my lips and tap furiously on the screen.

> Helloooooooooo??????????

What fucking gives, Hank? The asshole's probably punishing me. I throw the device to the opposite end of the sofa and slump against the cushions with a huff. I survey the growing mess in the living room and adjoining kitchen with disdain. I just cleaned this place yesterday!

I lean over and snatch my cell. Fine, I'll call.

It rings three times.

"You've got some nerve calling," Henrietta says.

Great, the battle ax answered. "Skip the bullshit. Is Hank there?"

"He's not available. And right now, you'll have to go through me. Good luck with that." If venom can be broadcast, she aces it.

I stand, bristling, my heart rate ticking higher. "Put my goddamned husband on the phone, Henrietta."

"Do you have any idea what you've done, you malicious, selfish hussy?"

My insides roar, and I pace the room, glaring at the woman at the other end of the call. "Do you have any idea what your son did? He brought everything on himself!"

"Oh! Of course. My *son* is responsible for you having an affair with another man…right in his own bed to boot." She snorts. "You're a real piece of work."

My free hand jabs at the air. "Hank is a wife beater. No matter what I've done, it doesn't justify his actions, and you raised him, so part of this is on you, Mother of the Year!"

Henrietta cackles, then her voice hardens. "I'm going to bury you, dear. Stay away from my boy. Far, far away."

"Give it your best shot, Henr—"

The mobile silences in my ear. High and mighty bitch! How dare that vindictive, hairsprayed old hag. And why did she answer Hank's cell? I have no doubt my husband and I would be talking right now if his phone hadn't been commandeered. In his eyes, the sun rises and sets with me. I will not allow Henrietta McCallister to fuck things up, no matter how hard she tries.

———

HENRIETTA MCCALLISTER: THAT TRAMP IS THE SPAWN OF SATAN, AND I MEAN LITERALLY. I LOOKED UP HER NAME AND IT TRANSLATED TO *THE DARK ONE*. I KNOW HER TYPE WELL…SHE MANIPULATES, LIES, SCHEMES AND CHEATS, ALL BY WIGGLING HER TITS AND ASS IN SOME POOR SUCKER'S FACE. SHE USES ONE MAN AND MOVES ON TO THE NEXT, LIKE TARGETS AT A SHOOTING RANGE. I DETEST WOMEN LIKE THIS, AND I WILL NOT ALLOW HER TO RUIN MY SON OR MY GRAND-CHILDREN. I'VE HIRED THE BEST ATTORNEY IN THE COMMONWEALTH TO MAKE SURE OF IT. IN THE LONG RUN, HANK WILL THANK ME.

CHAPTER 63
HANK

I ENDURE two more sessions with Dr. Nicholson where he tries to root around in my brain. Although I convince him I don't have a death wish, he stresses violence is never a solution, whether inflicted on me or others, and lobs some shrink-speak diagnosis at me. He urges me to find a psychologist and pursue ongoing counseling to equip me with insights about my behavior. *Thanks, but no thanks.*

With his sign-off, Dr. Lee approves my release from the hospital with clear marching orders. Besides tending to my wound, she wants me to suck on that damn spirometer daily and return for follow-ups. I still have a pain in my chest the size of a football field, but healing is not a priority when the wreckage of my life awaits.

My parents pay for a hotshot Virginia lawyer. When we consult by phone, he has good news. The Emergency Protective Order expired, and Adrienne didn't file for the extended version, prolonging this nonsense. I have no idea why, but don't look a gift horse in the mouth.

The most pressing matter is turning myself in to the authorities to deal with the existing warrant. My attorney orchestrates my surrender. Immediately following my arrest, he'll argue for release on my own recognizance and post bail. With no prior domestic disputes and my other two misdemeanors relating to bouncer altercations, he's confident we'll prevail. I'm scared shitless. This takes the kind of trust I don't like placing in human beings, but what choice do I have?

Next, I must address the divorce and custody of the twins. My mother vehemently opposes anything but sole custody, removing Adrienne as a rightful parent in perpetuity, but I'm not sure I have grounds, or the stomach, to go there. I've barely spoken to my wife, and I want her to tell me—in the flesh, to my face—she doesn't love me and wants the split. Her ongoing, hard-ass attitude floors me. I've gotten no calls or texts, nothing but a fuck-you-very-much.

My workplace poses another problem. When my parents contacted my employer to tell them I was in the hospital after "an accident," they furloughed me, and couldn't promise my position would be available upon my return. I understand, accepting I kissed an excellent job goodbye and there isn't a soul to blame but myself.

My folks lobby me to move home and help run the ranch with a focus on the machinery and equipment. They remind me I'll be surrounded by my entire support system, and what a wholesome place it is to raise the twins. What they don't say: the near impossibility for my soon-to-be ex-wife and I to share custody. Ergo, it doesn't seem a likely scenario.

We agree in the short-term I'll fly to Virginia and return to Sweetwater in time for my next medical appointment. I arrange to rent a car and stay with Jimmy—and out of trouble. Wyatt wants to tag along, but I don't need a babysitter, despite my entire family disagreeing. Can't say I blame them.

They plead for me to wait until the tropical storms run their cycles. On the heels of Hurricane Gustav (who names these things?) is tropical storm Hanna, gaining momentum in the Atlantic. Superstorms are often overrated with dubious strength and landfall predictions, so I blow off their concerns. Frankly, a hurricane is the least of my worries.

If I'm unclear before getting on the airplane, my parents are the bom diggity. They booked me a first-class ticket, so I don't have to cram into a coach seat in my condition. A perky flight attendant flirts with me across the country and brings me a few extra chocolate chip cookies. I finish *The Worst Hard Time: The Untold Story of Those Who Survived the Great American Dust Bowl* by Timothy Egan. Talk about a book to hoist you off your pity pot. It forces me to look gratitude square in the face.

And yet, it doesn't stop my shoulders from hunching toward my ears every fifteen minutes. It doesn't prevent me ruminating about my impending surrender and possible outcome, the one we hope doesn't come to fruition. And it doesn't quell my simmering anger at Adrienne calling the police when *she* was fucking dickless wonder in our own bedroom and one hundred percent in the wrong.

But I can't afford negativity. I've got to keep my wits about me. And when I tense up, my chest wound shows me who's boss. It hurts like a motherfucker.

As we near Dulles International Airport, I rub my aching neck and shoulders. My stomach quivers as the plane lands. I deboard, my scalp prickling when I glimpse the sign broadcasting my name, held by my attorney. No turning back now.

At first glance, Mitch Cook oozes confidence, a real Slicky Boy. Sharp suit, hair gelled in place, a disarming smile, the kind of guy who could sell ice to an Eskimo—exactly what I need.

We talk as he drives us to the police station, going over my part, which mostly amounts to me shutting the hell up.

We arrive and reality closes in fast. My stomach churns as we approach our destination, and I rethink my options as I scout an exit strategy. Turning yourself in never sounds like the right move. No one thinks, *Sure, let me volunteer to go to jail.*

The bail bondsman my attorney arranged for joins us, a character named Ike who may or may not have been behind bars in his lifetime. Ike sports a mess of long, brown hair corralled into a ponytail, two sleeves of tattoos and tells me he was born the day Dwight Eisenhower was elected president. Somehow, it all makes sense.

"Ready?" says Mitch.

The doubt clanging in my ears drowns out the sound, but I manage to nod. Sweat trickles from my pits down my torso, anxiety swirling in my bloodstream, as I inch forward on quaking legs all the way to the front desk.

My lawyer does the talking, explaining the arranged voluntary surrender. Things progress smoothly and efficiently. The police question me, with Mitch present and guiding me. After I'm processed, I appear before the magistrate where my attorney does what he said he would with the outcome we planned. The bond is set, and I'm released on my own recognizance. Slicky Boy done good.

Outside the station, still a free man, I'm damn near jubilant. I've never experienced such a polite exchange with the heat. I thank Mitch and Ike, shaking their hands. Ike reminds me he knows where I live, cackling like a madman, but I don't think he's joking.

Mitch and I discuss next steps while he drives me to the rental car facility. Rain taps the windshield, the first signs of Hurricane Hanna making her way up the coast. He talks about my impending civil case, which he predicts will be thrown out. Still, it looms large. He reminds me to steer clear of trouble, namely my wife, violent offenses and firearms. I assure him I'll lay low, despite the itch begging to be scratched. I *will* see Adrienne.

I have to.

———

Ike: I got mixed messages from the kid. Hank's a big guy, but he looked a little dazed. Could he kill someone? Sure. Is he going to? Doubtful, although his mental state seemed shaky. Nine times out of ten with guys like this, some woman has fucked him over. Chicks never understand the power they have. It's the power of the pussy, man...and they hold it all.

CHAPTER 64
ADRIENNE

RAIN PELTS the house for the third day in a row. I can't take one more second alone in this house. I'm like a caged animal. Thinking about nasty, helmet-haired Henrietta makes me want to claw her eyes out. And caring for the twins 24/7 is the definition of tedium. Booze and cigarettes only go so far. I need outside stimulation, a conversation with an adult, a first-rate fuck.

Hey, there's an idea.

I reach for my phone and tap in the number. As it rings, I picture his gorgeous face, bottomless eyes and deft hands. By the anticipation flooding my center, you'd think I was about to shoot heroin.

"Dude! I told you to bury the arms and throw the body in the ocean. Sorry… hello?"

Sophomoric as ever. "Hi, Nate."

"Who is this?"

"Adrienne."

"Well, well, well. She's baaaaaaaack."

"Shut it. You know you miss me." *Like I do you right now and your exquisite, chiseled hardbody etched in my mind.*

"Don't flatter yourself, sweetheart."

"Am I wrong?" I recline on the sofa and whip up my feet. My free hand flutters down my stomach.

"I'm seeing someone."

Whatever. "Come over. I miss you. I want to do dirty deeds."

"Tempting, I admit. But you're kind of a using bitch, you know that, Adrienne?"

A feral smile crosses my lips. "You used me too—don't deny it. We're perfect for each other, and right now, I only want you."

"What about your husband?"

"History. I'm divorcing him. Now drive your ass over here and let me lick every inch of you."

Nate groans. "I swear to God, woman…"

"I'm touching myself just thinking about you." No lie.

"But the hurricane…"

"Fuck the storm—and fuck me instead. Stay over. And hurry, before I make myself come." I force my fingers away from my crotch.

"Screw it. Text me your address."

I grin like Bud Fox after bagging the elephant in *Wall Street*. "That's the spirit."

"You're going to be the death of me."

I perform my best evil laugh.

"You better get ready for Hurricane Nate."

The wind howls on cue, rain pelting the roof as if angry. "Oh, I'm ready."

We end the call and I kick my heels into the air. My insides are already gushing. Now to prep the kids—and myself.

I peek out the window to assess the weather situation. The trees sway and bow. The babies cry. I change their diapers, feed and bathe them and put on a silly cartoon while I dash into the bedroom to doll up and don my sexiest lingerie. I wriggle into a racy red teddy that hugs my curves and stand back to admire my assets, imagining Nate's face when I reveal this little number.

My cell rings. It's Hank. "Finally!" I mutter. Despite repeated efforts, he's never called, and I blame his meddling crone of a mother. She can try and ruin everything I've carefully planned, but I have four words for Henrietta: *over my dead body.* Unless it's *her* calling now. Shit!

I answer. "Hank?"

"Hi."

Thank fuck. "Hi."

"How are you?"

I sit on the edge of the bed, the underside of my teddy wedging into my ass crack in the process. "Okay. You?"

"Uh, it's been a bit of a roller-coaster ride." He sounds melancholy but calm.

"Did you get my messages?"

"What? No. You called?"

"I've called, texted, you name it, many times over the past week."

"I'm…sorry. I had no idea. Nothing came through."

"Ask your mother." *Take that, Shrewella.* He'll be pissed about her intervening.

"Christ. I'm…not surprised. My mother, well, never mind. Why were you trying to reach me?"

"To apologize." Well played, Adrienne.

"Really?"

"I regret…how things went. I don't want bad feelings between us." I need him to believe this.

"I'm relieved to hear you say that. I was hoping we could talk. Face to face."

He's in town? "You're here?"

"Yes."

"Have you been in jail?" I thought the police were supposed to contact me when he got arrested. Incompetents.

"I turned myself in and was released on my own recognizance."

I'm sure he wants to add *no thanks to you*, but refrains. "I'm sorry, Hank. But you mega freaked me out. I thought you were going to kill me."

"I would never…" He sighs. "You, of all people, should know that by now."

I do but won't admit it out loud. "So, what now?" The rain beats harder against the windows, and I hear an intense crack. Craning my neck to peer through the sliding glass door, a sizable limb from the neighbor's tree crashes to the ground.

"You and I still have to show up for the civil suit, whenever it happens," he says wearily. "But I'd like to see my babies and talk to you. Can I come over?"

"Tomorrow."

"That's probably a smart idea with this storm. You and the kids all right?"

"We're fine. Listen, I've got to go." I want to put the twins to bed before this hurricane gets any damn louder.

"Thank you. I miss you all." He sounds like he might cry.

"Uh…sure. Goodnight."

Nate arrives with a bottle of champagne and a single red rose, the cheap variety they sell in convenience stores, but he's the real present. Even dripping wet, he dazzles—his sea-green eyes boring into mine, his lips curving into a wicked grin. I'm like Pavlov's dog, salivating at the mere sight of him.

He shrugs out of his coat, and in route to the kitchen, I whisper the babies are sleeping and to keep quiet. Without a word, he pins me against a wall and his mouth possesses mine. I moan as our tongues tangle, my insides quivering as pleasurable heat shoots down my center. My hands roam his back, skimming the taut muscles through his cotton shirt. I yank it off, exposing his tanned magnificence and a smattering of hair leading the way directly down his bulging Levi's. He guides me to the island and hoists me on top, my ass grazing the cool tiled counter. I fling off my minidress, and his eyes bug.

"Wow," he says, drinking me in. "Spectacular. And all for me?"

Wordlessly, I nod.

He kisses my neck and heads south with his talented mouth. His tongue circles my right breast, sucking the nipple until I squirm. His fingers skim the outside of my teddy, then deftly unsnap the enclosure and plunge into my wet depths. I shudder, on the verge of exploding. I moan as his lips and fingers work their magic, driving me insane.

"I fucking missed this," he utters.

"Me, too," I rasp.

He removes his fingers and smells them appreciatively. It's a massive turn-on. I recline on the island, sprawled across it like a buffet. I dip my head so it hangs over the edge, and Nate meets me on the other side, shedding the rest of his clothes. He slides his rigid cock between my waiting lips and groans. With my head upside-down, the angle allows him—and me—to go deep. He fucks my mouth, blazing eyes fastened on me the entire time, and I'm so tuned up, my gushing juices drip down my thighs.

Nate stills his strokes, keeping my mouth and throat deliciously stuffed with his magnificence as he leans over to strum me like an instrument. Two fingers plunge inside my slick center while his thumb deftly maneuvers the hot button. I combust into a thousand pieces, my screams muffled by Nate's cock. He pulls out, whips me around, aligns our bodies and slides into me forcefully. My pussy shudders with orgasmic waves, and the heady combination with his thrusts leaves me breathless. He begins his onslaught, muttering filthy endearments and cuss words as my eyes loll back in my head. I fling my legs out as far as they'll divide, wishing he could slam into me forever. And he gives and gives—and takes and takes. There is nothing but this hedonistic moment.

When he comes undone, our eyes lock in mutual admiration. Sweat dampens his curls, and I fall into those eyes. He thrusts into my pelvis for good measure.

"Goddamn," he mutters with awe.

"Round one," I say, licking my lips and reveling in the aftermath.

"I'm tapping this fine ass all night long, sweetheart."

"Promises, promises."

We disengage, wipe ourselves with kitchen towels and tug our clothes on. Outside, the storm rages, pounding the house with driving rain. When booming thunder rattles the windows and lightning paints the sky, I flinch and scoot closer to him.

"Scared, baby?"

I nod. "It sounds like it's going to rip the house to shreds. Are we safe here?"

"As much as anywhere, I'd wager." He holds me in his arms and kisses my head. "How about some champagne?"

"Alcohol? Hell yes."

He pops the cork at the same moment we lose power.

"Crap," I say, groping around in the dark, trying to remember where we keep a damn flashlight. I can't see my hand in front of my face, so I inch along the island to the counter next to the fridge. Nate chuckles and flicks his lighter, illuminating the junk drawer, where I find tea lights and matches.

"Mighty exciting," Nate says, his teeth gleaming in the dim light as I ignite the candles.

I'm suddenly grateful he's here for more than mind-blowing sex.

He fills our glasses, and we clink them together. I drain mine and a shiver runs through me, a persistent eeriness clinging like a second skin.

I disperse the candles, leaving some in the kitchen, living room, bathrooms and bedroom. Nate follows me, toting the bubbly.

We climb on the bed, talking and sipping champagne. When the thunder cracks again, I crawl into his arms and he holds me, lightly stroking me from shoulder to fingertips. He tilts my head and kisses me, the intensity building until we're clawing each other with need.

In the flickering light, he murmurs, "Ready for round two?"

———

Mrs. Kincaid: Can you believe this storm? I wish it were raining men, like the words from that old '80s disco song.

Mrs. Brown: You and me both, Gladys—no offense to my husband, of course. He's not exactly a hardbody anymore, in all senses of the word. Which reminds me, did you notice the vehicle parked in the McCallister's driveway? A handsome young man was driving...I'll bet he has a hardbody. That McCallister woman is shameless. Then again, I guess it's true you should use it before you lose it.

CHAPTER 65
HANK

JIMMY and I watch the news in his spartan apartment, frosty longnecks in hand and a decimated pizza before us. The weather remains the top story. Hurricane Hanna, which made landfall at the Carolina borders, now wreaks havoc as it races up the coast. Storm surges, power outages and flooding are reported in her wake.

"There's a reason they name brutal storms after chicks," I say.

Jimmy raises his bottle. "Amen, brother."

The rain beats mercilessly against the windows, coming in horizontal sheets as vigorous wind gusts rattle the glass.

I set down my beer and stand, igniting the pain in my recovering wound. "I need to check on my wife and kids, man. It's driving me nuts."

Jimmy's stares at me like I have ten heads. "You already look like death warmed over, now you want to take your sorry ass into a hurricane? Wait out the storm, dude."

"I can't. Need to know they're all right." My chest aches in more than one way since talking to Adrienne. I have hope. If I show up, maybe she'll let me hold my babies, and her. And Diesel…God, I miss him. Seeing all of them is a reunion I desperately crave. The thought of waiting until tomorrow devastates me. I can't.

"It's your funeral."

I chuck a pillow at him, wincing at the effort. "I can always count on you for an encouraging word."

"Go fuck yourself," he says, followed by a smirk.

"If only I could."

I slide into the waterproof jacket Jimmy loans me and don my Rangers baseball cap before scurrying to the car. I can't run with my injury, but a man doesn't let a little rain perturb him. My lame-ass rental? *That* perturbs me. Adding further insult, it's a Ford.

The night galvanizes the storm's powerful presence. Trees bend to ninety degrees, limbs and debris cover the roadways, flashes light up the sky and thunder growls from the heavens as buckets of unrelenting precipitation flood the streets. I hydroplane across the wet roads, and my wipers can't keep pace with the avalanche of rainfall, forcing me to creep along as I strain to see through the storm. Fucking midsize piece-of-shit car.

Bleary-eyed, I enter our development sixty-three minutes later, the slowest twelve miles I've ever clocked. Every house is enveloped in darkness. Power's out. I was right to come. Can Adrienne handle an emergency, or even find the flashlights I've stowed strategically around the house? She isn't the sharpest tool in the shed.

The driveway is blocked. Parked next to my wife's minivan is some beater van I don't recognize. I let out the breath stuck in my throat, palpably relieved NimRod isn't here. No data on the status of asshat, but Adrienne led me to believe she wanted to work things out with me. I think. I pull to the curb and switch off the ignition.

Through the inky gloom, light flickers within. But what's with this sorry excuse for a van? It's suspicious, putting me in caution mode. I don't even have my Kershaw for a weapon since I couldn't bring it on the airplane. What if my gal is in trouble?

With the power out amidst this deafening storm, the situation is ripe for a stalker or crime. I leave the car, stealthing up the front walk and peeping into the living room windows. Two candles flicker dimly but there's no sign of activity. My senses kick into high alert. If a friend of Adrienne's was here, they'd be visible.

I work my way around the side to the bedroom, preparing myself for worst-case scenarios. The rain soaks through my jeans and pours off the brim of my hat. Water seeps down my neck and coats my bare hands. Gripping a fallen limb as a makeshift weapon, I peer cautiously through the sliding door. Two candles flank the bed, emitting scant light, but I make out two figures.

Straining to see anything through the mottled glass and pouring rain, I adjust my line of sight, sharpening my focus and tightening my grip on the branch.

In ten seconds, I take it all in: my wife, clad in a sexy lace getup, reclined on the bed, her legs splayed. A naked man kneeling on the floor lapping at her pussy. Adrienne thrusting her hips to his mouth, her hands grasping at the sheets, eyes closed in bliss.

She's with *another* motherfucker.

The fuse ignites and like a twelve-pack of dynamite, I explode into the room, shattering the glass with the tree limb and the force of my six-four frame.

Adrienne screams and the man scuttles into a corner, eyes wide, one hand out for protection—as if that will do him any good. Through the thunderous storm, the twin's cries reach my ears. My heart flips at the sound but cannot deafen the murderous thoughts speeding through my brain.

"What the hell?" the stranger says.

"Hank! Stop! What are you doing?" Adrienne's eyes are panicked, but mine take in the scene, confirming not a word she spews can be trusted ever again.

The stranger attempts to cover himself without losing sight of me. "You know this guy?" he barks at her.

"I'm her husband, asshole. Who the fuck are you?"

He continues to cower. "Look, man, I've got no beef with you. Adrienne said you two were broken up, so if it's all right with you, I'll grab my shit and go. I'm sorry, dude. Seriously."

I weigh the situation, ignoring the burn in my chest, but not my labored breathing. It's hindering me. "Get the fuck out. Now."

Pretty boy scrambles to find his clothes, pulling them on as he hops down the hall and out the front door. My glare stays fixed on the woman I thought I loved. As she tugs at the scrap of material she's wearing, a ridiculous attempt to cover herself, she mouths off a litany of cuss words and insults I barely register. Anything she emits is worthless and meaningless, a lie or manipulation.

I lunge at Adrienne, slam her against the wall and pin her there. Her eyes bulge, wide with shock. I clench my hand around her delicate, pale throat and squeeze. A gurgle spurts from her mouth, the very mouth I'd eagerly kissed just a few weeks ago. Her hands claw at my chest in vain, not gaining any purchase. Through the sharp tunnel of my fury, a sense of calm emerges.

Snapshots of our life together parade across my thoughts. The memories I'd walled off in my brain buzz like static on the radio. They come in short, disconnected snippets. And then the night we met replays, and it's crystal fucking clear.

Except…it's all bullshit, orchestrated to use me and spit me out like a rancid piece of chewed meat.

Nothing feels righter than watching the light die from her eyes. This woman has no business raising our children. To play me and every other man for the fools—all at her whim?

But I'm no murderer. Or a lowlife scum-sucking wife beater.

I loosen my grip, and she sputters and coughs. Letting go, I step back, and she slumps to the ground like a wet towel. No matter what justice I want to mete out, it isn't in me. It's not who I am and I sure as hell won't waste the rest of my life rotting in a jail cell, leaving my children to be raised by her sorry ass or complete strangers.

It dawns on me Diesel hasn't barked or shown his face. I gaze, impassive, at the woman lying on the floor. "Where's my dog?"

She manages to gurgle out a laugh. "I got rid of the mother-fucker, asshole."

"Come again?"

"Left him in the middle of nowhere," she rasps. "Without his tags. He's gone, the miserable piece of shit."

A lump lodges in my burning chest even as the embers of fury are stoked, creating a hot new flame. I shut my eyes, and his wolf-like features loom in my mind...and his innocence. I didn't protect him. I failed him. A scream wells from deep inside and echoes into the room, matching the thunderheads rolling over us.

Adrienne's heartlessness is fathomless. I yearn to kick her in her face, her lying mouth, those bulbous lingerie-clad tits, the legs she's spread for every swinging dick. I'm torn between my pain, impulses, hunger for justice and ethics. It's too much to process.

My head jerks when a deafening crack drags me from my thoughts, light blazing into the room. I bolt to the window. Our tree—the mighty oak I thought a beacon of our solidarity—has splintered in two, with one half lodged through our roof. A second flash of lightning illuminates the charred, shredded remains, smoldering as the rain pelts against the heat. A moment later, the smoke alarms shriek.

———

NATE: I SAW THE LOOK IN HIS EYES. DUDE WAS ABOUT TO BLOW, AND I MEAN GET MEDIEVAL. AND HE HAD EVERY RIGHT TO BE PISSED. FUCKING ADRIENNE...THAT'S THE LAST TIME I HAVE ANYTHING TO DO WITH THAT CRAZY BITCH.

CHAPTER 66
ADRIENNE

HANK FLINGS OPEN the door and runs from the bedroom, unleashing a wall of acrid, bitter smoke. As it snakes its way into my strangled neck, I struggle to breathe, each hack compounding the problem. The outside air pulls the plumes toward the shattered glass door, until it collides with what's left of Hurricane Hanna, still pummeling the house with force.

"Hank," I squawk. My voice is weak and distant, like it's not coming from my own throat, as I fight to sit upright.

He returns, his breathing thick and labored, and crouches by my side. "The tree came through the house. It's on fire and spreading fast. It's bad…we need to get out of here. Can you stand?"

"I think so." Tanner and Cassidy wail, muted from the uproar raging around us. "Save our babies!"

Our eyes meet, his tortured and frantic. A flicker of guilt washes through me.

"I'm not leaving you. We can all make it out if we move fast." He helps me up. "Let's go."

I lurch. "Wait! The locket."

He stares with shock and confusion. "There's no time! Leave it!"

"I…I can't. You go! Get the kids," I implore.

"This is crazy! Don't do this."

"I'm right behind you." Our eyes lock.

He grabs me by the shoulders, his eyes pleading. "Hurry. You don't have much time." In a flash, he disappears.

Tanner and Cassidy's cries intensify, then fade. I trust Hank is ensuring their safety. Searching my memory for where I stashed the locket, I dart toward the dresser. I need it and some clothes—I will not walk out onto the street clad only in a red lace teddy. The last of the candlelight burns out, leaving me in pitch darkness. I stagger a few steps, groping the air.

Goddamn this storm. Its ear-splitting ferocity lashes through the smashed door, unnerving me with every massive boom. Finally, I reach the dresser. My brain reels with other items to take as I yank open various drawers and fumble for jeans and a shirt. *Find the locket.* Jerking on the narrow top drawer, I blindly search. The smoke is thicker now, suffocating. The clock is ticking.

My fingers close around the locket, the last tangible reminder of my sweet, dead sister. *Thank God.*

Turning, I inch toward the door, arms flailing in the dark. Sharp glass slices deep into my right foot and I shriek, losing my balance and falling to the floor. I land hard on a pile of broken shards, and pain stabs my body in a hundred places. The sick stench of blood reaches my nose, competing with the all-encompassing smoke.

I laugh-cry. Goosebumps flutter across my skin as blood oozes from my wounds. Surely Hank will come back. He'll realize I'm taking too long, understand something must be wrong. He'll save me, my cowboy.

The irony my house is on fire isn't lost on me. I'm catapulted back in time, to shortly after my eleventh birthday, to that pitiful farmhouse in the depressed small town where I'd been born.

My mother had berated my baby sister and me all through dinner, describing the countless ways we were losers…and always would be. She and my father, drunk on moonshine, cackled when my sister cried. I'd grown tough and hardened, fueled by sheer hatred of my parents, and told my mother to quit picking on us. My mother backhanded me in response, my cheek swelling from her cheap ring slicing through it.

When I tried to run, my father reached out his hairy arm and plastered me against him, forcing me to apologize to my mother while resting his hand squarely—intentionally—on where my budding breast poked out. It wasn't the first time and I hated it, hated him and his grabby, grubby hands touching me in my private places. I wriggled in his grasp. He spanked my bottom, telling me to clean the dishes.

Before long, my parents were passed out in front of the TV, watching reruns of Hee Haw. I spied the cigarette burning in my mother's hand as she snored like a chainsaw, head back in the recliner, and envisioned, with a chilling clarity, what must be done.

I pushed Annabelle outside, ordering her to play in the woods and not return until I called for her. I darted out to the shed and got the can of spare gas and splashed it throughout our humble first floor, trailing it from the kitchen through the living room and all the way to the front door. I took my parents' precious moonshine and dumped it out, too. Without a shred of remorse, I lit the newspapers I'd wadded up, scattered them in each room and ran like hell.

Fire engulfed the house at a surprising speed. Hiding in the woods, studying the angry smoke spewing from the wreckage, I wondered if my folks were fighting to escape. Moments later, when an explosion ricocheted through the house and sent a blast of flames sky high, in my bones, I knew they were gone. I'll never forget the sight—it's burned into my memory.

The fire trucks rounded the bend, sirens blaring, and I

remained hidden as they fought to douse the blaze. When it was safe, I ran through the forest calling Annabelle's name, but she didn't answer. I searched everywhere—down by the stream, back in the copse of pines, in our favorite, old hollowed-out tree, all our secret places—but I couldn't find her. Stumbling back toward the house, reality dawned.

I broke into a sprint, hell-bent on entering the inferno, but a fireman grabbed me by the waist, swinging me back.

"My sister! My sister! I can't find her!" I shrieked, tears streaming down my face. "She was outside, but now...what if she's inside? Please, mister. Help me! Save my sister!"

He wouldn't let me pass, keeping me captive as they drenched the flames. I watched in horror, powerless to do anything but wait. By the time they entered the house, I knew Annabelle had disobeyed me and went back inside before I'd set it ablaze. I'd killed her…and she'd died a grisly, horrible death.

I'd lived with this secret every single day of my life. It hardened me, plagued me, turned me into an empty vessel of regret.

I thought marrying Hank and having Tanner and Cassidy was my redemption. I could make it right with them, give them everything I never had. Create a happy family. Heal my soul. But maybe there's no such thing.

Flames breach the bedroom, licking the walls. Where is my husband? Why is he taking so long? Where is the fire department?

The faint wail of sirens filters in through the deafening pandemonium. *They're coming for me.*

Unable to stomach the rusty tang or the gooey wetness, I suck in a shallow breath just as a wave of nausea hits. Still prone on this bed of glass, I buck, bile rising in my throat. With the force of my vomit, the razored shard embedded in my chest inches further, impaling me. My eyes widen as I gasp a shocked inhalation. My face falls to the ground, and my world turns silent.

———

MRS. KINCAID: They say a piece of glass sliced right into her heart, killing her instantly. And between the tree and fire damage, they're going to tear the whole house down. It's not salvageable—just like that marriage.

CHAPTER 67
HANK

I GLANCE BACK at our burning house, flames providing the only light as my eyes strain through the unrelenting rain and darkness. My children howl in my arms, and I hasten to the car, their safety my entire focus. Adrenaline flows through my veins like a drug as the house groans behind me and debris falls. Envisioning rooms collapsing, I quicken my pace, tormented by the impossibility of saving everyone.

I set Tanner in the passenger seat and hustle around to the driver's side holding Cassidy. Soaked to the bone, chill bumps ripple across my flesh. I turn on the ignition and crank the heat, soothing my frightened babies as I fight to regain my bearings. My lungs are fried and the pain ferocious, like a hot poker stabbing my chest. It's a miracle I'm not dead or unconscious.

I sneak quick glances at the house. "Come on, Adrienne!" I say under my breath.

Where the hell is she?

Still searching for her damn trinket? She's never even mentioned it, and now she's risking her life for it?

What if she's hurt? Trapped?

My knuckles scrub my cheek, torn about what I should do.

Stress and anxiety radiate from the twins. I kiss Cassidy on the temple and stroke Tanner's leg. I don't want to leave them—and shouldn't. But Adrienne might die if I sit here one more second, and I can't let that happen. She's the mother of my children, for better or worse. And the love of my life. Or so I thought.

A flicker of indifference creeps in. So what if she croaks after all she's done? I bent over backward loving her, helping her, providing for our family—anything to counterbalance her fucked-up childhood and show her she was loved, worshipped, and valued.

And how does she reward me? With lies, infidelity and protective orders. And abandoning my trusty dog. I'm gutted thinking about Diesel roaming adrift…alone, hungry, scared. Without ID. *She took his tags so he couldn't be found.*

I groan through gritted teeth.

The thing is…despite everything, I can't wish her dead. She's broken. And what was that stupid catchphrase I heard a couple of years ago? *Hurt people hurt people.* Maybe it's not so stupid after all.

My eyes burn, fixed upon the unfolding destruction, fire engulfing over half the house now. Panic grips every muscle in my body tight.

And still no sign of her.

Walk out, Adrienne. Please…

I utter some prayers, fast and pleading. I'm going to owe a lot to the bank of God after this year.

Come on…

Damn it, I can't sit here and do nothing. Setting Cassidy next to her brother, I scuttle back outside, rain and wind whipping my face. You'd think the downpour would douse the fire, and yet, it rages on, probably fueled from the inside, the walls and furniture like tinder. As the front entrance is completely unpassable, I start for the side when sirens wail through the storm. *Thank you, God.*

It takes a full excruciating minute before fire trucks screech to a halt at our house. Emergency personnel spring into action. I shout that my wife is inside and where I saw her last. Pacing by my car, I crane my neck, waiting. Watching them work is fucking agonizing. And achingly slow.

Too much time passes.

Thunderheads rumble to the north, and the rainfall slows to a sprinkle as I stare at the pale blue house caving in on itself, smoke wisping from doused embers from both firehose and hurricane.

I know she's gone before they tell me.

They said she couldn't be saved; it was too late. I can't help thinking not only from this, but from herself.

Emergency workers swirl around me. The police arrive and pepper me with questions. Privy to our recent legal history, they are at turns cautious, aggressive and accusatory, asking about our relationship, what occurred, my state of mind and a litany of details I answer through a fog. They promise a thorough investigation and full autopsy, advising me to stick close to home. I get it. After the last go-round, I've got flight risk written all over me.

They carry my dead wife out of the house zipped up in a sobering black body bag. The finality of that image is so intense, I don't even try to stop the flood of tears.

One by one, everyone leaves. Numbness fills me. Staring at the rubble that is now my house and my life, I spy remnants of the fallen mighty oak, split in two and burned to cinders. *How poetic.* The tree turned out to be a symbol all right, but not in the way I'd envisioned.

The first inklings of dawn break, casting a glow across the wreckage. And it's suddenly so clear.

Struck by overwhelming gratitude, I fall to my knees.

I'm being given a second chance.

The profundity of it lodges in my throat and my eyes well again. I glance at the heavens, silently vowing not to blow it. I've got two little ones counting on me. And I'm counting on me. I'm keenly, painfully and poignantly aware I've got work to do. Changes to make. Possible criminal charges. A headshrinker to visit. It won't be easy. But I'm willing.

I will redeem myself.

"No human being is so bad as to be beyond redemption," I murmur. Mahatma Gandhi said it. Believed it. And I'm clinging to it now.

Standing, I wipe my tears and approach the minivan. The spare key is on my ring, but it's unlocked. The car seats are missing their carriers, surely burned to smithereens now. Shuddering, I open the back hatch and remove the emergency blankets I'd stowed months ago. Adrienne's sarcastic comments filter in: *It's the dead of summer, Hank. We don't need stupid blankets.*

Hearing the faint but distinct clink of metal, I whirl. Grief chokes my challenged lungs when I realize it's Diesel's collar and tags.

"I'm coming for you, buddy," I whisper. "I *will* find you."

Opening the sliding door, I prepare the space, return to the rental car and collect my children. Carrying them to the minivan, I nestle them in the blankets and secure them with seatbelts as best I can.

Looping the dog collar over the rear-view mirror, I give our destroyed house one final glance. I back out of the driveway, and don't look back.

———

Mrs. Kincaid: Poor Hank's got to raise those two babies by himself now. I hope he finds a nice girl. I always liked him, and his porn-star mustache.

Mrs. Brown: Tragedy strikes and you're still talking about porn stars and mustaches. Honestly, Gladys. Hank will be fine in time. I'll miss him too, though. I can't imagine anyone moving in across the street that will be as exciting as the McCallisters.

EPILOGUE

HANK

IT TOOK NEARLY four weeks to sort out the mess, but in the end, considering the circumstances, I couldn't have asked for a better outcome.

I called every animal shelter and missing pet reporting website in Virginia and found Diesel at a humane society in Farmville. Call it a hunch, but I figured Adrienne took him to her old stomping grounds. Damn if I didn't shed a lot more unmanly tears. I've been an emotional wreck, but these were happy fucking tears. I drove down to get him straight away, and we had one hell of a reunion. Even though I don't plan to let him out of my sight, I'm getting him one of those newfangled microchip IDs the vet injects under their skin…just in case.

I stopped by Grandma Betty's on my way home to pay my respects, deliver Adrienne's ashes, and get the closure we both needed. It slayed me to see her, to feel the weighted burdens I carry seem even heavier than usual. She held me tight, reassuring me her granddaughter suffered from the load of her parents' failures, and not to blame myself. She blew my mind disclosing how she'd guessed Adrienne set fire to the house that killed her daughter, son-in-law and other granddaughter, plus a host of other, kinder memories. She offered to put together a box of items for her great-grandchildren, so they'd have something to remember their mother by. We shared an emotional visit that left me fried. And yet I hated to leave knowing she was now all alone in the world. I told her our door was always open to her.

I was exonerated of any wrongdoing associated with Adrienne's death, which the authorities definitively determined a freak accident. My only regret is wishing I'd yanked her from that room instead of allowing her to remain and look for a trinket. She'd be alive today if I had. I try not to dwell on it, and my feelings still fluctuate by the hour: raging anger to feeling like the dumbest, most gullible idiot ever, to guilt, to missing her and the mother she might have been to these babies.

Tami has saved my ass in more ways than one. She's helped care for the twins, let us all stay in the finished basement at her house, and been a listening ear. We've been there for each other, both grieving the loss of our marriages. She kicked NimRod out and already set the wheels of divorce in motion. She's one strong broad and a sympathetic friend. I'm beyond grateful she's hugged and held my little nitnoys, because I have no idea how all this is affecting them. I'm anguished wondering about the void it will leave on their little hearts. I can't fathom them growing up without their mama. My heartbreak is one thing, but theirs? Unspeakable.

There's been an errant thought gnawing at me, now that I understand Adrienne was unfaithful, and that's whether these two precious young people are actually my flesh and blood. But I've decided two things: 1) I love Tanner and Cassidy with all my heart. They're absolutely mine. 2) If biology were to say any different, I don't give a shit. So, I've laid it to rest. I don't need any more proof than what's in my heart.

I lost nearly everything in the house. But I'm not sure it's a bad thing. Makes moving to Texas easier. I'm headed home, where we can stay with family as we sort this new life out. My parents and brothers have been nothing but gracious and supportive. Betting I have a small grace period for that, and I'll take it.

I finish packing what little I've accumulated over the past month and load it into the van. Tami is in the living room, watching over Tanner and Cassidy, already tucked into their car seats.

I take one last lap around the premises to be sure I haven't missed anything. When I'm done, I amble into the room where they all wait. Diesel, splayed at Tami's feet enjoying a rubdown, glances at me before popping up. It's as if he knows we're splitting.

Tami rises from the chair, her expression mirroring my own. Neither of us wants to be so far apart—1,576 miles—not when we've been each other life rafts. Not with how close we've become. It smarts more than I'd like to admit.

I half grimace, half smile as I approach then draw her in and hold her tight. Her arms wrap around my midsection, and it feels…comforting. She fits like she belongs there.

"You've been a true friend, Tami," I murmur, still clutching her in my grasp. "I don't know how I would have gotten through this without you."

She swallows hard, and I feel it against my chest. "Same."

I can tell she's fighting back tears, so I pull back. "You all right there, darlin'?"

She laughs softly, fanning away those unshed buggers as she pulls away. "There you go again, dripping your Texas charm at me."

I grin, my mustache stretching wide for the first time in weeks.

"I'm really going to miss you, Hank."

"I'm really gonna miss you too. But this isn't goodbye. I'm going to haunt your phone, plus convince you to move to Texas…" I wink.

She smiles bigger now. "You're crazy, you know that?"

"So I've been told."

She helps me get the kids in the car while Diesel leaps into the front passenger seat, claiming shotgun. Telling me to wait, Tami darts back in the house. She returns bearing sandwiches, snacks and drinks for the road, because that's the kind of thoughtful she is.

"Call me and let me know you're okay," she says.

I chuck her under the chin. "You do the same."

She rolls her eyes. "Very funny."

I try to keep it light, but the moment turns somber. "Thanks again. For everything." There's so much more I want to say. But it would all be woefully inadequate.

She reaches over and takes my hand. Hers is warm and soft as silk. "So long, Hank. Safe travels."

I bend down and kiss her cheek tenderly then give her hand a squeeze. Before I get all water-logged again, I get in the van, wave, and head for home.

———

Tami: I don't think I've shared anything this deep with anyone in my life. You think you have...until something so unimaginable, so far beyond your comprehension happens and you find yourself in a place you never expected, baring your soul to a person you never expected. The past few months have been a living hell, but if there's any silver lining, it's Hank...he's the bright spot, the little bit of heaven that hell can't keep quiet.

WANT A LITTLE MORE?

Score the bonus epilogue (link on website) and find out what's happening in Hank's world now.

Visit my website to check out all my books, order a signed copy, get freebies and subscribe for emails so you never miss a thing.

And if you enjoyed this wild ride, I'd be grateful for your review on Amazon, Goodreads, etc., and hope you'll share about it with your reader friends.

ALSO BY KATHERINE COBB

FICTION
Falling (a coming-of-age novel)
Fifty, Four Ways (a chicklit momcom novel)
Break Out the Dawn (a parody romance microvella)

NONFICTION
The Self-Loathing Project
It Is What It Is
Panhandle Portraits

CHILDREN'S
Weeza's Great Escape (picture book)

PLAYLIST

"At the End of a Bar" by Chris Young and Mitchell Tenpenny

"Bar Fight Song" by Dale Tyge

"Hurricane" by Luke Combs

"Two to Two Step" by Midland

"A Guy with a Girl" by Blake Shelton

"One Beer" by Hardy (featuring Lauren Alaina and Devin Dawson)

"I Need You" by Tim McGraw and Faith Hill

"Wait in the Truck" by Hardy (featuring Lainey Wilson)

"Who's Cheatin' Who" by Alan Jackson

"Achy Breaky Heart" by Billy Ray Cyrus

"Ring of Fire" by Johnny Cash

"The Cowboy Rides Away" by George Straight

"God Blessed Texas" by Little Texas

ACKNOWLEDGMENTS

A humungous thanks to my husband, Greg, for so many things. Like becoming a book widower once again…and surviving. For allowing me to pilfer some of your experiences. For being an early reader, especially since you don't like anything but nonfiction books about cars, military stuff, history or biographies. For your spot-on insights, including your encyclopedic brain totally correcting me from making that "Dust Bowl" faux pas. I appreciate so much that you are my biggest fan. I'm yours, too. And you'll never know how incredible it feels that you love me so much, you do crap you don't even want to do so I can write almost full-time, simply because you know how much I love it. Your love is so big, so unconditional, it blows me away. Yup…if I was a songwriter, that's what I'd name our first song: *Your Love Blows Me Away.* Since we both know I can't sing, that probably won't come to fruition. But it's the thought that counts, right?

A special mega-thanks to early readers Cathy Baldau, Natalie Ekvall, Kim Maeda (*twice!*), B. Muze (aka 2AMayze), Claire Stibbe and Amber Tischio. Your insights were invaluable, helped me make this a better book, and I appreciate you ALL so much!

Thanks also to Claire Taylor with FFS Media, who is an author, coach and all-around cool gal who turned me on to enneagrams and helped me with author and story alignment. I'm not ashamed to admit I cried working some of this out and learning my spot-on enneagram type and wingman.

Thanks to editor Jeni Chappelle for her comments and guidance on an early draft. P.S. I hope I never have to do another reverse outline ever!

There were a lot of moving parts to keep this story credible, so I did several enlightening consultations. Thanks to:
1) Tom Fitzgerald and Zach Tischio, former Virginia law enforcement, for clear direction on police procedures;
2) Dave Camilletti, Family Court Judge and former attorney, for his insights on legal procedures;
3) Stan Beall, former firefighter, for his consult on fires in the home;
4) KT Cobb, physician's assistant (and my smart, lovely daughter-in-law), for her medical consult;
5) Margie Stockton, RN, for her medical consult, especially regarding nursing;
6) Karen Sawyer, for sharing her experience of carrying twins and some of the complications she faced;
7) Monica Kincaid, for sharing her experience with the NICU; and
8) the Appomattox County Rescue Squad, for clarifying EMT practices.

Some of the phrases uttered by my Texan characters were taken from the Texas Monthly's roundup of "More Colorful Texas Sayings Than You Can Shake a Stick At" and the book, Fixin' to be Texan, by Helen Bryant. Using them made me happy as a clam at high tide!

Last but never least, thank you READERS! You make this all worthwhile, and your comments, reviews and enthusiasm always make my day. Cheers to you and more great books!

ABOUT THE AUTHOR

Katherine (Briganti) Cobb writes books exploring love, relationships and our shared, often messy, humanity. She believes dreams come true, love conquers all, and reading and chocolate are the perfect pairing. She writes fiction, nonfiction and picture books because…why choose? Connect, subscribe and a whole lot more at www.katherinecobb.com.

   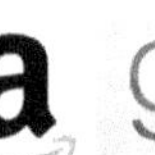